ROMANCE IN THE BADLANDS COLLECTION

BY
VICKIE MCDONOUGH

MBI

Romance in the Badlands Collection
Published by Mountain Brook Ink
White Salmon, WA U.S.A.

The website addresses shown in this book are not intended in any way to be or imply an endorsement on the part of Mountain Brook Ink, nor do we vouch for their content.

This story is a work of fiction. All characters and events are the product of the author's imagination. Any resemblance to any person, living or dead, is coincidental.

Scripture quotations are taken from the King James Version of the Bible. Public domain.

ISBN 9781953957-19-1

The Team: Miralee Ferrell, Alyssa Roat, Cindy Jackson
Cover Design: Vickie McDonough and Alyssa Roat

Mountain Brook Ink is an inspirational publisher offering fiction you can believe in.
Printed in the United States of America

CONTENTS

WILD AT HEART

Chapter One

"Of all the nerve!" Mariah Lansing crumpled the letter in her fist. Her grandmother scrunched her white brows together as she glanced up from the new Montgomery Ward catalog resting in her lap. "What is it, dear?"

"A letter from a reader." Mariah crossed the parlor and dropped onto the couch beside her

grandmother. "A rancher—Mr. McFarland—from North Dakota. He says I don't have my ranching facts correct."

"I would imagine the man knows what he's talking about." Grandma crossed her wrinkled hands over the catalog. "You knew when you decided to write dime novels that you would have an uphill climb in a man's world. It doesn't help that you've been raised in Chicago all your life. Perhaps it is time for you to take a trip out west."

Mariah shrugged. If only she could travel out west. But her grandma was too old to make such a journey, and Mariah wasn't about to leave her alone. "I'll just have to do more thorough research."

Grandma peered at her over the top of her round spectacles. "Did the man state anything specific that you got wrong?"

Smoothing out the letter, Mariah scanned the rest of the missive then gasped. "He's invited me to visit his ranch in the Badlands."

"What an opportunity. Perhaps you should consider it."

Mariah's gaze traveled around the parlor they had recently redecorated in pastels. Her grandmother loved to read, and Mariah had wanted to make her a cozy room for entertaining her closest friends and for relaxing. The soft blue wallpaper, hand painted with a myriad of butter, peach and rose-colored flowers with sea green leaves brightened up the walls that had once been a faded gold shade. Could she really leave home again and leave the only family she had left, even for a short adventure?

Such a journey would enhance her ability to write about the West and make her stories more authentic. But no, she couldn't—wouldn't—leave her grandmother. She owed her too much to go running off the first chance she got.

Grandma chuckled as she held Mariah's letter up so that the light from the nearby window illuminated it. "I fear, dear, you may have met your match with this gentleman. He says that men are the true heroes in the West, not women, and if you want men to keep reading your novels, you need to change your way of thinking."

A very unladylike snort erupted before Mariah could contain it. "That's one man's opinion. I see nothing wrong with a woman being the hero of a story."

Grandma gave her a patronizing look. "Surely you realize that more men than women read those paperbacks. Perhaps you should take Mr. McFarland's advice and let a man save the day sometimes. Men have delicate egos, you know, especially cowboys and ranchers who live such a rough life. They live a hard life. They're outside in all kinds of weather, facing dangers daily, and battling rustlers, outlaws and wild creatures. I imagine they see themselves as heroic."

Mariah would consider her grandmother's advice, but not some faceless stranger's. It had been a woman—her grandmother—who'd come to her rescue when her parents died. *Her* hero was a woman, so why not in her stories?

"I think you should at least pray about this man's invitation. He says here that he lives on a ranch of over four thousand acres with his mother and two siblings." Grandma peered over the top of her spectacles at Mariah. "I would never suggest your going if not for his mother being there. Of course, you'd need to see if she's willing to serve as a chaperone."

"I don't want to leave you alone."

"Pish posh. I'm perfectly fine. I was alone while you were away at college."

"That's different." She couldn't explain her nagging need to stay close to home. Was it a premonition of something to come? Grandma hadn't been sick, but she had seemed frailer of late.

Mariah shrugged off her concern. Her grandma was of sturdy Dutch stock and would probably outlive her. "What with the World's Columbian Exposition opening here soon, I'd probably be the only person leaving Chicago."

A soft smile touched her grandmother's lips. "That may be true. I can't tell you how I'm looking forward to visiting it this weekend."

"I'm excited to see all those grand buildings and exhibits." Mariah picked up a pamphlet about the huge Exposition from the coffee table in front of her and studied the photographs. They had been making plans to attend for two weeks—another reason she couldn't head west now.

"I know we'll enjoy sampling the concessions instead of taking our own food along. I may even try some of that Oriental food, if I get my nerve up."

Mariah giggled. "I can see you trying to eat noodles with those chopsticks the Asians use."

"I would make a fine mess, I'm sure." Grandmother shook her head. "I still can't believe the authorities are allowing concessions to be sold on Sunday. Whoever heard of such a sacrilege?"

Mariah stood and crossed the room to look out the window. From her bedroom upstairs, she could see the top of a steeple on one of the Exposition's taller buildings. "Times are changing."

"Don't I know. Who would have thought a woman would be writing dime novels?" Though Grandma shook her head, Mariah knew she was proud of her.

"I think you should reconsider and pray about this gentleman's offer. Perhaps God has provided this opportunity for you."

"You can't be serious about sending me off to the Wild West alone?"

Grandma shrugged one thin shoulder. "We could most likely find an escort for you to travel with. I think you should write the man, get more information, and ask if his mother would be willing to act as chaperone."

Mariah gasped. "I can't ask that of a total stranger. Besides, even if I wanted to go, Silas would never allow it."

Grandma smacked the catalog on the coffee table, sending a soft whiff of her floral

perfume Mariah's way. She slanted a glance at her grandmother, noticing her pursed lips.

"This isn't the Dark Ages. We're almost in the twentieth century." She lifted her chin, her eyes narrowed. "What do you mean that Silas won't allow you to go? You are not married to that man yet."

Mariah didn't want to argue with her grandmother again about Silas. "I don't mean he wouldn't allow me to go, just that he wouldn't want me to. You know how he doesn't like to let me out of his sight."

"That's because he's a controlling—" Grandma slammed her mouth shut.

Heleen Vanderveer was sweet but opinionated. Though Mariah's grandma had lost her Dutch accent after being in America most of her life, she was still a stubborn Dutchwoman at times. They had knocked heads more than once over the eleven years that Mariah had lived with her. She simply didn't understand Silas.

Sighing, Grandma laid her hand on Mariah's arm. "I don't want you to marry him because you think that will advance your writing career. He may have a prestigious position at Goodwell Publications, but you're very talented, dear. Chances are you won't write dime novels for the rest of your life, but you *will* be stuck with the man you wed. It's important that you marry a kind, God-fearing man you dearly love."

"I know. I do have feelings for Silas, as he does for me." She wasn't sure exactly what they were, even though she had decided to marry him. His constant querying had worn her down, and when he promised to allow her grandmother to live with them, she finally agreed to marry. That he was concerned for Heleen endeared him to her, even if he was overly bossy at times.

She glanced at the mantel clock. "You need to take your nap, Grandma, and I must prepare for the Chicago Writers Banquet tonight. Silas will pick me up in a few hours."

Grandma rose without further comment, picked up her cane, and shuffled into the hallway. Her disapproval of Silas was evident in the upturned tilt of her chin. Mariah's shoulders sagged.

She'd tried all her life to please Heleen and hated disappointing her. Silas seemed to be about the only bone of contention between them. Her grandmother, after an initial hesitation, had even supported and encouraged her in her writing career, although she had suggested Mariah use a pseudonym, which she'd agreed to. Most readers thought Drew Dixon was a male and started their fan letters with a "Dear sir," something that always tickled Mariah's funny bone. If she fooled so many men into thinking she was one of their cohorts, she couldn't be that far off the mark with her details.

She folded up Mr. McFarland's letter. Even though she disagreed with him, she longed to accept his offer and travel to his ranch. She'd never realized before that there were ranches in North Dakota. She had read in the paper about the many foreigners from Scandinavia and Russia who traveled there in hopes of owning farmland, but nothing about ranching. Visiting Mr. McFarland's Rocking M Ranch would help her to add realism to her stories, not to mention it would be an exciting journey.

She walked upstairs toward her bedroom, wondering what the Badlands looked like. She'd never set a story there before nor had ever even read one set in North Dakota. The spark of an idea flickered in her mind. *Belle of the Badlands.*

What if a Southern belle got lost in the Badlands and found a treasure from a Northern Pacific train robbery? Her mind swirled with ideas, and she hurried down the dim hallway to her room to grab pen and paper.

"Your Silas is looking well tonight." Amelia Winfield followed Silas's tall, lithe form as he wove through the crowded room to talk to the *Chicago Times* editor.

Mariah wasn't quite sure how to respond to Amelia's blatant admiration of her fiancé. She cleared her throat. "Yes, he's quite well."

"Gray is a good color for him. It matches his eyes."

Mariah swung her gaze toward Amelia. There was no mistaking her infatuation with Silas Wellington. Mariah's fiancé stood taller than many men in the room, but he was thin as a lamppost. And his nose was a bit too pointed for Mariah's taste, reminding her of a fox. She hoped their children would get her nose. Suddenly, a cold shiver zigzagged down her back at the thought of being intimate with Silas. Why hadn't she ever considered that before?

"Well, I must be off to chat with Margaret Sprague. I simply must get her to introduce me to that handsome cousin of hers. He's a captain in the army, you know."

Mariah watched her sashay off, relieved to be rid of the talkative woman. She studied the room filled with high-society people and newspapermen. The giant ballroom buzzed with conversation, and the mouthwatering scents of a smorgasbord of food battled that of women's perfume and men's cologne. She noticed her editor, Marc Taylor, across the room and made her way toward him. He was talking with a large man she didn't recognize, but then she was fairly new to writing and didn't know all the names and faces yet.

"Ah, good evening, Miss Lansing." Mr. Taylor smiled at her. "Let me introduce Harlan Otis of the *Philadelphia Daily*. Harlan, meet Mariah Lansing, an up-and-comer at Goodwell Publications."

Holding a glass of punch in one hand, Mr. Otis gave a stiff bow in her direction, and then looked her over as men often did. "A pleasure, Miss Lansing."

"Mr. Otis." Mariah nodded at him.

"So, are you a clerk at Goodwell?" Otis twirled one side of his handlebar mustache.

Mariah held back her sigh and glanced at her bemused editor.

"Uh. . .no, actually, Miss Lansing is one of our writers."

Mr. Otis's fuzzy brows lifted, and then he slurped his cup of punch, leaving droplets of liquid on his mustache. "Ah. . .a fashion reporter? Or perhaps a cooking column?"

Mariah prepared herself for the regular reaction when people learned that she wrote dime novels. Some folks considered them sleazy, even though they were only action-oriented stories. So what if occasionally the hero and heroine fell in love? There was nothing sordid about that. She made sure of it.

"Actually, I write dime novels."

Mr. Otis's mustache danced as he burst out laughing, and Mariah exchanged a "not again" glance with her editor.

"Too funny, Miss Lansing. I do love a woman with a sense of humor."

Mariah scowled and opened her mouth, but Mr. Taylor beat her to it.

"It's the truth, Harlan. Mariah, here, has seven dime novels to her name, with several more contracted. People all across America are discovering her stories and have been writing fan letters."

"Writing is a man's business. Dime novels are dying out, just like the penny dreadfuls in Britain." Mr. Otis harrumphed. "I can't believe there's a market for ones written by a female. Women should be busy tending the home, not writing stories."

Mariah lifted her chin. "Sir, my grandfather came to America with dreams of settling in the West. He only made it as far as Chicago before my grandmother dug her heels in and refused to travel farther. I've thoroughly studied the West and write my stories for people like him— people who can't travel as far as they can dream."

Mr. Otis waved his beefy hand in the air, and he turned to her editor as if she were nothing more than a pesky fly. "Take heed, Taylor, that venture is doomed to fail." He turned and marched off.

Shaking her head, Mariah sighed. "Why is it so hard for people to believe that a woman can write something exciting?"

Mr. Taylor gave her a consoling pat on her shoulder. "Give it time. Folks are often slow to adjust to new things. I'm pleased with your work and sales figures."

"Thank you. That's good to know. By the way, I've finished *Sergeant Samuels and the Indian Maiden*. I'll turn it in tomorrow."

"Great! Excellent. I'll have Mildred cut a payment draft in the morning so it will be ready when you come in. I wish all my writers would beat their deadlines as early as you."

Mariah basked in his offhanded compliment. They were few and far between for a woman working in a man's field. Mr. Taylor excused himself and followed some men outside, so Mariah looked around the room for Silas. Normally, he was at her side, even to the point of being annoying, but tonight, he'd been strangely distant.

The room buzzed with conversation from small groups of people dressed in their best. When she didn't see him in the masses crowding the buffet tables, she crossed to the open double doors and went out on the veranda. Clusters of two to five people sat chatting at the small, round tables brought in especially for the evening. On the fringes where the light turned to shadows, a few couples could be seen standing too close to one another, but no Silas.

With her feet aching from her new shoes, Mariah was ready to call it an early night, but first she must find her missing fiancé. He was most likely off conversing with one of his business associates from the paper. She wandered back through the crowded parlor and dining room, down the hallway. Peering inside the music room filled with the gentle sounds of a string quartet, she studied the faces in the packed room but didn't see the object of her search.

She started to bypass the library but noticed the door ajar. From previous evenings at Sterling House, she knew the library was off-limits. Mr. Sterling had a vast first-edition book collection and didn't want anyone accidentally spilling anything on his volumes. She skirted past the door, but whispers and a woman's giggle drew her back. Probably just young sweethearts looking for privacy. Her curious nature made not opening the door impossible.

A lone electric lamp illuminated a man and woman in a passionate embrace. Mariah's cheeks heated at the blatant display. She reached for the handle to close the door but accidentally jiggled it, causing the man to look up with startled gray eyes.

Mariah gasped. *Silas?*

Amelia Winfield peered over her shoulder, her mouth tilted in a scathing smirk.

Pressing her hand to her chest, Mariah caught her breath and spun around. She hurried down the hallway, dodging the curious glances of those she passed. She quickly claimed her cloak, and a doorman opened the front entrance, allowing the cooler outside air to soothe her scorching cheeks. Lifting her long skirts, she trotted down the steps and suddenly stopped at the bottom. Now what?

She'd ridden to the banquet with Silas. It was too far to walk home, and a lady shouldn't be alone on the streets at night. Oh, why hadn't she heeded her grandma's reservations instead of being her normal stubborn self? Had her heart suspected what her mind refused to allow her to believe? Was that why she'd had doubts about her fiancé?

The valet, evidently not expecting anyone to be leaving so early, hopped to his feet from his perch on the low stone wall that bordered the walkway. "May I help you, madam?"

"I need the Wellington carriage, please."

"Yes, madam." He hurried down the walkway and turned the corner, disappearing from sight.

Silas's quick footsteps clattered down the stairs. "Mariah, wait."

Not wanting a public confrontation, she looked for a nook or cranny in which to hide, but no such place was at hand. With resignation, she straightened her back and turned to face her *former* fiancé.

"It's not what you think, Mariah, darling." He straightened his tie and brushed his hand over his slicked-back hair. His normally thin lips looked puffy. "Amelia forced herself on me."

Mariah huffed. "I'm supposed to believe little Amelia Winfield overpowered you and forced you to kiss her? What is she? All of five-foot-two?"

Lamplight illuminated the desperation that flashed through his eyes. "Uh—yes. That's exactly what happened. She's been chasing me for months."

"And I guess she also forced you into the isolated—and might I add *restricted*—library?" She crossed her arms over her chest, guarding her heart, as Silas fumbled for a response. Never had he kissed her as he had Amelia. Mariah hadn't minded his chaste goodnight pecks on the lips, thinking that showing any more ardor should be reserved for married life. In fact, she knew nothing of passion—except what she'd recently witnessed. And that was plenty.

"Just take me home."

He glanced toward the door. "I—uh—I'm not ready to leave yet. There are some important people I need to talk to."

"That's fine. I've already called for your carriage. The driver can return here after he drops me off."

"Mariah." He laid his hands on her shoulders. "Don't let something so petty ruin our evening. People will think it odd that you've gone and I'm still here. As my fiancée, it's expected that you'll be by my side all evening."

Her mouth dropped open. "Of all the insensitive cads. I am no longer your fiancée." She jerked away from his touch, pulled off her engagement ring, and tossed it at him. The diamond glinted in the lamplight then bounced off Silas's hands as he struggled to catch it. The ring clinked on the stone walkway just as the carriage pulled up. The valet opened the door, and Mariah glanced up at the driver. "Please take me home and then return. Mr. Wellington wishes to remain here."

She took her seat, and before the door shut, she saw Silas on his hands and knees, searching for his mother's ring. A tiny shaft of concern stabbed her. She hoped her impulsive reaction hadn't caused the antique to get lost. Even though she no longer wanted it, the diamond-and-ruby ring was a cherished family heirloom.

The door closed on the future Mariah had thought she'd wanted. Leaning her head back, she closed her eyes. How could things change so fast? Most women would be crying over the loss of a fiancé, but betrayal and anger scalded away her tears.

A trip out west sounded better and better with every turn of the carriage wheel as it bumped along the brick road.

Chapter Two

A hairy tarantula skittered across the top of Adam McFarland's head. He jerked and tried to lift his hand to brush it away, but his arm felt weighted down, his body sluggish to react. A loud train whistle and the feeling of his body slipping sideways on the bench jarred him fully awake. He shoved out his left arm to halt his slide and grabbed his new Clay Barton felt hat lying on the seat next to him before it slid into the aisle. He rubbed the sleep from his eyes as the Northern Pacific clattered and shimmied its way west.

Though he knew he'd only been dreaming, Adam's head itched as if the spider were actually there. He scratched the top of his head, his hand encountering something light and fluffy. Looking upward, he let out a quiet groan. Now he remembered. Ever since the pretty gal with the garishly frilly hat had taken the seat behind him, Adam had warred with those stupid feathers. He pivoted back around, resisting the urge to yank them off the woman's hat. He knew his thoughts were unmannerly, but a man shouldn't have to fight birds on a train ride.

He struggled to keep from smiling as he imagined the woman's face if he were to toss her hat in the air and shoot off the offending plumage. Why did a pretty gal think she needed a headdress to improve her appearance? He shook his head, glad his twin sister, Anna, was more levelheaded and practical.

Adam stared out the window as the flat landscape of North Dakota gradually yielded to the bumps and mounds, which would soon reveal his beloved badlands. He didn't leave home often and missed the rugged beauty of the area where his family's Rocking M Ranch was located.

The contract he'd received while in Chicago was safe in his jacket pocket, but he tugged on the lapel anyway for a quick glance. Art dealer and gallery owner, Trenton Howard, had been far more excited about Adam's drawings of the West than he'd expected. He'd bought all ten, right out of Adam's portfolio, and commissioned him to draw a dozen more, with the promise of a gallery showing and future business if the pictures sold as he thought they would.

Scratching his head again, Adam wondered how he'd break the news to his sister and brother that he'd be leaving. He'd dreamed for years of traveling farther west and maybe even down south to Texas, where his family originated, to sketch pictures of cowboys, ranch settings, and even some Indians.

Anna wouldn't like him leaving. As twins, they'd always been close. His hardworking brother, Quinn, kept the ranch running well but was quiet and preferred to work in his office most evenings rather than socializing with his family.

Would Quinn listen to Anna during her chatty spells? Would he hug her when she was lonely or discouraged?

The view of his mother waving goodbye at the depot after his visit in Bismarck stayed with him. She felt pulled between her children and her own needy mother, but with her children all grown now, she had decided her mother needed her more. Anna would be disappointed to learn Ma would be staying in Bismarck awhile longer tending their grandmother who'd broken her leg.

Adam looked out the window at the scenery whizzing past. Quinn would do what he needed where Anna was concerned, of that he was certain. His older brother wasn't the most affectionate person in the world but had been a father figure ever since their pa died years ago.

For the first time, Adam considered what leaving the ranch meant to him. No more family. No familiar bed to sleep in at night. And no more of Leyna's delicious German cooking.

Adam scratched the top of his head. Sure, there were things he'd miss, sacrifices to be made, but still the adventure of traveling called to him. Lured him like a honeybee to a flower or a lost calf to its mother. His fingers tingled as he thought of all the beautiful sights just waiting for him to discover and to draw.

A tickle, as if a broken egg had been spilled on Adam's head and was running down the sides, forced him to scratch his head again. The lady across from him gave him an odd look and hugged her sleeping son a bit tighter. She probably thought he had lice or another infestation.

He'd had enough. Grabbing his hat, Adam thrust himself up. He held on to the back of the wooden bench to keep from losing his footing as the train rocked down the track at an amazing speed. Looking around, he realized with a sigh that the only available seats were either next to the woman in the hat or directly across from her. Evidently, most other folks on the train were steering clear of that pesky bonnet, too.

A rugged cowboy, slouched with his leg across the seat opposite the woman, gave him a disgusted look as Adam motioned that he wanted to sit beside him. The man scowled but slowly slid his leg down and straightened in the seat. He glared at Adam as he stood, almost looking eye-to-eye. Holding his ground, Adam kept his expression neutral. Suddenly, the cowboy grinned and then plopped down beside the woman. Surprise engulfed her countenance, and she hastily gathered her skirts to keep them from touching the dirty cowboy.

Adam eased down, glad that the confounded feathers would no longer pester him. He much preferred looking at the citified gal and couldn't help wondering why she was traveling alone. He laid his hat on the seat beside him and relaxed, glad to have solved that problem. The woman scooted as close to the window as possible, and guilt stabbed at him that he'd caused her to have to share her bench. The cowpoke slouched back in his seat, allowing his left thigh to ease closer to the woman than was proper. Adam glared at him, but the man wasn't intimidated.

Fancy Feathers pulled a lace hankie from the cuff of her sleeve and discreetly held it to her nose as she stared out the window. The cowboy had reeked of body odor and cows when he'd stood. Adam considered offering to swap seats but figured the man wouldn't want to move again.

Adam's gaze drifted to the right. Soft wisps of light brown hair had pulled free from Fancy Feathers's oval face, making her look young and innocent. She couldn't be much older than twenty. Her navy travel suit was wrinkled and dusty. A pretty gal like her shouldn't be traveling alone. How far had she journeyed? Was she going home or perhaps visiting someone?

"Been traveling long?" The words were out before he could rein them in.

"Pardon me?" Her coffee-brown eyes darted in his direction.

His stomach flip-flopped. He hadn't realized how pretty she was until she lowered her hankie and turned her full attention on him. He cleared his throat. "I said, have you been traveling long?"

She nodded, looking a bit suspicious of him. "A few days."

I'm harmless, he wanted to say. His drawing hand tingled. He didn't encounter many women of her caliber around Medora. He must have stared too long, trying to memorize her features until he was free to sit down with his paper and pencil, because she blushed and looked out the window again, the lace hankie firmly hiding all of her face except those expressive eyes.

Mariah tried not to squirm under the man's steady gaze. She refocused on the boring landscape, hoping he'd get the idea that she didn't want to talk. At least the flat farmland had given way to hills, which added a little variety.

Out of the corner of her eye, she peeked across the aisle. Given a different time and circumstances, she might have liked getting to know the handsome man, but she'd recently sworn off men. His tanned complexion made her wonder if he was a rancher or farmer, though he currently resembled neither. His gray Western suit perfectly fit his broad shoulders and blended well with his black hair and boots. Vivid blue eyes emanated kindness and curiosity, and he was mannerly enough not to force her into conversing.

At least she no longer had to avoid the lascivious stares of the smelly cowboy, although she preferred that to his sitting so close to her. She needed to make sure that she included more scents in her stories. Men out west tended to be less tidy and not as worried about daily ablutions as easterners. Why. . . oh my. . .the cowboy even had something greenish-brown smeared across his boots.

Oh dear. She tugged her skirts away, but the boot edged closer.

Except for appearance, the cowboy's arrogant behavior reminded her of Silas. The day after the writers' banquet, he'd come to her house saying that she'd imagined he and Amelia kissing and blamed her for ruining the evening. He insisted she take the ring back and stop her silliness. How had the situation become her fault?

Now that she'd finally seen Silas for the snake he was, she wanted nothing to do with him. Grandma had invited her sister for an extended visit and encouraged Mariah to go west for a while. Mariah just hadn't expected things to be so different out here.

Sharp needle pricks jabbed her left arm, which ached from being crushed up against the window frame for so long. She tried to straighten it without moving any closer to her unwanted seatmate. The train started a wide turn to the left, and the cowboy leaned even nearer. When he slid over another inch, Mariah's heart lurched.

She'd had an escort all the way from Chicago to Bismarck, but Mrs. Hannady got off there to visit her daughter. With less than a half day's train ride to Medora, her companion felt that Mariah would be fine alone, as long as she avoided talking to men. Now she was surrounded by them.

She turned her head to see if there were any other free seats and encountered the cowboy's whiskery face. A slow grin tilted his lips, revealing yellowed teeth, with one eyetooth missing.

"The name's Mitchell Sparks, ma'am. Where're you headed?"

His foul breath washed over Mariah, making her stomach churn. She longed to shove her handkerchief in front of her nose again but didn't want to appear rude.

"I would appreciate if you'd move over a little, Mr. Sparks."

His eyes twinkled, and he grinned fully. "Be happy to oblige."

He slid even closer—if that was possible. Mariah's heart lodged in her throat, but she couldn't resist mentally capturing every detail she was experiencing so she could recreate them in her stories. A writer simply must take full advantage of every situation that presented itself. Still, she couldn't allow his impropriety to continue. She narrowed her eyes. "Please scoot over *the other way*, sir."

"I'm fine right here. In fact, little darlin', you can sit on my lap if'n you've a hankerin' to."

Mariah gasped.

Irritation simmered.

She simply could not put up with such insolence—and if he didn't slide over soon, she feared she'd faint from his foul odor. The handsome man across from her leaned forward as if he might come to her aid, but she was quite able to defend herself. She reached up with her partially numb left hand, extracted a hatpin, and shifted it to her right fist. The handsome man's blue eyes widened, and he shook his head. He opened his mouth the same second she jabbed the pin in the cowboy's thigh.

"Ow! What the—" The cowboy jerked and held his leg. He stared unbelievingly at her with catlike amber eyes. Quickly, surprise turned to anger. He lifted his left arm, as if he were going to backhand her. Mariah raised her arm and prepared for the slap.

Would she ever learn to think before acting?

Adam fired off the bench like a bullet out of a pistol, grabbing the cowboy's fist before he could punch the woman. Years of wrangling ornery cattle made wrestling the cowpoke off her bench and onto his a simple chore. He shoved the cowboy down. "Now you sit there and behave."

The man jumped up and glared at Adam, his loose fingers lingering dangerously above the pistol on his hip. He took a quick glance around the crowded car then flopped down, arms crossed. Leaning against the side of the railcar, he placed his legs on the seat, kicking Adam's new hat onto the floor. Taking up the whole bench, he crossed his arms and gave Adam a satisfied smirk.

Adam took the vacated seat, being careful not to get too close to the hairpin-wielding woman. He picked up his hat, dusted it off, and laid it in his lap. Keeping his eye on the cowboy, he couldn't help wondering how such a prissy greenhorn gal could have the gumption she'd just displayed. Her hands were empty now, but she had snatched that spike from her bonnet faster than he could draw his revolver. His body slowly relaxed with the action over. He couldn't wait to get back home and away from all these crazy folks. Not that he'd be staying home for long.

A scent of something flowery drifted his way every time his seatmate moved, mixing with the pungent odor of coal smoke and many sweaty bodies in a confined space. She turned her head, looking out the window, and that pesky feather tickled his nose.

He blew out a loud sigh and swatted at it as if it were an annoying fly then scooted toward the aisle.

Suddenly, the woman turned to face him. "Thank you for your assistance, sir."

With her face so close, he could see a pale smattering of freckles across the bridge of her nose. His tongue seemed as tied up as a calf in a roping contest. "Uh. . .you're welcome, ma'am."

Her cheeks turned an appealing rose color; then she shifted toward the window, leaving her sweet scent behind. Adam pondered asking her where she was headed. Was she perhaps a mail-order bride?

He nearly laughed out loud. What weapons would she pull on her unsuspecting spouse when he irritated her? Throw hard biscuits at him in a fit of rage? Perhaps she'd sling her rolling pin at the poor man? Adam chuckled at that thought, receiving curious glances from both the cowboy and Fancy Feathers. He glared at the man but flashed a grin her way.

Her dark brown eyes widened, and then she turned away again. Adam hunkered down in the seat, arms crossed, ready to have this trip over. What would Quinn say when he told him he'd soon be leaving the Rocking M?

Probably be happy. Adam couldn't work hard enough to please his competent, slave-driving brother. Quinn didn't need him there, what with all the ranch hands. He doubted he'd even be missed—except by the womenfolk. Besides, after what he'd done, he didn't deserve to live on the Rocking M.

Mariah massaged the crick in her neck that she'd gotten from keeping her face turned toward the window. It was the only way to avoid the gawking cowboy. She felt relieved when the handsome man had come to her rescue but was disturbed by his closeness. What had he been laughing at? Was it her?

She hadn't minded traveling alone when Mrs. Hannady disembarked in Bismarck, but now she understood a woman's need for protection in the West. Things out here were far different than in Chicago. Manners and propriety were rules few seemed to care about west of the Mississippi River, and she never dreamed the odors could be so overpowering.

Dabbing her perfumed lace handkerchief below her nose, she covertly studied the man who came to her aid. Though probably only in his early twenties, he had a commanding presence and encountered no difficulty in overpowering the discourteous man, who seemed familiar somehow.

Suddenly she sat up straighter. The uncouth cowboy reminded her of Snake Slaughter, the vile villain in one of her stories. All he was missing was the jagged scar on his left cheek. He noticed her stare, and his seething gaze sent shivers up her spine. Would this trip ever be over?

She longed to see a forest, river, or hills. That flat North Dakota prairie lay open as far as the eye could see, but once in a while, they'd pass odd round-top hills that resembled dinner rolls rising in a pan more than landscape. The steep hills and pretty trees near Bismarck had been a pleasant diversion after the boring prairie.

Mariah yawned. Every part of her body ached, and she longed for a hot bath and soft bed. Leaning her head against the warm glass, she watched the patterns made by the coal smoke as the train veered to the right.

She wondered if Mr. McFarland had received the telegram she'd sent saying she was coming. Would he meet her at the train? She imagined he must be older—perhaps a widower with several children—since his mother lived with him. What would he say when he discovered she was a woman? There simply hadn't been time to write and wait for a letter back from him. After Silas's fiasco, she couldn't leave town soon enough.

Her eyes drooped, and she yawned. She didn't want to sleep again, but there was little else to do. The gently swaying railcar rocked her into a limp, relaxed state.

Mariah jumped at a loud noise and realized she'd fallen asleep. She'd dreamed of a train robbery and glanced down to make sure her reticule was still snuggly wrapped around her wrist.

"Nobody move—unless you want to get shot."

Jerking her head up, Mariah stared at a masked man at the front of the car, pointing a gun in her direction.

Her nightmare had become reality.

Chapter Three

Now wide awake, Mariah clutched her reticule against her chest. Her mouth went dry, and her whole body trembled. Women screamed. A baby wailed.

Thank goodness she'd had the wisdom to pack most of her money and jewelry in a secret compartment in her trunk, exactly like the heroine in *The Perils of Jane Bolin*.

The annoying cowboy seated across from her jumped to his feet and pulled out his gun faster than she could sneeze. For a second, Mariah thought he was going to attack the masked robber and save them all, but he slowly turned the pistol on her seatmate. "Throw down your gun, real slow like."

A muscle in the handsome man's jaw twitched. Ever so slowly, he pulled a gun from his holster using only his fingertips then set it on the floor. The cowboy nudged it with his foot, sending it sliding under their seat. Mariah's fears increased with her champion disarmed. If she sat still and did as the robber said, hopefully they would get out of this ordeal alive.

"Fork over your valuables." From under his vest, the cowboy jerked loose a small flour sack and shook it open.

She peeked at the passenger beside her, wondering how he felt at being bested by the man he'd so recently put in his place. Lips pursed, he glared at the cowpoke as if ready to charge into action at any moment.

"Don't try to be a hero. I'd be happy to give your belly button a back door. Figure I owe it to you." The cowboy smirked. "Now, pull out your valuables and drop them in the bag."

Her seatmate looked as if he'd swallowed a quart of vinegar, but he reached into his vest pocket and pulled out a wad of dollars. He held on to them as if trying to figure a way out of this predicament. She hoped he wouldn't do anything stupid that might get him shot. With a heavy sigh, he dropped the money into the bag.

"Now the watch." The cowboy waved his gun at the man's vest.

He pulled out his pocket watch and rubbed his fingers lovingly over the face, as if it held special meaning to him.

"My trigger finger's gettin' mighty itchy, mister." He jiggled the bag.

The man heaved a sigh and dropped the watch. The sack moved in her direction, sending her heart skittering faster than the train, still barreling down the tracks.

"You, too, *princess*." His sarcastic tone sent chills down her spine.

With shaking hands, she loosened the drawstring on her reticule and withdrew the two dollars and change that she had left from her traveling funds. Fortunately, she was near the end of her journey. As she dropped the money in the bag, she leaned forward and stared at his pistol.

"What are you gawking at?"

Mariah looked up. She knew she should keep quiet, but the words came out before logic could restrain them. "Do you perchance have any notches on your gun?"

Both men stared at her as if they'd seen a cow fly over a rainbow.

"Hurry up, Slim." The masked robber in the front of the car glanced their way then shoved his canvas pouch in the face of a plump, red-cheeked man. "Fill 'er up."

"Gimme that thing." The rude cowboy pointed his gun at the broach on Mariah's shoulder.

She gasped, covering her beloved jewelry. "You can't have that you. . .you fiend. Why, that was my great-grandmother's. It came all the way from Holland."

He blinked a moment, and then a cruel grin twisted his lips. "Fine then, I'll take the whole works."

Confusion blurred Mariah's thoughts. He grabbed her wrist, yanking her to her feet. With the pistol, he motioned for her startled seatmate to move over by the window. Mariah's heart stampeded as the man did as ordered. She knew the West was a dangerous place, but she'd never expected a situation could go from ho-hum to disastrous so quickly.

A half hour ago she'd wanted only to forget about the man who'd harassed her, but now she tried to memorize the thief's gravelly voice and menacing glare, hoping she could describe the man to the authorities should she be fortunate enough to escape.

As he shoved her across the aisle, her thoughts veered to the heroine of a shocking dime novel that she'd recently read. The heroine in *Dancing Under the Brazos Moon* had suffered horribly at the hands of outlaws until she escaped. Mariah wasn't prepared to suffer like that, not even for the sake of authenticity.

Her mind raced. She had to find a way out of this predicament.

Adam gritted his teeth. He despised handing over his father's watch even more than his family's hard-earned money. He didn't have many treasures in this world, but that watch was top on the list. Fancy Feathers wrestled the cowboy as he dragged her from the seat. Adam wanted to help her but didn't dare move since the pistol was still pointing at his gut.

He couldn't believe that woman had the gall to ask the thief if he had notches on his gun. What kind of gal would say such a foolish thing?

Women sniffled all around him, but the feisty greenhorn gal just looked irritated. Didn't she have the sense to know that she was in serious danger?

He had to do something. As annoying as she had been, he couldn't allow her to be kidnapped.

He glanced out the window at the cloudy sky. *Lord, You and I haven't exactly been on speaking terms for a while, but I could use some help here.*

He turned his attention back to the dilemma at hand. Like a cougar ready to leap on his prey, Adam bided his time, staying alert to the location of both robbers.

The cowboy turned the woman loose, thrust the bag into her hand, and shoved her across the aisle. His gaze darted to the couple nearest to them. "Make a donation."

The thin passenger scowled but pulled a thick leather wallet from his coat pocket and dropped it in. The woman next to him cowered against her husband's shoulder and whimpered like a critter caught in a snare. With a shaking hand, she pulled her wedding ring off, tossed it in the sack, and started blubbering.

From the corner of his eye, Adam could see a rider with two spare horses racing toward the train up ahead, waving a rifle. The getaway man. The train didn't slow, so the thieves would have to jump. Maybe the fast-moving leap would finish them off.

The cowboy shoved Fancy Feathers down the aisle toward the back half of the train. He pointed his gun upward as he passed it quickly behind her back. In the second that the revolver was aimed toward the ceiling, Adam dove at the cowboy. A shot rang out as he plowed into the robber.

Screams erupted all around. He grappled with the cowboy for the gun. They landed in the laps of the couple who'd been robbed. The woman shrieked. The thin man, much stronger than he looked, shoved at them, causing Adam to lose his balance. He fell backward, grabbing for a handhold, and stumbled into the aisle. At the front of the car, two men were trying to wrestle the pistol away from the other robber.

Adam hit the floor with a hard *thud*, the cowpoke landing on top. The robber suddenly regained his balance, sitting on Adam's chest and pinning his arms down with his legs. He raised the gun toward Adam's head, but Adam didn't look away.

Dear God, help me.

"I knew we'd come to blows." The cowboy cocked the gun. "Looks like I win."

Adam bucked and twisted but couldn't get free. In that instant all manner of thoughts galloped through his mind. His family would never know he'd planned to leave the ranch. Would they miss him when he was dead? Would he go to heaven after what he'd done?

A shadow rose up behind the man, and Fancy Feathers lifted one of her long hatpins in the air. Adam's eyes must have widened at the foolhardy action because the cowboy glanced over his shoulder. She jabbed the pin downward, impaling the robber's shooting arm.

"Ahh!" the man yelled as he lurched sideways. Gunfire blasted. A razor-sharp burn radiated through Adam's upper arm and shoulder. The screams in the railcar dimmed. He shoved away the pain and ringing in his ears and pushed to his feet. A wave of dizziness threatened to buckle his knees as smoke stung his eyes. The acrid odor of gunpowder mixed with the metallic scent of blood. *His blood.*

A burly man grabbed the struggling robber and held him to the ground. Vile curses echoed around the car before the captor punched his fist into the cowboy's cheek, knocking him out. At the front of the car, the masked man roared and threw a skinny youngster off him and dove out the front door. The train whistle screamed a lonely wail.

Bonnet askew, Fancy Feathers sat on the floor behind the unconscious robber. Her face looked as pale as the inside of an apple, but her brown eyes danced with excitement. What kind of crazy woman got excited over a train robbery and a shooting?

He ought to take pleasure that her annoying feather had broken in half, but he plumb hurt too much. Warm liquid dampened his sleeve. Adam winced and pressed the ball of his palm against the gunshot wound in his arm. His drawing arm.

His vision blurred. It suddenly hit him that he wouldn't be able to meet his deadline. His gut twisted as he saw his dreams go up in the lingering gun smoke. He fell backward, clutching at a nearby seat. The noise and pain faded as everything went black.

Chapter Four

Mariah waved her hand to clear away the smoke and the pungent sulfur odor of gunpowder. A brawny man punched the robber in the jaw, rendering him unconscious. Thank heavens for that.

She heard a ruckus behind her and pivoted toward the front of the train. The other thief flung an adolescent boy off him, glanced her way, then rushed out the door before anyone could stop him. The train hadn't slowed a speck, and she held on to the back of a seat to keep her balance. Out the side window, she saw the robber fly through the air then hit the ground, rolling. The train quickly passed him and another man on horseback, who was leading two other horses.

Mariah turned back to see if anyone had been hurt. Now that her fear had fled, her creative side kicked into full gear. She sniffed the air, trying to memorize the odor of gunpowder, which still made the inside of the car hazy. Passengers coughed, but nobody opened a window, knowing it would only allow in more coal dust and smoke.

An intruding ray of sunshine poked through the hole in the roof that the robber's gun had blasted when her seatmate had come to her rescue. Mariah sucked in a gasp, suddenly remembering the man who'd assisted her. She stared through the haze, concerned for his welfare. Her heart jolted when she saw him lying in the aisle. Two curious young boys leaned over their seats, peering down at him.

Holding her skirts, she cautiously made her way past the downed outlaw and his guard to where her champion lay. Her heart skittered. His right shoulder and arm were covered in blood. In spite of the steady rocking of the car, she worked her way to his side. She had to help him.

An inch-long gash accompanied an egg-sized bump where he must have hit his head. He lay deathly still. Mariah lifted the back of her hand to her mouth at the sight of so much blood. What if he died because of her?

"Excuse me, ma'am. Let me through. I'm a doctor." A short, bald man carrying a black satchel tried to squeeze past her.

"Oh yes. Please hurry." She backed into a seat that already held a man and a half-grown boy, but she wasn't budging. Relief flooded her when she saw her hero's chest rise and fall with each breath.

The boy behind her shinnied over the bench in front of them. Mariah sat in his seat, realizing her still legs trembled.

The doctor squeezed in beside her hero then glanced up at her. "You won't faint if I have you assist me, will you?"

She shook her head, hoping that she could keep her senses about her. She'd never attended anyone who'd been shot before. The doctor pulled several squares of surgical dressing from his black leather bag and placed them on the gash above the man's right eyebrow.

"Hold that down, please." Mariah did as requested, trying to keep steady in spite of the rocking train. The doctor deftly tied strips of fabric around the man's head to hold on the bandage.

He unbuttoned the man's vest and shirt, revealing the wounded arm, and prodded area around the wound. Mariah's cheeks heated at the sight of her hero's solid chest. She never knew a man's torso could be so tanned and appealing. She fanned her face and looked away for a moment.

The doctor dabbed the wound with cotton then poured a foul-smelling liquid on it. The man didn't flinch, so Mariah suspected the medicine must not have felt as awful as it smelled. The doctor pressed a thick wad of dressing over the entry wound.

"Help me roll him over a bit."

Mariah complied then grimaced when she saw more blood on his shirt.

"Yep, just as I thought. The bullet went clear through his upper arm. Hopefully it missed the bone, but there could be some muscle damage." He grabbed another dressing and pressed it against the back of her hero's arm. Glancing up at Mariah, he pursed his lips. "Not a lot that I can do here, except try to stop the bleeding."

She nodded, not sure why the doctor kept talking to her as if she and the man were related.

The doctor laid the injured man's right forearm across Mariah's lap. The improper action shocked her, but she kept silent. The bare hand and wrist were a sun-kissed brown with dark hairs coloring them. His forearm felt solid, hard—not soft like Silas's.

"Hold him steady, so I can get his wound wrapped tightly."

She secured his warm arm with both of her hands. While the doctor made quick work of bandaging the wound, she studied the injured man's face. Long, black lashes fanned his tanned cheek. His nose was straight, and his mouth pleasant to look at.

When the doctor moved away, she stared at the red dot on the man's head dressing. Black hair matted with blood hung over the fabric. Would he need sutures? Would he have a scar that marred his fine features?

His face was clean shaven, and she couldn't help remembering his vivid blue eyes. Did he have a wife or other family waiting on him to return home? Children, perhaps?

"All right, that's as good as I can get it for now. It's best we leave him on the floor, ma'am." The doctor looked at Mariah again. "He's lost a lot of blood, but I think he'll recover. You need to take him off at the next stop and get him to the local doctor. I've only got limited supplies in my bag, but I think we've slowed the bleeding down. If you wouldn't be opposed to sitting in the aisle, your husband might be more comfortable with his head in your lap."

My husband? Mariah knew she ought to correct the kind doctor, but she desperately wanted to help her champion, and there seemed only one thing she could do at the moment, no matter the impropriety of the action. She nodded and moved into the aisle.

"I reckon you'll get more blood on that pretty outfit."

She looked down at her wrinkled travel garments. She owed this man her virtue and possibly her life. Who knows what would have happened if he hadn't helped? Hers was a small sacrifice compared to his, and she sat down in the dirty, bloodstained aisle, knowing such an action would have shocked her grandmother. If she knew Mariah had nearly been kidnapped by an outlaw, she'd have her granddaughter on the next train headed home.

The doctor and another passenger lifted the wounded man and laid his head into her lap. She didn't know where to put her hands. Finally, she looped one arm around his head and wrapped her other arm around his chest, holding his shirt closed. The man's steady breath warmed her face. Her cheeks burned. Never had she been in such an intimate position with a man. But she owed him so much.

Before long, her shoulder burned from the strain of holding his head steady. Who would have thought that a head could be so heavy?

The doctor checked his patient's pulse and nodded. "Nice and steady. He's a young fellow and in good shape, so I'm sure he'll come around soon. Try not to worry overly much."

"Is it normal for him to be unconscious for so long?" she asked.

The doc shrugged one shoulder. "Could be from the shooting, but it's more likely he has a concussion from that blow to his head when he fell."

"Here's your money and the gentleman's belongings." A thin man handed the robber's loot bag to the doctor, and he passed it to her. She peaked inside to make sure her reticle was in the bag. At least the man would get his watch and money back. She clung tightly to the sack, thankful to have a bit of good news to share when he awakened.

Mariah glanced around the railcar. It looked odd and unnatural from this viewpoint. The thief squirmed on the floor, where someone had tied him to the iron legs of a bench seat.

He glared at her. "I'm gonna get you," she thought he mouthed. Her heart jolted. Surely she was mistaken. Gratitude swelled when a man moved into the aisle, shielding her.

People had finally stopped staring at them and had gone back to reading or sleeping or whatever else they were doing before the robbery. She tried leaning her head against the edge of the nearest bench, but the rough ride jarred it too badly.

Silas intruded into her mind. Though they'd courted for nearly a year, she didn't miss him in the least. He would never have been brave enough to come to her aid as this stranger had. She brushed strands of his hair away from the bandage on his forehead. His ebony hair felt softer than she'd expected. She didn't even know her hero's name, but there was so much more to him than Silas. Why hadn't she realized sooner how low a caliber of a man her former fiancé was? Was she merely taken with him because he had an enviable position at the newspaper?

A low moan drew her gaze back to her patient. His head lumbered to the left. She wanted to do whatever possible to make him comfortable. If Mr. McFarland was at the depot waiting on her, he would just have to continue waiting or return another day for her. She'd get her champion to a doctor and find a room in Medora until he no longer needed her assistance.

Adam struggled to open his eyes. He rubbed a hand across them, trying to figure out why the floor was shaking. His ears rang and a campfire burned in his right arm. Where was he? What happened?

Someone forced his arm down. Suddenly he remembered the gun pointed in his face and the sneering robber. His heart pounded as he blinked his surroundings into focus. An intense ache radiated from his forehead down through the top half of his body. Something shifted under his head, and he looked up. Fancy Feathers stared down at him, abnormally close. The sweet fragrance of her perfume drifted around him. Concern dimmed her brown eyes. What in the world?

He tried to sit up, but something held him fast. Her arms?

"Lie still. You've been shot."

Shot!

Now everything came back into focus, and he remembered Fancy Feathers stabbing the robber. The man had jumped when she jabbed him, and his gun had gone off.

Had she saved his life by causing the robber to shoot him in the arm instead of the chest or head? Or perhaps he wouldn't have been injured at all, if not for her crazy action. Thank the good Lord that the shot wasn't fatal. At least he hoped it wouldn't be.

Adam shoved his pain aside and sniffed the woman's feminine scent. He didn't like being so close that she could impale him with one of her long pokers, but he felt weaker than a newborn colt. Besides, cushioned with all her skirts, her lap was so soft. He didn't think he could get up without help and didn't want to make a spectacle, so he allowed himself to relax. His strength would be needed soon enough.

"Next stop, Medora," the purser shouted as he stepped through the door. When his gaze landed on Adam, his eyes widened. "What happened in here?"

A woman in calico near the front of the car explained the situation. The purser shook his head and continued his spiel as if a robbery were an everyday occasion. "Medora ain't much of a town, folks, but you can get something to eat at the café and get a look at the Marquis de Mores' big house on the hill. Course, he don't live there no more, but it makes for an interesting story. We'll be making a long stop to talk with the sheriff and get these men off-loaded."

Adam realized he was one of the men the purser was talking about. At least he was in Medora and not in some other town along the rail line.

But how would he get home? The buckboard was at the livery, but he wasn't sure if he could drive it one-handed, the way he felt right now. If he could only get his buckboard and the supplies loaded at the depot, surely his horses could find their way home.

Chapter Five

"That should take care of it, for now." The doctor, who'd recently arrived in Medora, also served as barber in the small town. He swiped his hands on a towel. "Change the dressing daily until it scabs over. Looks like the bullet went straight through. It missed the bone, but there could be muscle damage, so don't use that arm for several weeks or so. And bed rest would be best for the next few days."

Wonderful. There went his deadline—and his hopes of leaving the ranch.

"How much do I owe you?"

"Two bits'll be good."

Bracing his wounded arm against his chest, Adam slid off the table. His knees threatened to buckle as his feet hit the ground. He checked his jacket pocket and remembered the robber had stolen his money. Had his watch and money been recovered since the thief was captured?

Fancy Feathers darted around the curtain that separated the barbershop from the doctoring room. Had she been there the whole time, watching and listening?

Adam glanced down at his bare chest. The shirt that had been new when he left Bismarck this morning was now bloodied and dirty with a hole in the right sleeve. The shirt covered his shoulder but gaped open since his injured arm wasn't in the sleeve. He attempted to pull it together. What was she doing here, anyway?

"I'll pay for your services." She rummaged around in that little bag of hers and pulled out three coins and handed them to the doc.

Adam preferred to pay his own debts, but since his money was gone, he kept his mouth shut, swallowing back his embarrassment. He could square up with her later.

He leaned against the table, hoping the floor would stop swirling. Somehow he had to get to the livery, pick up his wagon, then get over to the depot and collect the supplies he'd bought in Bismarck.

He hoped news of the train robbery and his getting shot didn't make it all the way back to Bismarck. His mother would be concerned if she figured out his train had gotten held up. He wouldn't mind being back at his grandmother's nice home now, though, and letting them coddle him a bit with good cooking and loving attention.

He breathed in a deep breath, pushed away from the table, wobbled, then leaned back.

"You'll be weak for a while. You lost a barrelful of blood." The doctor pulled back the curtain that separated his operating room from the barbershop. "And that small dose of laudanum I gave you will make you sleepy. You can stay here if you like, but I've got several women about to deliver babes that I need to check on."

Adam shook his head, instantly sorry. "I need to get home."

The doctor frowned. "It'd be best if you stayed in town tonight rather than trying to travel on."

"I'll make sure he does what he's supposed to." Fancy Feathers hurried to his side and hooked his good arm around her thin shoulders before he could object. "Let me help."

He hissed at the biting pain the movement caused.

"I'm so sorry. Oh, this is all my fault."

Adam clenched his jaw as sweat trickled down his neck. If only she had given the outlaw her cameo, perhaps the man would have left her alone. Perhaps Adam's arm wouldn't have two holes in it.

But in all fairness, she was as green as they came. She had no way of knowing how dangerous the West could be. The person he should be angry at was the one who let her travel alone.

She glanced up at him and smiled as if they were going on a Sunday picnic. "Ready?"

"Looks like you'll have plenty of good nursin'." The doc smiled and waggled his brow. He pulled a clean triangle of white fabric from a drawer, tied it around Adam's neck, and then carefully placed his forearm in the sling. "That should help to keep your arm injury from being jostled so much."

Adam nodded his thanks and realized he didn't even know the man's name. Lots of folks had left Medora after the bad winters of 1886 and '87. A few new folks like the doctor had come to town, but since he was rarely in Medora, he didn't know all that many people.

Fancy Feathers took a step forward, but he pulled away. "I can walk just fine, lady." She scowled and looked to be holding back a comment.

Her gentle touch had stirred something in him that he didn't want to consider with everything else he had to worry about right now. He made it a whole three feet to the doorjamb and sagged against it.

C'mon, McFarland. Buck up. Quinn's occasional taunting rattled in his brain.

"Sir, my name is Miss Mariah Lansing, and it's obvious you need help. Please, allow me to assist you. It's the least I can do after you came to my rescue like you did."

The pungent scents of antiseptic, hair oil, and shaving cream from the barbershop made his empty stomach revolt. He needed to get outside before he embarrassed himself any further.

At the fervent pleading in Miss Lansing's lovely eyes, something inside Adam yielded. Maybe she would feel less responsible for his getting shot if he let her help him a little. "All right."

Her sweet smile made him long to stand up straight and put his arm around her shoulders—because he wanted to, not because he needed help. *Whoa!*

Where had that thought come from? This was the lady with the spikes in her hat, remember?

He made it out the front door. The glare from the bright afternoon sun stabbed his eyes; his headache doubled in intensity. Adam squinted and leaned against Fancy Feathers for support more than he wanted to.

"I think maybe you should sit down for a minute." She led him to one of the chairs lined up in front of the barbershop, and he dropped down without arguing.

"I intend to help you, but I need to know where you want to go."

The blow on his head must be the source of his wooziness— or maybe the laudanum was. Adam hated feeling out of control and dependent on a stranger—a woman, no less. If he could just get to the wagon. . .maybe he could get home and let Quinn send one of their hands back in town for the supplies.

He needed to check at the depot and see if his money and his watch had been turned in. And what happened to his new hat?

Mariah stared at her hero. She didn't think he had the strength to even make it across the street. "Do you need to go back to the depot and wait for the next train so you can continue your journey?"

He shook his head—slow and easy. "This *is* my stop."

Well that certainly simplified things. Mariah smiled and looked around the small, rustic town of Medora, set in a valley between big mounds of hills and rocks that were part of the Badlands. They didn't look all that bad to her. She turned toward the depot. Would Mr. McFarland be waiting there for her? Hopefully he'd received the telegram she'd sent yesterday from Bismarck.

Perhaps she should have sought him out before coming to the doctor's office. He might have returned home when he couldn't locate her.

A smattering of mostly one-story wooden buildings dotted the area, along with several brick buildings. She swallowed back her unease. Medora sure wasn't like any place she'd ever been. Never had she imagined it would be such a rustic setting. "So, do you live here in town?"

"On a ranch." He leaned his head back against the barbershop wall and closed his eyes.

Her heart leaped. What a coincidence. Perhaps he knew Mr. McFarland.

He swatted a pestering fly and grimaced. Mariah hated seeing him in pain. He'd been so commanding when he pulled that smelly thief off her seat and had swapped places with him—and then again when he saved her from being kidnapped and who knows what else. Why, just the jump from the fast-moving train would have probably killed her.

"Got a buckboard at the livery. If you want to help, you could fetch it and bring it here." His right eye opened to a slit.

She gulped. How hard could steering a wagon be? She'd never done it before since her grandma had a carriage driver, but maybe the livery owner could instruct her. For her champion, she'd give it her be. When she nodded, he closed his eyes again.

"Just tell them you need the McFarland wagon."

A spasm started in Mariah's neck and skittered down her spine. *McFarland? As in Adam McFarland?*

Surely it couldn't be. But how common of a name was that in these parts? "Um. . .shouldn't I give a first name also?"

"We're the only McFarlands in the area. Just tell Jake that Adam sent you and I'll settle up what I owe him in a few days."

Mariah grabbed the nearest post and clung to it. *Oh dear.*

Should she tell him who she was? Or would it be better to wait until they arrived at the ranch? Surely he wouldn't force her to go back to town once he learned her identity. But would he allow the person responsible for his getting shot to stay at his ranch?

First things first. *Get the wagon from the livery to here. Worry about the rest later.*

She pulled down the brim of her hat to cut the glare of the sun and retied the sashes under her chin. Just where was the livery anyway?

Mariah turned left and walked a few feet.

"It's the other way. Past the depot."

She halted and pivoted, thankful his eyes were shut. His smirk and sarcastic tone indicated he didn't have much confidence in her abilities. Hiking her chin, she marched past his slumped form. So far she'd failed to show him that she was capable, but that would change.

Dust stirred in the streets on the warm breeze, assaulting her with the odors of manure and cattle. Mariah retrieved her handkerchief and held it to her nose. She made her way back to the depot then hurried past a malodorous holding area for cattle. Ignoring the pitiful cries of the penned creatures, probably doomed for the butcher block, she made a beeline for a lone barnlike structure with Livery crudely painted over the double doors.

Mariah brushed at the dried blood on her travel dress and winced at the dark splotches. If she didn't get it soaking in cold water soon, the outfit would be ruined.

She stepped into the dimly lit building. Dust motes danced on shafts of light streaming through the cracks in the walls, and the strong odor of animals nearly overpowered her. Following a pounding sound, she located a giant of a man nailing a board across a stall. His back was to her. Mariah cleared her throat. "Um. . .pardon me."

The man swung around, his hammer in the air. She took a step backward. He was huge—had to be well over six feet tall. Sweat dripped off his dirty face into his beard, and he stared at her as if she were a mirage. He suddenly jerked into action, set his hammer on a bench, and wiped his face with a dirty bandanna.

"Excuse me, ma'am. I didn't know you were there." He swiped his filthy hands on faded overalls and stepped forward. "What can I do for you?"

The rancid scent of stale body odor and tobacco wafted past her. It took all of Mariah's willpower not to shove her perfumed handkerchief back under her nose.

"I'm here to get Mr. McFarland's wagon for him." A horse stuck its head out of a nearby stall and nickered at her, as if asking for a treat.

The man's beady eyes narrowed, and he spat a dark stream of something vile toward a nasty pot in the corner. He missed. "Where's McFarland?"

Mariah swallowed down her nervousness. Another horse whinnied for attention. "He was shot in a train robbery. He saved my life, and now I'm trying to help him get home."

The man snorted and ran his gaze down her body. "You know how to drive a team of horses?"

Mariah forced a sweet smile and batted her lashes. She despised flirting but this was for a noble purpose. She simply must get Mr. McFarland home before he collapsed. "I don't suppose *you* could drive it over to the doctor's office, could you?"

He softened his stance, and one corner of his thick mouth turned up. He scratched his chest. "Reckon I could—to help out a lady. Let me get the team hitched."

Mariah swallowed back a relieved sigh as he entered a stall at the back of the livery and walked out one of the largest horses she had ever seen. In spite of its size, the dappled gray had a smooth grace to it.

"This here's Samson. Mighty fine animal, isn't he?" He didn't wait for a response but kept talking. "After their pa died, them McFarlands started raising these here Percherons. Folks from all over the area go to the Rocking M now to buy stock from them."

The man's deep voice rumbled as he talked, and Mariah filed the information away to consider later. He moved into the shadows in the back of the big barn and then reappeared with a near twin horse to the first one. This animal snorted and shook its head. Mariah moved back a few feet.

The man chuckled. "This here's Delilah. Samson's a sweet ole boy, but his sister. . .well, she's a bit persnickety."

Perfect. Just what she needed—a horse with an attitude.

"My name's Jake, by the way."

"Miss Mariah Lansing."

"Miss, eh?" Jake grinned, revealing yellowed teeth and a dark stain inside his mouth. He spat another black stream and wiped his chin with the back of his hand.

She stepped back at his suggestive leer, feeling quite vulnerable alone with him. He chuckled and moved into motion, attaching yards of leather harnesses to the big animals.

When finished, Jake surveyed the team. Samson lowered his head and sniffed a stray clump of hay on the ground while Delilah pawed the dirt and snorted, as if anxious to be on her way. A trickle of sweat slid down Mariah's temple, and she dabbed it with her hankie. The pair of matched blacks that her grandma owned looked half the size of the McFarlands' team. How would she ever manage to steer such big horses?

"You ready?"

Mariah nodded. She studied the wagon. How in the world was she supposed to climb up to the seat and still resemble a lady? Jake stepped to her side, and she forced herself not to grimace at his filthy outstretched hands. Before she could attempt to climb up herself, he spun her around. She nearly screamed as he grabbed her waist from behind and tossed her upward. Mariah grabbed the side of the wagon and climbed on board, her cheeks burning. The big oaf may know how to handle horses, but he sure didn't know how to treat women.

She rearranged her bunched skirts as she gathered her composure; then she sat. The padded leather cushion did little to soften the seat. The wagon lurched dangerously to the side as Jake climbed aboard. His bulk filled nearly the whole bench. Mariah scooted as far to the right as she could. She longed to keep her face turned away from the man's overpowering body odor, but she needed to watch how he drove the team.

He used both hands, separating the long leather lines between his fingers, then grunted a "Step up."

In unison, the horses lifted their big heads and moved forward. That seemed easy enough.

At the end of the road, Jake called out, "Gee."

Mariah made note of the odd word and the wide right turn the team made. She watched how Jake held his hands out in front of him. Mariah relaxed in the seat. She could do this, and Mr. McFarland wouldn't have to know she'd never driven a team before.

At Samson's familiar whinny, Adam opened his eyes. It didn't surprise him a bit that Jake drove the wagon instead of Miss Lansing. He had to hand it to her, the gal was resourceful. He imagined her blinking those long lashes and Jake nearly swallowing his chaw at her request for help.

Adam pushed up from the chair and hated the dizziness. His arm ached, and the bright sunlight made his head hurt. If only he could locate his hat, at least he could eliminate one problem. Clinging to a post, Adam waited for the wagon to stop. When Fancy Feathers turned her concerned gaze his way, his heart skittered. What would it be like to have a pretty gal like her taking care of him all the time?

He shook his head, driving the unwanted thought away. How could he forget so quickly how she so lethally handled those hatpins of hers?

Adam was grateful for the shadow created as Jake stopped the wagon in from of him. The buckboard creaked when the big man climbed down. "Thanks, Jake. I'll square up my bill next time I'm in town, if that's all right?"

Jake nodded. "Take care of that purty little gal and that arm of yours." Jake tipped his cap to Miss Lansing and lumbered away.

Adam glanced up to see a worried expression on her face. Was she concerned about him? Or driving the team?

The wagon's bench looked a mile away, but with some heaving and tight-fisted grappling using his good hand, he managed to climb up without embarrassing himself. After taking a moment to catch his breath, he reached for the reins. Miss Lansing snatched them up before he could get them. He frowned at her.

"You're wounded. I'll drive."

He wanted to ask if she knew how but sat back and decided just to watch.

It took her a moment, but she managed to get a set of reins in each hand. Confusion wrinkled her brow; then her lips curved up in a smile, and she shook the reins. "Stand up."

Samson and Delilah jerked their heads but didn't move. Adam couldn't help grinning. "They're already standing up. Did you perchance mean 'Step up'?"

Red flamed across her pale cheeks, and she hiked her chin. "Yes, I believe that is the correct phraseology. Step up."

The team lurched forward. Miss Lansing flopped back ward, the beleaguered feather in her hat flapping as if waving goodbye. Relief washed across her pretty face. Women in this part of the country rarely had skin as fair as hers. He couldn't help wondering if it would feel as soft as it looked. She struggled with the long reins and held them close to her chest, with the right side dangling a bit. Samson veered that direction, nearly plowing into a black horse tethered to a post. The surprised animal danced sideways then looked back to see what was behind him.

"Haw, Samson! Delilah." The Percherons shifted to the left at his firm command and away from the near collision. Miss Lansing avoided his gaze, her cheeks red. "Keep the same tension on both reins. And hold your arms out a little so you're able to pull back, if needed."

The woman scowled at his instructions but did as he said. Samson headed straight again. After several minutes and two more near misses, the wagon slowed at the depot. She pulled hard on the reins, leaning back so far her body nearly formed a straight line. Adam bit back a smile at her tenacity.

The horses stopped. Miss Lansing heaved a sigh and rose. "I need to get my things."

"Don't forget the brake."

"What?" She whirled to face him. "Oh, uh. . .yes." Her gaze traveled the bed and sides of the wagon. She nibbled one edge of her bottom lip. "I'm afraid I don't know where it is."

Adam pointed to the wooden lever on the side, and she struggled to pull it back. She wrestled with it a few minutes then huffed out a sigh. "I can't seem to get it to budge."

Adam resisted shaking his head. His first opinion was correct. Greenhorns had no business in the West. "I'll do it."

"But you're injured."

He ground his teeth together. It wasn't the first time he'd been hurt. Shot, yes. Wounded, no. He stood. "Go ahead and get down."

He held out his hand to assist her, but she glared at it and climbed down alone, fighting her skirts all the way. He half expected her to fall but was glad she didn't. He shoved the brake in place and wrapped up the reins then struggled himself to get down one-handed. While Miss Lansing flagged down the purser, he went into the depot.

Horace Grimes nodded at him. "Glad to see you back on your feet. Got your gear back here."

Horace disappeared for a moment then returned, holding out Adam's hat and pistol. Glancing at the holster around his hips, he was surprised he hadn't noticed the weapon was missing before now. He shoved the gun into the holster, chastising himself for getting lax. Being without his gun could be dangerous out here. Many men in North Dakota didn't even wear a weapon, but as a boy growing up in Texas, he learned the smart thing was to wear a gun. He pressed the shape back into his smashed hat. This one sure hadn't stayed nice for long.

"Got some mail and a telegram for you and yours." Horace handed him a stack of envelopes with the telegram on top. "Folks say you helped stop the robbery."

Adam shrugged, uncomfortable with Horace's evident admiration. "Just trying to save a lady from getting kidnapped."

Horace nodded. "Well, the railroad is grateful, as I'm sure the woman is. Your crates of supplies are at the west end of the depot. Otis and Jasper can load them into your wagon for you."

"Thanks. I don't guess you've seen the robber's loot bag? My pocket watch and money were in it."

Horace pursed his lips and shook his head. "Can't say as I have. Sorry."

Adam needed to find his family's money, but instead, he found an empty bench and dropped onto it. He yawned and opened the telegram addressed to himself.

Arriving Medora depot June 4.
Drew Dixon

He turned the paper over, as if the back held more information. Why did that name sound so familiar?

Leaning his head against the wall, his body felt heavy from the numbing effects of the laudanum. He wished he were already home.

Drew Dixon. Adam rummaged around in his mind, finally grasping hold of the name. The dime-novel writer. The one he'd invited to the ranch—was arriving today. Adam bolted upright and searched the platform for a stranger. What lousy timing. He was in no mood to host another greenhorn from the city. But he *had* made the invitation.

He pushed to his feet, blinked his vision clear, then approached Horace's cage again. "Has a man by the name of Dixon been looking for me?"

"Nope. Can't say as he has."

"Mmm. . .must have missed his train or had something come up." Adam looked for Miss Lansing and noticed the porter loading a huge trunk he didn't recognize onto his wagon, as well as his own crates of supplies. He scowled, wondering if she planned to move in. He turned back to Horace. "If the man shows up, have him stay at the hotel. Someone from the ranch will probably come to town on Saturday, and he can catch a ride then." Adam stepped back.

Miss Lansing smiled at him and slipped up to the window. "I need to send a telegram."

Leaning against a post, he tried not to listen—sort of.

"To Heleen Vanderveer." She relayed a Chicago address that for some reason sounded vaguely familiar. "Arrived safely in Medora. Mariah."

Who was this Vanderveer woman? Was Miss Lansing from Chicago? And had she planned to stop in Medora? That's how it sounded. He couldn't for the life of him figure out why a city gal like her would come here, unless she had something to do with the Marquis de Mores' family.

Adam's gaze drifted to the huge house on the hillside, which townsfolk called "the chateau." The marquis rarely visited Medora anymore. Not since his business had failed. The town had been named after the marquis' spunky wife, who still visited occasionally. The Marquis de Mores had been a visionary. He built a huge meat processing plant right across the Little Missouri River. Adam could see the tall smokestack from the depot. But the marquis' dream of shipping refrigerated cattle back East had collapsed after two killing winters, where ranchers like De Mores had lost the majority of their herds. Adam was glad they hadn't had such rough winters since his family had arrived in North Dakota.

"Ready to go?"

Miss Lansing's voice near his ear startled Adam out of his thoughts. He helped her down the depot steps and then assisted her as she climbed onto the buckboard. He clambered aboard the wagon again, realizing it was harder this time than the last. He reached for the reins out of habit, receiving a glare from Miss Lansing.

"Let me drive. That's why I'm here—to help you."

He still wasn't sure how much help she was but didn't feel like arguing the point with the laudanum making is limbs sluggish. He passed the reins to her and leaned back in the seat, thankful to have his hat again.

"Just get the team out of town and down the road a ways, and they'll get us home."

He slouched down, ready to rest. When the wagon didn't move, he pushed his hat off his forehead. "Something wrong?"

She nibbled her lip in so appealing a manner that he hated being such a grouch. "Um. . .which way is your home?"

Chapter Six

With each step the horses took, Adam McFarland drifted farther in Mariah's direction until his head finally rested against her shoulder. She'd watched him fight to stay awake and upright, but finally the laudanum had taken effect. Soft puffs of his warm breath tickled her neck. She longed to scratch the area but feared losing control of the team.

Mariah braced her foot against the floorboard. The weight of Mr. McFarland's heavy body pushed her sideways, closer and closer to the wagon's edge.

"Back on your on side, buster." Using her upper arm and elbow, she gently pushed him over as best she could.

At least he'd been right in that the horses seemed to know the way home. At each fork in the dirt road they'd come to, she'd held her breath and watched as the horses turned in unison without her assistance.

Samson nickered, and Delilah answered. They picked up their pace as they crested a hill covered in knee-high grass and prickly bushes. Mariah exhaled a sigh at the sight of the wooden uprights supporting a sign that read Rocking M Ranch. The sign looked odd standing there all by itself with no fences leading up to it. From her research, she knew much of this land was still open range, without wire and wooden boundaries.

The ranch landscape appeared much the same as what they'd been traveling through for over two hours. Steep hills covered in rock gave way to valleys of grasslands. Sages and junipers provided excellent hiding places for the birds that made a *ka-squack* sound and the quick, light gray rabbit that had darted across their path. Here and there small trees provided a smattering of shade, while wildflowers of violet, lemonade yellow, and white made the grasslands and rocky areas beautiful. The gentle breeze whipped her cheeks as she enjoyed the palette of nature.

A prairie dog peeked out of its hole, sniffed the air, and froze. It stared at her and squeaked before scurrying back into its mounded home. Other nearby prairie dogs followed suit.

A sharp pain in her neck drew her attention away from the comical critters. Her shoulder ached from the pressure of Mr. McFarland's head. It hadn't seemed so heavy when it had rested in her lap. Using her shoulder, she pushed him to the right again. He mumbled something incoherent but didn't awaken.

Now that they were closer to his home, anxiety swirled in her stomach, reminding her that she hadn't eaten since breakfast. The biscuit in her satchel was probably hard by now. If she hadn't been so thirsty, she might consider trying to figure out a way to remove it from her bag. But holding the leather reins with both hands and keeping Mr. McFarland from falling off the seat took all of her physical capabilities.

Mariah tightened her grip on the reins to keep the horses from going too fast. They must be close to home since she had to fight to keep them at a slower pace. She wished she felt so enthusiastic. Would Mr. McFarland's family hold her accountable for his injuries? Would they welcome her or send her packing?

Mariah licked the dust from her lips and grimaced at the grittiness in her teeth. She swallowed the dry lump in her throat and thought of the long walk back to town. She hadn't seen any nefarious creatures like wolves or coyotes but knew they were around. The western horizon gradually turned plum and orange as the sun sank lower. The total silence, except for an occasional bird squawk and the sound of the wind, was eerie after the noise of Chicago. What kind of critters ruled the night way out here?

Surely Mr. McFarland's family would be hospitable and let her stay until morning—and hopefully longer. She had a little money but hadn't brought a lot, knowing that she'd be staying at the ranch. What would she do if those plans fell through?

They topped another hill, and a large log cabin came into view, as well as a big barn and other smaller structures. Two brown horses stood side by side in a corral, their tails swishing. Mariah's heartbeat picked up as the team increased their pace again.

She'd dreamed for two years of visiting a ranch and learning things to make her stories more authentic, but she'd never once thought of arriving in such a manner. The horses headed straight for the barn in spite of Mariah's struggles to turn them toward the house. "Haw, haw," she yelled, sounding more like a flustered crow than a driver in control.

A woman exited the front door of the house and stood on the porch, her hand shading her eyes. She was certainly young enough to be Mr. McFarland's wife.

"Adam!" she cried, her hand flying to cover her chest. She pushed into motion, lifted her skirts, and jumped off the porch, ignoring the steps.

Mariah gasped at her unladylike behavior but concentrated on stopping the team before they plowed into the barn. She jerked back on the reins and pressed her feet hard against the floorboard. "Stop. Halt. I mean, whoa. Please, whoa."

Mr. McFarland jerked awake and sat up. "Samson, whoa!"

He grabbed the reins with his good hand and assisted her efforts. Thankfully, the animals stopped just outside the barn. Mariah had no idea if the barn's double door opening was wide enough to accommodate the wagon. The last thing she needed now was to destroy the McFarlands' barn and wagon and injure his fine horses.

Her passenger rubbed his eyes then pressed his palm against his bandaged forehead. The woman's steps pounded as she ran toward the wagon. She skidded to a halt at Mr. McFarland's side, honey blond braids flapping, and climbed up onto the wagon wheel. She glanced at him and then to Mariah. "What happened?"

"He was shot in a train robbery." Mariah laid down the reins and attempted to wrestle the brake into place.

"Quinn!" the woman yelled toward the barn, "Adam's hurt!"

"I don't need him." Mr. McFarland stood, wobbled, and then sank back onto the seat. "Gimme a minute, and I'll be fine."

"Good grief, Adam, you're not invincible. It's not a shame to ask for help." The woman reached for his hand, but he shook it off.

A tall, broad-shouldered man ran out of the barn, followed by two more. His concerned brown eyes mirrored the woman's. In fact, they resembled each other so much that Mariah felt sure they must be related.

Her hero stood again and climbed down, albeit very ungracefully. He landed on the ground, grimacing, and grabbed his arm. Her heart ached for him, and she wished she could ease his pain.

The man named Quinn hurried to Mr. McFarland's side, and ignoring the protests, assisted him into the house. The young woman followed then stopped and looked back at Mariah. "Thank you for bringing my brother home. Would you please come into the house and wait while we get Adam situated?"

Mariah nodded and allowed a skinny ranch hand to help her down. *Her brother.*

Now why was that such welcome news?

Adam hated leaning on Quinn, but he doubted he'd make it all the way to the house on his own. He'd tried ever since their father died to prove himself responsible to his big brother, and once again he'd failed.

Quinn's strong arm upheld Adam and half dragged him through the front door Anna had left open in her haste to get to him. He figured he'd be coddled and babied by her and Leyna for the next few days, not that he'd mind some of Leyna's fine cooking. But rather than enjoying their fussing over him, it would remind him that he wasn't pulling his weight.

Anna took his hat and Quinn's and hung them on their pegs inside the front door. Quinn shouldered him down the hall to Adam's small bedroom then set him on the bed and removed his boots.

"Lie down and tell me what happened," Quinn ordered.

Adam complied, only because he didn't have the energy to argue. "There was a train robbery a few miles outside of town."

Eyes wide, Anna clung to the doorframe, listening. "How did you get shot?"

He explained how the robber had taken Miss Lansing captive and how he'd gotten shot trying to rescue her.

"You're a hero." Anna smiled.

"You were stupid to interfere." Quinn glared at him.

Adam struggled to sit again so he didn't have to look so far up to Quinn. "I couldn't very well let those thieves take an innocent woman with them, could I? You know what would have happened to her. I kept thinking, 'What if it was Anna?' "

"At least you're all right." Quinn sighed and stood. "Stay in bed for the next few days."

He strode out the door, and once again Adam felt his big brother's disappointment.

Anna crossed the room and hugged him. "Don't listen to him. He's just worried about you."

"He's got a funny way of showing it."

"I'm so thankful to God that you're safe. Let's get that dirty shirt off." Anna tugged at his sleeve, freeing his good arm, then wadded up the soiled shirt. She sat on the edge of the ladderback chair in the corner by the window, brown eyes dancing. "So, tell me about the woman you brought home."

"The horses brought me home." Adam harrumphed. "She wanted to help me as a way of saying thanks, so I let her."

"She's pretty."

"For a greenhorn." Adam scooted down, trying to get comfortable. Every way he moved made his arm ache. Exhaustion weighed down his eyelids. He yawned. "Make sure someone gets her back to town in time for the next train—and let's pay for her ticket. She probably has family wondering where she is."

Anna pressed her lips together and studied the floor. After several moments, she looked up. "I'd like to ask her to stay awhile."

"What? Are you crazy? She's a stranger. We know nothing about her."

Anna shrugged one shoulder. "No, but I do get lonely for a woman's company, especially now that Ma is in Bismarck."

"She's not your playmate, sis."

Anna pulled a face. "Do you need anything right now?"

He didn't miss how she deftly changed the subject, but he didn't feel like arguing.

"Another dose of laudanum," he considered saying. But he despised how the pain medicine had made him woozy. Adam shook his head then reconsidered. "Maybe a glass of water?"

"Sure."

In what seemed like a few seconds, Anna returned. She helped him sit up enough to drink a glass of cool water then assisted him down again. She stuffed a pillow under his wounded arm, which allowed him to relax it without as much pain. "Thanks."

"You rest for a while. I'm going to see to our guest."

Adam was grateful Anna was tending to Fancy Feathers. With the lateness of the hour, hospitality dictated they should invite her to stay the night. Though he was embarrassed for her to see him in this lacking physical state, he didn't know how he would have managed to get home without her help.

Another yawn tugged at his lips. What would Miss Lansing look like without her big hat and her soft, brown hair hanging down around her face?

Perhaps in the morning he'd feel good enough to find out where she was going, so he could send her on her way. Greenhorns had no business leaving their big cities. Just look at all the trouble this one had caused.

Mariah rubbed at her blistered hands and wondered how long they'd smell of leather. She alternated between studying the parlor and worrying about Adam McFarland. For some reason, he'd seemed irritated to have the big man assist him. She wondered if the man called Quinn was Adam's brother. They didn't resemble each other much in coloring but were similar in build, except that Quinn was a few inches taller. Both were long in the legs and broad in the shoulders.

Her gaze landed on a family portrait. A handsome, dark-haired man stood behind a pretty woman with pale hair who sat in a chair. The man's hand rested on her shoulder. Beside them stood three children. One a tall, gangly adolescent, and a shorter boy and girl, who were equal in height.

"That portrait was taken in Texas over ten years ago, when my father was still alive."

Mariah swung around to face Mr. McFarland's sister. "It's wonderful that you have something so nice to remember him by. So, is your mother still living?"

"Yes, she's in Bismarck tending my grandmother, who broke her leg." The woman stopped beside Mariah. "I can still remember how I hated standing so long while the painter was working. The boys kept tickling me and getting me in trouble for squirming. But I'm glad we have the painting now. I often gaze at it so I don't forget what my father looked like."

"You favor your mother."

The woman's eyes lit up. "Thank you. That's kind of you to say. If you couldn't tell by the painting, Adam is my twin brother. We look a bit alike. Our mouths and noses are similar, but Adam has dark hair like our father's. I'm Anna McFarland, by the way."

"Mariah Lansing. Pleased to meet you." Mariah nodded at the colorful canvas. "And the man who helped your brother inside is the taller boy in the painting?"

"Yes, that's Quinn. He's five years older than us. He's been in charge of the ranch ever since Pa died."

"I'm sorry for your loss. I lost my parents when I was young." Mariah hugged her satchel to her chest. The day's journey and excitement had finally caught up with her, and she longed to rest.

"Thank you. I'm sorry for your loss also."

A heavyset woman scurried into the room. Mariah's gaze landed on the tray containing a teapot and cups and a plate of breads and cookies. The fresh scents made her mouth water. The woman set the tray on a coffee table in front of a leather couch. "Welcome to the Rocking M."

"Thank you." Mariah nodded. Welcome sounded more like *velcome* and the more like *de*. With her accent and the woman's braided buns curled onto the sides of her head, Mariah surmised she must be German. "Might I clean up a bit before taking refreshments?"

Anna scanned Mariah's travel dress then pursed her lips. She captured Mariah's gaze. "I'm thinking we should soak your dress in cold water. We might yet be able to salvage it."

"*Ja*, I will do the soaking and get the guest room ready for the visitor."

"This is Leyna. She's our cook and much more. Come to my room, and you can clean up and change."

Mariah followed her, unable to stem her curiosity as they passed a small bedroom with the door open. Her heart thudded. Adam McFarland lay sprawled out with his good arm over his forehead and his feet hanging off the end of the bed. Quickly she averted her eyes but was happy to know that he was finally resting. She would forever be grateful that he came to her defense.

She followed her hostess into a whitewashed room with a colorful quilt and curtains on the lone window. A small wardrobe sat in one corner and a chair in the other. "This is my room. Please make yourself at home. Once Leyna has the guest room ready, we'll move you in there."

Mariah hesitated, not wanting to impose, even though Anna's smile was warm and hospitable.

"There's fresh water in the pitcher, and the towel is clean. Do you have something to change into, or do you need your trunk?"

"I have a dress in my satchel." She omitted mentioning that it was most likely full of wrinkles by now.

"I'll step out while you refresh yourself. Come on back to the parlor when you're finished." Anna stopped at the door and turned. "You were traveling somewhere when all this happened. Are there people who will be expecting you, wondering what happened?"

"I telegraphed my grandmother from Medora to let her know I would be here for a few days."

"Good. At least she won't worry. I'd love if you could stay awhile. We don't get many visitors, especially women near my age."

Mariah wondered how to respond. Should she reveal her true identity to this kind girl?

Something made her hesitate. Maybe tomorrow would be soon enough. "Thank you, Miss McFarland. I'd love to stay and visit with you, if I'm not imposing."

The young woman grinned. "You're not, and call me Anna. We're not too formal out here."

"And you must call me Mariah."

Anna nodded. "That's such a pretty name." She closed the door before Mariah could respond. She mostly despised her odd name and had never thought of it as pretty.

She set her satchel on the bed and opened it. The robber's loot bag stared up at her. How could she have forgotten to return Mr. McFarland's watch and money?

"How long did the doc say for you to rest up?" Quinn lounged against Adam's doorframe.

"A day or two."

His brother lifted a brow.

"All right, he said several days, but I feel fine now that I've had a good night's rest."

"Good enough to bust broncs?"

Adam blinked. "Well, no, but I can pull my own weight."

"Let's get you into some clean clothes."

Adam didn't like how Quinn deftly ignored what he said or the fact that he needed his brother's help to get his pants on. "We can leave off the shirt. Leyna said she'd be back in a few minutes to change the dressing."

Quinn stood after helping Adam into his boots. "I don't want to see you outside until the end of the week. If you rest up now, you'll recover quicker and can get back to work sooner."

Not waiting for a response, Quinn hurried out of the room. Adam laid his head back against the chair, taking a moment to catch his breath. He'd never take good health for granted again.

His gaze landed on the small desk along the opposite wall. His siblings didn't know it, but under the roll top rested his drawing supplies. After not drawing for years, the urge to sketch became more than he could resist. Adam flexed the fingers of his right hand, wincing at the burning sting it caused in his upper arm. Could he still draw, even with a gunshot wound?

His looming deadline dangled before him like a hangman's noose. He'd finally been given the chance he'd dreamed about for so long, and he wasn't about to give up now. If he rested his arm a few days maybe he could draw again.

And then there was the missing money. He needed to tell Quinn about that but couldn't bring himself to do so. Not yet. The matching Percheron pair he'd sold in Bismarck had brought good money. He'd purchased supplies and still had a wad of cash left over. So where was it now?

Anna walked into his room without knocking. Adam shook his head. His sister was sweet, but in spite of his mother's efforts to make her a lady, Anna often surprised him with her brazenness.

"Leyna is busy with breakfast, so I'm going to play doctor." Her smile warmed him. Anna had done her fair share of tending wounds, so he allowed her to remove his bandage, grimacing as it pulled loose. She gasped. "Oh, Adam. That looks dreadful. Does is hurt much?"

"What do you think?"

"I'm sure it does. The bullet went clear through. I'll be careful and try not to hurt you more."

Grateful that she ignored his crabbiness, he kept quiet and concentrated on the hillside view out the window while she cleaned and rebandaged his wound. She helped him into a fresh shirt and put his arm back in the sling. Adam brushed her hand away as she reached for the buttons. "I'm not a baby. I can still button my own shirt."

"Perhaps you're not a baby, but you sure are a grumbly ol' bear." She stuck her tongue out at him, making him grin.

He formed a claw with his fingers and swiped at her. "Grr." She giggled as she fled the room.

At noon, Adam sat at the dinner table with Anna and Mariah. He'd eaten breakfast earlier then made it back to his room and had fallen asleep again. He was determined to eat well and regain his strength as quickly as possible, even though eating with his left hand was a challenge he hadn't anticipated. Quinn hadn't said anything about him shirking his duties, but he knew the other men would have more work with him laid up.

Leyna set a steaming pot of *knoephle* on the table. His mouth watered at the thought of the chicken-flavored soup with potatoes, carrots, and little dumplings. From the breadbasket, he snagged a slice of *Bauernbrot*, Leyna's delicious sourdough bread.

"This looks great, Leyna. I missed your cooking while I was in Bismarck."

She beamed at him and patted his shoulder. "Leyna's knoephle will make you feel better."

"It smells delicious." Miss Lansing smiled at Leyna then glanced at him.

Adam stared back until she looked away. A week—at least. Anna had gone and invited her to stay a whole week. Why did she have to go and do that? Did she forget that writer was supposed to visit? Didn't Fancy Feathers have people somewhere wondering what had become of her? There was nothing extraordinary about her light brown hair, but her eyes as dark as coffee intrigued him. And the things she did with that appealing mouth. . .

He shook those thoughts from his head and waited for someone to dish up his soup. Testing his arm, he clenched his fist, wincing as pain radiated through his upper muscles. He pitied all the men he'd ever known that only had one arm or hand. Even the simplest tasks were difficult.

Anna finally set his bowl in front of him, the scrumptious odors making his mouth water. He fiddled with the spoon with his left hand, trying to hold it correctly. Using a fork was one thing, but eating soup with his left hand was another. He awkwardly fished out a dumpling and brought the spoon to his mouth. He slurped up the dough ball but dribbled broth onto his clean sling. Adam smacked the spoon back on the table, receiving a glare from Anna. Mariah jumped and gawked at him. He snagged up his bread and shoved it into his mouth. How was a man supposed to get his strength back when he couldn't eat?

Anna slapped her spoon on the table, making Mariah jump again. "Really, Adam. Stop being such a baby." His sister took his napkin and covered his chest and the sling with it, making him a bib. Embarrassed, he darted a glance at Mariah, who was studying her soup.

Leyna tsked and snatched up his bowl, carrying it into the kitchen.

Great! He wasn't ready to call it quits simply because he'd bobbled his first spoonful.

Mariah stared at her food then ladled a spoon of soup like a queen and took a bite with feminine finesse. Had he stooped so low that he was jealous of a woman eating soup?

Leyna marched back into the room, carrying a large, steaming mug. She set it in front of him, smiling. "I fix it so you can eat my knoephle."

He picked up the mug and took a sip then held it up as a thank-you to his cook. Suddenly, shame and embarrassment flooded him as he considered the spectacle he'd made.

Yep, he was definitely right. This was no time to be having company. This was going to be a long week.

Chapter Seven

Anna stormed into the parlor and flopped into a chair. "I can't believe how grouchy Adam is. He's never liked being sick, but he's much grumpier this time."

Mariah laid aside the book she'd been reading. "Maybe it's because he's not actually sick and thinks he should be out laboring with the other men." Or perhaps he didn't like having a stranger witness his difficulties at lunch.

Anna leaned her head back against the chair and stroked one of her braids. "You're probably right. He keeps saying he should be doing something. He's the hardest worker on the ranch but never seems to think he's done enough. I don't understand what drives him."

"Perhaps it's simply a male thing. Most of the men I know are driven to work hard." *Except Silas.* Even though he had a very nice job in his uncle's publishing company, he much preferred socializing and taking extra-long lunch breaks to working hard. Mariah shook her head. Silas was the last thing she wanted to think about right now.

"I have a yearling I need to be training, but someone has to watch over Adam and make sure he doesn't do too much. I have the feeling if I don't keep an eye on him, he'll slip out back and chop wood or try to break a mustang or something else every bit as foolish."

"You work with the horses?" Mariah studied the woman, who was close to her in age. Anna's thick, golden braids hung down clear to her waist. Her brown eyes were so dark that Mariah couldn't make out her pupils, even from such close range. The girl had a gentle wildness about her, an unabashed freedom to be herself that Mariah envied.

Suddenly, Anna leaned forward, eyes glistening. She snapped her fingers. "I know, *you* could watch over Adam. He won't argue with you like he does me and Quinn."

Mariah blinked. "It wouldn't be proper for me to um. . . enter a gentleman's private quarters."

Anna brushed her hand through the air. "Oh, pshaw. Adam's dressed. There's no reason you can't sit and talk with him."

Mariah considered how much she owed Adam. Surely she could do this one thing—but she wouldn't dare tell anyone back home about it. "All right. If it will help you, I'll keep watch on him."

"Oh, thank you." Anna smiled and leaped to her feet. She hugged Mariah's shoulders. "I've got a few hours before dinner, so I'm going out to the barn. If Adam gives you too much trouble, get Leyna, and tell her to bring her biggest wooden spoon."

From a peg near the front entrance, Anna grabbed a Western hat much like her brothers'. She hurried out the door, leaving it open behind her, and jumped off the porch. Someone needed to teach that girl how a proper lady behaved herself.

Perhaps Mariah could somehow help in that area while she was here.

She closed the front door, then tiptoed toward Adam's room, unsure if she had the nerve to cross the threshold or not. She couldn't help wondering how Leyna's stirring spoon would help keep Mr. McFarland in bed.

"Anna!"

Mariah jumped at the loud shout and stepped to the bedroom doorway. Mr. McFarland scowled.

"Where's Anna?"

She moistened her lips. "Outside. She said she had a horse to work with."

He looked out his window, even though the barn was on the other side of the house.

Mariah ached for him, knowing how miserable he was. "Is your arm hurting, Mr. McFarland? I could ask Leyna to make more of her tea, or perhaps you need another dose of laudanum?"

He shook his head. "I don't want tea. And that medicine makes me sleepy. I'm just bored. You might as well call me Adam, since you're staying a while."

She liked his name. It was a strong moniker that suited the commanding man on the train, but not so much the malcontent in bed. Still, if not for her big mouth, he wouldn't be here now. "Would you like me to read to you?"

"No, thanks. There's nothing wrong with my eyes." As if to prove his point, he glanced toward her hand. "What's that you've got?"

Ignoring his brusqueness, she held up the book she'd been skimming through. "*Ivanhoe*."

He shook his head and ran his hand through his hair, mussing it even more than it had been. It gave him a roguish appearance that she found appealing. "I've read it three times. Read all our books, in fact. Too bad there isn't something new to read."

She thought for a moment, excused herself, and then hurried to the guest room that Leyna had so graciously made up for her. In the bottom of her satchel, she found what she was looking for. A copy of her April release, *The Red-Headed Rustler*, and one of her competitor's novels that she'd read a few days ago. Without thinking, she snatched the pen off the desk and signed "Drew Dixon" on the title page of her book.

At her doorway, she paused. There were two details she needed to take care of—and now was as good a time as any. First, she needed to return Adam's belongings. She pulled the loot bag from the drawer she'd stuck it in and returned to his room. At the threshold, she halted. The second detail was more difficult. She had to tell him who she was.

Mariah wrestled with the improprieties of entering a man's bedchamber. She shouldn't even be standing at his door. Perhaps she could talk him into moving into the parlor.

His lovely blue eyes perked up. "What's that you've got there?" He sat up straighter on the bed.

She held out the loot bag.

"Is that what I think it is?"

Mariah nodded. "I made sure to collect your watch and money since you were, um. . . unable to at the time. I'm sorry I didn't return it sooner, but with your injuries and all, I forgot I had it. I hope all your money is there." She already knew his watch was, because she'd looked at it once.

"Let me see."

She wavered a moment, stepped a foot into the small room, and tossed the bag onto the bed. Just as quickly, she scurried back to the hall.

Adam chuckled at her. He opened the bag and pulled out the pocket watch and money. He glanced at the wad of dollars as if mentally assessing if it was all there then turned his attention to the watch. Lovingly, he stroked the gold cover then opened it and studied the face of the timepiece. "This belonged to my pa. I'm sure glad to have it back again. Thank you."

His warm smile gladdened her heart. Seeing him happy for the first time in days made her realize how badly she wanted him to get well. He was much more handsome when he smiled, and a man so robust shouldn't be stuck in bed.

"What else do you have there?"

She held up the dime novels.

"Hey, that's new. Haven't read that one before." He struggled to sit up straighter and winced. "Let me see it."

Mariah glanced at the threshold. She simply couldn't cross it again.

"It's all right for you to come in. We don't hold much on propriety way out here. Besides, I'm a perfect gentleman." His roguish grin made her question his words.

Her hand trembled. He had no idea that entering a man's room went against all she'd ever learned, but she knew if she didn't enter then he'd probably get up and hurt himself again. Taking a breath, she rushed to his bedside, shoved the dime novels into his hand and hurried back outside the door again.

"I don't bite." Laughing, he looked at the booklets then held up the competitor's dime novel.

Gathering up her nerve, Mariah opened her mouth to confess her identity. "There's something I need to—"

"I've read that one." Scowling, he tossed her novel onto the bedside table. "Even wrote the author and told him he needed to get his ranching facts straight. I invited him to visit the Rocking M, but he hasn't shown up."

The confession lodged in Mariah's throat like a hard biscuit. "J–Just what was it the author got wrong?"

Adam shook his head. "For one thing, he gave a steer a calf." He chuckled. "That'd be interesting to see."

The blood rushed out of Mariah's cheeks, making her skin feel tight. She didn't understand the nature of her error, but it was clear that she'd made one.

"And besides that"—Adam flipped over her competitor's novel and looked at the back cover—"he made a woman the hero of his story."

Mariah narrowed her eyes, irritation rising at his know-it-all attitude. "What's so wrong about that?" Hadn't she saved Adam's very life by distracting the train robber who meant to kill him?

"Whoever heard of a lady rustler rescuing a rancher and saving his cattle? It's too far-fetched to be believable."

"It's fiction."

He glanced up. "Yeah, well, it still needs to be realistic. No steer is ever gonna have a calf. Just proves the author doesn't know beans about life out here."

Mariah hiked her chin. "I—uh—need to go do something."

She hurried from his room toward her own, embarrassed that she'd obviously made a grievous error in her research. How could she tell him who she was now that he'd shoved her mistakes in her face?

Adam slanted his face toward the warm sun, grateful to be outside again. His days of inactivity had left him restless and anxious to be back at work. Stretching, he watched Cody exercising a green broke mustang in the corral. Every lap or two, the mare bucked as if she weren't quite ready to give up her freedom.

"She's really pretty."

Adam glanced sideways at Mariah. He wasn't sure why he'd agreed to give her a tour of the ranch, probably simply to have a legitimate excuse to get out of the house. She looked pretty in her blue dress and small, tidy hat, much less of a threat than her big floppy one with the feathers.

Since yesterday, he'd had the feeling she was perturbed at him. As much as he'd wanted her gone at first, she was growing on him, and he didn't like seeing her upset.

He'd never been around women much except for his mother, Anna, Leyna, and the women he saw in town or at church, but most of those were married. And then there were the city gals that his grandma had invited to dinner when he was in Bismarck, but most of those thought of him as a country bumpkin. Mariah was the first woman with whom he could let down his guard. That made him want to get to know her better, but at the same time he wanted to shove her away.

"So, what is that man doing? Is that a freshly broken horse?"

He swallowed back a sigh. Since she'd decided to be his nursemaid, she'd pelted him with one ranch question after another. He'd never met a woman so interested in ranching.

If she hadn't been easy to talk to, he probably would have been more tight-lipped. But she had a way of getting under his skin and making him want to share more than he had in ages.

"We call it a *green broke horse*. She's a three-year-old mustang that we recently caught in Wyoming."

"How long will it take to train her? Will you use her to herd your cattle?"

Adam shrugged. "Depends."

"On what?"

"On the horse—how stubborn or willing she is. On how much time we have to work with her."

The warm breeze cooled his sweaty neck and swirled dust into a little dust devil off in the distance. A sweet, floral scent drifted from Mariah's direction. The womenfolk he knew rarely smelled that nice.

"What's that funny bridle on that horse?"

"It's called a hackamore. It doesn't have a bit. We find that some horses respond better to them."

"It seems to me you wouldn't have as much control without a bit." She stepped up onto the lowest rail of the corral and leaned her head through the bars, her eyes dancing with delight.

"Careful."

The mare approached, watching her warily. As the horse neared, it stretched out its head and nipped at Mariah's bonnet.

"Oh my!" Fancy Feathers gasped and jumped backward, arms flailing as she fell off the rail. Adam caught her with his good arm and helped her to regain her balance.

Hand to her chest, she stared up at him with ruby cheeks. "Thank you. She took me by surprise."

"You've gotta remember many of these animals are still half wild." The sun glimmered off the end of Mariah's silver hatpin. He removed his hand from her arm and stepped back, irritated with himself for enjoying her nearness. He'd do well to remember Miss Lansing could turn into a wildcat faster than he could unholster his gun. Those hatpins of hers were dangerous. "You want to see inside the barn?"

"I'd love to."

The sling's knot pinched his neck. He shifted his arm and loosened the pressure. Thankfully, the pain from the movement wasn't as sharp as a couple of days ago. He'd give it a few more days then try drawing again.

"Is your arm hurting?" Mariah's face puckered with concern.

He shook his head, tired of having his injury at the forefront of everything. "You never mentioned why you're traveling in this part of the country."

Her gaze darted to the left as she entered the barn. She wrinkled her nose in an appealing manner. "Several reasons, actually. The main one being. . .um. . .I need time to get away and think."

"Seems a long ways to go just to think."

Suddenly, she twisted around to face him. "Would it be possible for me to ride a horse while I'm here?"

Adam got the distinct impression she was trying to change the subject, but he didn't press her further. She had a secret, and that made her even more interesting. Maybe if she learned to trust him, she'd share it with him.

"There's no other way to see the ranch except by horseback. That black mare is yours." Adam nodded toward the two horses Hank had saddled at his request. Hank tightened the cinch on the black horse then untied the reins and walked toward Adam, leading the mare and Adam's gelding.

"Your horse is named Sugar. This is my blue roan, Chief." Adam patted his horse, glad to be able to ride his old friend again.

Anna's shadow darkened the barn opening as she rode in. Her horse nickered, as if it were happy to be back home. "Going for a ride? You sure you're up to that, little brother?"

Adam scowled at his sister's reference to his birth order. She loved to point out the fact that she was eleven minutes older than him. He ignored her question, studying Mariah instead. She stared at the black horse, the color fading from her face. She looked petrified. Had she changed her mind about riding?

"I—uh—don't you have a sidesaddle?" Mariah asked.

is owned by the marquis' wife."

"Would it be possible to borrow it?"

Adam shook his head. He held on to the bridle of Anna's horse as she dismounted. "I don't think anyone is living at their house anymore. They've been gone for years."

Anna walked over to Mariah. "You can't truly appreciate the West riding sidesaddle. Much of the country is too rugged. You can borrow one of my split skirts, if you don't mind wearing it. I believe it should fit you, even though you're thinner than me."

Adam handed the reins to Hank, and he took Anna's mare into her stall. Anna followed. "I'll groom her. We had a good ride today, and she deserves a treat."

Mariah glanced at the horse again and then at Adam, her face even paler than when the train robber first took her captive. She leaned closer to him and whispered, "I'm sorry, but I can't wear Anna's skirt. It's simply too immodest."

Adam watched her flee the barn, irritated that her high ideals made her too good to try something new. Anna's skirt covered everything a dress did. There was nothing improper about it. As much as he'd hoped he was wrong, Mariah Lansing didn't belong on the Rocking M.

Mariah stomped up the steps and into the house. Now that her initial embarrassment had fled, anger moved in. Had Adam deliberately tried to put her to shame by suggesting she ride astride?

No, she didn't believe that he'd stoop that low.

At breakfast and lunch, she had pleaded with him to take her on a tour of the ranch, thinking it would be something he could do to occupy an hour's time. She hadn't thought about needing a horse for the tour. Wouldn't a buggy work for that?

Mariah plopped on a stuffed chair in the parlor. What truly irritated her the most was that she really wanted to try riding astride. Surely a Western saddle would be easier to stay on than a sidesaddle. But it was so unladylike. Grandmother would have a fit if she learned that Mariah had ridden Western style.

A tiny smile tugged at her lips. Hadn't she come west to learn all its secrets? How could she pen life-like horseback riding heroines if she wasn't willing to ride astride like them?

She had to do this. There was no other option.

If only there were some way to do it without wearing that scandalous split skirt.

Chapter Eight

Mariah swayed forward and then back in the saddle, holding on to the horn with a death grip.

"Try to relax. Don't hold on to the saddle horn if you can keep from it." Adam leaned against the top rail of the corral watching her.

Relax? Mariah nearly let a sarcastic laugh slip. How was she supposed to do that while risking her life on the back of a horse? She loosened one handhold slightly and took a deep, calming breath.

Adam nodded at her. "Good. Hold the reins looser, otherwise the horse will think you want to stop."

Mariah was so thankful her grandma couldn't see her. First, she'd lowered herself to wear that horrible split skirt. Her ruffled shirtwaist looked much too fancy with it, but she wasn't about to don one of Anna's flannel tops. She had her fashion limits, after all.

She pressed down Anna's Western hat. Adam's sister had tried to talk her into wearing her hair in two longs braids like hers, but Mariah wouldn't agree. Her normal hairstyle, plaited and pinned in a bun on her nape worked well since the Western hat sat atop her head.

Mariah peeked at Adam as the horse plodded past him and circled the corral.

"You're doing fine. Think you could handle riding out of the corral, or do you want to save that for another day?"

She wanted to tour the ranch, and to do that, she had to leave the corral. To prove her ability, she released her death grip on the horn and sat back, her body rocking gently with the horse's slow gait. This wasn't so bad. As long as walking was all they did, she could manage.

"I believe I'm game." How was it possible to be so nervous and so excited all at the same time?

Adam grinned and pushed away from the railing. He looped the reins over the head of his sleek, gray horse and mounted as easy as could be. Having only one hand didn't seem to faze him when it came to getting on a horse. He rode up to the gate, flipped the rope loop off the top, and opened it. "Let's go then. I'm ready to see something besides the house."

He waited until she walked past him then closed the gate and rode up beside her. Mariah's heart pounded now that she was free of the corral. What if something scared her horse and it took off running? Could she stop it?

"Quit frettin'. You're doing fine."

She tried to calm herself by studying the landscape, a wild combination of stones, grasslands, and big mounds of rock with few trees. Some places looked as if the hillside had been cut in half, revealing flat layers of brown, black, and even orange rock. An artist's palette of wildflowers brightened the barrenness. A warm breeze feathered her cheeks, reminding her of outings along the shores of Lake Michigan, except the wind here was dryer.

"How big is the Rocking M?" She remembered the size of his ranch from his letter, but she couldn't very well tell him that. A shaft of guilt stabbed at her.

"Over four thousand acres."

"Your sister said your family originated in Texas. How did you end up here?" She followed him down a short grade, pressing her feet into the stirrups and holding on to the saddle horn. She was certain that any second she'd go flying over the horse's head, but they leveled out, and she settled back in the saddle again.

"Lean back a little when you go down a hill. It's easier."

Mariah tried to envision that but failed to see how it would make things less difficult. She held the reins loosely, wondering if Adam was going to answer her question. She learned that he talked more freely if she could get him conversing about the ranch.

"We had several years of drought back in Texas, and our herd was shrinking because much of the grass had dried up, so Pa decided to go north. He'd seen advertisements about good land up in North Dakota, so he went for a visit. He had received an inheritance from a wealthy uncle in Ireland and ended up buying out a couple of ranchers who'd about gone under; then he moved us all up here."

"Must have been exciting to move so far away."

Adam grunted but made no comment.

She watched a bird circling high above, making a tinkling sound.

Suddenly, it dove at a frantic speed straight for the ground as if it had been shot. Mariah held her breath, but at the last second, it angled off and glided upward again. "What was that?"

"A male lark. Kind of fun to watch, isn't it?"

She nodded, amazed at the different creatures there were out here. Her heart soared at the rugged beauty of the place. They rode through prairie grass that swished in the breeze and sometimes touched her shoes and smacked against the horses' bellies.

"We'll have to canter a bit if we're gonna see much of the ranch."

Run?

Mariah swallowed. She had begun to think that riding astride could be fun. As much as she hated to admit it, astride was far more comfortable than a sidesaddle and easier to stay on. Although she suspected she'd be every bit as sore afterward.

Adam didn't wait for a response but nudged his horse into a gallop. Hers followed suit but fell behind in a bone-jarring, teeth-rattling trot. Mariah gripped the horn, certain any moment she would fall. "Whoa. Stop."

Instead of obeying, the black mare broke into a run. Eyes watering, Mariah clung on with her hands, her knees, and feet, but she gradually realized that a gallop was easier to take than a trot. Slowly, she began to relax with the smooth, rocking gait.

Adam looked over his shoulder and grinned. Evidently, the faster speed hadn't hurt his wounded arm. He rode as one with his horse, his broad shoulders barely rising and falling as he raced forward. She hadn't expected to admire the man, but how could she not?

He saved her virtue and probably her life. Except for being cranky from his injury, he'd been kind and patient with her endless questions. His blue eyes reminded her of her grandma's Delft pottery that had come from Holland and was scattered throughout every room of her house. She had come here partly to forget Silas, but she'd never planned to be attracted to another man. She'd do well to guard her heart. Soon she'd be headed back to Chicago, back to her grandmother, and she couldn't leave part of her heart behind.

Adam bit back a smile but kept a close eye on Mariah. She'd surprised him when she'd come to breakfast this morning wearing one of Anna's split skirts. He didn't know what had changed her mind, but he was glad that she didn't let her apprehension keep her from learning to ride.

He knew he was pushing her, but he wanted to see what her limits were. He hadn't expected her to make it past a trot, but other than looking a bit nervous and bouncing up and down like a baby on her father's knee, she'd done fine—and earned his admiration.

How many of those silly gals that his grandmother had invited to dinner could hold a candle to Mariah?

None, he was certain.

He reined Chief to a walk, hoping that Mariah would do the same. After grappling with the reins and yelling "Whoa" several times, she jolted to a halt.

"Good riding."

"Wipe that grin off your face, cowboy. It's lousy riding, and you know it." She fidgeted in the saddle then smashed Anna's hat back down. Her frilly white top looked out of place with the Western hat, skirt, and his sister's old boots.

After dismounting, Adam held the reins of Mariah's horse while she got down. He steadied her when she landed on the ground, giving her a moment to regain her balance. Her head came up to the bottom of his nose, allowing him a whiff of her floral-scented hair.

"I can't believe how shaky my legs are after such a short ride." She turned and looked up at him, pushing her borrowed hat off her forehead.

Adam's mouth went dry. Her trusting brown eyes stared at him. What would it be like to have a woman other than one in his family depending on him? To love him? When he didn't release her, Mariah's gaze turned questioning. He cleared his throat and stepped back, recovering from his moment of insanity.

This was the wild hatpin-wielding woman who attacked train robbers. He couldn't be attracted to her.

And yet, he knew that at some point, she'd gotten under his skin, and if he wasn't careful, she might steal a hunk of his heart.

"Was there something here you wanted to show me? Why are there so many trees in this area when they are so sparse everywhere else?"

"Water." That's what he needed. A douse of cold water over his head. "Come here. I want to show you something."

He took hold of Mariah's elbow and guided her toward the edge of the bluff, tightening his grip as they reached the drop-off. She glanced down the steep gorge and stepped back.

"That's a long way down. What's that creek called?"

"That's the Little Missouri River."

Mariah snorted a laugh. "Not much of a river."

Adam held her arm tight as she crept forward, standing near the edge. She wrapped her arm around his waist and leaned forward. He knew she wasn't aware of her actions, but he enjoyed having her close all the same.

"It may not look like much right now, but don't let it fool you. The Little Missouri floods quite often after a heavy rain or snowmelt."

"It's deceptively quiet now."

Adam nodded. Mariah peeked up at him, obviously realizing where her arm was. Her cheeks turned bright red, and she stepped back.

"Ready to ride again?"

Mariah stared at the horse, heaved a sigh, and finally nodded. She swaggered to the mare, evidently still getting used to the split skirt and boots. Adam bit back a grin, imagining tomorrow when she was in her dress again and still walking the same. Her legs would be sore after today's ride. He'd best make it a short trip to ease her discomfort.

They rode on for another hour. Adam pointed out a herd of Black Angus they'd recently acquired.

"Oh, those are pretty cows."

"They're not all cows."

Her brow crinkled. "They're not?"

"Some are steers."

"What's the difference?"

Adam's neck and ears turned red. "Big difference. Maybe you should ask Anna about that."

Mariah stared at him for a long moment then looked away. "All right, I will."

In another pasture, he pointed out the Herefords.

"These red and white cattle are pretty too, but I like the solid black ones best," Mariah said.

"You should have seen the longhorns we brought up from Texas. Many had horns six feet from tip to tip or even longer."

"I've seen pictures of them. It seems like they would be dangerous."

Adam reined Chief toward home, dreading their ride coming to end. Being back in the saddle again felt wonderful, and he could get used to riding with Mariah, even though her questions never ended. Was she writing a manual about ranch life?

He chuckled at that ridiculous thought.

She rode alongside him, looking more at ease in the saddle. Her hands no longer strangled the saddle horn, and her body swayed with Sugar's easy gait. What would it be like to come home to Mariah every day?

"May I ask you a question?"

Adam chuckled. She'd been asking him questions ever since she arrived, but she'd never asked his permission before. "Sure."

"Why have neither you nor your siblings gotten married?"

Adam shrugged. They were all plenty old enough to be married now, but the subject rarely came up. "Except for Quinn, we were too young for marriage at the time our father died and have worked too hard since then to take time to find a suitable spouse, I guess. Mother hints every now and then that she'd like grandchildren." Adam chuckled. "It sure will take a special man to tame Anna and a very patient woman to woo Quinn."

Mariah nodded, as if she agreed.

Adam scowled and swatted at a fly. How could he even think of courting a woman and marrying? It would mean the end of his dreams of traveling the country and recording the West through his drawings. Every day, more folks were moving westward. Soon this way of life would be a thing of the past. Why, two decades ago, there'd only been a handful of white folks in North Dakota and now look at all the immigrants who lived here.

He nudged Chief into a canter, and Mariah followed after a short hesitation. Women wanted the security of a home, where they could cook, sew, and raise children. No woman would want to give all that up to spend her days traveling the western half of the United States with him.

His upper arm ached, pulling him from his thoughts. He'd probably be as sore as Mariah tomorrow.

On the trail up ahead, a trio of turkeys waddled into view. His mouth watered at the thought of fresh meat. He yanked his rifle from the scabbard and fired, downing the largest bird.

Sugar lurched to the right, away from the gunfire. Mariah squealed and flew through the air, landing hard in a patch of stinging nettles.

Chapter Nine

Adam paced from the dining table, into the parlor, and back. After Mariah's fall into the nettle patch, she had stayed in her room the rest of the day and during this morning's breakfast. He missed seeing her sweet smile across the table at mealtime and hoped that she was feeling better today. He flopped down on the settee, guilt eating at him for causing her pain.

He heard a shuffling sound and saw Mariah limping into the parlor. She rubbed her shoulder then noticed him and frowned.

He stood and hurried to her side, offering his good arm. "Here, lean on me."

"That's not necessary. My ankle is fine today." As if proving her point, she limped to the settee.

"I'm really sorry, Mariah. I shouldn't have shot my rifle without warning you." He resumed his place at the other end of the settee.

Anna strode into the room, carrying a tray of coffee and cookies. "I still can't believe you did that." She set the tray on the table in front of the sofa.

He glared at his sister, feeling guilty enough without her lambasting him. "It was a gut reaction. I saw game and knew we could use the meat. I didn't stop to analyze my actions."

Anna paced in front of them. Mariah scratched at the red welts on her nape.

"That's right, you didn't think. Mariah could have been badly injured." She flung a glance at their guest. "She's covered in nettle stings. Don't rub them, Mariah. You'll only make it hurt worse."

Mariah gripped her hands together in her lap. "Leyna's salve helped quite a bit, although the stings do still hurt some." She studied the floor, as if the topic wasn't proper for mixed company.

"Can I do anything for you?" Adam ran his hand over the back of his neck, wishing he could take away her discomfort. He hopped up, and using his good hand, carefully poured a cup of coffee. He handed it to Mariah, spilling a bit onto the saucer.

"Thank you." She accepted his gift with a shy smile and sipped the hot brew. Adam poured himself a cup and stuck a cookie into his mouth then reclaimed his spot on the settee. His injured arm tingled, as if wanting to be rid of the confining sling as much as he, but at least the sharp pain had subsided.

"I've been praying for Mariah and trust that God will ease the irritation." Anna flopped into the chair next to the parlor window, sticking her legs out in front of her, and crossed her ankles like a cowpoke.

Adam had prayed, too, though the words hadn't come easily. Lately, he'd felt as if God were calling him to come back to Him. After his father died, he hadn't wanted to go to church, feeling unworthy for causing the accident that killed his pa. But Quinn said they needed to go whenever the weather cooperated and there was a parson in town. Adam had listened to the preacher's word about forgiveness over the years until they were finally soaking in. God's love was unconditional. God had already forgiven him, but how could he forgive himself?

Mariah slipped her hand up to her neckline and ran her fingers back and forth until she caught him watching. He hated knowing he'd caused her pain and wondered if that's how she felt about him getting shot.

"What do you plan to do today?" Anna leaned forward, her elbows on her knees.

"I thought I should stay close to the house. Perhaps write a letter to my grandmother." Mariah picked at lint on her navy skirt. "I suppose I should pack my things and prepare to leave."

"Why? Aren't you happy here?" Anna looked distressed at the thought of Mariah leaving. He knew his sister was often lonely for female companionship, especially with their mother gone. She had Leyna, but their cook was more like a loving aunt than a friendly companion. Anna needed to spend time with girls her own age.

Mariah smiled at his sister. "You graciously invited me to stay for a week, and tomorrow is seven days."

"We don't want you to go. Do we, Adam?" Anna stared at him with hopeful eyes.

What could he say? At first all he wanted was to be rid of Fancy Feathers because he was embarrassed for her to see him fumbling about with his injury. He wanted her to see him as the man who'd come to her rescue, not an invalid. But then she started growing on him like a stray pup. He didn't want her to leave but knew if she didn't soon go, his heart might be shattered like a glass shooting target. And yet he longed to get to know her better. How did he answer his sister's question when the truth was scrambled eggs in his own mind?

Mariah stood. "It's all right. I've overextended my stay as it is."

"No!" Adam lurched to his feet. "I—don't go. I mean, it's all right if you stay—unless of course, you have somewhere else you need to be."

Mariah stared at him; then a soft smile pulled at her lips, and her cheeks turned pink. Anna grinned as if she'd won the Fourth of July horse race in Medora and gave him a knowing glance.

Uh-oh.

Adam swigged down the last of his coffee and fled the room, banging the front door on his way outside. Mariah would never leave if Anna learned of his attraction to her.

He had a gut feeling that it was too late to worry about that.

"So, what do you think of my brother?" Anna lifted her brows.

Adam's strange reaction to her comment about leaving the ranch left her stunned. He sure departed the room quickly afterward. Was he possibly growing to care for her as she was him? Or perhaps he simply didn't want to admit that he wanted her to leave.

Anna waited for an answer, a cocky grin dancing on her lips. Mariah could tell Anna was fishing for information, but she didn't know why.

"Which brother would you be referring to?" Mariah wasn't going to fall into her trap that easily.

Anna giggled. "You know good and well who I mean." She jumped up from the chair and plopped down on the settee next to Mariah. Anna didn't know what the word *glide* meant. She moved like a cowboy and acted like one. She'd never capture a man's interest if she didn't settle down.

"Of course I like your brother. He saved my life, after all."

"But don't you find him handsome? I've always wished I had blue eyes like his. It hardly seems fair to be twins and not have the same coloring." She fiddled with the end of her braid. "I think it bothers Adam that he doesn't resemble Quinn and me more."

Mariah considered that and wondered if it weren't true. Adam seemed unsettled, as if he didn't quite fit in here in his own home.

"So, do you think Adam is handsome?"

Mariah nodded, catching the fragrant scent of the roasting turkey that Leyna was cooking. Her stomach gurgled in spite of the pain she'd suffered because of that bird. "Of course. Both of your brothers are exceptionally fine-looking. They *are* quite different, though, other than their appearance. Aren't they?"

Anna nodded. She nibbled at a cookie and gazed at the family portrait on the wall. "When we were children, Adam was a tease, often getting in trouble for his practical jokes. He changed after our pa died, became moody and withdrawn. He's a gifted artist, and Ma had always hoped he might sell his drawings one day, but he up and quit sketching after Pa's accident. Quinn's always been quiet, as if he carries the weight of the world on his shoulders. And I guess he does, in a way. He was only nineteen when Pa died. Quinn became the man of the family and had a ranch to keep going."

"Seems to me he did a good job." Mariah pulled a pillow from beside her onto her lap, trying to imagine Adam as an artist. Why would he quit drawing because his father died?

She gazed out the window and saw Quinn ride past on a fine-looking bay horse. "I don't know a lot about ranching, but your herds are large, and your house is one of the finest I've seen in the area."

"Yes, the ranch is doing well, now, but it's been a struggle, especially the first years after Pa's death. And you can tell, I'm not much of a lady, much to Ma's chagrin. It's simply not practical. I'd wear pants if she would let me, but she draws the line at my split skirts."

Mariah grinned. "I never thought I'd admit this, but your skirt is much nicer for riding than a dress. Although it sure felt odd having all that fabric between my legs. Made walking difficult at first." She hoped her grandmother never found out what she'd done.

"Split skirts are better for fighting the winds we have, and I don't have to worry about all the cowboys seeing my unmentionables."

"That's certainly true." They shared a giggle, and Mariah felt as if she'd gained a new friend. "I want to thank you for your hospitality and your prayers. I've gone to church most of my life, but praying was always something the minister did."

Anna leaned forward and picked up Mariah's hand. "Prayer is for everyone. God is my best friend, and I can't imagine not talking to Him every day."

Mariah had never thought of God as a friend. He always seemed like a distant deity waiting to squash her if she did wrong.

"God helps me through each day, especially with difficult situations. I don't understand everything that happens, like Pa dying, but I trust that God is in control."

Mariah stood and walked to the window. She wished she knew God as Anna did, but because she didn't, the conversation made her uncomfortable. Or maybe it was guilt over the secret she held.

Determined, she whirled to face Anna. "There's something I need to tell you."

Anna smiled and leaned forward, curiosity shining in her eyes. "What is it?"

"You know the writer that Adam invited to stay here at the Rocking M?"

Anna nodded. "Yes, he mentioned it. I thought he was crazy to invite a complete stranger to visit, even though I have to admit I do enjoy the man's stories when I can sneak them out of Adam's room." Anna blushed as if she'd revealed a huge secret of her own.

Mariah swallowed the lump in her throat, finding her confession harder to make than she'd expected. "Well. . .I'm the man he invited. I mean, Drew Dixon is my pen name."

Anna looked confused; then her eyes brightened. "*You're* the writer?" She slapped her leg and hee-hawed as if that were the funniest thing she'd ever heard.

Mariah fought a niggling of irritation and scratched her arm. Did Anna think it funny that she wrote dime novels? Hadn't she confessed to enjoying them?

Anna bent over laughing, holding her stomach. "Oh, that is a hoot. Adam doesn't know, does he?"

Mariah wrung her hands together. "No. I didn't know how to tell him. I plan to, though. Soon."

"No!" Anna sat up, suddenly sober. "Don't tell him. It really doesn't matter anyway. You're my guest now, not Adam's."

Chapter Ten

Mariah read through the final pages of her latest dime novel, *The Preacher's Outlaw Sister*. Toward the end of the story, her heroine had a bad encounter with a stinging nettle plant. Smiling, Mariah knew for certain that the scene would be realistic.

She shook her head, still unable to believe that people around here actually ate the pesky plants and used them for tea. She hadn't been able to force herself to taste the greens Leyna had made after being in irritating discomfort for over a day from her encounter with the beastly plant, even though everyone else wolfed it down at dinner. The turkey was a different issue. She figured she deserved to eat it after the distress it had caused her.

She penned a letter to her editor, telling him several other ideas she had recently thought up for future novels. Seeing the West and being here truly did stir her creativity; she'd caught Adam's passion for the area. She wondered if he knew how poetic his words were at times and how he stirred her to want to be a better writer. Mariah folded the note, laid it on the cover of her manuscript, then wrapped the whole thing in the brown paper and twine that Anna had given her.

After pinning on her hat, she studied her reflection in the small mirror hanging on the wall. In spite of wearing a hat most of the time she was outside, her skin had definitely darkened. Her friends in Chicago would most likely consider her tan ghastly, but she rather liked it. She turned her head and checked her hair then grabbed the manuscript and hurried out to catch Adam.

Anna had mentioned he was driving to town today for supplies that were due to arrive by train, and Mariah hoped to catch a ride. Anna giggled when she told Mariah that Adam wanted to see if the writer had arrived yet. Mariah still struggled with keeping her secret from Adam, but after his comment about her writing and Anna's encouragement to not tell him, she'd remained silent on the issue.

Two hours later, Mariah walked into the small mercantile, thankful that Adam hadn't put up a fuss about her riding along. In fact, she was almost certain that he had enjoyed her company as much as she had his.

He'd regaled her with stories of the Marquis de Mores and the meat processing plant he'd built across the Little Missouri River, next to Medora. The tiny town that had popped up on the west side of the river had the nickname of Little Misery. The marquis hadn't liked that, so he started a new town east of the river. She thought it romantic that the man had named the town for his wife, Medora. What kind of man did something that sweet?

He must have loved her very much. Mariah sighed, wondering if a man would ever care for her that much. Silas was too ambitious and selfish. How could she have ever been enamored with him? Now that she'd met real men like Adam and Quinn, she'd never look at a man the same. Pale-skinned city men didn't hold a candle to these wide-shouldered, tanned, good-hearted cowboys.

Her eyes adjusted to the dimmer interior of the mercantile, and shadows began to change to shape. She breathed in leather and spice scents, and her mouth watered as she passed a small pickle barrel sitting on the counter. After paying the clerk to mail her package, she scouted out the quaint store.

As she read the label on a jar of hand cream, her nape started tingling. Mariah glanced up. A scruffy-looking man resembling the train robber tore his gaze from hers and moved into the shadows across the room. Her heart skittered. Had the heinous thief escaped from jail?

On second glance, she decided he wasn't the man from the train. Perhaps he was merely a man looking at a woman in a town with few females—or did he have a nefarious purpose?

Adam had instructed her to stay at the store, and he would return for her after picking up his supplies at the depot. She had a sudden urge to be back in his presence. She set the lotion down and hurried to the door, looking over her shoulder. The man was no longer in sight.

Was she overreacting? Had her creative writer's imagination conjured up something that didn't exist?

Her curiosity wouldn't let go, and she stepped out onto the covered walkway in front of the mercantile. Darting her gaze to the left, she scanned the sleepy town to see if Adam was coming. Lifting her skirts, she walked down the steps to the ground. Suddenly a hand clasped her wrist. Someone yanked her into the shadows between buildings. A cry escaped her lips before a nasty-smelling hand covered her mouth.

Mariah shoved an elbow in her captor's chest. He grunted. She was spun around and came face-to-face with the scruffy stranger. He shoved her up against the rough weathered planks of the mercantile. She was certain her heart would burst clear out of her chest. A nasty saltiness from the man's hand filled her mouth, making her want to retch.

"Don't guess you know who I am, little missy." His leering grin turned Mariah's stomach even more. Stringy blond hair hung out from under his filthy hat. His front tooth was chipped a quarter of the way off. The man's foul body odor made her want to faint just to get away.

But she'd never been the fainting type.

She struggled against his overpowering hold and kicked him in the shin. He shoved her harder against the wall and pressed his body against hers. A whimper struggled for escape, but she forced it back. Better not to let him know how scared she was.

"You promise not to scream if I let go of your mouth?"

Mariah considered tricking him but reconsidered. She nodded and wiped her mouth with her sleeve when he complied.

"Tell me what you want and let me go." Her voice sounded far braver than she felt.

He grinned. "My brother's in jail because of you and that cowboy he shot on the train."

I'm a dead woman. The thought of her grandma mourning her instilled her with a strength she hadn't felt before.

"Stop wiggling." The man pressed his forearm against her throat, cutting off her breath. Mariah froze.

"I ain't gonna hurt you. Not yet, anyhow. Just need to deliver a message." His leering grin sickened her, and he leaned even closer, as if breathing in her scent. "My brother wants you to know that after I bust him out of jail, we're coming after you and that low-down McFarland."

The man's dull gray eyes sparked, and he pressed his foul mouth against her lips, his whole body molding with hers. She shoved against his chest, but he ravaged her mouth further. Suddenly he broke the kiss, leaving Mariah gasping for breath.

"Be expecting a visit soon. I plan to finish what I started here."

He released her so fast that she fell to the ground. Leaning over, she spat and swiped her mouth with the back of her hand. Anger simmered, pushing her to her feet. Who did he think he was that he could take such liberties?

At the corner of the alley, she watched the vile man cross the street, never looking back. He headed directly for a lone house standing a few hundred feet from the rest of the town. Mariah darted across the street, unsure what to do.

She should wait on Adam, but she had to know if the man was alone or if he had accomplices. He loped up the steps of the stone house and went in the door. Mariah's feet were moving before she could stop them. Hunkering down, she ran toward the structure, knowing if he looked out the window that he'd see her. There were no bushes or trees to hide behind.

Mariah held down her hat, and her heart pumped as fast as her feet. Her grandmother's words echoed in her head, *"A lady should never run."*

Mariah thought, in this case, where her life could be at stake, those words didn't apply. She darted around the corner of the stone building. In spite of the heat from the sun, the rock walls felt cool to the touch. She caught her breath and peered through the corner of the open window. She heard a man's playful growl and a lady's high-pitched giggle. Mariah squinted to see inside the dark structure. Her attacker stood next to a woman dressed in something that looked like fancy lace undergarments.

Gasping, Mariah covered her mouth with her hand and took a better look. The man swigged back a drink of liquor, most likely. He laughed and wrapped his arm around the woman, and they disappeared through a doorway. Another female clothed in a silky dress smiled with red painted lips at a man sitting in a chair. He stood and kissed her thoroughly on the mouth.

If Mariah had any doubts, she now knew exactly what this place was.

"Are you sure, Doc?" Adam grimaced as he looped his arm back in the sling.

He nodded. "Yep. Keep it immobilized for a few more days. It's healing well, but you don't want any permanent damage."

Adam heaved a sigh and paid the man. He squinted at the bright sunshine outside and pulled the brim of his hat down. He might not be able to pull his full weight on the ranch yet, but at least he was able to draw if he did a little at a time. It might still be possible to meet his deadline, after all.

If nothing else, this injury had shown Quinn that he was easily able to get along without Adam. That might help things when he told his family he'd be leaving. He thought of traveling the West and drawing pictures. Quinn would call him foolish and say he didn't want to work hard, but Adam longed to give folks back East a taste of the West. And he craved to see more of God's great earth. How could he explain that to a brother whose roots went deep?

He'd always had itchy feet. That's why he made the trips to Bismarck for supplies and Quinn stayed home. The Rocking M truly belonged to Quinn. He'd earned it from the day he'd first set foot on the ranch, and especially after their pa died. Adam had known all along that he wouldn't end up on the ranch. Sure, it was plenty big enough for them all, but it wasn't where his heart was.

With the rough winters they often had this far north, you never knew what to expect or whether you'd lose most of your livestock. The fewer people the ranch had to provide for, the better.

He nodded to a man and his wife as they passed in a buggy. His mouth suddenly went dry when the buggy pulled past him and he saw Fancy Feathers running toward the town's only house of ill repute. What was the crazy woman doing now?

He didn't want to walk in that direction. Didn't want the townsfolk to think he frequented the place, but he had to get Mariah away from there before she saw something she shouldn't.

What in the world would make a lady like Mariah snoop around such a place?

She had to be the most frustrating—and interesting—woman in the whole world.

He jogged toward her but slowed his gait because the jolting stabbed his arm. As he stepped up beside her, he heard her gasp. He didn't want to imagine what she'd witnessed.

"What. Do. You. Think. You're. Doing?" He spat out each word.

Mariah whirled around, holding her palm to her chest, her face pale. She laid her small hand on his sling.

"Oh, Adam. You frightened me half to death." She looped her arm around his good one. "Come on. We have to get away from this dreadful place before someone sees us."

A little late for her to be thinking that.

He allowed her to guide him back toward the depot. After they passed several homes, he stopped in the shade of a small grove of quaking aspen trees. The leaves dangled in the cool breeze, making a soft clattering sound. A blue jay screeched at them before flying away.

Taking a calming breath, he stared at her. How was he supposed to keep her safe if she refused to do as he asked? "Did I or did I not tell you to wait at the store?"

She swallowed and nodded. "Yes, but—"

He shoved his hand to his waist. "Didn't I tell you that it's dangerous to go unescorted around here?"

Again she nodded. "But, Adam—"

"Don't argue, Mariah. A woman who hopes to maintain her good reputation has no business

anywhere near that place." He pointed back at the stone house.

Her pale face brightened with irritation, her brow wrinkled in an alluring manner. "Would you please let me tell you something?"

When he kept silent, she lifted her chin and leaned forward. "For your information, I was accosted outside the mercantile a short while ago by a heinous villain."

His heart jolted, and he grasped her upper arm with his left hand. "Who was it? Why didn't you stay in the store?"

Adam trained his focus on Mariah as he scanned her length. "Were you hurt?"

She shook her head, and Adam noticed that her hat was askew and her hair mussed. Her lips looked puffy, and his gaze leaped to her eyes. He moved his hand up to her shoulder as tears puddled in her lovely eyes. He thought his heart would break. "Tell me what happened."

Chapter Eleven

Mariah swallowed her discomfort and gazed at Adam, his concern evident in his intense stare. "A man was watching me in the store. He looked like the train robber, and he went outside, and I followed." She shrugged one shoulder and flashed Adam an apologetic half smile. "Sometimes my curiosity overpowers my common sense."

His presence and concern warmed her heart and calmed her jittery nerves. He brushed back a strand of hair the wind had blown across her face. His touch, so much gentler than that atrocious man's, brought more tears to her eyes.

"Shh. . . Don't fret. You're safe now." He tucked his hand behind her neck and pulled her against him. His curiosity about the incident was obvious, but he seemed more concerned about her well-being than hearing her story. That made her care for him even more.

She leaned her head against his solid chest, being cautious not to press against his injured arm. He hugged her close to his left side and rested his chin against her head, the warmth of his tall, masculine frame making her feel safe and secure. She inhaled his unique scent of soap, dust, and leather. If not for the fact that they were standing in a public place, Mariah was certain she could have stood there an hour, holding on to him, but after a moment, she stepped back. Had Silas ever once comforted her in such a gentle manner?

She told Adam what the man said and how he manhandled her, grimacing at Adam's stunned expression. He tugged her back into his arms, hugging her fiercely. "I'm so sorry I wasn't there to protect you."

After a minute, he stepped away, looking like he had on the train when the cowboy had harassed her. Adam took her arm and tugged her forward. "We need to talk to the sheriff."

She longed for a bath to wash off the filth that she felt from her attacker's manhandling and from peeping into the house of ill repute.

Thank goodness nobody had seen her except Adam.

As Adam escorted her to the sheriff's office a story started swirling in her mind. Dare she put one of those scantily-clad ladies in her story? Could a soiled-dove-turned-heroine somehow save the day?

A cool north wind whipped the crocheted shawl away from Mariah's shoulders. She snatched the flapping garment and tucked it back around her neck then leaned closer to Anna on the bench. Quinn stood by the side of the barn, a Bible open in his hand. He read from Psalm 42:5.

"'Why art thou cast down, O my soul? and why art thou disquieted within me? hope thou in God: for I shall yet praise him for the help of his countenance.'"

Mariah glanced around the ragtag group of ranch hands standing or squatting around the campfire, all whose attention focused on Quinn. Adam stood outside the group, twisting the brim of his hat. Something about the rustic gathering touched her heart. She felt closer to God here at this smoke-scented, outdoor assembly than she'd ever had in her grandmother's formal church with its beautiful stained-glass windows and fancy decor. Lifting her face, the chilly breeze teased her hair and coated her lips with dust—something she was getting used to.

" 'Hope thou in God.' "

The words Quinn quoted beckoned her—or was it God calling?

Faith in God seemed an intricate part of life out west. Not something talked about but rather a firm belief. Mariah longed to know God in a more personal manner and to have that assurance in her heart.

Anna stood and sang "Amazing Grace." Tears pooled in Mariah's eyes at Anna's sweet songbird voice. The words called to her. She was lost. She'd been blind to the ways of her heavenly Father—and now that she could see, she longed to become a part of the family of God.

But how did one do that?

An old man stood with the help of another ranch hand. He shuffled to the front where Quinn and Anna had stood. Mariah admired the McFarlands for employing such a man at their ranch. He obviously couldn't perform most of the difficult tasks that needed doing because of his age and lack of physical prowess.

The bent man looked at the group through round spectacles and faded blue eyes. A straggly, misshapen beard covered the lower part of his face, and his overalls were well worn. Mariah wondered what such a man would say to a group of ranch owners and cowpunchers.

"In Exodus 33, the Bible says that our Lord spoke face-to-face with Moses as a man speaks to a friend. In 2 Chronicles 20, the Word refers to Abraham as God's friend forever. God wasn't just the friend of these men who lived thousands of years ago; He wants to be your friend, too."

Mariah listened as the man continued talking for the next ten minutes. She'd never considered that she could be a friend of God. As if a flame flickered to life in her chest, she had a burning desire to have a relationship with God. Not the One her grandmother's minister told of—a God of wrath and vengeance, but the God this man talked about—a God of love and friendship.

He walked around, taking time to look each person in the eye. When he glanced at Mariah, her stomach flip-flopped. "In John, the Good Book says: 'Ye are my friends, if ye do whatsoever I command you. Henceforth I call you not servants; for the servant knoweth not what his lord doeth: but I have called you friends; for all things that I have heard of my Father I have made known unto you.' Imagine that, Jesus, the Son of God, calling us friends. It's such a simple thing, but mighty hard to understand."

He finished with a final verse. " 'A friend loveth at all times, and a brother is born for adversity.' " With an apologetic grin, he glanced at Quinn and Adam. "The Lord loves us all the time, no matter if we're walking with Him or not. No matter where you are in life or what hardships you're facing, God is there for you. He wants to be your friend. All you have to do is call on Him, confess your sins, and let Him into your heart."

He ambled back to his buddies. Quinn stood, hat in hand. "Thanks for that thought-stirring word, Claude. Let's close in prayer."

As he prayed, Mariah considered the man's message. Surely reaching God couldn't be as simple as just asking Him into your heart. There had to be more effort involved than that.

Adam carried three sticks of wood into the kitchen and laid them in the box near Leyna's stove. It took him awhile to fill the bin, but this was a job he could do one handed. The fragrant odors of rabbit stew simmering on the stove and fresh bread baking made his belly growl, even though he'd eaten breakfast a few hours ago.

He snatched a leftover biscuit, receiving a mock glare from Leyna, and headed outside. He couldn't shake the words that Claude had shared the day before at their Sunday gathering. *"A friend loveth at all times, and a brother is born for adversity."*

He and Quinn had never been very close, but he never thought of his brother as the enemy. Sure, as a boy, he had resented the times their pa took Quinn out to work and left him behind. His brother had said something in anger one time about Adam having it easy while Quinn had to do the hard work all the time. It wasn't his fault that he was five years younger and had to help his ma with duties around the house.

Adam dumped another load of wood into the bin. Mariah glided into the kitchen, her eyes sparkling when she saw him. She was so pretty, graceful, and kind. As she moved in his direction, his heart skittered. A woman like her could make a man forget he had other plans and dreams.

Mariah stood before him, wringing her hands like she did when she was nervous. "Just the man I was looking for."

Just the woman he wasn't looking for, but the one who had ambushed his heart.

"I was wondering if I might have a word with you." She stood like a princess with her hands folded in front of her. The gold-colored dress she wore looked nice with her brown hair and eyes and the lightly tanned glow of her skin. His mouth went dry, and he nodded.

He held the door for Mariah as she swished outside. Lately, Anna had attempted to walk more ladylike than her normal bouncing and running motions. She'd even worn a dress to their Sunday service and had actually walked down the front steps instead of jumping off the porch as she usually did. Mariah was influencing his sister in a positive way, and for that he was grateful.

Mariah worried the lace on one sleeve with her fingers. She glanced up at him then looked away, but not before he noticed the pink tinge on her cheeks. She definitely had something on her mind.

They walked away from the house toward the creek that ran along the bottom of the hill. He thought of all the times he'd lugged buckets up and down that incline before they'd rigged up a rope-and-pulley system.

"I was wondering if I could talk to you about something."

"Sure. What's on your mind?" Adam broke off a stem of blue gama grass and fiddled with it.

"Would you please tell me how one goes about becoming a friend of God?"

He shot her a look. Was she serious? Of all the things she could have asked him, he'd never seen that one coming.

Why ask *him*? A man who'd been at odds with God for a third of his life?

And yet, he knew the answer that she sought. As a child, he'd prayed daily and felt that God was his best friend, but when his pa had died, he'd grown distant and had misplaced his faith.

"Uh. . .I'm not sure I'm the best person to be asking." He rubbed his nape.

"Why not?" Her innocent brown eyes stared up at him, imploring him to answer.

He sighed. "I haven't been on talking terms with God for a long while."

"Oh." Her shoulders sagged, and she stared at the ground. "That man who shared Sunday made it sound so easy to be God's friend, but it seems difficult to me."

They stopped beneath a cottonwood and sat on a flat, sun-warmed boulder near the creek bank. The water rippled over rounded stones, making a soft gurgling sound he never failed to enjoy. Above them a blue jay ranted at their invasion of his territory.

Mariah arranged and rearranged her skirts, her nervousness evident. He wanted to answer her question, but he had his own struggles. Still, if he could make things easier for her, he'd muddle through. He may have been estranged from God because of his own confusion and hurt, but he wanted her to know the peace he'd once known.

"It really is a simple thing to ask God into your heart. You only need to believe that His Son, Jesus, died for your sins, repent of those sins, and then invite God to come into your heart. He will come."

She swatted a fly away. "The reverend at my grandmother's church in Chicago preaches that you must be obedient to God's Word, and then goes on to tell about all the people God destroyed for their disobedience. He makes God sound distant and fierce."

Adam noted how she referred to the church as her grandmother's rather than hers. "I won't deny that the Lord can be fierce, but He is also a loving, caring heavenly Father. He wants us to fellowship with Him and be His friend. For a friendship to grow, friends need to spend time together." Guilt needled him at all the times he should have turned to the Lord and didn't.

Mariah shrugged. "I don't know how to be friends with a mighty God that I can't see." The breeze whipped at Mariah's hair, and she tucked the strand behind her ear.

"You can't see the wind, but you know it's there."

"I can *feel* the wind and see how it blows the trees and flowers."

"But you can feel God, too. In here." He tapped his chest. His own words ladled more condemnation on him. In his grief over causing his father's death, he'd shoved God away when the Lord would have comforted him. And he was still shoving. Unshed tears stung his eyes as he realized the grief he'd caused his heavenly Father. He turned his head away, blinked back the tears, and focused on helping Mariah understand.

"God can also help you know what to do when you face difficult times in your life." Adam tossed a pebble into the creek and watched the ripples, wishing now that he'd let God help him through the rough days.

"Did He help you. . .I mean, through a rough time?"

Adam clenched his jaw, thinking about how alone he'd felt after his father died. But it hadn't always been that way. There'd been a time he felt God answer his prayers. "I remember crying out to God when we left Texas. I was angry at Pa for making us leave. I didn't want to come here. Then my horse stepped in a gopher hole and had to be put down. I felt like I'd lost my best friend."

She laid her hand on his arm. "I'm sorry, Adam. We don't have to talk about that if it bothers you."

He breathed in deeply, feeling a release of tension. "No, it's all right. I think I need to talk about it. After my initial ranting at Pa, I ran off alone and cried out to God. It felt as if He took me and cradled me on His lap. Perhaps that sounds odd, but that's how it seemed to me."

"That's beautiful. I wish I'd had God to comfort me when my parents died." Mariah plucked a nearby wild prairie rose and rubbed her thumb over the dark pink petals. The flower's beauty faded next to hers.

"Things changed after Pa died."

Mariah gazed at him, obviously wanting to know what had changed, but she remained silent. Adam stared at the bank across the creek, unable to believe he was ready to share the secret he'd held for all these years. "Pa would be alive today if not for me."

She gasped. "What do you mean? Anna said your pa had an accident."

Adam rubbed his wounded arm. "That day, Pa told me to change the wagon wheel because he was going into town for supplies. I was. . .uh. . .doing something else and wanted to finish that first. I never did change the wheel. It broke, and Pa and the wagon tumbled off an icy bluff near the trail."

"Oh, Adam, I'm so sorry." Mariah laid a soft hand on his cheek.

He wanted to lean into it, but he didn't deserve her comfort. "Later, after Pa was buried, Quinn and I went to the accident site to see if we could salvage anything. I saw the busted wheel and knew that the accident was my fault. If only I'd repaired it. . . ."

Mariah turned so that she faced him. "You have no proof that you're responsible. You might have repaired the wheel and your pa still could have had the accident. You said it was icy then."

"I should have done what I was told instead of—" *Drawing.* He couldn't tell Mariah that he'd been drawing a picture of a cow with her newborn calf instead of doing the work his father had instructed him. That's why he'd given up drawing—as a penance. Only recently had the call to draw become too strong to ignore.

Mariah remained quiet, as if she didn't know what to say.

"The point I'm trying to make is that I walked away from God. I felt too unworthy to ask Him to comfort me after what I'd done."

"You were only a boy."

"I was fourteen. Out here, a fourteen-year-old does a man's job—is a man. I know now that I should have turned to God instead of away from Him. It would have made things much easier." He thought of how he'd pulled away from his mother and his brother and sister, too, not consoling them in their loss or allowing comfort from them. He'd been stubborn and stupid, causing his grief and anger to drive a wedge in his relationship with his siblings, especially with Quinn.

Adam stood, feeling the need to be alone. "I don't know that I've helped you any."

Mariah accepted his offered hand and allowed him to pull her to her feet. He caught a whiff of her sweet scent and remembered how nice it had felt to hold her in his arms. But the comfort he needed now wasn't a woman's, but from a higher source.

"Thank you, Adam. I know what you shared must have been painful for you, but it helped me."

He watched her walk back to the house. At the door, she turned and waved at him. His heart thumped as it did when he'd been running.

He crossed the creek at the bridge he and Quinn had erected when they'd first come to this area and climbed up to the top of a rocky butte. A cool north wind whipped at his hat, threatening to steal it away. He closed his eyes and turned his face to the breeze. Tears dripped down his cheeks, leaving their saltiness on his lips. He swiped them away, embarrassed for his weakness even though nobody was there to see them. He dropped to his knees, thinking of how he'd turned his back on God.

"I'm sorry, Lord. Forgive me for the anger I've held all these years. I was the one responsible for Pa's death, but I blamed You for not saving him. I'm sorry."

Sometime later, Adam rose, feeling fresh and renewed for the first time in years. The sun dipped behind a butte, painting shades of orange and pink in the sky. Hope swelled in his chest, and he felt true joy for the first time in years. He needed to apologize to Quinn and Anna for his bad attitude of late and for shoving them away.

As he walked back home, he stopped on the bridge and looked up again. Feathery black clouds disappeared against the darkening sky in the east. "Thank You, God, for forgiving me. Help me to forgive myself, and show me what to do about my growing feelings for Mariah."

Chapter Twelve

Mariah stood at the window in the parlor watching Adam walk to the barn, his long-legged gait smoothly carrying him away from her. His arm, free of the sling now, held something that looked like a pad of paper against his side. Her affections for the man grew daily. *Oh, what am I going to do?*

Something had happened after their talk at the creek. Adam seemed lighthearted and happier. She'd even seen the confused looks that Anna and Quinn had shared at the dinner table when Adam told a joke he'd heard while in Bismarck. Her heart had warmed to see him laughing at the corny joke.

Mariah heard a shuffling noise, and Anna joined her at the window.

"Adam seems different lately, don't you think?" Anna sidled a glance her way.

"Yes, I've noticed. He seems happier than he ever has since I've known him, not that that's been such a long while."

Anna stared at Mariah. Uneasiness edged up her spine. What could Anna be thinking?

"Hmm. . .please be careful with Adam. He's suffered a lot since our pa died." Anna turned back toward the window. A wistful smile tilted her lips. "He seemed to take Pa's death much harder than Quinn and me. I never figured out why, since they weren't particularly close.

"I'm so relieved to see him smiling again. It's like having my brother back. I know something's happening between you and Adam. I like you a lot, Mariah"—she turned to face her again—"but I don't want my brother to get hurt."

Mariah opened her mouth to respond, but nothing came out. Did Anna think she was responsible for Adam's current state of joy?

"I've got to work with my yearling. I'll see you later." Anna went outside and actually walked down the steps. Mariah smiled at the small victory.

She sat down on the couch and considered Anna's words. Could Adam's joy possibly be that of a man in love?

Her feelings for Silas had never compared to those she felt for Adam. She admired him even on the train when he first protected her from the antagonizing cowboy and then saved her from being kidnapped. She shivered to think what could have happened if he hadn't been brave enough to challenge that heinous, gun-toting train robber.

Suddenly she bounced to her feet, feeling almost guilty for Adam's happiness. If his current attitude had something to do with his affection for her, what would happen to him when she returned home?

Wringing her hands, she considered how her own heart would ache when it came time to leave. But what hope was there for her and Adam, even if he did hold affections for her?

She simply must return home to Grandma, and Adam belonged here. There wasn't much use for a cowboy in Chicago—or a city girl in the country. She blinked back the tears stinging her eyes. Her throat tightened.

The walls of the house closed in, seeming to strangle her. She needed to get out and away where she could think. A ride would do her good.

She paused at her bedroom door, thinking of the man who'd accosted her in town. Was his threat real? Or simply meant to scare her?

If she stayed close to the ranch where there were people working, she should be fine. She headed to her room to change into the split riding skirt that she'd grown to appreciate.

At the barn a short while later, Hank held on to Sugar's bridle. "I hope I don't get fired for this. You sure it's all right with Adam for you to ride alone?"

"I promise not to go far, but I need to get away for a bit."

He didn't look convinced but let go of the bridle. "Make sure you keep the barn or house in sight, you hear?"

Mariah nodded, giddy to be on horseback again. How could she come to love riding in such a short time? And did she love Adam or merely admire him?

She guided the mare out of the yard and down the hill, amazed at how quickly her riding skills had improved.

A smile tugged at her cheeks. A little over a week ago she'd argued with Adam about finding her a sidesaddle, but now she actually liked riding astride. Staying on was much easier, and her right leg didn't cramp like it had with the sidesaddle.

She rode down the hill, away from the house and barn and through the shallow creek. At the top of the next hill, she reined Sugar to the west, keeping the house in sight. Gusty fingers of wind yanked at her hat, threatening to steal it away. "Whoa, Sugar."

She looped the reins around the saddle horn and retied her hat. The straw of her summer bonnet flapped like a bird's wing. The heavier weight of the Western hats were far more practical out here than her lighter head coverings. If she ever came west again, she'd invest in her own Western hat and more practical clothing. Perhaps even a pair of boots.

Loosening the reins, she allowed Sugar to lower her head and nibble at the grass. Mariah hadn't been able to get Adam's words out of her head. It pained her that he felt responsible for his father's death. She could see why he thought that but still wondered if it were the truth. With icy roads, accidents happened fairly often, even when a wagon was in perfect condition. She'd seen plenty of them in Chicago's inclement weather.

And what about the things Adam had said about God? She gazed heavenward, watching a hawk spiraling in the azure sky. "Do You truly want to be my friend, God? It's all so confusing. Do I believe the reverend or Adam and his family?"

Adam's God seemed so much more approachable. The longing to have a faith like that of the McFarlands nagged her. Perhaps if she could talk to Adam some more, she could make better sense of it all.

She glanced toward the tiny house in the distance and realized she'd wandered too far. Turning around, she leaned back in the saddle as Sugar picked her way down a rocky incline. The mare's back hooves skidded suddenly, sending Mariah's heart ricocheting in her chest and her hands grasping the saddle horn. Sugar righted herself before Mariah could react further and slowed down on level ground.

Mariah remembered losing her own parents and thought how awful she'd feel if she'd been in any way responsible. Her heart ached for the fourteen-year-old Adam, a boy who had suffered not only his father's loss, but also felt as if he were responsible.

"Please, God, if You're the loving, caring God I've heard about recently, please help Adam to forgive himself. Take away his pain."

A warmth, as if she'd drunk steaming coffee, heated her chest. Praying felt so right. Perhaps she should try talking to God again.

The house disappeared as she rode up another hill then reappeared as she reached the peak. In the valley south of the house, the large herd of black cattle Adam had told her about grazed peacefully. They were sleek, pretty cows—and steers. Thanks to a private talk with Anna, she now understood the difference, although from a distance they all looked the same.

Under the shade of a cluster of quaking aspen trees, she saw someone sitting in the grass. She pulled down the brim of her hat to block the sun and stared at the figure. Was it someone spying on the ranch? Should she ride for help?

But the person was between her and the house.

She nudged Sugar closer. Perhaps if she could get near enough, she could kick Sugar into a sudden run and charge right past the man before he could mount his horse.

"Shh, Sugar." The horse plodded forward, unaware of the potential danger. Just when Mariah was certain she'd faint from nervousness, the man stood and stretched. Adam.

Relief made her limbs weak, and she heaved a deep breath.

Adam must have heard her, because he spun around, one hand resting on his pistol. With his other hand, he shoved something behind his back. His frown turned into the semblance of a smile, making her wonder what she'd interrupted.

"I'm happy to see you riding, but you shouldn't be out alone and unarmed after being threatened." He held Sugar's bridle, giving her a stern stare.

Mariah ignored his rebuke, knowing she'd done her best to stay close to the house. She loosened her hat and allowed it to drop to her back, leaving a loose bow across her throat.

"You're alone." She lifted her brows at him.

"I'm a man and can take care of myself. Besides, I'm armed." He rested his hand on his pistol, as if to prove his point.

"A weapon wouldn't do me any good, you know. I've never even fired a pistol."

"I would have ridden with you if you'd asked."

"You weren't home." She cocked her head in a sassy manner.

Adam pursed his lips and sighed.

"Besides, I needed to get out and think, and I had a burning desire to ride again."

Adam smiled. "I know what you mean. My grandmother insists I drive her buggy whenever I visit her in Bismarck. I'd much prefer riding alongside, but she seems to think she needs me, even though she often drives herself when I'm not there." He shrugged.

She stared at his empty hands. Several pencils rested in his shirt pocket. Shavings he'd whittled off littered the area where he'd been sitting. "So, what were you doing when I rode up?"

Adam shrugged. "Not a lot. I tried to work, but Quinn chased me off. He's being overly stubborn. I filled the woodbin again and did some things for Leyna, but I guess I'm bored."

He obviously wasn't going to tell her, so she'd have to figure it out on her own. She drew her leg over Sugar's back and fumbled to get her other foot out of the stirrup. The wind whipped her skirts, startling the mare. Mariah held on, hoping she wouldn't fall in another patch of nettles.

Adam grabbed the reins. "Whoa, there. You're all right, Sugar. Shh. . ." With the mare steadied, he dropped the reins and helped Mariah dismount. As her feet hit the ground, a pad of paper tumbled from behind Adam. He stepped in front of it, blocking her view.

"Sure is windy today." Her cheeks felt as if they were on fire at the thought of Adam seeing her bare leg, but as he shifted his weight to his other leg, she noticed the expert drawing on the paper. The top page fluttered, revealing the perfect muzzle of a horse on a second page.

"Oh, Adam, did you draw those?"

He picked up the pad and held it behind his back. A muscle in his jaw twitched. Why would he hide such talent? Was he embarrassed that he could draw? She wondered now if he'd been the one to pen the detailed pictures of cattle and horses on the walls of his bedroom.

She shoved her hands to her waist. "Well, are you going to answer me? Did you draw those pictures?"

Adam clenched his teeth. Why couldn't she leave well enough alone?

Hanging his head, he knew she'd give him no peace until he told her. "Yes, I drew them."

"Oh, can I see them?" She clapped her hands together like a child at Christmas.

Her excitement was infectious, and he couldn't resist smiling. "I guess so."

His hand trembled slightly as he handed her the pad. She reverently dusted the dirt off the landscape scene he'd been drawing when she'd interrupted.

Mariah glanced up, looking at the tranquil hillside covered in wildflowers, then back at the picture. She smiled up at him. "Why, Adam, you're an artist. This is absolutely amazing!"

Her enthusiastic praise warmed a spot deep within him that had been cold for a very long while. Though his ma had encouraged him to draw, his father had never understood his desire and had even chastised him for wasting time. Adam hadn't realized how much he longed for someone to support him and to tell him that his pictures were decent. Yes, Mr. Howard had, but having someone he cared about cheering him on meant much more. Holding his breath, he watched Mariah flip page after page, alternating between smiling and studying the drawings.

His own family didn't know he'd taken up drawing again. He didn't know why he was ashamed to tell them. Was his secret safe with Mariah?

Mariah held the pad of paper to her chest. "Adam, these are so good. You could sell them."

"Thanks."

Suddenly, tears pooled in her eyes, she looked away. Sniffing, she wiped the tears away with her finger.

Adam's chest tightened. "What's wrong?"

Her lower lip quivered. "I caused you to get sh–shot in your drawing arm. Y–you might never have been able to draw again. How awful that would have been."

He hadn't expected her remorse, and it melted another section of his cold heart. He pulled her into his arms before he stopped to think whether he should or not. Holding her close, he rested his cheek against her hair. She sniffled and clung to the back of his shirt.

"Mariah, look at me."

She shook her head and tightened her grasp.

"When my pa died, I gave up drawing. If I hadn't been so stubborn about completing the picture I was working on then, I would have fixed the wheel, and he wouldn't have died. I figured it was penance to sacrifice my drawing since that's what caused Pa's accident."

Mariah leaned back, her face red and splotchy. "No, Adam. You were only a boy. You have a God-given talent that should be used and cherished by others."

A God-given talent. He'd never really considered his ability a talent that the Good Lord had bestowed on him.

"You should be sharing your talent with others, not hiding it away. Isn't there a Bible verse about that or something?"

"Possibly." He shrugged. "Quinn and Anna don't even know that I started drawing again."

Mariah pulled a lace handkerchief from her sleeve and wiped her eyes and dabbed at her nose. "Why ever not?"

"I don't know. It's been so long since I've done any drawing that I guess I was ashamed to tell them I'd started again."

She shook her head. "They would be proud of you, just like me. I know people who would buy your drawings in a heartbeat."

Her faith in him made him feel ten feet tall.

"Mariah." He slipped his hand behind her neck, ignoring her widening eyes, and kissed her soft lips.

This woman had sneaked in and shaken his world, and he had a feeling he'd never be the same.

Chapter Thirteen

The next morning, Anna guided the buggy toward town. Mariah braced her feet against the front of the buggy as it jostled down the rough trail. About thirty feet in front of her and Anna, Adam sat atop his gray horse. Adam's head continuously turned as he studied the horizon to the east and west and the road ahead. The butt of his rifle rested on one thigh with the barrel of the weapon pointing toward the sky. His dark hair hung shaggily past his collar in a manner she'd never found appealing on a man until now, and his wide shoulders looked strong enough to bear the weight of whatever came his way.

Mariah heaved a sigh. Even from the back, he presented the epitome of a Western cowboy. She touched her lips, remembering his kiss—so unexpected, so wonderful.

He hadn't wanted them to ride to town after Mariah had been threatened, but Anna had insisted she needed items from the town's mercantile, and Mariah wanted to post another story to her editor. In the end he agreed, because he, too, had a package to post. She'd seen the curiosity in his eyes when he noticed her manuscript packet, but he'd been polite enough not to question her about it. If she happened to finish another manuscript while she was at the Rocking M, she'd wait and turn it in after she returned to Chicago.

She wasn't used to quiet evenings at home and had used her newly acquired knowledge of ranching and Western life to quickly pen *Penelope of the Union Pacific*, the tale of an undercover female law official who captures a train robber. A smile tickled Mariah's lips as she considered how much the train robber in her story resembled the one who shot Adam. Except Penelope used her six-shooter to capture the outlaw instead of hatpins.

Mariah's shoulder collided with Anna's as they hit another rut, pulling her out of her musings.

"Sorry, but the trail through here sometimes gets washed out during a heavy rain, and that makes things rough going after it dries. I much prefer riding horseback, but Quinn insists I take the buggy when I go to town. He thinks a lady shouldn't ride in public. As if anyone would mistake me for a lady." She curled her lip.

"I suspect he's trying to watch out for your reputation. It seems a man can get away with appalling behavior, but a woman is always expected to behave like a lady."

"Ain't that the truth!"

They shared a sisterly giggle. Mariah waxed sober. She would miss Anna nearly as much as Adam when she left—and she needed to leave soon. She couldn't continue to impose on the McFarlands' hospitality much longer.

"You know," Anna whispered as she sidled a glance at Mariah, a teasing grin dancing on her lips, "Adam is falling in love with you."

Mariah stared at Adam's back, desperately hoping what Anna said was true and yet hoping it wasn't. She knew now that she'd never truly loved Silas. Perhaps she'd simply been infatuated with his status in Goodwell Publications and all the people he knew and the connections he had.

Now she sounded like Amelia Winfield. Could she possibly be that shallow?

"Aren't you going to say anything? I mean, I've confessed that my brother—who's never shown interest in any particular woman before—is in love with *you*. I think that demands a response." Anna's eyes twinkled. "Has he kissed you yet?"

"Anna!" The skin on Mariah's face tightened at such a personal question. "Shh. . . You do realize he's right over there, don't you? He's going to hear you."

"He has, hasn't he?" Anna grasped Mariah's forearm. "Oh, this is wonderful. We might be sisters soon."

Adam peeked over his shoulder at them, his neutral expression calming her fears that he'd overheard his sister. He winked at her then turned back around. Her stomach danced at his forwardness. Anna grinned as if she knew a huge secret.

"Adam hasn't said anything to me about how he feels, Anna." How could she tell Anna about that kiss? That sweet, wonderful kiss that took her by surprise?

"Well, Adam's not as quiet as Quinn, but he's probably more likely to *show* you how he feels rather than talk about it. Soo. . .I ask again, has he kissed you?"

Mariah's cheeks burned. "Don't you think that's a rather personal question?"

"No."

"Well, if you must know. . ." She leaned close to Anna's ear and whispered, "Yes, he did kiss me. Once."

Mariah thought of all the things Adam had shared with her. . .things she wouldn't tell his sister. That was up to him.

Anna slapped her thigh. "I knew it!" The mare jerked her head and squealed. Adam reined his horse around, evidently checking to see if they were all right.

"Easy, girl," Anna said, suddenly sober.

Adam lifted one brow but turned his horse and guided it down the trail again. He obviously didn't want to get involved in female chatter. He nudged his horse into a trot and rode over the next hill.

"Anna, I have to tell you, I'm feeling guilty about keeping my identity a secret from Adam. I feel I should tell him the truth." Mariah hoped the new topic would steer her friend away from talking about Adam's affections.

Anna shrugged. "I suppose you'll have to tell him sooner or later. Maybe I was wrong in suggesting you wait. I really don't see as it will matter to him. Did you know he's an artist? He drew those pictures in his room—a long time ago."

"He's very talented."

"Yes, it's too bad he quit drawing. He never told me why, but after Pa died, he didn't want to draw anymore. It's really a shame."

Mariah thought it odd that Anna didn't know Adam had started drawing again. It didn't seem like the kind of thing to keep secret. What was the point of that? "Yes, you're right. It is a shame."

"He tore up all but the few sketches on his walls after Pa died. For some reason, he couldn't stand to look at them anymore. I never understood it." Anna shrugged. "Maybe after we return home, we could pick wildflowers and put them in vases throughout the house."

Anna's topics changed direction faster than a weathervane in a thunderstorm. Mariah figured it was time to broach a new subject of her own. "I'm going to telegraph my grandmother and let her know I'll be coming home soon."

Anna's head swung around. "But why? Don't you like it at the Rocking M?"

"Of course I do." She laid a consoling hand on Anna's arm. "But I've stayed far too long already. Grandma always said fish stink after a few days, and so do visitors."

Anna giggled. "Well. . .if you ask me, fish always stink, and so do a few men I know."

They laughed together, and Adam glared back at them as if he thought they were laughing at him. Mariah placed her hand over her mouth to hold back her giggle. She'd never had a friend close enough to find silliness in the small things.

"Well, I'm not letting you go, no matter what you say." Anna looped her arm through Mariah's and tugged it close to her side as if she could keep her from leaving. Her loneliness for female companionship was obvious.

Mariah's mirth died as she realized all that she'd be leaving behind when she left North Dakota. The rocky hills and grasslands had grown on her. She loved the *swish* of the grass on the steady breeze and the kaleidoscope of wildflowers. But it was the people who'd truly stolen her heart. The McFarlands to be exact.

Mariah sighed. She'd accomplished her goal in coming west. She'd learned a lot about ranching and life in the Badlands, and her heart had mended from Silas's betrayal.

She couldn't stay here much longer, not when her grandmother needed her. Though not as steady as she had been, her grandma still had many years ahead of her, and Mariah planned to cherish each one.

As much as she would like to, it wouldn't be fair to ask Adam to wait for her—even if he were so inclined. She touched her lips, her insides tingling at the reminder of Adam's kiss. The sooner she left, the sooner she'd forget Adam and Anna, and even stoic Quinn.

She stifled a sarcastic snort.

Who was she kidding?

"Hold the barrel up. Now, look through the sight and aim toward those tin cans."

Adam stood to the side, watching Mariah. She did as he asked and closed one eye as she pointed the rifle toward the target. She'd asked him half a dozen times to show her how to shoot. At first, he thought it was a silly notion, but then he reconsidered. Who knew how long she'd be here, and as feisty and independent as she was, he couldn't guard her every minute. Her few days' visit had turned into several weeks, not that he was complaining. Still, he couldn't help wondering where she'd been going when she'd come to his aid on the train. Why had she been traveling alone?

The barrel slipped downward again, and he lifted it with two fingers. "Hold it up. You don't want to shoot your toe off."

Mariah scowled at him then pressed the rifle into her shoulder and hefted it up again. "It's heavier than I expected."

"Shoot it a few times, and then we'll switch to my pistol. That will be easier for you."

He longed to wrap his arms around her and help her hold up the rifle but shoved his hands into his pockets instead. How had he become so enamored with Mariah in such a short time? Was it because he was rarely around women?

No, it was because she'd stolen his heart when she bravely—or maybe foolishly—stabbed that train robber with her hatpin. A smile tugged at his lips as he remembered her gumption. The rifle blasted, and he jumped. Who was he kidding? He no longer cared where she'd come from or where she was going. He was just grateful she was here and hoped she'd stay long enough for him to win her heart as she had his.

"Phooey, I missed." She swung around, the rifle pointing straight at his belly.

He gently pushed it away. "Watch it. Never point a weapon at a person unless you intend to shoot them."

Her cheeks flamed. "Sorry. I doubt I need to be concerned with shooting people."

"Nobody hits the target on their first attempt. Try again." He spun her around by her shoulders. "Hold the rifle steady."

She lifted it to her shoulder, and this time, against his better judgment, he wrapped his arm around her, helping her to hold the Winchester upright. She smelled like some kind of flowers, and he couldn't help inhaling her sweet scent. He liked the feel of her in his arms and tightened his embrace.

"How's that? Any easier?"

Mariah stiffened at first but then relaxed. "Yes, um. . .thank you."

"All right, aim it where you think it needs to be then gently pull the trigger when you're ready. Slow and easy."

The rifle report made his ears ring, and the scent of gunpowder hung in the air. The tin can on the left pinged and jumped sideways.

"I hit it!"

He took the rifle from Mariah's hands as she turned in his arms.

"I did it."

Her face illuminated with joy, and all he could think about was kissing her again. But this wasn't the time or place. Emotion clogged his throat, and he cleared it. "Good job."

He stepped away, noticing Mariah's confused look. He reloaded the rifle then scanned the valley below and the hillside to his right. The train robber remained in jail; he'd made certain of that while in town yesterday. But the man who'd threatened Mariah was still out there. Though there were plenty of ranch hands working the herds in the area, a man couldn't be too cautious—not after the woman he loved had been assaulted.

And he did love her. He'd be lying if he didn't face the facts.

The problem was she was leaving. She'd told them yesterday at dinner after they'd returned from Medora. Said her grandmother would need her after her aunt returned home in a few days. Adam clenched his jaw.

Didn't she know that he needed her? She filled a void in his heart that had been there for a long time, and her questions about God had prompted him to make things right with his Savior.

But how could he ask her to stay with him when her grandmother needed her? But how could he let her go?

At times, he wished it were easier for him to confront issues head-on like Quinn and Anna did. To talk—or even argue—until a difficult situation was resolved. But God hadn't made him that way.

He yanked his pistol from the holster and spun the barrel, double-checking to make sure it was fully loaded. He'd prayed for hours and couldn't find a solution.

As much as he wanted to keep Mariah here, he couldn't ask her to stay and leave her elderly grandmother alone. Besides, he hadn't even planned to stay himself. Mariah might consider traveling with him, but they couldn't take an elderly woman.

There was no solution that he could rope and cling to. He sighed and handed her the gun. She watched him, obviously struggling with her own thoughts. He'd love to know what they were, but he wouldn't ask.

"You should find this a lot easier. Cock the gun, point it at the target, holding it with both hands, and shoot." He swung the revolver toward the can and fired, hitting it once, and then again before it touched the ground. Okay, so he was showing off. He grinned. "Think you can do that?"

"That's amazing. . .and, uh. . .no. I'm sure I can't." She reverently took the pistol and fired at the target, missing it every time. "It's harder than I thought."

"Hopefully you'll never have to shoot anyone, but a person is lots bigger than a tin can, so in some ways, it's easier to shoot a man. Course, a tin can doesn't move like a person does."

Mariah shivered and handed the gun back to him. "I don't ever want to have to shoot a person. I was just curious about how a gun worked since I'd never fired one."

He reloaded, using the last of the bullets he'd brought with him. He deftly spun the pistol around on his finger and dropped it into the holster.

"Showoff." Mariah's lips curved upward, revealing her nearly straight teeth.

He shrugged, enjoying her amusement. He wasn't ready for their time to end and searched for a way to prolong it. "How'd you like to try herding cattle?"

"Truly?" Her brown eyes widened.

He nodded.

"I'd love to."

Adam headed toward Chief. "It might be easier for me to show you how if we rode double."

"What about Sugar?"

He untied the mare, fastened her reins loosely around   the horn, and smacked her on the rear. Sugar galloped off in the direction of the barn, sending dust flying. "She'll head home where she knows she'll get a rubdown and a pan of oats."

Mariah lifted her brows but followed him. He boosted her into the saddle; then, using the stirrup, he climbed on behind her. With his left arm, he guided Chief to the top of a butte, allowing his right arm to rest on his thigh. The wound didn't pain him much anymore, unless he overdid things, but it didn't hurt to rest it now and then.

Atop the butte, he scanned a plateau to the south and east, looking for the herd of Angus. He remembered how Mariah mentioned liking the black cattle. His arm lightly grazed her waist, and wisps of soft brown hair tickled his cheeks and clung to his whiskers. He brushed them away, enjoying Mariah's nearness.

The herd wasn't in sight, so he nudged Chief in the other direction. He'd check the valley to the west where a branch of the Little Missouri pooled into a wide pond.

After asking him probably a hundred questions about ranch life when she'd first arrived at the Rocking M, Mariah now seemed content to ride quietly. In fact, she'd been quiet for the past couple of days. He wondered if leaving would be as hard for her as it was for him.

He was certain she'd developed feelings for him. On several occasions, he'd caught her staring. She was quick to look away, but not before he caught a shy smile on her pretty lips.

In town yesterday, he'd noticed how the men watched Mariah. He assumed they were intrigued with the city gal and her fancy dresses instead of his tomboy sister.

The parcel with his four latest drawings was on its way to Chicago, along with a request for an extension of his deadline. He was a man who kept his word, and it went against everything within him to ask for an extension, but he had no choice because of the shooting. He could only hope Mr. Howard wouldn't consider it a breach of his contract.

"There's the Angus herd." Mariah pointed down in the valley where a hundred or so head of cattle were spread out, enjoying the warmth of the summer sun. Some lazily munched grass while others slept on the ground. A calf frolicked in the grass and received a *moo* from its mother when it drifted too far away.

He wished he could be at home here, content to tend cattle and raise Percheron all his life. It wasn't that he hated it here, because he didn't. He simply felt that God had something else for him, at least for now. Who knew where he'd be a few years down the road? All he knew was that he hoped Mariah would be by his side. It was time he had a long talk with his brother and sister—and Mariah.

"The babies are adorable."

"Calves."

She peered over her shoulder. "I know what they're called. But they're still babies, and they're cute." She turned back to watch the cattle. "I wish I could pet one."

"They're dinner and coats and rugs, not pets."

Mariah gasped. "Adam, that's atrocious." She jabbed him in the belly with her elbow.

A puff of air slid out on a chuckle. "It's the truth. No sense getting attached to them." He rested his cheek against her head. The wind whipped a strand of her hair across his face, and he couldn't help feeling its softness between his fingers as he brushed it off.

"I know, but when you say it that way it sounds dreadful." She leaned back against his chest, and he enveloped her with his good arm. "So how does one go about herding cattle?"

"Hmm? Who said anything about chasing cattle? I'm pretty content to stay here like this all day." His belly growled.

Mariah giggled. "I don't think your stomach would be too happy if you did."

The warm breeze brought with it the scent of cattle and sage and the swishing of buffalo grass. A hawk screeched high above him, and the sun glistened off the pond. He'd never felt this content. He'd made things right with God and was drawing again. The two things he'd thought most important were back in his life, only now there was something else he wanted. He just couldn't see how to work it all out.

At first, Mariah had been a nuisance, and he'd wanted her gone. But then she started helping Anna and puttering about the house like she belonged there—belonged in his heart. He admired her bravery and spunk, even when it got her in trouble. If only she'd turn her heart to God and stay here.

Clicking out the side of his mouth, he urged Chief forward. Best get this herding lesson over with and put some distance between him and Mariah before he turned into a pile of mush.

"We're heading for that lone steer over there by the pine, and then we'll persuade him to rejoin the herd."

"Persuade?" Mariah threw a saucy smile over her shoulder.

"Yes, ma'am. In a minute, he'll want nothing more than to join his cousins."

He felt Mariah's side vibrate as she giggled, and his chest swelled that he could make her so happy. Tightening his grip on her waist, he guided Chief down an incline.

Yep, at this moment, life was just about perfect.

Mariah turned sober and fidgeted with the lace on her cuff. She cleared her throat. "Adam, there's something I need to tell y—"

A shot rang out, and Mariah jumped. His heart jolted. Had she been shot?

He tightened his hold on her and rolled them off his gelding as Mariah let out a squeal. Adam landed on his injured arm, gritting his teeth as blinding pain shot across his shoulder, but he cradled Mariah to soften her landing.

Another shot blasted the dirt two feet from his face. He jerked away and grabbed Mariah around the waist, rolling her behind a big boulder jutting up from the ground.

She didn't move. Didn't make a sound.

He grabbed his pistol and peered through a bush growing in a crevice on the warm boulder. His heart thundered. Had his carelessness and daydreaming caused him to lose the woman he dearly loved?

Chapter Fourteen

Mariah lay in the dirt, her heart pounding faster than it had when she accidentally set fire to her grandma's heirloom tablecloth. Gasping, she tried to catch her breath. Adam's body had shielded hers, but her side ached from landing on his arm. Hopefully it hadn't been his injured one.

Bullets pinged against the boulder shielding her and Adam from the shooter. Mariah lay perfectly still. One late night at finishing school when the girls were telling stories instead of sleeping, Sarah Jane Carson had whispered across the beds, "If anybody ever shoots at me, I'm playing dead. That way they'll quit shooting and leave." Mariah's heroine in her first dime novel had done the same thing, but now Mariah realized what a foolish notion that was. Playing dead wouldn't dissuade a man with a gun intent on killing someone.

"Mariah," Adam whispered. "Sweetheart, are you all right?"

Her heart thumped even faster at the endearment. Moving carefully to keep her body behind the boulder, she rolled over. "I–I'm fine."

"Thank God."

She pushed up from the ground, her head spinning as her eyes struggled to focus. Perhaps she'd been knocked out and hadn't realized it. She spat dirt from her mouth and wiped it off her lips with her fingers.

Adam grabbed her arm and pulled her against the warm boulder. "Keep down and stay close to me."

He peered over the rock, fired once, then ducked back down. He gave her a once-over then plucked a stem of grass from her hair and brushed the dust off her shoulder. His concerned smile made her want to lunge into his arms and cling to him, but she sat still.

"My rifle is with Chief, but he's gone. I don't have much ammo left." He twirled the chamber of his pistol.

Mariah's mouth went dry. Before the ambush, she'd been worrying about leaving Adam and going home, but now she might never make it that far.

Adam rubbed his gunshot wound. Had he reinjured it in the fall?

She scooted closer, looping her arm around his and laying her head on his shoulder for a moment. He patted her back.

"Don't worry. Someone will see Chief or Sugar soon and come looking for us."

She wondered if they could hold off their attackers that long. Loosening her hold, she looked around for something she could use as a weapon. She thought about her heroines and wondered what they'd do in such a situation.

The attackers resumed firing. Mariah jumped. What did she know about being brave? She was a city gal from Chicago who made up stories about valiant men and women. Tears blurred her eyes at the thought of her grandmother suffering when she learned Mariah was injured or killed.

Adam peeked up and fired. He ducked down again and checked the chamber. "Four more shots." Leaning to the right, he scanned the trail.

Mariah hoped help would come in time. She'd been such a fool to not take the man's threat more seriously when he assaulted her. Turning to the side so Adam wouldn't see, she wiped her eyes with her sleeve. If she were going to die, there were two things she wanted to do. She'd opened her mouth to tell Adam who she was when the firing started. Once again, she'd failed.

But more importantly, if this was her last day on earth, she wanted Christ to come into her heart. *Simply ask.* It still seemed too easy, but now wasn't the time to argue. She glanced heavenward as Adam fired another shot.

God, if what Adam and the others say is true, then please come into my heart. Forgive me of my sins and for my stubborn ways. I believe Jesus is Your Son, sent to save me from my sinful ways. Please watch over us, and send help in time.

"Got one!" Adam slid down beside her. "There's only one left."

"Bullets or men?"

Adam grimaced. "Both."

"Don't you think someone will hear the gunfire?"

He shrugged. "They'll probably think that we're still shooting targets."

She lowered her head and fiddled with the dirty lace edging of her blouse. It looked as if they might not make it out of this, but inside, she felt lighter. Perhaps God would give her the courage she needed in her last hour.

"Hey, don't give up yet." He lifted her chin and traced her cheek with his finger then rubbed his arm. "I'm not good with words. I wish I could draw you a picture to show you how I feel about you."

She couldn't help wondering what that drawing would look like. Would the love she saw in Adam's eyes show forth in his artwork?

"You're very talented. No matter what happens, I hope you'll keep drawing."

"I'd like you to have one of my sketches—once we get out of this, uh. . .predicament." His melancholy smile tugged at her heart. He peered over the boulder again. "The man I shot hasn't moved, but I can't see the other one."

"Adam, there is something I need to tell you. I'm not who you think I am."

He darted a gaze at her but went right back to keeping watch. "Let it wait. I need to keep my attention focused right now."

Mariah hung her head. How many times had she debated telling him—tried to tell him?

As much as she longed to have the news of her identity off her chest, she feared Adam would feel lied to. Would he still care after she told him?

The tone of Mariah's words scared him. Sweat trickled down his temple, and he swiped it against his arm. What did she mean she wasn't who he thought?

Adam could hear the gunman calling to his partner, but he couldn't see him. And he wasn't sure if he'd killed the downed man or just winged him.

He despised killing. As an artist, he longed to show people the beauty of God's creation, not the dark side. But both were part of the world. If not for the dark things of life, many people would never realize their need for God. When troubles come, many people turn to God. But sometimes they let their problems stand between them and their God.

That's what he had done.

But no more.

One more shot—that's all he had. But no matter what, he couldn't let that man get Mariah. He'd die before letting that happen.

Lord, You reckon You could help us out here?

Pebbles dug into his knees, and his arm ached. Mariah sat next to him, her head resting against her knees. He wanted to believe she was praying.

She'd asked enough questions about God and the Bible the past few days to fill a book.

God, please don't let her die without giving her heart to You.

He thought of his mother. Thought of Anna and Quinn. He should have told them his what he longed to do instead of worrying about their reaction. Quinn probably would encourage him to follow his dream. Adam had shortchanged them both because of his own feelings of guilt and inadequacy. Having renewed his heart with God made him see how he'd been living under the shadow of guilt for far too long.

"Hey, McFarland. You ain't getting out of here. I've got plans for that pretty city gal."

Mariah gasped. "It's him. The train robber."

Adam recognized the man's gravelly voice, too. Since the man had most likely broken out of jail last night, the sheriff would be looking for him—and the sheriff would probably come straight to the Rocking M— unless he was dead.

"I know y'all's been doing some shooting practice and gotta be low on ammo."

Adam's skin crawled. They'd been watching? Why hadn't they attacked back then instead of waiting?

Because this was the perfect spot for an ambush. If he hadn't acted so quickly and pulled Mariah to the ground when he had, he and Mariah would have been exposed without any place to hide. This boulder was the only thing big enough on this side of the trail to hide behind within a hundred yards.

And yet the outlaws had lots of cover—and water. With the creek behind them, the outlaws could far outlast him and Mariah. The sun crept overhead. Soon it would shine on them, making them hotter and thirstier. How long could Mariah hold out without water?

C'mon, Quinn. Hank. Anybody.

He hunkered down as the outlaw fired off another volley of shots. The shuffling of quick footsteps moved his way. Adam peered at the train robber, who dodged behind a tree. He was making his move—getting closer.

The man's evil chortle sent shivers up Adam's spine.

"What's he doing?" Mariah rose up to get a look, but Adam shoved her back to the ground.

"Stay down. He's trying to get closer."

The trunk didn't totally cover the man's body, but Adam wasn't willing to risk using his last bullet for less than a sure shot.

The vile laughter came again. "I'm guessin' you're out of bullets or you'd be shooting at me. Gonna have to kill you, McFarland, for shooting my little brother."

"What's that?" Mariah leaned sideways. "Oh, look!"

The sound of horses' hooves was music to Adam's ears. Help was near.

The train robber muttered a curse and ran toward his horse. Adam stood, knowing he'd get one chance to stop the man. Mariah wouldn't be safe with him on the loose.

He fired.

The man lurched and fell. Adam darted toward him.

"Adam, no. Wait." Mariah's cries echoed behind him.

Though shot in the leg, the outlaw stood and hobbled for his horse. Adam ran after him, his mouth dry. The man lifted his gun and fired again. Adam dove for the dirt.

The outlaw cursed and raised his pistol. Adam knew he was done for.

The empty chamber of the gun clicked. The thief threw it away and lunged at Adam. The weight of the bigger man's body landed hard on Adam's. They struggled, grunting and throwing punches. Adam swung his fist at the man's jaw. Pain spiraled through his hand.

The outlaw seized Adam's wounded arm. Adam cried out. The man grinned and threw a punch right in the same arm, as if remembering the gunshot wound. Blackness swirled, sucking Adam under, but he fought back.

He forced his eyes open. The outlaw blurred from one to two. A sickening grin twisted the man's features. Adam looked over the outlaw's head to see the rock he held. The man drew his arm backward, readying to strike. Adam lifted his left arm to block the blow.

Suddenly, Adam saw a shadow and heard a *thud*. The rock dropped behind the outlaw. His eyes rolled up in his head, and he fell backward. Wielding his own pistol like a club, Mariah came into focus. She turned concerned eyes on him.

"Are you all right?" She knelt beside him. "You saved us, you know?"

Four horses skid to a halt, slinging dust and pebbles. Mariah sneezed and squeezed his hand. "It's over, Adam. How badly are you hurt?"

"Whoo-wee, did you see that little lady club that man?"

Adam recognized his ranch hand's voice as he laid his head back down, thanking God for sending help in time. Give me a minute, and I'll be fine."

"What happened here?"

Adam opened his eyes, unable to ignore Quinn. Mariah patted his chest and looked up.

"Those men attacked us. That one"—she pointed to the man she'd knocked out—"he's the train robber who shot Adam. The other man is the one who accosted me in town."

For once Adam was relieved that Quinn took over, barking orders and making sure the outlaws were tied up and on their way back to jail. Relief washed over him to learn the other outlaw was unconscious and not dead.

After a few minutes, Adam allowed Mariah to help him sit up. His arm still throbbed, and his knuckles were swelling, but the rest of him wasn't in too bad of shape.

"Here, drink this." Mariah lifted a canteen to his mouth, and he drank fully, grateful for the cool water.

He offered it to her, and she, too, had her fill. Then she pulled out her handkerchief and dabbed her mouth. He'd love to place a kiss on those pretty lips, but that would have to wait until they were alone. But he wouldn't wait long—wouldn't make the mistake he had before in not telling her how he felt.

He'd come close to losing her today, and he was so thankful to God for second chances.

Mariah walked over to Chief, who was tied behind Hank's horse, and patted his nose. "You're such a good boy, going home and getting help for us."

She kissed Chief's muzzle, bringing a smile to Adam's lips and making him not a little envious of his horse.

Rubbing the back of his neck, he thought about how Mariah had risked her own life to save him. She bravely, without hesitation, knocked out the outlaw who was bent on sending him to his Maker.

Adam swallowed. Perhaps Drew Dixon was right. Maybe a woman does save the day—once in a while.

Chapter Fifteen

Mariah stood at the parlor window watching for Adam. In spite of her objections and Quinn's, he'd insisted that he go to town to give a report to the sheriff about the ambush. She worried about his arm. When the train robber had grabbed it, Adam's handsome face had contorted in pain. Anger had surged through her, and all she wanted was to help him, even if it meant rendering the outlaw unconscious.

"Feeling better?" Anna stopped beside her and handed her a cup of water.

She nodded and accepted the glass. "Yes, a bath works wonders."

"I may enjoy working with the horses and even the cattle, but I do relish a nice, warm bath. Leyna's fixing bratwurst. I'm going to see if she needs help. You stay here and wait for Adam. I'm sure he'll want to see you as soon as he returns." With a saucy grin and a giggle, she sauntered out of the parlor.

Mariah took another sip of water. It was odd how being stranded without water for such a short time had made her crave the refreshing liquid now. She drank half three-fourths of the cup.

Anna and Leyna had peppered her with questions while helping her undress and filling the washtub. Leyna seemed stunned by an ambush right here on Rocking M property, but Anna acted as if she was disappointed to have missed out on the action.

A horse nickered, and she looked up. Her heart skipped a beat at the sight of four men riding into the yard. She set the glass down, thankful she'd had time to bathe and rest while Adam was gone. She wanted to look nice for him, and they *had* to talk. Nothing was going to stop her this time from telling

Adam that she was Drew Dixon. Picking up her skirts, she rushed out the front door and down the steps.

Adam's lips tilted in a tired smile as he turned Chief toward her. Her steps faltered at his fatigue, and she wondered if maybe she should wait until he'd rested, too.

He dropped from the saddle and looped one arm around her neck, pulling her against his chest. She clutched him, thankful the frightening event was over, but at the same time, she couldn't help wondering if Quinn and the ranch hands were watching. She pulled away, hoping to rein in her emotions and avoid a public display of their affections.

After he learned her secret, Adam might no longer want to hold her.

He took her hand. "Walk with me to the barn. I want to give Chief a good rubdown."

Thankful that nobody was watching them, Mariah took his warm, callused hand. His wasn't what one expected in an artist's hand, but rather a laborer's. His fingernails were chipped and even had dirt under them, and yet his hands were gifted—able to recreate God's creation in amazing lifelike drawings.

Since returning to the house, she'd also spent a little time reading the Bible. Some things encouraged her, but others were confusing. She couldn't wait to ask Adam about them.

The light dimmed in the barn, and the scent of hay, horse, and leather wafted, along with dust motes, in the air. Adam unsaddled Chief and brushed him down while the ranch hands who'd ridden along with him to town finished tending their own mounts. Mariah grabbed a comb and worked on Chief's silvery mane. One by one, the men drifted outside, leaving only Adam and her.

He gave his horse a bucket of feed then closed the stall gate. He put the brush and comb away in the small tack room. Mariah wondered what he was thinking. He hadn't said a word but smiled and even winked at her a time or two. Anxiety over their needed conversation battled with her growing love. How was it possible to have such feelings for someone you'd only known a few weeks?

Adam took off his hat and dipped his hands in the fresh bucket of water that Quinn had fetched earlier. He scrubbed his face and hands. He shook his head like a wild stallion, flinging water, but a few droplets clung to his tanned jawline, darkened with whiskers. Mariah stepped forward, gently wiping each droplet with her finger. Adam closed his eyes and breathed deeply.

Her heart ached with love for this man. But would he still care for her once he learned she'd not been fully honest with him?

Suddenly Adam's eyes opened. They sparked like blue fire, and he grabbed her hand, tugging her back in the barn.

In the privacy of the shadows, Adam pulled Mariah into his arms. He pressed his face against her sweet-smelling hair and clung to her. He'd come so close to losing her today.

There was something on her mind; he knew that. He'd sensed something was bothering her for a while but figured she'd tell him when she was ready.

All the way to town and back, he'd struggled with what to say to her. How to tell her how he felt. Why couldn't words come as easy as sketching did?

He took her gently by the shoulders and pushed her back so he could look into her face. She was lovely but not perfect. Her skin had browned, and tiny freckles dotted her pert nose. Her big brown eyes stared back with curiosity and affection. He swallowed hard. He'd never been in love before—and he was finding it wonderful—and a bit scary. Mariah licked her lips and brushed a tress of hair off her cheek.

He was nervous, too, but leaned forward, closing his eyes. His lips met hers, and he tried to show her how he felt—the depth of his love. After a few moments of pure joy, he pulled back, his breath ragged. "You have to know how I care for you. Love you."

Tears glinted in her eyes, and she nodded.

"Don't leave, Mariah. Stay with me. Marry me."

Surprise widened her eyes, and an *O* formed on her lips. Then her thin brows dipped, making his heart stumble. Tears filled her eyes—tears that didn't look like happy tears. He prepared to slam and lock the door of his heart—fearing her rejection.

Had he imagined she felt the same way he did?

Hadn't she kissed him and clung to him like a woman in love?

"Adam, I care for you, too. Deeply. But I've been trying to tell you something. Something that may change the way *you* feel."

She fiddled with the edge of her sleeve, and the faint aroma of soap tickled his senses. She'd bathed and changed while he was gone and looked pretty in the blue and white dress that swished when she moved.

"Too much happened when we first met—when you got shot." She gazed at him, an apology written on her pretty features. "I thought I wouldn't be here long enough to bother telling you, and then when Anna invited me to stay, I decided to wait until you were better."

She turned away from him, his concern growing by the second. "Whatever it is, just say it."

"All right." She pivoted around, her skirts swinging. "I'm not who you think I am."

"You've told me that before. So, who are you?"

Chief nickered as a horse galloped into the yard. Adam glanced outside the double doors. He hated the intrusion but wondered why someone was riding up to the house so fast. It usually meant a crisis somewhere. A tall, thin stranger wearing a suit and derby hat struggled to stop his mount. Adam glanced back at Mariah. She looked over her shoulder and scowled at the disturbance.

"Hell–o–o? Anyone there?" the stranger called.

Mariah gasped and covered her mouth with her hand. "Silas?"

She gazed up at Adam, sorrow and confusion in her eyes. Who was this Silas guy?

Chapter Sixteen

"Good day to you." Quinn approached the stranger from the house. Silas dismounted and turned away from the barn, evidently not seeing Mariah in the shadows. She searched for a place to hide but knew there was no getting away. How in the world had Silas found her way out in North Dakota? And why had he bothered?

"Who is Silas?" Adam hissed in her ear.

She jumped, almost forgetting him at the shock of seeing her former fiancé. A shadow darkened the barn before Quinn and Silas entered. Mariah hoped her expression conveyed her apology to Adam. Why did Silas have to show up at that moment?

"Mariah," Quinn called, looking not as congenial as he'd been the past few weeks. "There's a man here to see you." His concerned gaze darted to Adam.

Silas, tall and skinny as ever, stepped into view. His eyes sparked when he saw her. "Mariah, darling. I thought I'd never find you."

Mariah stepped back, closer to Adam, but to her disbelief, Adam moved away. Silas grabbed her up in a hug, pinning her arms to her side. His thin form was so slight in comparison to Adam's muscular build. She struggled to get away, but he held her tight.

She cast a plea for help over her shoulder to Adam, but he stood there with arms crossed, glaring. It cut her to the core to know that Silas's unwanted display had hurt Adam.

Finally, Silas released her after holding her far longer than was proper. Quinn now stood next to Adam, as if forming a unified front. Mariah's heart sank. Adam would never trust her after this.

Silas turned to the two brothers and held out his hand. "I'm terribly sorry to disturb your day. I'm sure you have cows to herd or other menial work to be done." He waved his pale hand in the air.

Both Quinn and Adam glared at him, but Adam also cast confused glances her way.

"My name is Silas Wellington, and I'm Mariah's fiancé."

A bullet to the chest wouldn't have hurt Adam worse than those words. His eyes fired daggers at Mariah. She looked stunned, and for a moment, his hurt and anger dimmed.

"No!" Mariah held up her palm. "That isn't true. Silas is my former fiancé. There is nothing between us now."

Her pleading gaze beseeched Adam to believe her, and for a moment, he wavered. Was that what she was trying to tell him? That she was engaged to be married?

How could he believe anything she said now? He was such a fool.

Silas took hold of Mariah's hand, but she yanked it away. "Now, Mariah, darling, I know we had a disagreement, but I never consented to dissolve our engagement. I thought you just needed time to get over your little snit."

Mariah gasped. "Well, you're wrong, and you wasted your time coming all this way. I have no intention of ever marrying you." She hiked her chin at the man.

He leaned closer to her. "We should discuss this when we don't have an audience." He rubbed his thin mustache with his index finger and darted a glance at Adam and Quinn.

In spite of his roiling emotions, Adam couldn't help feeling things weren't totally on the up-and-up. Something wasn't right here.

The question was, who was right? Had Mariah simply run away from her fiancé after an argument? Was the engagement actually absolved, or was the not-so-happy couple still planning to be married?

He clenched his jaw. Had Mariah been trying to tell him that she planned to marry another man?

He never should have let his emotions get involved. He'd done a good job over the past years since his father's death of keeping them locked away. But a hatpin-wielding imp had pried open the lid.

Silas turned back to Mariah. Adam wanted to step between them—to protect her still, even though he no longer knew if she wanted his protection. But he didn't. Whatever was wrong, Silas and Mariah needed to hash it out, so she would be free to move on—to him.

If she truly wanted to be married to him. She'd never actually said she loved him.

"There's something else I need to tell you, darling. Your grandmother had a fainting spell and fell down the steps in her house."

"Oh no." Mariah laid her hand against her chest. "Is she—is she all right?"

"She's alive, but it doesn't look good. She broke her hip, and I'm sorry, dear, but the doctor doesn't think she'll live much longer." Silas pressed his thin lips together.

"There's a train heading east in the morning. If you get packed quickly, we can return to town tonight and catch that one. Otherwise, we'll have to wait several more days."

The pain in Mariah's eyes mirrored that in Adam's heart. He ached for her and wanted to comfort her but didn't know where things stood with this—fiancé.

She turned to him. "I'm so sorry, Adam, but I've got to go. Grandmother raised me and is very precious to me. I have to see her before she—"

A *squeak*, like an animal in fierce pain, erupted from Mariah's mouth. Picking up her skirts, she rushed out of the barn. Adam wanted to follow—to tell her everything would be all right, but his feet felt as if they were trapped in quicksand.

"Come into the house, and I'll get you some refreshment. You've had a long journey and have even farther to go." Quinn ushered Silas away, casting Adam a concerned glance.

He sank down onto a nearby bench. How could things change so fast?

Mariah had whirled into his world like a cyclone, stirring up things, making him want things he'd never desired before. Now she was leaving behind a shattered heart. A path of debris that Adam wasn't sure he'd ever recover from.

Had she loved him at all? Did she still?

With his arms on his knees, he hung his head. *What do I do, Lord? Did she lie to me?*

Should I go after her?

Mariah slung a spare dress into the satchel, caring little if it would wrinkle.

All she knew was that she had to get to her grandmother before she died. She had to kiss her goodbye and thank her for all she had done.

Anna sashayed into the room, and her eyes widened. "You're leaving? Why?"

"My grandmother's been injured in a fall and isn't expected to live."

"Oh, I'm so sorry." Anna rushed to her side and enveloped her in a bear hug. "Let me help so you can get on your way. You'll need to get to town before dark."

Mariah wiped her tears and nodded. In a matter of minutes her satchel was packed and her other items secured in her trunk. She picked up a copy of one of her dime novels and handed it to Anna. "Will you give this to Adam for me?"

Anna's brows crinkled as if she thought it an odd goodbye gift, but she nodded. "You go on. I'll have somebody take your trunk into town tomorrow. We send it on the next train."

"Not Adam. Please don't ask him to do that."

Anna stared at her, concern etching her pretty features. "Did something happen between you two?"

Mariah sighed and looked away. She picked up her straw hat and tied it on. "I have to go. I'm sure he'll tell you what happened."

She pulled Anna into another hug. "I've always wanted a sister. You're the closest I've ever had." Tears blurred her vision, and she dashed out of the room.

"You're coming back, aren't you?" Anna's hopeful words echoed behind Mariah.

She shook her head. "I don't think Adam would want that."

The pungent scent of Leyna's sauerkraut filled the air. Mariah glanced toward the kitchen on her way past the parlor. She wished she had time to say goodbye to the kind cook and to eat another of her delicious meals.

She swiped away more tears, knowing she'd never step foot in this home again. The rustic log house with its Western-style furniture had become familiar and homey. It was here that she first learned that God could be her friend. That He was a loving Father who wanted a relationship with His children, and not a scary icon bent only on vengeance. She may be leaving the Rocking M, but at least she was taking God with her.

Mariah's heart broke with each step she took. She longed to talk to Adam, but there was no time. She and Silas *had* to get to town before dark or they risked getting lost in the barren wilderness.

As she exited the house, she saw that Quinn had prepared a buggy and tied Silas's horse to the back. Hank, scowling down at her, sat atop his horse.

"Hank will guide you into town and then bring the buggy back tomorrow. So you don't need to worry about it." Quinn glared down at her. She wanted to explain. Wanted him to believe she'd never hurt Adam on purpose, but she climbed in the buggy, her throat too clogged for words.

The buggy tilted slightly as Silas crawled in beside her. He clicked the horse forward, and they started walking out of the yard.

Impatient and frustrated with all that had happened, she yanked the reins from his pale, effeminate hands. She was sure he'd never had a callus. "He-yah!"

The buggy jerked as the surprised horse lunged forward into a run. Silas fell back against the seat, mouth open and staring at her like she was crazy.

She looked back as they left the ranch yard. Adam was nowhere to be seen.

Her heart broke, and she saw the future she'd hoped for dissolve before her eyes.

Adam stared at the blank pad of paper lying on his bed, unable to stir up his creativity in light of all that had happened. The lamp cast eerie flickers of light and shadows. The only thing he could think of to sketch was Mariah.

He flipped back to one he'd done of her standing at the corral, watching Anna working with her yearling. Her interest was obvious in the way she stood on the bottom rung of the railing and leaned her head between the bars, in spite of the fact the she'd almost been bitten by doing that before. A claw gripped his chest. He missed her—longed to have five more minutes with her.

Five minutes to hear what she'd wanted to tell him.

Five minutes to hold her close.

He tossed the pencil down before he cracked it in two. Shoving up from the chair, he went and stood in front of the small window. The sun had set and the moon wasn't out yet. Leaning his head against the cool pane, he prayed for God to heal his hurting heart. He prayed Mariah and her greenhorn companion made the morning train, so she could get home to her grandmother.

His stomach curdled at the thought of Mariah with another man. Why hadn't he kept his distance from her like he'd wanted originally?

"Are you all right?" Anna stood at the door, leaning against the jamb. "Quinn told me what happened. I'm so sorry."

"Yeah. Me, too." He straightened and sat on the edge of the bed. "Did you want something?"

Anna nibbled her lower lip, a sure sign she was contemplating something. "I really believe Mariah loves you."

Adam snorted a laugh. "She has an odd way of showing it, don'tcha think?"

"She told me she came here to get away from a troubling relationship. I feel certain that she broke off her engagement before she left Chicago."

"Well. . .that Silas fellow sure didn't seem to think that." He rubbed at the pinch in the back of his neck.

Anna pulled the ladderback chair away from the desk and spun it around on one leg. She sat down, and Adam noticed she had something rolled up under her arm.

"I know when Mariah first came here something was bothering her. I don't think her fiancé was very kind to her."

Adam sat up at the news, concerned for Mariah's welfare. "Why do you say that? Did she say something?"

Anna shrugged. "It's a feeling I got. She rarely talked about her home, except for mentioning her grandmother."

Adam pursed his lips. "I knew she was hiding something, but I never considered it could be a fiancé."

His sister stood and hugged him. "Hopefully she will write and explain everything. She did ask me to give you this, odd as it seems."

Adam's gaze latched on to the dime novel a second before his hand did. This was a different one from those she'd given him before, but the author was Drew Dixon. He narrowed his eyes. How did she know the author? And why hadn't he ever heard back from the man after receiving a telegram saying he was soon to arrive?

"I probably should go help Leyna put supper on the table. I'm here for you if you need me, little brother." She sent him a sympathetic smile as she left the room.

He'd never liked her referring to him as her little brother, but he ignored it, knowing, this time, she meant the words as an endearment and not a jibe. Adam turned the colorful paperback book over in his hands. He wasn't in the mood to read, but then perhaps an interesting story would take his mind off his own confusing troubles. Flipping open the front cover, he noticed a folded sheet of paper, and his heart bucked.

With shaking hands, he unfolded the page.

Dear Adam,
Please know that I broke my engagement with Silas before leaving Chicago. I have no intentions of marrying him, despite what he says. I care for you and hope you and I can talk soon.

Adam fingered the paper, his hopes soaring. Mariah wasn't engaged. Silas had been acting the part of a loving suitor. Or perhaps he wasn't acting but really was in love with Mariah. He couldn't blame the man for that.

He folded down the bottom flap of the paper to read Mariah's signature, and the breath whooshed out of him.

Love,
Mariah aka Drew Dixon

Mariah was Drew Dixon?

He hurriedly looked at the inside cover page and saw that this novel also held the author's signature, only this time it was signed to him—by Mariah.

The signatures on the note and inscription were the same. He crumpled the sheet of paper.

Mariah had lassoed his heart and then dragged it through an emotional pile of stinging nettles. Now all the questions made sense. She was doing research for her books.

Hadn't he told her in the letter he wrote that her ranching facts were sometimes inaccurate?

Why hadn't she simply told him the truth?

He shot off the bed and marched through the parlor. Quinn glanced up from the desk in the corner where he often looked over the bookwork that Anna diligently recorded. Silverware clinked at the table where Anna was setting it for dinner. Ignoring their questioning gazes, he stormed out the door into the cool night air.

The darkness called to him. It was a place where he could hide from everything except the battle going on within him.

The woman he loved had used and betrayed him. Had her kisses merely been research, too? Just so she'd know what it was like to kiss a cowboy—so she could describe it accurately in her paperbacks?

He'd wanted to marry her and give her his name. He was even willing to give up his dream for her, but she'd deceived him.

How was a man supposed to forget about something like that?

Chapter Seventeen

Mariah sat on the sofa in her parlor with her two best friends, staring into her lukewarm tea. Grandma was gone. Mariah had been through too much to refuse Silas's offer to escort her to the funeral, but it was Adam's comforting arms she longed for. Arms that would never again surround her.

"Are you ever going to tell us about your journey west?" Angela Carter asked as she reached for another cookie.

Sarah Beth Jennings glared at Angela. "She doesn't want to talk about that on the day she buried her grandmother."

"I was simply trying to get her mind off. . .well, you know." Angela cast Mariah a repentant gaze.

They were her closest friends, women she'd gone to college with, but both were shallow and insensitive at times. She knew they were trying their best to cheer her up now that the others had left the gathering that was held at her home after the funeral.

Mariah longed to go upstairs, shed the stiff black dress, and go to sleep. The last week as her grandma had slowly gotten worse had been dreadful. And after two months of pining for Adam, he'd not answered a single one of her letters.

Anna had written and told her to give him time. But Mariah was sure he'd never forgive her for what she'd done to him. She could barely forgive herself.

Over and over she rationalized things in her mind, trying to figure out where she went wrong. She should have told Adam who she was the first time he mentioned Drew Dixon. But that was hindsight.

Even if she didn't have Adam to comfort her, her heavenly Father had been with her each step of the way.

Angela stood, looking apologetic. "I suppose we should be going. The sun will be setting soon, and Papa will be furious if I'm not home before then."

Mariah called to her housekeeper. "Thelma, please have Miss Carter's carriage brought around front."

Thelma nodded and glided out of the room, her eyes still red. The woman had worked for Mariah's grandmother longer than Mariah had lived in the house and missed her dearly. Heleen Vanderveer's death had been hard on all who knew her.

A short while later, the women left, and Mariah retired to her room. She breathed a sigh to be out of the ugly black dress. She pulled the pins from her hair and brushed out the tangles then braided it. A nap before supper would do her good—if she could actually sleep.

Looking at the reflection in the mirror, she studied the walls decorated in light blue floral wallpaper. White eyelet curtains and a matching bedspread gave the room a soft, gentle atmosphere. Still, given her choice, she'd leave this big home with all its beautiful furniture and decorations for that tiny, whitewashed room in North Dakota.

Tears blurred her eyes. Her grandma may be gone, but Mariah's love for the dear woman would endure forever.

But Adam was a different story. How did she *stop* loving a man who no longer wanted her?

She'd pleaded with God to soothe her breaking heart and to take away the pain, but two months had passed, and she felt no different. Dabbing her nose with a lace handkerchief, she stood and crossed the room to her chest of drawers. On top lay her most recent novel. The story of a woman who goes west to tend her sister's three children after her sister's death. The city woman had quite an adjustment to ranch life, including learning to ride astride and shooting a gun. The main difference in the heroine's life and Mariah's was that the heroine got her man. She eventually fell in love with her sister's husband—a man she'd despised for years for stealing her sister and taking her far out west.

Sometimes Mariah envied her fictional characters. She could give them problems, but in the end, the hero always got the woman. Too bad real life wasn't the same.

She caressed the cover. A picture of a man and woman riding double while herding cattle.

Adam's picture.

He'd told her she could have one, and that's the one she picked, mainly because the man resembled Adam and the woman looked quite a bit like her.

Had he received the check and copies of the book that she'd sent to him? Would he be upset to see one of his pictures on the cover of a dime novel?

She'd probably never know.

With a sigh, she crawled under the covers of the bed, her body instantly chilling in the cold sheets. Tears dampened her pillowcase. She held back a sob and prayed for God to help her through yet another lonely evening. One of these days she needed to look to the future, but right now, all she could manage was to get through the next hour.

The next minute.

"Everything looks to be in order for your showing, Mr. McFarland." The art gallery's hostess stared at him with soft green eyes, her interest evident. "Could I get you a glass of punch?"

"No, thank you. I'm fine." Adam resisted the urge to tug at the collar of his new suit and to scratch his arm. The garment felt stiff and confining compared to the comfortable chambray or flannel shirts he preferred.

The gallery owner, Trent Howard, strode around the big, open room with his hands behind his back, looking at the framed pictures Adam had drawn. Several of them had already sold for a surprising amount, and he had assured Adam that probably the others would also before the end of the evening. His share of the money would enable him to realize his dream. Before winter set in at the ranch, he planned to be on a train, heading south.

He glanced at the door, disappointed to not see the one face he was looking for. Important officials and supporters of the gallery had been granted early admission, but it was still too soon for the general public to attend. Quinn and Anna stood in a corner with his mother and grandmother, looking at a rendition he'd done of his siblings sitting on top of the corral fence. Both Quinn and Anna had been excited and supportive when they learned he had started drawing again. His mother had been ecstatic.

The group of four turned and walked toward him. The women were all smiles, but Quinn looked as uncomfortable as he felt.

"I'm seriously thinking about buying that drawing of Quinn and Anna." His grandma looped her arm through his. "My only wish is that you were in the picture, too."

"You don't have to buy that. I'll give it to you."

"Pish posh." She smacked him on the arm with her wrinkled hand. "I can afford it. Besides, what would Mr. Howard think if you gave away all the drawings he commissioned?"

"He'd probably sue Adam, and then he'd be too poor to leave the ranch." Quinn grinned.

"You only want me there so you don't have to work so much," Adam shot back. He enjoyed his brother's good-natured teasing. Ever since he'd confessed to Quinn and Anna that he felt responsible for their father's death, things had been different between his brother and him.

"I want that picture of your father, too." Adam's grandma tugged him toward the drawing of his pa on his horse, Carlos. "I'm amazed how you captured his likeness so well. You were only fourteen when he died."

"We may get into a bidding war for that drawing. I rather like it myself." Adam's mother smiled and wiggled her brows.

Adam flinched at the mention of his father's death, but Quinn lifted a brow. His brother had assured him that he wasn't at fault in their pa's accident. The ice storm that moved in while their father was returning to the ranch had been to blame. Quinn even told Adam that the bad wheel had mostly likely broken as a result of the fall. Nobody blamed him, except himself. All these years he'd suffered needlessly. He shook his head, wishing he had turned his problems over to God years earlier, instead of mere months ago.

He glanced at the door again. There was still one big unsettled issue in his life. He walked over to the framed sketch that hung on the wall near the refreshment table. Mariah sat on Sugar, her long hair flowing in the breeze. Her head was lifted up as she watched a red-winged blackbird in the sky. Adam had struggled whether or not to include that particular picture in the showing but needed it to complete the quota he'd promised Mr. Howard. Maybe he'd get lucky and it wouldn't sell.

Pursing his lips, he remembered how Anna had told him she'd encouraged Mariah to not tell him who she was. Anna had wanted him to heal first, and then one thing after another had happened, and Mariah had never gotten a chance to tell him that she was Drew Dixon. He was certain now that was what she'd been trying to get off her chest.

He sighed and poured a cup of punch to quench his dry throat. He'd been such a fool—wallowing in his pain instead of riding after the woman he loved.

Mr. Howard approached with a couple of his supporters. Adam knew he needed to make himself available to talk with them, but it wasn't something that came natural to him. He cast a final longing glance at the door, hoping and praying Mariah received her invitation.

Mariah lifted up the skirt of her lavender party dress as she climbed the steps leading into the Trent Howard Gallery of Art. Waiting to get inside, she wrapped her cloak firmly around her to keep out the blustery chill. Since returning home, she'd shunned anything that had the sound or smell of artistry, but when she received the invitation to attend a showing of Western art, her curiosity had gotten the better of her.

Sarah Beth stepped up the final stair, stopping beside Mariah as they waited for the people in front of them to enter the crowded lobby. "I'm so glad you agreed to come tonight, even though it's colder than a polar bear's nose. It's been over a month since your grandmother passed. I was afraid you were going to become an old maid, lingering away in your big, old house."

Mariah shook off her friend's comment, eager to see if the artist's drawings resembled Adam's. His were certainly good enough to be in a gallery, and she wondered if he was still drawing. The crowd shifted, and she hurried inside, rubbing her palms together. They quickly passed their cloaks to the cloakroom attendant and allowed themselves to be pulled along by the crowd.

"Oh, these are good." Sarah Beth stood on her tiptoes, looking over a short man's shoulders.

Mariah struggled to see around her friend's taller form. The people in front of them moved on, allowing her to step up beside her friend. Mariah couldn't hold back her gasp.

Sarah Beth sidled an odd look her way. "What's wrong?"

"This is Adam's work."

Sarah Beth's eyes widened. "Your Adam?"

Mariah nodded then shook her head. He'd been hers for a short, sweet time. But no more. She moved to the next picture, holding her breath. Sarah Beth stood beside her and leaned forward. She looked at Mariah and then back to the drawing and back to Mariah. Her mouth gaped open. "Why. . .that's you—riding a–astride on a horse. You didn't—" Waving her fingers, she shushed her friend. "Not so loud. Please."

The couple beside them cast curious glances their way then moved on to the refreshment table. They looked at a picture there, whispered some words to each other, then stared back at Mariah. The woman nodded excitedly to her husband.

Mariah was curious what picture they'd seen but didn't want to be too obvious.

"You never told me how good Adam is. Why, he has his own show. How exciting." Sarah Beth scampered over to the next exhibit.

Mariah took the moment alone to study the picture of herself. It was a good likeness. Peeking over her shoulder, she scanned the crowded room, hoping to see Adam. Her heart skipped a beat when she saw Quinn and Anna laughing with two older women. Mariah turned to her left, and there stood Adam, gazing at her with those sapphire eyes she loved so much.

Her heart all but stopped. She held her breath, afraid she was dreaming. He looked so handsome in his fancy black suit that matched his hair. His gaze held uncertainty. A shy smile tugged at his lips.

"I was hoping you'd come tonight."

"Adam." She reached out, needing to touch him, but pulled her quivering hand back, unsure if he'd welcome the contact. Tears stung her eyes, and she struggled to blink them back. As hard as she'd tried to forget him, her loved for him burned even stronger today. "I—I missed you."

"Could I talk to you? Privately?"

Holding a hand to her chest, she glanced around for Sarah Beth. She found her friend drinking punch and talking to a nice-looking gentleman.

"Are you with someone?" Adam's lips pursed.

"Yes, well. . .I mean a friend—a lady friend."

Adam's tense expression immediately relaxed. Had he thought she was there with Silas?

He held out his arm, and she looped hers through his. As he stepped forward, the crowd parted with many curious glances sent her way. He led her into an office and shut the door then stood there gazing on her face. Finally, he lifted his finger and brushed it along her cheek.

"I'm sorry, Mariah."

She crinkled her forehead. "What do you have to be sorry for? I'm the one who needs to apologize."

"No, I should have come after you instead of stewing in my own pot of self-pity and pain for so long."

Tears blurred her vision, but this time she didn't even try to stop them. "I feel horrible for hurting you. I should have told you right from the beginning who I was, but I was afraid."

"Of me?"

"No, not you personally, but I thought you'd send me packing if you knew the author you invited to your ranch was a woman. You made it clear that you were expecting a man."

Adam took her hands and pulled them against his chest. "I'm sorry I was so insensitive. Can you ever forgive me?"

The hum of voices and music from a stringed quartet and harp player could be heard through the wall. Mariah smiled. "Of course, I forgive you."

His gaze turned hopeful. "Do you think we could pick up where we were when that Silas guy interrupted?"

Mariah nodded, her mouth suddenly gone dry. "Silas is no longer an issue. I told him shortly after Grandmother's funeral that I wouldn't be seeing him again."

Adam smiled. "I can't tell you how happy that makes me." He pulled her into his arms, hugging her tight. "I missed you, Fancy Feathers."

She pushed away. "Fancy Feathers?"

He grinned. "That's the name I gave you on the train when the feather from your hat kept poking me in the back of the head."

"I never knew. I'm sorry for that."

"Don't be. I think that crazy feather was just trying to get me to notice you. It worked." He wiggled his brows, sending delightful shivers through her body.

"I have something I want to give you." He took her hand and led her to a chair. Suddenly he looked shy and unsure.

From inside his jacket, he pulled a folded piece of paper that looked very similar to the note she'd left him. Her breath quickened as she reached for it.

She opened the paper and stared at another sketch of herself dressed in a white blouse and a split riding skirt. Western boots covered her feet, and a cowboy hat hung down her back, held by a cord against her throat.

The picture spoke attitude. Gone was the unsure city girl, replaced by a woman who knew where she belonged—in the arms of the man she loved.

The letter *M* peeked out from the edge of her thumb, and she slid her hand down, revealing a message.

Mariah,

Marry me and love me forever.

All my love,

Adam

Tears blurred the writing, but the words had found root in her heart. She let out a sob. This is what she'd prayed for—dreamed for.

Adam knelt in front of her. "Are you all right?"

She smiled at him. "Oh yes. I'm wonderful. And I can't wait to marry you, Adam McFarland."

His grin rivaled that of the noonday sun, and she threw her arms around his neck. He lifted her to her feet. His mouth found hers. His kiss held a promise of sweet things to come, but he pulled away much too soon for her.

A charming smile tilted his lips as he brushed his forefinger across her face. "I love you, Mariah. You know that, but there's one condition to marrying me."

Mariah blinked. Condition? She felt herself pulling back away from Adam as she found her voice. "What condition?" she said with no inflection.

Adam's grin tripped her heart. "That you never use those hatpins on me."

Her apprehension instantly dissolved, and she tugged him closer. "You've got a deal, cowboy."

With a chuckle, she went back for seconds, kissing the man she dearly loved.

Epilogue

Three weeks later

Mariah glanced up at her groom. She and Anna had managed to alter her mother's wedding dress with a few minor adjustments. She wished her parents and grandmother could be there to share this most wonderful of days with her, but at least she had Adam's family. She listened to the reverend's words in the small Medora church and then shared her vows with Adam, pledging to love, honor, and cherish him all of her days. Just one more thing. Well. . .two.

"Adam, you may kiss your bride." The pastor's pale blue eyes gleamed, as if he rather enjoyed this part.

Adam leaned down, a gentle smile on his handsome face. "I love you, Fancy Feathers." And he kissed her.

"Yee-haw!" Behind them cowboys cheered.

"Kiss her again, Adam." Claude waved at her, his face glowing.

Adam chuckled and straightened. "I will, Claude, but not when there's a crowd watching."

Everyone laughed, and Adam turned her to face the minister again. He looked past them to the crowd. "It gives me great pleasure to present to you Mr. and Mrs. Adam McFarland."

Whoops and hollers resounded as they made their way down the short aisle of the small church. Adam had promised her a church wedding, and he'd kept that promise.

He lifted her into a decorated buggy for a short ride to the Metropolitan Hotel, where dinner would be served to those who attended the wedding.

"I can't believe we're finally married," he said as he climbed into the buggy.

He stole a kiss and gave her an ornery smile. She looked forward to seeing that expression often in the future.

"Don't forget, I need to mail in my latest manuscript so it will be there before the deadline."

"Already done. Quinn did it before the wedding."

She leaned against his arm—the same one the train robber had shot. "Ever the thoughtful husband."

"I aim to please, ma'am." He stole another kiss. "So, what's the name of this book?"

Mariah smiled. "*The Greenhorn Gal of the Dakota Badlands.*"

OUTLAW HEART

Chapter One

Rocking M Ranch, Southwestern North Dakota, 1894

"You want to do what?" Quinn McFarland shoved his hands on his hips. Anna resisted the urge to squirm under her brother's stern glare. "I want to find some type of employment."

Shaking his head, Quinn spun around and looked out the parlor window with his arms crossed over his broad chest. No doubt he was thinking of all the work he had to do and that he didn't have time to humor his little sister. He turned, slow, like a cougar about to pounce on its prey. "That's utter nonsense. We have more than enough money and plenty of work around here. Women are supposed to work at home, not some place else."

She knew he wouldn't understand. Anna plopped onto the parlor's settee, thinking that was the longest string of words her somber brother had said in a week.

She loved their large log cabin and helping Quinn around the ranch, but something was missing in her life. How could she make her work-all-the-time-never-have-fun brother understand how she felt? Why, Quinn woke up before the roosters each morning.

He rubbed the back of his neck and sighed. His dark brown eyes, so much like hers, softened. "Look, I realize you feel a bit lost since Ma's been staying at Grandma's for so long. And now Adam is gone too. I can't pretend to understand the connection you two have, being twins and all, but finding employment isn't the answer."

Anna stared at her hands. What he said was true. While she loved Adam's new bride, Mariah, she missed her twin terribly. He talked with her and joked. He knew when she felt sad, and if she was bored, he'd find something to challenge her mind or body. All Quinn did was work.

Twisting her hands in her lap, she glanced up at him. "It's been hard to lose Adam—"

"We haven't lost him. He'll be back."

"It's not the same. He has a wife now. He doesn't need me." Thick with emotion, her throat tightened. She poured herself a cup of tea from the pot that sat on the low table in front of the settee. The cup clattered on the saucer as she lifted it.

Adam had found the love of his life and was finally realizing his dream of drawing sketches of the west. His wife, Mariah, wrote dime novels for a Chicago publishing company, so traveling with Adam gave her the opportunity to get fodder for her stories. Anna was truly happy for Adam, but his leaving had left a hole inside her that nothing else could fill. Even praying hadn't helped.

"Have you written Ma about this crazy idea of yours?"

Anna couldn't look him in the eye, knowing she hadn't mentioned her desire for a job to her mother. Mama would have had the same reaction as Quinn. Hadn't she left her own children—albeit grown ones—to care for her ailing mother? She'd never understand Anna's longing for something different to do.

"I can tell by your lack of response that you haven't." He paced to the dining table and back into the parlor, his long legs making quick work of the short distance.

"I have an idea." Quinn snapped his fingers, crossed the room, and stood before her. Dressed in denim pants, a blue chambray shirt, leather vest, and boots covered in a layer of dust, he looked every bit the rancher that he was. His dark blond hair even had a perpetual ring from where his hat had pressed it down.

"I hadn't mentioned this to you yet, but I'd planned to take our annual trip to Bismarck next month to stock up on supplies before winter comes. What if we go earlier? Maybe this coming Monday? We can visit Ma and Grandmother for a week or so."

Anna set her teacup on the table and jumped up, clapping her palms together. "Truly? Oh, that would be wonderful! They'll be so surprised to see us this early."

She dashed around the table and embraced her older brother. He was solid, hard muscled, and a good three inches taller than Adam, who neared six-foot-tall. Not one to overly show emotion, he lightly embraced her and patted her back. She looked up at him and smiled. "Thank you, Quinn."

He cleared his throat and stepped back. "I've got work to do."

"Me too. I've got to get busy so I'll be ready. Three days is hardly enough time to prepare." All the things she needed to do before leaving raced through Anna's mind. Pack. Make a list of food supplies. Search the catalogs for anything else they would need over the long, cold North Dakota winter.

"We can wait and go in a few weeks, like I'd planned if it's too much of a rush."

"No! I'll be ready."

Quinn chuckled and shook his head. "Make your lists. Don't forget ammunition and restocking the medicines for the animals. I'll have Claude write down what we need." He grabbed his hat from the peg near the front door and left.

Anna hurried to her room and threw open the wardrobe door. Fluffing the skirt of one of her wool dresses, she noted of its thinness. She'd need to buy a new winter dress or two and another split riding skirt, and she and Leyna, their cook, needed to make a long list of food supplies.

Excitement surging through her, she grabbed the stack of catalogs from the floor of the wardrobe and hurried to the dining room table. She loved going to Bismarck to visit her grandmother and to shop, and she couldn't wait to hug her mother again. Oh, how she'd missed her. A smile tugged at Anna's lips. And just maybe, if she worked things right, she could find employment there and not have to come back to the boring Rocking M Ranch.

Standing outside of the U.S. Marshal's office in Bismarck, Brett Wickham rubbed his thumb over his deputy marshal's badge. Was he really ready to resign? To call it quits and go back to ranching with his younger brother?

"You sure about this?" Taylor watched him. "I'd love to have you back at the Bar W, but if you're not ready to quit, we can get along without you for a while longer."

It was time. Brett had put months of thought and prayer into his decision. He was ready to live a slower life. After five years of chasing outlaws, his ache for adventure had been satisfied. Two dollars per captured outlaw would never make a man rich, but then he hadn't done the job for the money. He'd served the new state of North Dakota by capturing numerous thieves and murderers and seeing them convicted for their crimes and making life safer for the decent folk.

"I'm sure. It's time I went home. You still got the draft from the cattle sale?"

Taylor patted his shirt pocket. "Right here."

Brett nodded. "You did a good job getting that herd here. Why don't you go to the bank and get the cash for the draft while I tender my resignation, then we can celebrate with a steak dinner."

Taylor smiled and rubbed his belly. "That's my kind of celebration. After I go to the bank, I'll find my wranglers and pay them their wages, and then I'll meet you at that little café across from the hotel, all right?"

Brett nodded and watched Taylor amble away until a wagon loaded with supplies blocked his view. His younger brother had been a skinny, pimple-faced kid when Brett left their Bar W ranch to realize his dream of becoming a lawman, but now Taylor was a man. His brother had stepped up when their father died and kept the ranch going, but now it was time for Brett to go home.

Maybe if he was lucky, some pretty gals had moved into the area or one of those giggly schoolgirls he used to tease had grown up and was still unmarried. He smiled, remembering how he'd tied a frog to one of Sally Novak's braids. The girl had squawked and thrashed like a chicken chased by a fox. Yep, he was ready to settle down and have a few ornery boys of his own, but a man needed the right woman to do that.

The window on the door rattled as he stepped inside the marshal's office. The scent of leather and gun oil mixed with cigar smoke. Brett nodded at the young deputy seated at the desk. "Marshal Cronan in?"

"Back there." The man jerked his head toward the rear office.

Brett saw his boss, Marshal Joseph Cronan, seated at the desk, his head down, as he studied a wanted poster. Brett knocked on the doorjamb, and the man looked up. His mustache twitched right before he smiled. He stood, offering Brett his hand. "Caught any more criminals, Wickham?"

They shook hands. Brett sat after the marshal did and hung his hat on his knee. "Not since yesterday."

Marshal Cronan chuckled. "Well…I don't reckon we can catch one every day, though I'd sure like to."

Brett let his gaze rove over the various posters mounted on the wall to his right. The office was rustic, messy, and reeked of cigar smoke, but that didn't keep the marshal from doing his job.

"So, ya ready for a new assignment?"

Brett resisted the urge to fidget like a schoolboy in trouble. He hated disappointing the man who'd been his mentor. He pulled off his badge, rubbed his finger over it again, and laid it on the marshal's desk. "No, actually I've uh...decided to...uh...resign."

Whew. That was harder to get out than he'd thought.

Marshal Cronan pursed his lips and studied him. He narrowed his eyes for a moment, then resignation dulled his gaze, and he sighed. "Real sorry to hear that. I sure hate to lose a good man like you."

"I've got a younger brother who's been running the Bar W since our pa died. It's time I go back and do my fair share."

He nodded. "A man's gotta do what he feels is best. I wish I could offer you a fair wage to stay, but..." He shrugged one shoulder.

Brett knew the deal. A marshal risked his life for his job. He didn't make a wage and only got paid if he captured and turned in an outlaw. If he and the outlaw were killed together, the marshal's family was expected to pay the burial expenses of both men. It wasn't right, but that was the way of things.

Brett laid his badge on the marshal's desk. "Thank you for taking in a rebellious youth and making a man of him."

The marshal nodded. His chair squeaked as he stood and shook Brett's hand again. "I've got train robbers, cattle rustlers, and the Sallinger gang acting up again. I'm hoping you'll change your mind."

Brett flashed him a wish-I-could-help-you smile, slapped his hat on his head, and walked outside, feeling freer than he had in a long while. Yes sir-ee, time for a new beginning.

Anna walked down a street that angled down a hill, taking in all the sights and sounds of Bismarck. The town seemed to sprout buildings as fast as her garden did weeds. Every time she came to visit there were new houses and stores going up.

Anna enjoyed having her mother walk beside her, after being separated from her for over a year. Ellen McFarland still turned heads at forty-seven. They greatly resembled one another with their blond hair and brown eyes. Anna hoped she looked as youthful when she was her mother's age.

"It's too bad Quinn had to return to the ranch so soon. I'd hoped he could rest and visit more than a few days." She looped her arm through Anna's. "I missed you so much."

Anna smiled. "I missed you too. Are you staying here much longer? Grandmother seems to be doing better."

Her mother's cheeks turned red, and she looked away. "Actually, I've met someone. You children are grown now. Adam's married." She stopped and faced Anna. "I'm not sure that I will be returning to the Rocking M."

Anna's heart fluttered. Her mother had met a man? She wasn't coming home?

"I can see this comes as quite a shock to you, darling. I'd love for you to stay here with Mother and me for the winter."

Anna started walking again. Was this the answer to her prayers? Her loneliness? Could she leave Quinn alone to run the ranch, not that she did much other than bookwork and helping herd cattle when needed?"

Her mother took her arm again. "It's a lot to think about. You don't have to decide right now. Let's just enjoy our time together. There's a wonderful little shop a few blocks over that has all manner of feminine accessories. They have the prettiest hair combs."

Anna thought of the long list of supplies she would have to purchase now that Quinn had returned home and found it difficult to get excited over a hair comb. People dressed in fancy clothing passed them by on both sides of the street. The large buildings blocked the view of the hills unless she looked up the street. She missed the wide-open spaces and quiet of the country.

"I do hope Quinn will be all right. I pray for you children every night."

"It's been a long while since we've had rustlers. I hope we didn't lose too many head of cattle. At least they didn't get any of the Percherons." Anna swatted at a fly buzzing her face.

"I worry about Quinn out chasing rustlers."

"He'll be careful." Anna flashed her mother an ornery look. "What he needs is a wife to settle him down."

Her mother smiled, brown eyes twinkling. "It will take a very special woman to do that."

"And a mighty patient one, too." They shared a laugh.

"If we don't find a dress you like in one of the stores here in Bismarck, we can try looking in Mandan."

"I'm not that picky. I'm sure I can find something here." Anna jerked to a halt as a man rushed out the doors of the Bedford Hotel and nearly plowed into them. He scowled and marched down the steps into the street.

Her mother shook her head. "Whatever happened to manners? I declare, folks these days don't know how to show even the simplest courtesy."

Anna scowled at the rude man and pulled her beaded reticule, the small handbag she saved for trips to Bismarck, further up her arm. "Most of the cowboys on the ranch are quite polite, but we do occasionally get one who isn't. Quinn soon puts them in their place if they act improper around me."

"He's a good brother. He did a wonderful job of keeping that ranch going after your father died. I still regret not helping him more, but I was suffering my own grief at the time. Besides, Quinn was always determined to do things himself."

They ducked into Harper's Mercantile. Anna's eyes took a moment to adjust after being in the bright sunlight. The scents of leather, coffee, and spices filled the air, exciting her. She loved purchasing supplies and seeing the new items that the stores in Bismarck carried.

Her mother had offered to make her a skirt, and Ellen fingered a charcoal gray wool, but Anna's eyes drifted to a dark green.

"Has it been hard for you since Adam and Mariah left?"

Anna shrugged, not wanting to burden her mother with her worries. "I do miss him—both of them, if you want the truth. Mariah quickly became the best friend I'd never had."

"She's a lovely woman and seems to be the inspiration that Adam needs. I'm glad I was able to go to their wedding." Ellen smiled as if remembering the small ceremony held on the Rocking M last summer. "At least you know they'll be back for part of the year. That should be a comfort."

"Yes, it is." But it would be a long time before they returned from their travels. Too long. Perhaps she'd be gone by then also. "I've been thinking of trying to find employment."

Her mother swiveled around, staring with her mouth gaping open like a wide-mouth bass. "Don't you have enough to do at the ranch? It's most unusual for a woman to work unless she's a widow with children to support or a schoolteacher. Really, Anna, that seems an absurd idea."

Anna sighed. Her mother's response was the same as Quinn's. Why did it matter if a woman worked outside the home? Surely there were jobs a woman could do better than a man.

"Would you live in Medora? I can't imagine there are many jobs available for a decent woman in that small town. " Ellen shook her head. "Besides, you wouldn't want to leave Quinn all alone, would you?"

How could she explain that Quinn was the one who deserted her? He worked all day away from the house, and in the evenings after dinner, his head was in a book on cattle breeding or ranching techniques or he was checking her bookkeeping. He simply didn't know how to relax.

"Why don't you stay a few months here with your grandmother and me? We could have such fun. There are so many more things to do here than on the ranch."

Maybe an extended change of scenery would do her good. But did she really want to be in a crowded town for so long? "I'll think about that."

"Do you see anything you like here?"

"What about the emerald?" Anna was glad to be on a different topic.

Her mother unrolled the bolt of green wool and held it up in front of Anna. "It looks good with your coloring, although a brown or gray would go better with your eyes."

"I think I will get this. I love the color."

They purchased six yards of the wool cloth and several other items then meandered out of the store. The streets of Bismarck were crowded with people. The one thing Anna disliked about the city was all the noise. People chattered everywhere, harnesses jingled as wagons passed on the streets, and the smells were so different than those of the ranch.

"I need to stop at the bank and make a withdrawal, then what do you say to eating lunch at a café?" Her mother tugged her across the street toward the Bismarck Federal Bank.

"Oh, I'd love to." Anna nearly bounced. The only time she ate out of the house was at a church social or when she came to town. It was a treat that she eagerly looked forward to.

They crossed the street and headed for the bank. Anna helped her mother up the steps and reached for the bank's door handle. Suddenly, the doors burst open. Someone rushed out and plowed smack into Anna. She gasped and spun around, snagging her heel on her skirt, and she fell down. The other person tripped and landed beside her. Gold coins exploded from a bag and plunged to the ground like shiny raindrops, clinking onto the boardwalk all around her.

Heart pounding, Anna looked up and caught the angered glare of the other person who'd fallen—a woman's glare. The woman jumped up and grabbed the bank bag, which looked to be only half full now and raced toward a nearby horse.

The door flew open again and clanked against the wall. A poorly dressed man with a full beard charged outside, lugging two more bank bags and waving a gun. He glanced down at Anna and the coins lying all around. The gun turned her way, and her heart dropped. Her mouth went dry. *Lord, help me.*

Chapter Two

The outlaw's gun hovered in Anna's face for only seconds, but it seemed a lifetime. Her breath caught in her throat as her heart stampeded. The man muttered a curse and ran to his horse, pocketing his weapon. Anna's whole body trembled, but she heaved a sigh of relief as the two galloped down the hill.

A skinny man with round spectacles ran out the open door. "Bank robbery. Stop them!" He shoved his hands to his waist as he watched the two riders disappear around the corner at the end of the street.

People from all around hurried toward the bank. The clerk looked down at Anna and scowled. His eyes widened when he saw the coins on the ground. "That money belongs to the bank."

He grabbed her arm and attempted to pull her up. "Someone hold her until the marshal comes."

Anna jerked her arm away. "No, wait. I didn't have anything to do with the robbery." As if she were telling a falsehood, a coin rolled from off her lap and clinked against one already on the boardwalk.

When no one moved to hold her, the clerk pursed his lips and dropped to his knees, frantically gathering up the coins.

Anna rubbed her aching wrist and remembered her mother. She twisted around, relieved to see her standing by the bank window, holding her handbag to her chest, shocked but safe.

"May I assist you, ma'am?" An older gentleman offered Anna his hand.

"Yes, thank you." She reached out to him, and as she stood on trembling legs, gold coins dropped from the folds of her skirt, plunking onto the boardwalk. "Oh, dear."

The clerk scowled at her again. "That's the bank's money."

"I—" Anna started.

"Listen here, Floyd," the man beside her said. "This woman is an innocent bystander. I saw it all. That first robber plowed out the doors and knocked this woman in a tizzy. The bank bag fell open, spilling coins everywhere. You should thank her. In a way, she actually saved some of the money by causing that first thief to drop the bag."

The flustered clerk's cheeks reddened. He picked up the last two coins and cradled them all in his untucked shirt. "Sorry, ma'am."

A heavyset man shoved his way out of the bank and looked from side to side. "A man's been shot in here. Somebody get a doctor."

Brett glanced at his pocket watch and resumed staring out the window. He'd been waiting nearly a half hour for Taylor to arrive for lunch. He must have had trouble finding his crew.

Brett sipped his coffee, marveling that he could be so relaxed after quitting law enforcement. Out of habit, he glanced at the others in the room, studying their faces, still remembering all the wanted posters he'd viewed on nearly a weekly basis.

"Can I warm your coffee?" A young woman offered him a coy smile.

He held up his cup, enjoying her pretty features and fresh look. "Thanks."

"Do you want to go ahead and order or keep waiting for the rest of your party?"

Brett shook his head. "I'll wait. He should be here anytime."

The café door rattled as a big man fumbled with the knob. Finally, he shoved the door open and searched the room. His gaze landed on the wiry man at the table next to Brett's.

"Doc! You're needed at the bank. A customer was shot during a robbery," the burly man shouted, not even taking the time to cross the room.

The man at the table beside Brett's jumped to his feet, tossed several coins down, and left his half-eaten meal. He hurried from the café, his napkin still tucked in his waistband.

Brett went rigid. The bank. A customer was shot in the bank?

He leapt up, dropping a handful of coins on the table and raced for the door. His mind pounded out a cadence with his fast-moving feet. *Not Taylor. Please, God, not my brother.*

A group of people crowded the bank entrance. "U.S. Marshal. Clear the way."

The crowd parted like the Red Sea had for Moses, and Brett followed the doctor inside. He blinked his eyes as he searched the room. Near the counter, a man lay on the floor. Brett's chest tightened as he stepped forward.

The doctor knelt beside the man and checked his pulse. He shook his head and stood. "There's nothing I can do. He's already gone."

As the doc stepped to the side, a force equal to a cannon ball hit Brett in the gut.

Taylor.

His brother lay dead on the floor. The bank draft for their cattle was still clenched in one fist and his gun lay on the floor a few inches from his other hand. Brett dropped to his knees.

No.

Not now.

Oh, God, why? He fought back tears. A marshal never cried.

He scooped up Taylor's still warm form and hugged it to his chest, fighting back a moan. As he held his brother's body in his arms, he listened to an accounting of what had happened. Taylor had simply been in the wrong place at the wrong time.

"If'n that young cock hadn't gone for his gun, he'd most likely be alive right now," a skinny clerk with round glasses stated.

Brett clenched his fist. He wanted to clobber the man for referring to his brother in such a manner. Taylor was as honorable as the day was long and mature for his twenty-one years. If he'd gone for his gun, it was to protect the others in the bank.

Brett pulled the draft from Taylor's fingers and pocketed it, berating himself for not cashing it himself. But Taylor had been the one who had raised the herd and driven it all the way to Bismarck. It was his place to reap the benefit.

Some benefit.

He lifted his brother and stood, Taylor's limp, muscled body weighing heavy in his arms. Brett clenched his jaw so tight it ached. Numbness blurred his vision as Taylor's blood soaked Brett's shirt.

Marshal Cronan left a group he was questioning and strode toward Brett. "You know him?"

Brett blinked, struggling to make his clogged throat respond. "He's my brother."

The marshal's eyes widened. "I'm sorry, Brett. Can I do anything for you?"

"You can give my badge back."

"You sure?" The marshal pursed his lips, his mustache twitching.

Brett nodded. "Just let me get Taylor to the m—mortuary." He nearly choked on that last word.

"You need help?"

Brett shook his head.

The marshal nodded, understanding that this was a job Brett needed to do alone. "I've gotta find Charley Addams. He draws sketches for me. From the descriptions, it sounds like Jack and Lottie Sallinger robbed the bank. I want to get clean drawings of them before the witnesses forget what they look like. I got a poster on Jack but nobody's ever gotten a good look at Lottie, until today."

The crowd of murmuring spectators stepped back as they walked outside. Brett hated their sympathetic stares and curious glances. How could things change so fast? Could he ever go back to the ranch knowing his brother wouldn't be there?

The first thing he had to do was bury Taylor. He nearly stumbled at that thought. His younger brother had always followed him around, wanting to be like Brett. And yet, Taylor had stayed home while Brett ran away from their overly strict pa and put his life on the line as a lawman. With all the risks he'd taken, he should be dead, not Taylor.

Brett bit the inside of his cheek until he tasted blood. If it took the rest of his life, he'd hunt down the Sallingers and vindicate his brother.

The next day, Anna pored over the ads in the newspaper, finally settling back in her chair, discouraged. She had hoped that if she stayed in Bismarck for an extended time as her mother had requested, she might find some kind of employment here, but it was no use. She heaved a heavy sigh. Nearly all the advertisements were jobs for men, and the ones that weren't sounded boring or involved too much work for the puny wages offered. Though Anna loved children, she had no desire to be stuck in a building teaching them all day. So what was a woman to do? She could be a cook, seamstress—if she learned to sew—or clean houses, pretty much the same thing she had done back home.

Flipping the paper closed, her gaze landed on an article about the bank robbery. She scanned it and gasped. The description of the female thief sounded exactly like her. Had that buffoon of a clerk given the law officials a description of her instead of the outlaw? She'd seen the woman up close, and she looked nothing like Anna except for their hair coloring. She'd never forget those cold hazel eyes glaring at her.

Anna shivered. She'd acted brave yesterday in front of her mother, but the truth was, that robbery had frightened her more than she could ever remember being frightened—and she wasn't one to scare easily. She'd read in the paper that a man had been killed, a rancher from southwestern North Dakota. A man not even as old as her twenty-two years. How sad to die so young. So needlessly.

She felt the city closing in on her, strangling her. Anna longed for the open fields and high buttes of her Badlands. A place where you could ride for days and never encounter another person. Where the only sounds you heard were those of nature. And yet, she didn't want to leave her mother. Who knew when she'd see her again?

"Are you sure you want to go home already? You've barely arrived." Her grandmother lifted Anna's beaded handbag off the coffee table. "What do you have in here? Stones? It feels like you brought half the Badlands with you."

Anna giggled. "A gal needs her stuff, doesn't she?"

"That she does." A smile tugged at her grandmother's wrinkled cheeks, then faded. "I do wish you'd reconsider staying longer. I so enjoy your visits."

Anna patted her hand. "Why don't you and Mama come to the ranch and stay a while? It would do you good to get out of town for a bit."

She shook her head. "No, these bones are far too old to withstand the shaking and rattling of a train all the way to Medora and then taking a long wagon ride to the Rocking M. I'll just have to be content and wait until you visit again in the spring. I do thank you for sharing your mother with me. I don't know how I would have gotten along when I broke my leg last year if she hadn't come to help me. I like to pretend, but in truth, I know I'm not as strong as I was before that happened."

Half an hour later, after hugging her grandma goodbye, Anna left with her mother for the mercantile. She still had numerous items to purchase and arrange to ship back to Medora. Once she was done, she would high-tail it home, away from the hustle and bustle and accusations of this town. Maybe by next spring, things would have quieted down, and she could plan a long stay in Bismarck.

Brett stacked his small pile of supplies on the mercantile counter and looked around the store. He still needed to fill his tin of matches, pick out a new shirt to replace the one that got ruined when he carried Taylor's body to the undertaker, and get more cartridges for his shotgun.

Along the wall, he grabbed an extra-large, blue chambray shirt and headed back to the counter, his boots echoing on the wooden floor. Two young women batted their lashes at him, and he tipped his hat to them.

"I need two boxes of those cartridges," he told the clerk as he pointed to the brand he wanted.

The bell over the entrance tinkled and a shadow darkened the doorway as two women entered, side by side. Brett nodded to the older woman and turned his gaze on the younger female. His heart nearly jolted out of his chest. Lottie Sallinger?

He ducked his head and turned. Surely, she wouldn't be so brazen as to march into a store the day after robbing the Bismarck Federal Bank. Out of the corner of his eye, he watched her examine a shelf of spices. The older woman stayed by her side like a shadow, chatting merrily. Were they related? Or merely friends?

He ambled to the window, feigning interest in a fancy tooled saddle on display. From his shirt pocket, he pulled out the sketch of Lottie Sallinger. The woman in the store looked exactly like the drawing. His heart pounded, but his thoughts warred with each other. Hadn't Marshal Cronan said this morning that the Sallingers had been spotted south of Bismarck?

And Lottie Sallinger wasn't a lady, from all reports. So could she be playing the part of one as a daring, elaborate disguise?

He studied the woman then looked at the picture. The same oval face with a small straight nose and pleasant lips stared back. Of course, he couldn't see the color of the woman's eyes, but he wondered if they weren't the same brown as Lottie's were reported to be.

The two women took their armloads of purchases to the counter. The clerk scooted Brett's measly pile over, and his eyes gleamed as the women deposited theirs.

"I have a list of supplies that I need filled and delivered to the train depot by ten tomorrow morning. Will you be able to fill such a large order?"

The woman's voice was soft, delicate. Not at all what he would expect in an outlaw. That Lottie Sallinger was quite the actress.

Imagine the guts it took to order a wagonload of supplies in the same town you'd just robbed. Would she pay in double eagle coins, like those missing from the bank?

"I can easily handle this size order. What name do you want on the crates, ma'am?" The clerk held his pencil poised for her response.

"Rocking M Ranch. Medora."

Medora? Was that where the gang hid out when not on a robbery streak?

He'd been through the sleepy little town in the heart of the Badlands. Wasn't much there. A big, old factory that a French nobleman had abandoned after his business failed and a handful of smaller buildings east of the Little Missouri River.

Now that he thought about it, the Badlands was the perfect place for a hideout, except maybe during the frigid winters.

Should he arrest her now or follow her, hoping she might lead him to her brother—and the stolen money? And who was the older woman?

He couldn't even collect the money owed him for the cattle sale since the bank had no funds at the moment. But that was the least of his worries right now.

Brett rubbed his thumb and forefinger down a fancy leather belt. His last arrest had gone bad when he'd gotten in a hurry and hadn't taken enough care to gather the proper evidence. The outlaw had been set free, and he quickly kidnapped the thirteen-year-old daughter of the man who'd testified against him. Brett clenched his jaw, remembering the day he'd found her battered body. He released the crimped belt.

Lottie was at the counter, counting out a stack of dollar bills.

Brett didn't want to make the same mistake again. He'd never forget having to tell that girl's parents that she was dead. The mother's cries still haunted his dreams. This time he'd use caution and patience and make sure he had the evidence needed to convict the Sallingers—and see them imprisoned for killing his brother.

Chapter Three

With an ear-shattering squeal and hiss, the train shuddered to a stop. From his inconspicuous seat at the back of the train, Brett watched Lottie collect her few belongings and stand, as did the other half dozen passengers who were getting off at this stop. Clothed in a dark blue travel dress with her golden hair caught up in one of those net things, Lottie looked more like a woman going to church than an outlaw. But looks could be deceiving. Brett stood and stretched, gathered his saddle bags and rifle, and plodded down the aisle after the last passenger had debarked.

He spotted Lottie a few cars down, talking to the baggage clerk. She waved her hand at the boxcar in front of her, then turned and marched down the street.

Brett watched her then glanced back at the cattle car. He needed to follow Lottie, but he also had to claim his horse before the train left. It would take the baggage handlers a while to unload all the Rocking M crates he'd seen at the Bismarck depot, but he couldn't take a chance on losing Jasper. Brett jogged toward the baggage handler and gave the man his claim ticket. "I've got a quick errand to run. Just tie that big black gelding up over there"— he motioned toward the hitching rail in front of the depot—"and I'll get him when I return."

The man nodded. Brett handed him a couple of coins and hurried past the depot. He looked both directions and finally saw Lottie at the far end of town, going into a big barn he assumed was the livery. He walked past two buildings and leaned against the side wall of a barbershop. He figured Lottie was fetching a wagon for all those supplies she'd bought in Bismarck, so she'd have to return to the depot, but if not, he wanted to make sure to see in which direction she rode as she left town.

He glanced around as he waited. Medora hadn't changed much since the last time he'd ridden through. The town was tucked in a nice little valley with tall, rocky buttes surrounding it. The Metropolitan Hotel was still the largest building in town, unless you counted the abandoned meat packing plant on the other side of the Little Missouri River. A handful of houses surrounded a pretty white-washed church with a steeple.

After several minutes, Lottie came out of the livery driving a two-horse team hitched to a buckboard. Brett admired the matched pair of stock horses pulling the wagon. Sure enough, Lottie headed straight for the depot. Brett moseyed down the street, keeping his eye on her.

While she parked the buckboard, he headed toward Jasper. The gelding nickered to him and stuck out his big head for a scratch. Brett obliged the animal, slung his saddle bags over Jasper's rump, and shoved his rifle into the scabbard then tightened the cinch.

Lottie climbed down from the wagon, said something to the baggage handler, and then meandered down the street. The man beckoned another worker, and they carried a crate from the baggage car to the buckboard. Brett stopped at the depot's watering trough to allow Jasper a drink and watched Lottie enter a café.

His stomach gurgled, reminding him it had been a long while since breakfast. Next door to the café, he tied Jasper to a hitching post and then entered the small restaurant. Lottie sat at a table along the wall. A heavyset woman dressed in a faded brown calico covered with a stained apron stood beside her, rattling off the food items of the day. Brett ducked his head and sat at a table two away from Lottie's on the rear wall. With her back to him, he hoped she wouldn't notice him.

"Afternoon. Coffee?" A short man held out a coffee pot and pointed at the mug on Brett's table.

Brett nodded and turned over the cup. "What's good here?"

"Stew, chops, beans and cornbread." The man shrugged one shoulder. "Most everything."

"I'll take a bowl of stew, and could you wrap up some extra cornbread so I can take it with me?" Who knew when he'd get another chance to eat?

"I can do that." The man disappeared behind a stained calico curtain, and Brett could hear the clatter of pans and murmur of voices.

A woman dressed in white shirtwaist and brown skirt came through the front door. She glanced around the room and her gaze zeroed in on Lottie. She smiled and walked up to the outlaw's table. Brett couldn't see Lottie's expression, but was sure she stiffened. He leaned forward in his seat, hoping to learn something that would help him locate Jack Sallinger.

She cleared her throat. "Excuse me, Miss McFarland."

Lottie looked up. "Good day, Thelma May."

They exchanged pleasantries for a few moments.

"Care to sit down?" Lottie asked.

Thelma May shook her head. "I don't want to bother you, and I need to get back to the dress shop. I just wanted you to know we're having a sewing bee at Parkers' home on Saturday while the men are raising a new barn. I wanted to invite you and your brother."

The plump woman Lottie had been talking to earlier breezed past Brett, carrying a plate pile high with roast beef, potatoes and cornbread. The fragrant scent wafting in the air nearly did him in. The woman nodded to Thelma Lou and set the plate in front of Lottie.

Brett wished he'd gotten the roast beef now instead of stew. The old man who'd taken his order plunked a bowl in front of him, gaining all of Brett's attention. His mouth watered as he took the first bite.

"Well…I know you're not overly fond of stitching, but I wanted you to know that you're invited." Thelma Lou hoisted her handbag up her arm.

"Thank you. I'll let Quinn know about it if he's back. We've had trouble with rustlers."

Quinn? Was that Jack's alias? Brett mentally filed away that name as he shoved half the square of cornbread into his mouth. His lips quirked up at the ironic idea of outlaws having problems with rustlers. In a matter of minutes, he wolfed down the whole bowl of stew. It wasn't the best he'd had, but it was filling. The plump woman refilled his coffee, and he stared at the black liquid.

He still couldn't grasp in his mind that Taylor was dead. Right when Brett was ready to settle down. He remembered his father's stern discipline and how all he'd wanted when he was in his teens was to get away. After a brief stint as a sheriff's deputy in a small town, he knew he wanted the freedom a marshal had, rather than being tied to one place all the time. It took a long time for him to grow up and face his responsibilities, but after giving his heart to God, he was finally ready.

So why would the Good Lord allow his brother to be gunned down, especially now?

Brett couldn't wrap his mind around the thought. He was a fairly new

Christian, and except for when that freed outlaw had killed that girl, Brett's life had been good. He'd been happy for the first time in a long while. Lonely, but mostly content.

Brett sipped his coffee. He should have seen to Taylor's burying, but he sent his brother's body home with the Bar W hands. They'd make sure he was buried next to their parents. Guilt gnawed at Brett for not taking Taylor home himself, but he couldn't let the Sallingers' trail grow cold.

He glanced at Lottie's table, and his heart skittered. She was gone!

His gaze darted to the window as he lurched to his feet. Relief washed over him when he saw her talking outside to a bent old man.

"That Anna McFarland sure is a looker," the man who'd waited on him said. "Course, that older brother of hers won't let no man near her. It's odd to see her in town without an escort."

So he was right. The Sallingers lived somewhere near Medora. Brett sidled a glance at man. "What can you tell me about the Rocking M Ranch?"

"Depends. Why you want to know?" He narrowed his faded blue eyes and wiped his hands on his dingy apron.

Brett shrugged. "Heard it was a good place to work. I'm wondering if that's true."

The man visually relaxed and nodded. Brett kept his gaze traveling between Lottie and the man.

"The Rocking M is a good-sized spread—around three or four thousand acres, from what I've heard. Them McFarland brothers raise several cattle breeds and Percherons. Got some of the best draft horses in this part of the country. Course, Adam got married last year and ain't at the ranch now."

Adam? There were two Sallinger brothers? He'd never heard that before. "Have they owned the ranch long?"

The old man shook his head, sending the few hairs on his bald head to dancing. "Their pa bought out a bunch of small ranches back in '88, after two of the worst winters we've ever had in these parts. Lots of ranchers lost most of their herds. Plumb closed down that meat packing plant over in Little Misery."

Brett knew the snide nickname referred to the tiny town just across the Little Missouri River, but this was the first he'd heard of the Sallingers' pa being alive. "So I need to talk to the older McFarland about work?"

"That be right hard to do since he's dead. Quinn's the man you want.

He's tough, but fair."

"How did Mr. McFarland have enough money to buy so much land?" The old geezer shrugged. "Scuttlebutt says an Irish uncle left him a fortune."

Brett saw Lottie wave at the man she'd been talking to, and then she headed out of view. He laid several coins on the table. "Thanks for the meal."

"Oh, hey, forgot yer cornbread." The man darted behind the stained curtain.

Brett tapped on the table. Lottie couldn't move fast with a heavy wagon, but he didn't want to lose track of her. The trail from her wagon wheels could get lost among all the wheel marks in the rocky dirt from other wagons driving through the town. The man hurried toward him and handed Brett a package wrapped in waxed brown paper—still warm.

If he had time, he'd picked up a few more supplies at the local mercantile, but trailing Lottie was his priority. Hopefully by tonight, he'd have the Sallingers in custody.

Then maybe that aching hole from his brother's death would begin to heal.

"Whoa!" Anna pulled the wagon to a stop in front of her home. The log structure was big compared to many homes in the North Dakota Badlands, but it was rugged, like the weather here. It may not have the attractiveness that the fancier homes in Bismarck had, but it was far better than a soddy or dugout. And best of all, nobody here would confuse her with a bank robber.

"Afternoon, Miss Anna." Claude scratched his shaggy beard. "Boss man didn't say nothin' about you returning home so soon."

Anna set the brake on the wagon and climbed down. "He thought I was staying longer, but I had an aching to come home."

He grinned, revealing his crooked teeth. Claude wasn't a handsome man, but his heart was full of God's love. He spoke at the Sunday services they had at the ranch sometimes when there wasn't a minister in town. "I'll get Hank and Toby on this wagon. Where you want 'em to put all these crates?"

"The porch off the kitchen is fine for now. Leyna and I can unpack them and put things away. Most are food items. Those three," she waved at the trio of crates on the bottom of the pile, "are for the bunkhouse. Cookie will be happy with all the spices and other things I purchased." Claude rubbed his belly. "I reckon we'll all be happy if'n we get to eat somethin' other than beans and cornbread."

Anna laughed and headed for the house. Inside, she hung her hat on a peg near the door. After being in the bright sunshine, she could barely make out the shapes of the parlor's furniture, but the scent of the house was familiar. The delicious fragrance of baking bread made her stomach grumble, even though she'd eaten a few hours earlier.

"Leyna, I'm home."

The middle-aged German cook hurried through the kitchen door, smiling. An apron covered her dress, and her typical braids were curled up in two big buns, pinned on either side of her head. "*Fraulein* Anna! I not expect you home so soon."

Anna hugged the woman who'd been more like a dear aunt to her than an employee. "I'm glad to be home again." She pushed back, grinning. "And wait until you hear what happened to me."

Leyna looped her arm through Anna's. "Come, eat some honey cookies, and you tell Leyna. *Ja?*"

"The men are bringing the wagon around to the mudroom. Oh, you'll love all the wonderful things I bought. We'll be baking all winter."

"We?"

Anna grinned and shrugged one shoulder. Leyna's thick accent made 'we' sound like 've'. "All right, *you'll* enjoy using all the spices and canned items I bought."

"I should teach you cooking."

"I'd rather be out herding cattle or working with the Percherons." She poured herself a cup of water and drank it deeply.

"One day, a young man will take you to be wife. You will wish you know cooking and sewing then." Leyna waved a wooden spoon at her.

"Quinn won't let any man get close long enough for me to get to know him well enough to marry."

"The right man will not let that *störrisch* brother of yours stop him."

"My point exactly. Quinn is stubborn and hard-headed." Although she couldn't help wondering what kind of man could best her strong, capable older brother. That she'd like to see.

"We have rustler trouble. *Herr* Quinn, he has been gone since he returned from Bismarck chasing after those bad men."

"Did the rustlers get many cattle?"

Leyna shrugged. "What do I know? Those men, they do not talk with me." Murmuring something in German, the cook snatched a towel off the back of a chair and pulled two golden loaves of bread from the oven. Anna's mouth watered, but she worried for her brother and hoped they hadn't lost too many head of cattle.

After a snack of warm, buttered bread, they set to the big task of opening all the crates and putting things away. Two hours later, Leyna stretched, pressing her fists to her back.

"We will eat good this winter, but I must fix supper soon or we not eat tonight. *Ja?*"

Anna wiped a damp towel over her hot face. "I'm not too hungry after unpacking all those crates. Why don't we just eat sandwiches tonight?"

"Sandwiches not enough. I make soup." Leyna turned away and washed her hands in a basin.

Anna knew it was useless to argue. Leyna might claim Quinn was stubborn, but once the cook set her mind to something, there was no changing it. "I'm going riding."

Chapter Four

Following Lottie Sallinger had been more difficult than Brett had expected. Not because she didn't leave a clear trail, what with that wagon loaded down with supplies that she'd paid for with the robbery money, but because of the landscape. The rocky plateaus atop the buttes gave a clear view ahead, but if Lottie so much as turned her head, she'd have a perfect view of him.

There was little brush tall enough for a man on horseback to hide in and precious few trees. He felt grateful that the location of his ranch wasn't this barren. At least there were plenty of grasslands among the rocky terrain here for cattle to survive on. The Badlands held a rugged beauty of its own. Wind-whipped rocks in colorful layers similar to tree rings looked as if a giant knife had sawed off the side and left the guts exposed. Oranges, greens, browns, and even black layers created a majestic display of God's handiwork. Above him, a 'V' of Canada geese headed south, honking at the world below.

Brett dismounted and climbed to the top of the next hill. Lottie's trail had disappeared in a pass between two tall buttes. Brett crept through the grama grass and stuck his head up behind a small sumac bush.

He sucked in a breath at the unexpected sight. A green valley boasting a nicely laid out ranch with a huge log cabin spread out before him. Smoke curled from the chimney lending a deceptively peaceful, homey touch. There was a decent-sized barn, also made of logs, and a few smaller out-buildings. Whoever built this ranch must have hauled those logs a long ways and was determined to meet the harsh elements of North Dakota's weather head-on. Brett couldn't help admiring the spread but found it difficult to believe outlaws could have put in the work necessary to build such a place. His own ranch was a far cry from this. Of course, his place was built with sweat and hard labor, not with money stolen from innocent people.

Brett thought of Taylor's cold, limp body and clenched his teeth. The Sallingers had to pay. He wouldn't allow them to live as though nothing had happened. His world would never be the same. The temptation for vengeance was strong, but he knew that was wrong, both in the eyes of the law and God's eyes.

Justice. That's what he must focus on.

"I know, God, 'Vengeance is mine, sayeth the Lord.' But would you really mind all that much if Jack Sallinger got killed?"

Brett winced. Some Christian he was.

For a half hour, he watched two men unload crates from the buckboard and set them onto the porch. Then they drove the rig alongside the barn, unhitched the team, and carried the last of the crates into the what he assumed was the bunkhouse. All he saw of Lottie was when she'd step out onto the side porch and set another empty crate on the pile.

Brett wrestled as his ire grew. Good, decent folks had put their hard-earned money in that bank, and the Sallingers just helped themselves to it. Even when he caught them, most of the money would be gone. Course, there was this fine ranch that could be sold to make up the difference.

Lying low on the ground, Brett kept watch. A few men came and went from the barn, but none went into the big house. Was Jack out working for the day or off somewhere robbing someone else? And why had he left Lottie unprotected in Bismarck?

Maybe he should just ride in and capture Lottie and use her to bait Jack. Maybe he could get the drop on the few wranglers he'd seen and pick them off one at a time, especially since they weren't armed.

He rubbed his eyes and yawned. Grief and anger had overpowered his sleep the past few nights. A thick fog muddled his brain. "Help me here, Lord. Let me avenge Taylor and capture the Sallingers so they don't harm anyone else."

A sharp rock poked his belly. He fished it out and tossed it aside. A lizard zigzagged away from the spot where the rock landed. Brett rested his chin on his arm. No one could see him if he kept low, but he worried about someone stumbling across his horse. The ravine he'd tethered Jasper in hadn't offered much in the way of concealment.

Though the day was cool, the sun bore down on his back, warming him. Brett scratched his whiskery jaw and yawned again.

A horse's whinny jerked Brett awake. His blurry eyes focused, and he saw Lottie riding away from the house. He slithered back from the edge of the butte and hurried to Jasper. Was she going to meet Jack? Could he end this chase by tonight?

Anna loped her mare across the flat grasslands. The wind-sculpted buttes of the Badlands encircled her. Most folks would see nothing but a wilderness unfit for human life, but the odd combination of thriving grasslands and rocky barrenness reminded her of the Bible, where it talks of God creating life in the desert.

If one was tough enough, he could forge a good life here, but it was never easy. Snow could fall ten months out of the year at times, but in the summer, the temperature could be so hot you could fry an egg on a rock. Anna loved the challenge of surviving against the odds, but something was missing in her life. Something she hadn't noticed until her twin left.

She reined Bella to a walk near a four-foot-wide creek, a tributary of the Little Missouri that ran along the western side of Medora. After a hot, mostly dry summer, the creek ran low, sputtering its way over the myriad rocks and pebbles that made up its bed. Such a peaceful, soothing sound after the noise and feverish pace of Bismarck.

Anna dismounted and tied Bella to one of the cottonwoods hugging the creek line. She started to reach for her rifle but felt sure she'd be safe without it this close to the ranch. So many people coming and going kept most critters away, especially in the daytime.

Sitting on a flat, sun-warmed rock, she sighed at her disastrous trip to Bismarck. "I was a ninny, Bella. High-tailed it out of town as soon as I could after that bank robbery. Ma probably thinks she did something to upset me."

She'd never come so close to death as she had when she'd stared into that robber's pistol. The moment had only lasted a few seconds, but it had rattled her to the core. Then to have that buffoon of a clerk accuse her of being a partner in the robbery—simply because that lady thief knocked her down and dropped coins all over her.

Anna shuddered, pushing that horrible memory away. She had more important things to think of, namely finding something to fill her time. Oh, sure, Quinn let her help out with the cattle and horses, but more and more he seemed to be pushing her to do womanly things instead. But what did she know of cooking and sewing? All she'd ever wanted to be was like her brothers. Now, she wished she hadn't fought Leyna so much when the woman had tried to teach her to sew. It might be nice to make a colorful quilt during the long, cold winter. That would sure help to occupy her time.

The cool breeze blew a strand of hair across her cheek, tickling it. She brushed it behind her ear. Scratching her neck, she looked over her shoulder, feeling uneasy, as if someone or something was watching her. *Oh, stop it!* She'd been on edge ever since that robbery. A black and white magpie squawked at her, drawing her attention back to the creek, before it went back to hunting for its dinner.

Anna laughed and picked up a pebble and tossed it in the water, splashing a few sprinkles on the bird. The magpie scolded her and flew over to another rock a dozen feet away. Anna smiled at the creature, wishing she had a bread crust to give it.

Maybe she needed to focus on getting a husband instead of finding employment, which she doubted her stubborn brother would allow either. But the spouse pickings were few in Medora. Most men of the marrying type of were already settled with a wife, and the men who were left hardly inspired a young woman to matrimonial aspirations.

Anna heaved a sigh. She loved the Rocking M, but life was too lonely here. Picking just the right man was essential, and she wouldn't trade one bossy man for another. Maybe she could get lucky and marry someone like Adam, who was traveling the West, drawing his wonderful sketches. Maybe a merchant, but definitely not a rancher, or a banker, whose life could be snuffed out by robbers.

What she really needed to do was pray instead of trying to work things out for herself. Claude had preached recently on letting God ordain man's steps. She'd wanted to get employment in Bismarck, and look how drastic things had turned out there. Anna looked heavenward. "Show me what to do, Lord. Give me a direction for my life."

She closed her eyes and prayed, realizing now how she'd given in to her fear and fled Bismarck. The question was…should she go back and try harder to find employment? Or had God sent her home for another reason? She began humming, and soon started singing *Amazing Grace*. That song never failed to touch her heart.

A noise across the creek snagged her attention, sending the magpie to flight. Anna sat up, suddenly quiet. Listening. Her heart pattered. A half-grown bear cub poked its head past a clump of junipers and sniffed the air. It waddled toward the water and stared right at her. Bella snorted and pawed the ground.

Anna stood. Cute as it was, she would have enjoyed watching the creature, but where there were cubs, there were mama bears. Bella whinnied and pulled at her reins. Anna jumped off her rock and jogged toward her mare.

The bear cub bawled and backed up at her sudden movement. A loud roar answered back, and the angry mother plowed out of the brush and ran across the shallow creek straight for Anna.

Brett followed Lottie to a creek bed where she tied up her horse and then sat on a flat rock. Was she waiting for someone?

He crept down the boulder he'd been hiding behind, edging closer, careful not to make a sound. If she did meet with someone, he wanted to hear that conversation. Lottie sounded as if she were humming. It baffled his mind how a lowdown outlaw could be happy enough to hum.

Not to mention be so pretty. Her golden hair was now free of the confines of that net thing and hung down her back in a long braid, gleaming in the sunlight. He figured her to be about five and a half feet tall, and her slim shape with just the right amount of curves was pleasing to the eye—not his, but probably other men's.

What was that? Lottie singing? He edged closer, careful to not let his rifle clatter against the rocks, sure his ears were deceiving him.

Amazing Grace?

Surely not. How could an outlaw be singing a Christian hymn? Brett sat back on his heels, confused to the core. He tugged out the sketch of Lottie and stared at it. There was no doubt in his mind that the woman in the drawing was the same one sitting by the creek bed. *What's going on, Lord?*

Lottie's mare nickered. She pranced and tugged at the tree she was tethered to. The hairs on Brett's nape lifted, and he glanced around to see what had spooked the horse.

From his angle, nothing seemed out of place. Lottie's head jerked up and her singing halted. Suddenly, she jumped off the rock and hurried to her horse. The mare would have bolted if not tied so well.

Brett peered over the boulder to see what was wrong and noticed a cub by the creek. A split second later, a huge grizzly charged out of the brush, angry and roaring.

Without stopping to think, Brett raised his rifle and aimed at the bear's feet. Maybe he could scare it away. Lottie fumbled to free her mare.

If he shot, he'd give himself away and risk not capturing Jack. But he couldn't let Lottie be mauled to death.

He fired until his rifle was empty and jumped off the boulder, between Lottie and the beast. He yanked his pistol free, knowing a bullet from it wouldn't stop a charging bear. He fired at the grizzly's feet, but it continued on.

The snarling creature lunged at Brett. Its huge teeth glistened with spittle.

Lord, help me.

Chapter Five

Anna yanked at the reins and murmured soothing sounds to the frightened mare. The horse's jerking at the reins had twisted them into a knot around the low hanging tree branch. She fought to untangle them, knowing her swift horse would take her to safety. But she only had a few seconds before the bear would be upon her.

The knot wouldn't pull free. Anna's chest tightened as she yanked her Winchester from the scabbard.

Rifle fire and snarling growls sounded behind her. Anna spun around, her heart turning somersaults. The grizzly lunged at a man Anna had never seen before, swiping him across the chest with her big paw. The creature roared an ear-splitting growl in the man's face.

Anna fired two quick shots near the grizzly's hind paws. The huge creature jumped and lurched away from the noise, lumbering back to her cub. The mother thrashed across the creek and both bears disappeared into the bushes across the creek.

Heaving rapid breaths, Anna reloaded and watched to make sure the angry mother didn't return. After a few moments she dashed to her rescuer's side. If the man hadn't jumped between her and the bear, she'd most likely be dead now.

She quickly tore away the remains of the man's thick coat. At the sight of blood staining his chambray shirt, she winced. *Lord, show me how to help him. Please, save this man's life.*

She untucked her shirt and pulled a small knife from the top of her boot, then cut away as much of it as she could without exposing herself. Quickly, she unbuttoned the stranger's shirt and gently laid the folded fabric across his wound. Four of the bear's claws had cut tracks into his solid chest, but thanks to his heavy jacket, the injuries didn't look too terribly deep.

He moaned and rolled his head sideways, revealing blood on the flat rock beneath his head. Anna checked his head wound and wished she had something else to use for bandages, but the best thing she could do for this man was to get him home where he could be doctored properly. Looking over her shoulder, she checked to make sure the bear was still gone. They needed to leave before the creature decided to come back to finish her attack. But how could she move a man the size of Quinn all by herself?

He groaned and raised his knees as if trying to stand.

"Mister, can you hear me? We need to get out of here. You've been injured."

His brow wrinkled, and he gritted his teeth. Groaning, he reached for his chest. She grabbed his arm and wrestled it down. Pebbles bit into Anna's knees, but she tried to ignore her pain, knowing it was nothing compared to this man's suffering.

"Who are you?" Was he watching her? Or did he just happen to be riding by when the bear attacked?

That seemed too much of a coincidence. Anna sucked in a breath. Maybe he was one of the rustlers that Quinn was out hunting.

He tossed his head back and forth, uttering a low growl as if he were still fighting the bear. Anna rushed to the creek and scooped water into her hands, then dribbled it into the man's mouth. He coughed then swallowed. Using her hand, she wiped the blood off his dirty cheek. Slowly, as if he'd been in a deep sleep, his eyes opened. He glanced around, confused.

Anna took advantage of his moment of consciousness. "Mister, you've got to get on my horse so I can get you help."

Lifting hard and wedging her boot behind him, she managed to get him sitting. He cried out and clutched his torso but didn't fight her. Anna's heart stampeded. His life was in her hands.

Please, God, help me get him up.

Anna hurried to Bella, cooing to the still skittish mare, and untangled the reins, though her hands shook like the leaves of a quaking aspen in a windstorm. She led her horse right up to the man. The mare sniffed at the stranger but stood still. Anna got behind him and hooked her arms under his. "You have to get up. Please. I can't lift you by myself."

Surprising her, he struggled to his feet and fell against the horse. Anna strained to keep his heavy body upright. "Can you mount?"

He nodded. It took three tries for him to hook his foot in the stirrup, but with a loud grunt, he finally heaved himself up, holding one arm to his chest. Anna looped the reins over Bella's head and climbed behind the man. With one arm around his solid stomach, holding him tight, she guided Bella home with the other hand.

The short trip took a long while with Bella walking slowly. The stranger hunched over the mare's neck, and Anna couldn't tell if he were conscious or not. As they rode up to the ranch yard, Sam ambled out of the barn. He took one looked in her direction and jogged toward them.

"Who you got there, Miss Anna?"

"I don't know, but he saved me from a grizzly attack."

"A grizzly? There ain't been no reports of bear in these parts for a long while."

"Well...there is. A bear and her cub."

"Then that makes this feller a friend, I reckon. Where you want 'im?"

"In the house."

Sam took Bella's reins and led the mare toward the cabin. He looked over his shoulder and yelled, "Hank, get on out here."

The ranch hand ran out of the barn and looked around, then joined them at the stairs. Sam tied Bella to a hitching post, and he and Hank helped Anna get the stranger to the ground. The man would have collapsed if the ranch hands hadn't held him upright. They all but dragged him inside.

"Put him in Adam's room." Anna hurried past them and turned down the bed coverings.

They laid the stranger on the bed, and his feet hung off the end. Sam tugged his boots off and tossed them in a corner. "Who do you suppose he is?"

Anna shrugged. "Don't know, but God must have sent him to save my life."

"Where did you see that bear?" Sam asked.

"Down at the creek." Anna realized how she must look with her shirt half cut off, and she crossed her arms around her middle.

"I'll tell Leyna about the man and then me and Hank'll go after that bear."

"She's got a cub. Don't kill her, just chase her away. All right?"

Sam nodded.

"You might scout around and see if he has a horse tied up somewhere."

Sam and Hank left the room. Anna tugged the end of the quilt out from under the stranger's feet and covered them. His head wound had bled onto the pillowcase. She hurried to her room, grabbed some towels and the pitcher of fresh water Leyna always supplied and hurried back to her patient. She met Leyna at the door.

"We have an injured man, *Herr* Sam said."

Anna squeezed past her and set the supplies on Adam's writing desk. She dipped one end of a towel in the water and wiped a trail of blood off the man's temple.

Leyna moved closer and tsked her tongue. "We must stitch him up. I will get the basket of medicines."

Half an hour later, Anna stared at the man. They'd done the best they could to sew up his injuries. Only one had been overly deep, but Leyna had cleaned it well. If infection didn't set in and the man's head wound wasn't too severe, he should recover.

She couldn't help watching the man who'd saved her life. His thick dark brown hair hung over the white bandage on his forehead. Stubble darkened his jaw, giving him a ruggedly handsome look. What color were his eyes? She couldn't remember from the brief moment he'd opened them earlier. What would his voice sound like?

But more importantly, who was he? And why was he on Rocking M land?

Anna closed her eyes. "Heavenly Father, please save this man's life as he did mine. And please heal his wounds. Oh, and please, God, don't let him be a rustler."

Brett struggled to climb his way out of the dark pit. There was a light ahead, and he aimed to reach it. He blinked, then jerked awake, remembering the bear that had attacked him.

"Hey, settle down. You're all right."

A room slowly came into focus. Brett searched for the source of that sweet voice, but a consuming fire burning in his torso demanded his attention. He reached for his chest, needing to douse the flames. Someone yanked his arm back.

"Don't. A bear clawed you. The wounds have been stitched and doctored, and you need to leave them alone."

He turned his head toward the voice, and a woman's pretty features came into view. Her worried, tentative smile twisted his gut.

No. Not Lottie.

"I know you're hurting. I can give you laudanum if the pain is too fierce."

"No." His voice sounded scratchy. Off-kilter. The last thing he needed was to let Lottie Sallinger drug him, no matter how bad the pain was.

But, oh goodness, did she smell good. Up close, she was even prettier—and her eyes were brown, the color of coffee without cream. Beautiful. He must be delirious.

"Could you drink some water?"

That angelic voice couldn't belong to an outlaw. Brett nodded and struggled to sit up. His chest felt as if a giant fist had seized him and wouldn't let go, and he was sure his head had landed between a blacksmith's hammer and anvil.

"Careful, now. You don't want to bust out those stitches." Lottie reached behind him and lifted him up enough to drink. He guzzled the cool liquid until she took it away.

"That's enough for now."

Brett lay back, trying to catch his breath. He hated being at the mercy of outlaws, no matter how nice they treated him. He knew the truth. Still, how could this sweet, gentle woman be the same gal who robbed a bank? He must have hit his head hard when that bear plowed into him.

"My name is Anna McFarland. You're on the Rocking M ranch. What's your name?"

An angel with golden hair smiled at him. If not for the pain, he'd think he'd died and gone to heaven. But Taylor wasn't here, so he couldn't be in heaven.

No, he was in the lair of his enemy.

"You got a name?"

He licked his dry lips. "Brett." That was all she needed to know for now.

"Well, Mr. Brett, I don't know how to thank you for coming to my aid like you did. You most likely saved my life." Lottie twisted her hands, and a becoming pink shade stained her cheeks.

"You're welcome, and it's Brett. No mister." He might have to arrest her, but he was glad that snarly old bear hadn't damaged Lottie's beautiful skin. Was it as soft as it looked?

Brett turned away and pursed his lips. He had no business thinking such things. He chalked it up his current weak condition. A skillfully drawn picture of a herd of cattle on a peaceful hillside snagged his attention. Whoever had drawn that was very talented. On the wall opposite the bed, there hung a drawing of a pretty woman dressed in a flannel shirt, a split riding skirt, and boots. A western hat tilted on the side of her head gave the woman a cocky air.

"That's my sister-in-law, Mariah. My brother, Adam, drew all these sketches."

"He's very good."

Lottie nodded. "Yes, he is. He's traveling the West with his wife. He sketches western scenes for a Chicago gallery owner who frames and sells them. His wife writes dime novels."

Brett's gaze darted to Lottie's. "A woman writer?"

Lottie's warm smile tempted him to believe she was a good, wholesome woman. "Mariah is quite successful at writing dime novels. Maybe you'd like to read some when you're feeling better."

Brett grunted, neither a yes or no. He didn't want to become anymore beholden to the Sallingers than he was already.

Lottie rose. "You should rest. Is there anything you need first?"

He shook his head, instantly wishing he hadn't.

"Are you sure you don't want a dose of laudanum?" She stood and gazed at him with concerned eyes.

"I'm sure." He needed a clear head.

"Well…if you change your mind, let me know. I'll check on you in a little while."

Brett knew he should thank her, but the words tasted bitter on his tongue. How had he gotten himself in this predicament?

He glanced and lifted the sheet, taking small breaths to avoid the pain larger ones caused. His torso resembled a mummy with all those white bandages wrapped around him. He wanted to check out his injuries but didn't want to mess up the bandage. He'd just have to wait until they changed it.

The bedroom was small, but nicely furnished with a double bed, desk and chair, a small wardrobe and a wingback chair in the corner. A pale blue curtain fluttered on the breeze coming in the partially open window. The scent of cattle drifted in, mixed with the fragrant odor of something cooking. His stomach grumbled.

His gaze traveled to the ceiling. "Well, Lord, I'm in a fine predicament, aren't I? Thank you for protecting me—and Lottie—from that bear."

Now what? Would Jack recognize him for the lawman he was? His badge!

Brett hunted for his shirt and found it hanging on the bed post. He reached for it with his left hand, gritting his teeth against the knife in his chest, he searched the tattered remains of his shirt for his U.S. Marshal's badge. Where was it? Had Lottie already found it and kept it to show her brother?

He was wearing it before the attack, wasn't he? Brett stopped to remember what happened just before the bear charged. He'd put on his fleece coat because lying on the stony ground had hurt his belly. The jacket had offered a bit protection, even if it had made him sweat.

Maybe the bear had knocked his badge off. Ignoring the pain any movement caused, he checked his pants pockets. No badge, but there was a piece of paper. He pulled out the sketch of Lottie and glanced toward the open door. He quickly unfolded the single sheet. Anna McFarland was a dead ringer for Lottie Sallinger—and he'd just wormed his way into their hideout.

Chapter Six

Anna hummed as she arranged the breakfast items on the plate for her patient.

"That stranger, he is handsome, *ja*?" Leyna glanced sideways at Anna as she rolled balls of dough, her green eyes twinkling with mischief.

To disagree would be telling a falsehood, but she wouldn't play Leyna's game. "Yes, he is a nice-looking man. I think he's even taller than Quinn."

"*Herr* Quinn, he will not like that you have brought a stranger into the house with him gone."

Anna spun around toward the cook. "Why not? That man saved my life. I couldn't very well leave him to die."

"*Ach.* He should be in the bunkhouse with the other men."

"Well, he's not. It would be too hard to take care of him?" Anna yanked up the tray, sloshing coffee onto the saucer. Maybe it wasn't the wisest thing bringing a stranger into the house with her brother gone, but she hadn't stopped to think about that yesterday. All she'd wanted was to get the man's wounds treated so he wouldn't die. She couldn't bear it if that happened after he saved her life.

She peeked in the open door to see if Brett was awake. He lay sprawled out on top of the bed, one hand behind his head. He'd removed the tattered shirt and had tossed it across the foot of the bed, but he still wore his pants. What would he say when he noticed what they'd done to him?

She couldn't tell if he were sleeping or only looking out the window. The tray clunked as she set it on the desk. Brett turned his sleepy gaze on her, and her breath caught in her throat. With his hair tousled and a relaxed gaze in his eyes, instead of that wary, on-guard stare he'd worn the day before, he was quite handsome. He rubbed his whiskers and gave her a lazy smile. *Oh my!* Anna dropped into the chair before her legs could give out.

"Something sure smells good. What do you have there? I'm as hungry as a bear." Brett glanced down at his body, then reached to his right and grabbed the sheet, throwing it over him.

Anna shook her head at his bear reference and cleared her throat. "Eggs, bacon, and biscuits."

He pushed himself up in the bed, wincing.

"Are you in much pain?"

The dark look returned, as if he didn't like being reminded of his current situation. "I'm fine."

Anna handed him a pillow, which he placed across his lap, then she set the tray on the pillow. "Sorry, I spilled the coffee."

"Not a problem." He lifted the cup and slurped the coffee from the saucer, then sipped from the cup. "Mmm…hot and black, exactly how I like it."

He tossed her a hesitant glance, bowed his head for a moment, and then dug into his food as if he hadn't eaten in a week. Was he praying? If the man were a Christian that would certainly calm Leyna's nerves about having him in the house.

His ever-changing expressions confused Anna. One minute he looked like an outlaw with his two-day stubble and his deep blue eyes narrowed in a glare, then he'd lighten up and flash an intriguing smile that made her feel as if moths were fluttering in her stomach.

The question still remained…who was he?

"Very good food. Thank the cook, would you?"

Anna nodded. "I'll do that. Um…I've been wondering…how was it you happened to be right there when that bear charged out of the brush?"

He shrugged one shoulder. "Fortunate timing, I suppose."

"Yes, it was that. But that still doesn't explain why you were on the Rocking M."

Anna hiked her chin up, showing him she meant business.

"I heard in town that this was a good place to find work." He laid his hand on his chest. "Guess I won't be much good for work for a while though."

"Don't worry about that. You just concentrate on healing. I'm sure my brother would be happy to hire you once you're better."

Instead of looking happy about that, he scowled and stared out the window. Maybe he didn't like not pulling his own weight. Quinn hated being in bed the few times he'd been sick and not able to work. Maybe Brett felt the same way.

"There's not a lot you can do right now. Would you mind if I read to you?"

He shook his head. "No, I don't mind."

"Wonderful. Let me grab something, and I'll be right back." The chair creaked as she stood. Could this stranger be an answer to her prayer? Caring for him definitely gave her something to do. At least for now.

Brett wanted to throw something. Never had he been in such a frustrating situation. Accepting food and medical care from the very people who'd killed his brother didn't set right with him. His grip tightened on the sheet covering him. He felt the need to flee in the night and put distance between himself and the Sallingers, but at the same time, it seemed as if God had plunked him right in the middle of that nest of vipers. Besides, even if he wanted to leave, it would have to wait another day or two until he healed more. He could barely move without his chest burning with pain, and his ribs ached from the bear's heavy weight landing on him.

And where was Jasper? Was he still tied to a juniper shrub or had Lottie found his gelding and brought him back here. The time right after the bear attack was still foggy in his mind.

She re-entered the room with a thick leather book under her arm. He sure hoped she didn't plan to read that whole thing to him. She situated herself in the soft chair in the corner and opened the tome. A Bible?

Brett narrowed his gaze. What was going on here? Was this a ruse to throw him off the track? Were the Sallingers people who justified their deeds by misrepresenting God's Word?

"Ready for me to read to you?" Lottie's engaging smile withered under his stern scowl.

It was best he listen carefully to see if she tried to manipulate the Scriptures for her own purposes. A Bible reading bank robber—he'd seen everything now.

She cleared her throat. "Blessed is the man that walketh not in the counsel of the ungodly, nor standeth in the way of sinners, nor sitteth in the seat of the scornful. But his delight is in the law of the Lord; and in his law doth he meditate day and night. And he shall be like a tree planted by the rivers of water, that bringeth forth his fruit in his season; his leaf also shall not wither; and whatsoever he doeth shall prosper. The ungodly are not so: but are like the chaff which the wind driveth away."

Brett's mouth dropped open as Lottie's sweet voice softly read the words from Psalm 1. He scratched at the bandage around his head, trying to make sense of it all. Maybe that bump on his head had rendered him unconscious and this was nothing but a dream. Or maybe his mind had been knocked off-kilter and he was crazy now.

There had to be a mistake. Either this wasn't Lottie or a woman other than Lottie had robbed the bank. But the sketch he'd gotten from Marshal Cronan had been drawn on the day of the robbery, while the bank clerk's mind was still fresh and clear.

The only other possibility was that the clerk had described someone other than Lottie—maybe a patron at the bank? There had been a lot of confusion with Taylor's shooting and that bag of coins dropped outside the bank on the boardwalk. Was it possible the clerk had described the wrong person?

As he listened to the Scripture, his hands ached to pull out the sketch and compare it to Lottie.

She read for a solid half hour, and Brett gave up wrestling with the facts and let God's Word minister to him. God had a plan, even in this odd situation he'd found himself in.

Something clanked at the doorway, and he and Lottie both looked up. The older woman he remembered from yesterday entered, carrying a basin holding bandages and a jar of salve.

"*Guten morgen.* How is our patient this day?" She smiled and set the basin on the foot of the bed.

"He ate well, Leyna."

"Good! You like my cooking, *ja*?"

Brett couldn't help returning the German woman's warm smile. "*Ja.*"

Leyna chuckled. "You won't like so well the doctoring."

Brett laid his hand to his chest and glanced at Lottie. Maybe it was silly but the bandage covered him so well that he hadn't thought about being shirtless in her presence, but now…

"You must sit up so we can unwrap the binding then I will tend your wounds."

Trying to ignore the fact that Lottie was still in the room, Brett did as the cook ordered, hissing against the pain as he sat. He focused his attention on the cook. Was she one of the many Russian Germans who'd come to North Dakota looking for land and freedom? How had she gotten hooked up with outlaws? Was the kind woman even aware the Sallingers were thieves and murderers?

With the binding off, Leyna gently pushed him back down, and then carefully peeled off the bandages covering the wounds. Brett clenched his jaw. That old bear had made tracks on his chest, and with all those stitches and red welts, he looked like a scarecrow. He was lucky to be alive. Narrowing his gaze, he realized something was wrong. He sucked in a breath and looked up. "You shaved my chest?"

Lottie winced at his booming voice, but Leyna only tisked. "Hush your bellowing. It was necessary to avoid infection."

Brett started to rub a hand over the chest that hadn't been bald since he was seventeen, but Leyna smacked it away. He felt...violated somehow, which was silly since he knew the hair would grow back. At least he hoped it would. Leyna made quick work of her doctoring, and he lay back, more tired than he wanted to admit. Lottie handed her salve and clean bandages, watching him with a worried stare.

"I will get you one of *Herr* Quinn's shirts to wear." Leyna left as quickly as she'd come.

Lottie hugged the Bible to her chest. "Would you like me to read any more?"

He dreaded the thought of wearing one of Jack Sallinger's shirts and just wanted them to leave him alone. He shook his head. Lottie stood by the bed, looking disappointed. Guilt needled Brett.

The last thing he wanted was to feel sympathy for the Sallingers, no matter how nice they had been to him. He was a lawman, and they were outlaws. He supposed even outlaws had a little good in them. That was evident. But he couldn't afford to be swayed into lowering his defenses. Just as soon as he got the evidence he needed, Lottie and her brother were going to jail for a very long time.

He turned onto his side, almost grateful for the pain. The clomping of boots sounded in the next room and stopped at the bedroom doorway.

"Quinn! You're back."

Brett carefully rolled onto his back and saw Lottie hugging a man. He lightly patted her shoulder then pushed her away and glared at Brett.

"What's going on here? And why aren't you still in Bismarck?" He directed the last question at Lottie.

Up close, Jack Sallinger was taller and broader than Brett had expected. His blonde hair and brown eyes favored his sister's, though Lottie's hair was more a golden blond, and she was much shorter than her brother. There was no denying the affection between the two, but Jack seemed more interested in Brett than his sister.

"This is Brett. He saved my life." Lottie's warm smile of gratitude made Brett want to slink under his covers and hide.

"Yeah, the men told me what happened." His hard expression softened. "I owe you my thanks, mister. You got a last name?"

Brett couldn't abide lying, so he would have to give his real name and hope Jack hadn't heard of him. "Wickham. Brett Wickham."

Jack nodded. "What are you doing in these parts? It's a long ways from nowhere."

"I heard you might be hiring." That was true. Hadn't the man at the café in Medora said the Rocking M might be hiring?

"I can always use another good hand. You done any ranching."

Brett grinned. "Yep. Plenty. My pa owned a ranch down south a ways." He held the grin in place, even as thoughts of Taylor's limp body saturated his mind. The Bar W now belonged to Brett alone, and he would need to return soon. But first, he'd see the Sallingers behind bars.

"Well…you rest up and let the ladies coddle you for a few days, then I'll put you to work." Jack smirked, making Brett wonder if there was more to his words than the obvious. "Thanks for coming to my sister's rescue. I'm much obliged."

Jack stormed out of the room as fast as he'd come. Lottie cast him a hesitant glance and followed her brother. Brett lay back. God had placed him right smack in his enemies' lair. Now all he needed was to find evidence to convict the two.

"He's hiding something." Quinn stopped in front of the parlor window. He turned and scowled at Anna. "How could you bring a stranger into this house when I was gone? You know that could be dangerous, Anna."

She crossed her arms and mentally prepared to defend her stance again. "He was hurt bad. I didn't stop to think. The man had saved me from a horrible death or maiming, at the least, and all I wanted was to get him help."

She longed to protect her champion, but her couldn't let her brother's concern slide past. "Why do you think he's hiding something?"

"Just a feeling I have. It's too coincidental that he was right there when you needed him."

"Maybe God sent him." She lifted her brows, daring him to argue that fact.

He heaved a sigh. Standing there with his hands on his hips, his glaring may intimidate their ranch hands, but not her.

"Maybe so, but I'm still suspicious. Sam found a horse on the butte overlooking the creek."

"And?" Anna prayed Brett wasn't a rustler. *Please, Lord.*

Quinn turned up one side of his mouth. "Nothing. He had food supplies, a change of clothes, and ammunition. Nothing to show who he was or why he was on our land. Sam thinks he may have been watching you."

"Me?" Anna's eyes widened and her heart leapt in her chest. "Why?"

Quinn shrugged. "Maybe he's one of the rustlers and was keeping an eye on you. Maybe he's just a man watching a pretty woman."

If Anna hadn't been so concerned, she was certain she would have blushed at her brother's rare compliment. Had Brett been watching her? The thought sent chills up and down her spine.

"As soon as he can get around, I want him out in the bunkhouse where the other men can help keep an eye on him. That man is up to something. You stay out of Adam's room and let Leyna tend him."

Anna wanted to say he was making a mountain out of a molehill, but one had to be cautious in this wilderness they lived in. Still, Brett intrigued her like no man ever had.

Was it because he'd charged in like a medieval knight, risking his own life to save her?

Quinn could move Brett to the barn, but until the man was gone, he was still her patient…and tend him, she would.

Chapter Seven

Anna glanced at her reflection in the mirror on the wardrobe's door, admiring the fine job Leyna had done fashioning the emerald fabric she'd purchased in Bismarck into a lovely dress. Her mother had planned to make her something from the fabric but somehow the material had gotten placed in the supplies Anna had brought home. She glanced down at the hem she had stitched herself. She pressed her lips together. Was that a pucker?

Oh well, with the skirt as full as it was, who would notice anyway? She searched the wardrobe and found her beaded reticule in a drawer. She hadn't used it since her trip to Bismarck and didn't remember the bag being so heavy. Pulling open the drawstring, she dumped the contents onto her bed. Anna gasped at the two shiny gold coins resting on her quilt. Two shiny double eagle coins stared at her, sending stabbing shards of guilt throughout her. She felt as guilty as if she'd robbed that bank herself. The coins must have somehow fallen into her bag during the bank robbery.

What now?

Even touching money that didn't belong to her made her feel dirty. Could she be arrested for being in possession of stolen money? *Heavenly Father, what should I do?*

Who would believe that the coins had fallen into her reticule by accident? The bank officials would most likely accuse her of stealing them—at least that skinny bank clerk would.

Anna searched for a place to hide the coins until she could figure out how to get them back to the bank. If she walked in and tried to return them, that bank clerk might implicate her in the robbery. No, she'd have to find another way. They were far too heavy to mail. Maybe she could mail forty dollars paper money back to the bank.

Anna rifled through her drawers, finally deciding to hide the coins beneath her underwear. Nobody would dare get in that drawer except Leyna, and she would believe Anna's story of how the coins came into her possession. Should she tell Quinn? The bank clerk's accusations rang in her ears. No, it was best she find a way to return the money herself.

Quickly, she stuffed her belongings back into her reticule, affixed her hat, and hurried out to find Quinn. He'd promised to take her to town to hear the circuit-riding minister this Sunday. When she didn't find him in the parlor, she searched the kitchen. Leyna sat at the table, sipping coffee, her face pale.

"What's wrong? Has something happened?"

The cook waved her hand in the air. "*Herr* Quinn, he rode out early this morning. One of the hands, he found a dead cow."

Anna's heart sunk. "So he's not taking us to church?"

Leyna shook her head, but a smile tugged at her lips. "I will not go today. My head, it feels like a horse sat on it. But *Herr* Quinn says that *Herr* Brett will drive you."

Anna perked up at this news. "Truly?"

Leyna nodded, then grimaced. "*Ja*, it is the truth."

Her joy quickly turned to concern. "But is he ready for that? He's barely been out of bed the past three days since the attack."

"*Herr* Quinn is anxious to have him out of the house." The cook waved at the stove. "The stew, I will put it on for your dinner, then go back to *mein* bed."

Anna clasped the cook's arm. "No, you go to bed now. I can fix something when I return if there isn't a picnic after the services. Do I need to bring back the doctor?"

"*Nein*." When Leyna didn't argue about cooking dinner, Anna knew she must be feeling poorly. Anna nibbled her lip as Leyna pushed up from the chair.

"I could stay home and take care of you."

"*Nein*. You go. I sleep. But *danke*." A feeble smile touched Leyna's lips as she walked out of the room. The older woman was hale and hardy and rarely ever sick. Anna prayed she would feel better soon.

Outside on the porch, Anna searched for Brett. It was too soon for him to be driving a wagon to town and back. What was Quinn thinking?

She'd find Brett and tell him that she was quite capable of driving the rig herself. Before she could take a step, a horse and buggy came out of the barn. Brett guided it right up to the porch and stopped.

"Whoa."

He tipped his hat and smiled, sending Anna's stomach into spasms. Why did he have to be so fine-looking?

He stood and started to climb down.

"No!"

His brows lifted, and he halted at Anna's stern command.

Her cheeks turned crimson. "I mean, save your strength. You don't need to get down and help me up. I've been climbing into buggies since I could walk."

He nodded then reached out a hand to help her up. She stared at it, afraid he'd break lose his stitches if he did too much.

"Take my hand…Miss McFarland."

"I don't want to hurt you." Ignoring his hand, she climbed up beside him and arranged her skirts. He picked up the reins with a sigh and clicked out the side of his mouth to the horse. The buggy lurched and started forward.

Anna had to admit that in the light of day Brett looked healthier, less pale. He'd shaved this morning, revealing his strong jaw. Seeing him up and moving about sent a shaft of relief charging through her. If he had died saving her, she would have borne that pain her whole life. Brett was a fine looking man, broad-shouldered and tall, and those eyes….

Oh, bother! What was she doing admiring a man who might well be an outlaw?

He glanced out the corner of his eye at her and smiled. The buggy dipped, and his shoulder brushed against hers. She turned away, ignoring what that smile and his touch—albeit accidental—did to her insides and studied the landscape. Soon all the green would turn to brown stubble and the temperature would grow too cold for a two-hour trip to Medora for church—or anything else. She'd be stuck at the ranch for another winter. It had never really bothered her until Adam had left. What would she do cooped up for months on end?

"Nice day to go to church."

Anna turned to Brett. "You go to church often?" Maybe she could trap him into revealing his true purpose for being on the Rocking M.

"Yep. Every chance I get. There are too many troubles in this world. A man needs to be reminded of God's grace and love."

He pressed his lips together and looked away. What troubles was he talking about? Would a rustler go to church? If Quinn still suspected him, he'd never allow Brett to escort her, so that must mean her brother was satisfied that Brett wasn't a threat to them.

No, surely he wasn't a rustler. If he were, he would have been on edge in their home and not so relaxed. Brett confused her more than any man she'd met. And the trouble was…she liked him. More than liked him, she was attracted to him.

A churchgoing man couldn't be a rustler. That was all there was to it, and that's what she'd choose to believe.

Guilt surged through Brett. He'd all but told Lottie a lie, and that didn't sit well with him. Sunday service was the last place he wanted to go today. He hadn't yet made peace with God for his brother's death. But he had to see for himself that Lottie was going to church or he would never believe it possible.

His own words needled him. *A man needs to be reminded of God's grace and love.* Where had they come from? Was it a message from God to him, straight out of his own mouth?

For three days he'd lain in bed, stewing over Taylor's death. He knew God would comfort him if Brett would allow it, but he'd clung to his anger like a child clinging to a broken toy. How else could he keep his distance from Lottie and her constant, sweet nurturing?

Jack Sallinger hadn't been happy to find Brett in his house. Lottie's brother was suspicious of him, which was only natural, especially with his sister tending to Brett. Jack had shaved and looked little like the verbal description he had received from Marshal Cronan, but things had happened so fast at the bank. How much could he count on the eyewitnesses who'd been in fear of their lives? Most folks in such a situation would avoid looking a robber in the face.

The wagon dipped in a rut, knocking Lottie's shoulder against his. The fresh scent of something floral wafted in the air. His gut tightened. He didn't need to be attracted to her. Sure, she was a beautiful woman, but she was an outlaw. Remember Taylor? Remember all that stolen money?

Brett hated how his own mind and body threatened to betray his brother's memory. He couldn't allow his defenses to be broken down simply because Lottie doted on him and fed him—great food—and read the Bible to him. *God, help me. I don't want to like the Sallingers.*

"May I ask you a question?" Lottie peeked sideways at him.

His heart skittered. What did she want to know? How could he answer without lying and giving himself away? "Sure," he said, against his better judgment.

"Where are you from?"

Ah, that he could answer. "I grew up on a ranch south of here a ways."

"Why would you want to work for us if your family owns a ranch?" She turned curious, innocent eyes toward him.

He blinked. How could a thieving, gun-toting outlaw look so guileless? "Ah…my pa was quite strict. I left there over five years ago."

Lottie nodded. "Our pa was strict too, but he died a long time ago. I think that's why Quinn is like he is."

"Like what?"

She shrugged. "I don't know. He works all the time. He's been the closest thing to a father Adam and I have had since Pa's death, but he's never been affectionate—has always held himself away from us for some reason."

"Maybe he's afraid of losing someone else he loves."

Lottie looked at him with wide brown eyes, as if she'd never considered that notion. "You might be right. I hadn't ever thought of that. Our ranch in Texas wasn't doing very well after several years of drought, so Pa came up here, bought the Rocking M, and then moved us."

Brett held the reins loosely and watched a hawk circling in the bright blue sky. After three days of being shut up in that bedroom, he enjoyed the sun's warmth. Something pricked at the back of his mind…if the McFarlands were wealthy enough to buy all this land, why would they risk it and their nice home to rob trains and banks? Something else that didn't fit the picture. "That was a long move. Must have been hard."

"Actually…" Lottie glanced at him, her eyes dancing, "…I thought it was a big adventure. But I did miss my friends from school, and I felt sorry for Adam when his horse died. He was so sad for so long after that."

The slowly rocking buggy and warmth of the sun lulled Brett into a relaxed state. He yawned and stretched, instantly sorry. He sucked in a breath and rubbed his chest. Lottie cast him a worried glance.

"I can drive if you're in pain."

"No. But remind me not to stretch again."

Lottie's laugh kindled an awareness inside him that he didn't want fueled.

"Sorry, I shouldn't find humor in your pain."

Brett didn't respond. He tightened his grasp on the reins and clenched his teeth. He couldn't afford to like Lottie Sallinger—but those brown sugar eyes made him want to believe she was as innocent as she seemed.

Half an hour later, they pulled up to the church. The singing had already started. Brett escorted Lottie to a seat in back, then tended the horse, and returned. He was thankful they were on the last row so that no one could see him squirm. Vengeance wasn't right in the eyes of God; he knew that. Could he dispense justice without being overcome with vengeance? Would it be right to leave now and go home to the Bar W and let the Sallingers run free to wreak havoc on other innocent folks?

"Vengeance is mine, saith the Lord." The minister shouted the words and smacked his Bible on the makeshift pulpit. Brett jumped, and Lottie stared at him with wide eyes. She pressed her lips together as if holding in a smile, but it broke forth, dancing in her eyes. As she turned back to face the preacher, a grin twittered on her enticing lips.

He glanced around to see if anyone else had noticed his discomfort, but all eyes were pinned on the man up front. Brett settled in to listen, wondering how the minister had picked that of all messages to preach this day.

"Man seeks to avenge the wrong done him, but God's Word says to leave vengeance to Him. Anger and hatred drives man away from God. Satan feeds that anger until it becomes a raging fire that man can't put out on his own. God asks us to lay aside our anger and let Him deal with those who wronged you."

Brett hung his head. If he turned things over to God it would seem as if he deserted his brother. Exacting justice was his job as a lawman. How could he go home and do nothing?

The service complete, people filed outside shaking the preacher's hand as they passed him. Women set about pulling pots and platters of food from their wagons and putting them on makeshift tables the men had put up. Lottie nibbled her lip and walked over to him.

"We didn't bring any food. I feel funny eating when I didn't bring anything."

"Let's go then." Brett reached for her arm, right as a burly man stepped onto the bed of a nearby wagon.

"I know some of you folks live a ways out of town and didn't get word about our picnic today, but there's plenty of food, so we invite you to stay and eat."

The crowd erupted in a chorus of affirmation. Lottie shrugged. "Well...do you feel up to staying and eating?"

The minister's words still niggled at Brett. Letting go of his quest for vengeance was the right thing to do, but he didn't know how to release it. He wanted to hit the road, but if he started working at the Rocking M, he wouldn't get to town very often. Maybe he should take advantage of the chance to nose around and see what he could find out about the McFarlands. "Sure, I can always eat."

Brett wolfed down his food and went to check on the horse. The curious glances Lottie's unmarried women friends sent his way set his nerves on edge. He felt like a worm on a hook dangling over a lake with a dozen wide mouth bass ready to take a bite out of him.

He checked the mare and then led her over to the water trough. Another man, short and thin, was already watering a fine-looking bay mare. Brett nodded to him. "Afternoon."

The man smiled. "Name's John Cutter. Saw you in church with Anna McFarland. You her new beau?"

Brett sniffed a laugh. Him? Lottie Sallinger's beau? That would be the day. "Uh...no, I'm escorting her at her brother's orders. I work on the Rocking M."

"Lucky you, getting a peek at Anna McFarland every day. Most of the unmarried men in Medora would like to court her, but that brother of hers chases them all away." The man glanced past the crowd to where Lottie stood beneath a pine tree chatting with two men.

Brett followed his gaze, his hand tightening on the reins as one of the men leaned in close to Lottie and said something. She lifted her hand to her mouth, but stepped back, looking uncomfortable with the man's attention. Her gaze darted past the men, scanning the crowd. Was she looking for him?

Brett tied the mare to a tree where there was green grass within reach and let her graze. A desire to protect Lottie forced his feet forward. He strode toward her, wondering about his feelings. Was he actually jealous? Or did he just want to take good care of his charge? Jack had told him to guard his sister with his life. Brett huffed a laugh. He'd already done that once and had the scars to proof it, not to mention a bald chest.

The rocky ground crunched beneath his feet as he made up the distance in quick order. Was that relief in Lottie's gaze when she noticed him?

Anna watched Brett storm toward her. What had put a burr under his saddle?

Still, she couldn't help being relieved at his presence. Spenser Gilroy and Tommy Baxter had cornered her and wouldn't leave her be. How could she have ever considered either of them marrying material? All Spenser talked about was his business and how fast it was growing. Tommy bragged that he'd made more money last year than Spense. Neither seemed to care about what she had to say. As soon as she returned home, she'd scratch both names off her potential husband list.

Brett moved to her side, staring down the two shorter men. She introduced the three men, noting the scowls on Spenser's and Tommy's faces when she took Brett's arm. If he was surprised, he didn't react.

"You ready to leave yet?" He looked down at her.

"Yes, thank you." She said her goodbyes and allowed Brett to escort her toward the buggy, wondering at the tingles charging up her arm where hers touched his hard bicep.

Arm-in-arm, Pamela, Paula, and Phyllis Stewart intercepted them before they could escape. The three red-haired, stair-step sisters in their late teens giggled and looked at Brett as if he were their Christmas present all wrapped up with a pretty bow. He stopped three yards in front of their unified barricade.

"Aren't you going to introduce us to your *friend*, Anna?" Phyllis patted her hair, pulled so tightly into a bun that Anna wondered how her eyes weren't slanted upward.

"This is Brett Wickham. He's working on the ranch." She wanted to cling to Brett's arm merely to watch their response but turned loose of him instead.

"Ladies." He tipped his hat then turned to her. "I'll hitch up the buggy. It will be ready whenever you are."

The big chicken strode away, his long legs eating up the ground. Anna nearly giggled at his hasty escape.

"Oh, my." Paula fanned herself as she watched him depart.

Pamela turned back to Anna. "Where did you find him? He's absolutely delicious."

"And a church-goin' man too." Phyllis hugged her Bible to her chest.

"He saved me from a bear." Anna held back a smile as three sets of hazel eyes widened in unison.

Pamela puckered her lips in a smirk. "Anna McFarland, that is a falsehood. There's no bear in these parts."

Anna hiked up her chin. "It's true. I promise. I was down at the creek a short ways from our cabin when I saw a cub come out of the brush. I knew the mama bear would be nearby and tried to leave, but Bella's reins had gotten tangled and I couldn't get them free from the bush I tied her to. If Brett hadn't shown up when he did, that bear most likely would have killed me."

"*Ohh*…that's the most romantic thing I've ever heard." Paula fanned herself and peered over her shoulder at Brett.

"He's not married, is he?" Phyllis turned completely around, watching him.

Brett glanced their way then turned his back and busied himself with hitching the horse to the buggy. Anna wasn't sure but she thought he might be blushing. "I've had a lovely time today, but we must be heading back. The bear clawed Brett across the chest earlier this week, and I imagine he's getting tired. This is his first day up and about."

The three girls gasped. Anna sidled past them, feeling more than a little proud that she was the one leaving with Brett. She didn't know all that much about him, but she liked him anyway and thought they had become friends. He did save her life, after all, and she had probably saved his. As long as he didn't turn out to be a rustler, everything would be fine.

Maybe she should add his name to the top of her prospective husband list. *Hmm.* Anna Wickham had a nice sound to it.

Chapter Eight

Anna looked out the parlor window, hoping for a peek at Brett. She'd only seen him a little yesterday after returning from church. Quinn had assigned him light chores today, and he'd been outside since breakfast, when Quinn had told him it was time he moved to the bunkhouse.

Her brother strode out of the barn and soon entered the house. His gray cotton shirt had a long tear in it, and he walked by, not even noticing her. A line of dirt ran down his right cheek.

"What happened?"

He halted suddenly and spun around, squinting at her. "Didn't see you there." He peered down at his chest. "I was checking a cut on a calf's leg, and she got cantankerous. Her hoof got snagged on my pocket and tore my shirt."

"You're not hurt?"

"No."

"That's good. I need to go into town."

He scowled at her swift topic change and unbuttoned his shirt. "I can't take you today. Besides, you were there yesterday."

"But the stores are closed on Sunday." Anna stepped toward him.

Quinn peeled off his top and undershirt, revealing his tanned, muscled chest. Her brother was a fine-looking man. At twenty-seven, he should have been married and fathered several children by now, but he'd put his life on hold to make the ranch the success it was, so they'd all have a nice home. Did he ever regret working so hard? Not taking any time for himself?

"You bought a wagonload of supplies in Bismarck a few weeks ago. What else could you possibly need?"

Anna lifted her chin. "I want to make a quilt."

Quinn opened his mouth and shut it, probably shocked that she now desired to do something she'd always resisted before. "Well...uh, that's great news, but doesn't Leyna have enough scraps around here for that?"

If Anna was going to go to all the work and time to make a quilt, she wanted one that would last and look pretty, not one made of scraps. "If I buy new fabric for the quilt, it will last much longer."

Quinn sighed. "All right. Sam's not too busy. He can take you."

"Umm...what's Brett doing today?" Anna held her hands in front of her, hoping Quinn wouldn't know she was attracted to their new hand.

Her brother's brows dipped down. "Repairing and polishing tack. Why?"

"Oh, I thought maybe he could take me since there's not a whole lot he can do yet."

"He's not your personal worker. I've assigned him chores to do."

Anna hiked her chin. "Fine. Then I'll just ride Bella and go alone."

Quinn shook his head and headed for his room. "I'll have Brett hitch up the buggy."

Anna smiled. She would have enjoyed riding Bella, because the trip would have been smoother and taken less time, but this way, she could spend a good four hours with Brett. Maybe she could learn more about him.

As Brett drove the buggy out of Medora, Anna smiled to herself. Her timing had been impeccable. The train had come this morning and brought with it a dozen bolts of new fabric for the mercantile, which was normally low on such items. The indigo, rose, and cream fabric she'd picked out would make a beautiful quilt to decorate her bed. She sure hoped that sewing would be easier than the last time she'd tried it. Her fingers had been sore for a week and had resembled a pincushion with all the pricks they'd borne.

Though sewing was one of her least favorite things to do, she'd resigned herself to making a quilt. When Brett wasn't watching, she'd asked the store clerk about work in town. He'd been surprised by her inquiry but had directed her to a wall in the back where notices were posted. While there were notices for cowhands, a farrier, and a man to work in the livery, there wasn't a single position for a woman. It didn't seem fair, but that's the way it was. Women were stuck at home while men got to do all the interesting things.

She peeked at Brett. He hadn't talked much on the trip to town, and she wondered if he was angry with her for taking him away from the harness repair Quinn had assigned him to. "That was a tasty lunch, wasn't it? I particularly liked that apple cake. Mmm...."

He nodded but kept his gaze focused on the road ahead. Anna sighed and sat back. How was a woman supposed to get to know a man when he seemed determined not to talk?

"Tell me more about your parents' ranch." She swatted at a fly buzzing her face.

"There's not much to tell. It's a ranch. We raise several breeds of cattle, grow hay, have a garden."

"Do you have any brothers or sisters?"

When Brett didn't answer, Anna glanced at his face. His brows dipped down, and his lips were pressed tightly together. He breathed heavily through his nose. Why would such a simple question cause such a reaction? Had he lost a sibling? Her curiosity took her mind in different directions, but she kept her mouth shut, afraid she might say the wrong thing.

A quarter of a mile outside of town, they passed a trail that led up to a section of town Anna had never been to. She'd never had cause to visit there, but she doubted Quinn would allow it if she wanted to. Still, she couldn't help wondering what was around that bend in the trail. If she'd been on Bella, she might have satisfied her curiosity.

Deciding Brett wasn't going to answer her, she sighed and stared forward, thinking about what design she wanted to use for her quilt. On the butte overlooking the trail, she noticed three elk grazing. The majestic male had a rack that looked as large as a tree branch. He lifted his head and sniffed.

A loud scream rent the serene setting. Anna jumped. Brett yanked back on the reins to keep the spooked horse from bolting. He locked the brake, wrapped the reins around it, and grabbed his rifle.

Anna scooted closer to him and turned her head toward the sound. "What was that?"

"Don't know. A big cat maybe." He stood and jumped off the buggy. "I'll check it out. You stay here and calm the horse."

His boots crunched on the rocky ground as he walked away. Anna shinnied out of the buggy. There was no way she was staying behind when he had the only rifle. She glanced at the horse, which had already settled, and quickly tied it to a cottonwood trunk. Tiptoeing, she hurried to catch up with Brett.

He glanced over his shoulder and scowled. "You don't obey very well."

The eerie cry came again. Closer this time. Anna shivered and grabbed the back of Brett's shirt. He tiptoed forward, his rifle ready.

They heard a clunking sound, and Brett stopped just past the boulder that shielded them. Anna peeked around his arm, still clinging to him. She wasn't generally frightened easily, but that had been such a strange, creepy sound.

Another high-pitched shriek split the air as she rounded the corner. A dirty, shabbily dressed girl with dingy hair jumped up and down, barefoot on the rocky ground, crying. A boy not much bigger than she vigorously pounded a rattlesnake with an old shovel. Why were these children out here all alone?

A motherly desire to comfort them swelled in Anna's chest, and she rushed past Brett, keeping far away from the snake. She took the little girl in her arms. The child couldn't be much more than five.

"Shh...you're all right now." Trying to ignore the foul odor emanating from the child, Anna rubbed the girl's back, even though she remained stiff in her arms.

"Get back, boy."

Both children startled and looked up at Brett's command. The boy stepped back a half dozen feet. Brett walked over to the snake and nudged it with his rifle stock. "You killed it. That snake can't hurt you now, as long as you don't handle the head. You didn't get bit, did you?"

With the danger gone, the boy ignored Brett's question and spun toward Anna. "You let her go."

Brett laid his hand on the boy's shoulder, but the child shrugged it off. The girl wriggled and kicked her feet, so Anna set her on the ground. She limped over to the boy, who looked about seven or eight years old.

"Where you kids from?" Brett squatted eye level with the children.

"It don't matter. C'mon, Emma." The boy shrugged one thin shoulder.

Anna's heart nearly broke for the two urchins. Their clothes were little more than rags, and both were barefoot. Even with well-made shoes, Anna often found the rocky soil awkward to walk on. But barefoot? Why, their feet must be tattered.

"We have a buggy and can give you a ride," Anna offered.

"Please, Jimmy. I hurt my foot jumping on those rocks." Emma's soft blue eyes glistened.

The boy looked at her and Brett. "I don't see no buggy."

"It's around the bend. I can carry you, Emma, if you need me to." Brett's warm smile must have softened the child's defenses because she reached out her arms. Jimmy scowled when Brett picked up the girl, but he followed, grabbing his shovel as he passed the battered snake.

"We don't want to go back. Me and Emma are huntin' for our pa."

Brett exchanged a glance with Anna. These youngsters wouldn't survive out here alone. "It's best we take you back to wherever you came from. There are wild animals and all kinds of creatures in these hills that could hurt you, especially once the sun sets." Emma tightened her grip on Brett's neck.

"Besides," Anna smiled sweetly to him, "people could be out looking for you. If night falls and you aren't home, people risk their lives trying to find you."

Jimmy huffed a sarcastic laugh. "Ain't nobody lookin' for us, lady. I didn't figure my plan would work anyhow." Jimmy stared at the ground and kicked at a small rock. "Mr. Stout won't like you takin' us back. It's best we go alone."

Anna glanced at the boy. "Who is he?"

Jimmy shrugged. "The boss at the orphanage."

Anna blinked. How could there have been a children's home in Medora that she'd never heard of?

Brett loaded them in the crowded buggy and turned the horse up the trail. Anna didn't want to be rude, but the powerful stench of the children forced her to turn her head away. What kind of person could let such young children wander around alone and in such a horrid condition? She pressed her lips together, thinking she already didn't care for this Mr. Stout.

They traveled up the road Anna had wondered earlier about, and fifteen minutes later, they pulled up in front of an old clapboard house. The white paint had long ago lost its fight for survival with the elements. Two little girls maybe three years old, in the same physical condition as Jimmy and Emma, rocked back and forth together in one rocker.

A man finely dressed in a white shirt, black pants, and a sateen vest shoved his way through the door and stared at them. His guarded gaze shifted to a friendly smile that Anna felt sure was forced. He reminded her of a traveling snake oil salesman she'd once seen in town. "I see you've brought our runaways back. I'm deeply indebted to you folks."

Brett stopped the wagon and stepped down. Emma leaned against Anna as if she were afraid. Irritation fueled a fire growing within her. This man's clothing was new and of a high quality. His hair was oiled down, and his face cleanly shaven. She would bet he didn't smell like the children. How could he tend so well to his own ablutions and yet be oblivious to the children's needs? She wrapped her arm around Emma, wishing she could take the girl home. *Lord, protect these little ones.*

"Jimmy, Emma, hop on down. Miss Stout needs your help in the kitchen. We'll talk about your running away later." The man glared at the boy then his gaze softened as he looked at Anna.

Emma cast a final glance at Anna before following Jimmy into the shabby house. She feared for the children and hoped they wouldn't be punished.

"Thank you for returning our kids. Jimmy seems determined to leave here and find his father—the one who abandoned them when they were small." The man shook his head, a pitying expression on his face that Anna found difficult to believe.

"Forgive me for not introducing myself. I'm Lloyd Stout. My sister Haddie and I run this place. If not for us, these poor waifs would have nowhere to go. Most would probably be dead."

Brett touched the end of his hat but didn't offer Mr. Stout his hand. "Brett Wickham. And this is…Anna McFarland."

Anna's brow crinkled. Why had Brett stumbled over her name?

"My pleasure, Miss McFarland. It is Miss, isn't it?"

Anna nodded, uncomfortable with his unwavering appraisal. Brett watched the man silently with narrowed eyes. Did he, too, feel something was wrong?

"I do apologize for the condition things are in here. Donations to the facility have been lacking lately, even though we have more children than ever before."

Anna wanted to shout at him to spend less on himself and more on the children, but doubted it would make a difference. One thing for certain, even though Mr. Stout was rather nice looking, he would not be going on her list of potential suitors. She couldn't pin down what bothered her, but something wasn't right here.

"We need to get back on the road so we can make it home before dark." Brett climbed back into the buggy without even a goodbye. He made a smooching sound to the horse and jiggled the reins.

As the buggy jostled its way home, Anna realized she'd found something worthwhile to invest her time and money in. She could make life better for those poor orphans.

Chapter Nine

"You are not going back to that place alone." Quinn leaned toward her as if to emphasize his point.

"But I've been riding on this ranch alone as long as we've lived here." Anna figured it was futile to argue with her stubborn brother, she had to try.

"That's different."

Anna pressed her hands to her hips. She could be stubborn too. "How?"

Quinn blinked and straightened. "I don't have time to argue with you. If you insist on going to that orphanage, you'll take one of the hands with you."

Not Brett. She didn't like the confusing thoughts she had in his presence. It might be all right if he showed even the slightest interest in her, but most times, he was indifferent, even cold. On a rare occasion, though, she thought she caught a glimpse of admiration in his sapphire gaze. Was he fighting an attraction to her, knowing her brother would never let one of their hands court her? Or maybe he had someone back home that he'd already given his heart to?

Quinn rubbed the back of his neck. "I've already assigned jobs to the men for today. Brett is the only one I can spare since he's not totally fit yet. But I'm still not convinced he's on the up and up. Take your rifle with you."

Anna sighed, resigning herself to another day with quiet Brett. "He's never been anything less than a gentleman, and he did protect me at risk to himself."

"I know, and that's the only reason I've let him drive you to town. I reckon if he was willing to risk his life for you when he didn't even know you, that you're safe with him now." Her brother slapped on his hat. "I'll have him hitch the buggy."

"I really need to exercise Bella. Do you think Brett's healed enough to ride that far?"

Quinn nodded. "He's been riding some of the green broke horses and doing fine."

He strode out the front door. Anna headed into the kitchen to get the fresh loaves of cinnamon bread that Leyna had made for the children. The scent of sweet baked goods had permeated the house all morning.

"I wrapped the bread in paper and put in here." Leyna held up the burlap bag. "You will tie it onto your saddle, *ja*?"

Anna smiled. "That should work perfectly. The children will love your treat. Thank you for making it for them." She hugged the cook then Leyna handed her a smaller flour sack.

"I packed lunch for you and *Herr* Brett."

Anna lifted her brows at Leyna's humorous smirk. "How did you know Brett would be going with me today?"

Leyna shrugged. "I pray it is so."

"Don't bother trying to matchmake Brett and me. Quinn doesn't seem to like him for some reason, and Brett has shown no interest in me."

Leyna tsked and stirred a bowl of batter. "Young people, what do they know? I see how *Herr* Brett watches you."

Brett watches me?

A warm sensation started in the pit of her stomach and crept through her body, warming her down to her toes. Was it possible he liked her but was afraid to show it?

Anna took the bags from Leyna and moseyed outside. The day suddenly gleamed brighter, and she now looked forward to the ride to town and back with eagerness.

The last thing Brett wanted to do today was escort Lottie to town. The men in the bunkhouse were already teasing him that she was sweet on him. The problem was he liked this side of the female outlaw. The compassion she had for those smelly orphans nearly undid him. He had to keep a barrier up where she was concerned. He couldn't allow her soft side to sway him when he of all people knew what she and her brother were capable of. *Those Sallingers are such great actors they ought to be in the theater.*

Brett shook his head as he led Jasper and Bella out of the barn. Anna's brother had said he'd be escorting her back to the orphanage. He wouldn't mind another look at that dilapidated place. Something fishy was going on there, and he was glad for a chance to figure out what it was. Those poor kids looked mistreated and half starved, while the man who ran the children's home was well fed and immaculately dressed—so much so that he didn't fit there.

The lawman in him simmered. He had no patience for people who mistreated children.

"What's got you in such a dither?"

Brett stopped in front of Lottie, blinking. "What?"

"I said good morning to you, and you never even heard me—and you're scowling."

She looked beautiful in that baby blue shirt and brown riding skirt. Her straw hat hung on her back, and a thin cord cut along her soft throat, making a slight indentation. She carried a large burlap sack and a smaller bag, both bulging.

Brett swallowed and took the sacks from her, tying the smaller one onto Bella's saddle and the larger one to Jasper's. He shouldn't be wondering how soft Lottie's skin was. She pulled her hat onto her sun-kissed hair. He looped Bella's reins over her neck and locked his hands together to boost Lottie up. She quirked a brow at him, but allowed him to assist her. In spite of being over five and a half feet tall, she was light as a cloud. Brett shook his head, reminding himself to never do under-cover work again. He needed to maintain his distance to keep his perspective from getting skewed. His father's harsh words still haunted him. "You're too soft-hearted to be a lawman, Brett."

Lord, help me. Give me wisdom to see justice done and not be swayed by Lottie's beautiful smile or soft touch.

Things seemed overly quiet as they road up to the orphanage. On the trip there, Lottie had expressed her concern for the children. So, she'd noticed too.

On second look, the house was in worse condition than Brett remembered. Nearly all the paint had worn off, leaving a tired, weathered two-story structure that leaned a smidgeon to the right. Any grass near the house had been trampled long ago, leaving only dirt and rocks now. There were no children to be seen.

Lottie cast him a worried glance. "You don't suppose they cleared out, do you?"

The thought had crossed his mind, but he doubted Lloyd Stout would have gone to such trouble. And why should he? It's not as if the man cared about the children that much.

Lottie tied Bella to the porch. Brett removed the large burlap bag from his saddle as she knocked on the door. After a second knock, two tiny urchins came running to the open door, looking uncertain whether to invite them inside. The sun hadn't even crested to noon, and yet these toddlers were filthy. Their clothes were frayed rags, and their hair hung limp and tangled. Did they ever get a bath? Brett's heart twisted for the poor kids.

A tall, thin woman with sharp features appeared behind the children. "May I help you?"

"We were here yesterday. Met a Mr. Stout. We're the ones who found Jimmy and Emma and returned them." Lottie shifted the bag on her shoulder.

Brett trotted up the steps, keeping his eye on the children. While they both leaned against the doorframe, they didn't hide behind the woman's skirts like most shy youngsters would do. Interesting.

The woman's features softened a bit. "Oh, yes, my brother told me about you. I'm Hattie Stout."

Brett resisted chuckling. Stout might describe Hattie's brother, but she was the opposite.

Lottie held up the burlap bag. "We brought you cinnamon bread and a few other things. I also want to offer my services. Is there anything I can help you with?"

The woman's surprised gray eyes sparked a second before dulling again. "Thank you, but I don't think my brother would like me accepting help. He thinks I should be able to handle things here."

"Where are the other children?" Brett wondered where Lloyd Stout was too but didn't ask.

Miss Stout's expression looked panicked for a split second.

Lottie glanced over her shoulder at him. "Why…they're at school, of course."

School. *Sure.* If he were a betting man, he'd be willing to bet they weren't at school by the woman's reaction to Lottie's question. But where else could they be?

He stepped onto the porch, and Miss Stout stepped back—a typical response of a woman afraid of men. Her gaze darted from him to Lottie. Up close, he could see that one of the children had a runny nose. He reached down to pat the waif, but she dodged his hand and ran back into the house.

"They don't take too kindly to strangers, you know. They're afraid someone will take them away from us."

Uh huh. If he believed that, he'd be a sucker for every peddler in the country. More likely they'd been punished for talking to strangers.

"It must be difficult caring for so many children. Why don't you let me bathe these two little ones while you do whatever you were doing before we arrived?"

Miss Stout looked down at the floor. "I guess it wouldn't hurt none if you washed them young'uns, so long as you're gone before my brother returns."

"Wonderful!" Lottie's sweet smile made Brett wish she wasn't an outlaw. Made him wish for things that could never be.

She turned to face him. "I don't suppose you could work on things outside the house? Maybe fix the steps?"

Brett glanced at Miss Stout. "You got a hammer and nails? Spare wood?"

She blinked, then shook her head.

"You could get some at the mercantile. Put them on our account," Lottie said. "I'll probably be a while, getting those babies clean, so you'd have plenty of time."

"Will you be all right?" Brett's train of thought shocked him.

Lottie reached out and touched his arm, sending hot and cold chills charging upward as if he'd been hit by lightening. He wanted to step back and yet step forward at the same time, but he held his ground. "Thank you for your concern, but I'll be fine. See you in a bit."

The dilapidated house swallowed her into its dark mouth. Brett spun away, irritated with himself for worrying about an outlaw's well-being. He climbed onto Jasper, grimacing at the sharp ache that ran through his chest. He stared at the front door. Should he leave or stay? Shaking his head, he reined Jasper around. What had gotten into him?

Ten minutes later, he rode into Medora. A letter to Marshal Cronin burned his pocket, and he was thankful for the chance to get away from Lottie for a while. He'd wanted to send a telegraph but had chosen the more private letter to update his superior on where he was and what he was doing. The marshal should be pleased to learn he'd infiltrated the

Sallingers' hideout so easily. Brett rubbed his chest where the healing scars itched. Well...maybe not so easily.

He paid the postage for the letter and collected the supplies he needed to do minors repairs at the children's home. After tying the boards behind his saddle, he looked around town for someone who might be willing to give him information. He found the man sitting on a bench outside the saloon.

"Buy a feller who's down on his luck a drink, mister?" The bewhiskered old man glanced up with red-rimmed, amber-colored eyes.

Brett stopped and rubbed his chin. Whiskey had a way of loosening a man's lips, but as a Christian, buying liquor didn't sit well with him. "How about I treat you to a hot lunch at the café? I don't particularly like to eat alone."

The man licked his lips and glanced at the saloon door. "I guess I could eat something, if yer willin' to pay for it. The name's Ollie."

The café taunted Brett with it fragrant scents. The cooking in the bunkhouse mostly consisted of beans and cornbread. He missed Leyna's tasty food. He sat at a table in the back with Ollie, and both ordered the fried chicken. The soft hum of conversation blended with the clinking of silverware.

"So, what do you want to know?"

Brett looked at Ollie and grinned. The old timer was sharper than he looked. "What do you know about that orphanage outside of town?"

Ollie shrugged, and his suspender slipped off his frail shoulder. The man would need warmer clothes before winter set in. "Not much. I hear that kids come and go a lot. Seems they tend to get lost too often. Don't care much for the snake that runs the place. I'm betting he takes all the donation money for hisself."

"Where do the kids come from?"

"Don't know. Orphan train, maybe?"

That didn't make sense to Brett. The orphan trains tried to find good homes for children, rather than simply moving them to another orphanage. "Ever heard of kids gone missing in these parts?"

Ollie's eyes rolled up, as if he were searching his mind for an answer. "Nah. Most folks in these parts look after their own. They may be from somewheres else though."

"Know anything about the McFarlands?"

The old man grinned, his yellow teeth as crooked as a New York politician. "Yep, that I do know about. Their old man rode into town one day and paid cash for the Stonecreek Ranch. Then he bought several smaller ranches bordering Stonecreek and changed the name to the Rocking M."

The same woman Brett had seen at the café before set their plates in front of them. Ollie grabbed his fork and dug in. For a time Brett let the conversation subside while they ate. When his food was gone, Ollie sopped up the leftover gravy from his potatoes with his roll.

"Mmm, mmm. That sure tasted good. I thank ya kindly."

Brett nodded once. "You're welcome. I've heard a few folks around here don't like the McFarlands. Why's that?"

Ollie pushed his plate back. "Guess it's because folks didn't like how old man McFarland bought out their friends' ranches after we had a few terrible winters. Then too, them McFarlands shop mostly in Bismarck, and the store owners here don't like that neither."

"Seems like a petty reason to me."

Ollie shrugged and slid his suspender back over his shoulder. "Small town loyalties, ya know. Now me, I'm gonna find that big gold shipment that was lost in the Badlands, then I'll make ever'body happy cause I'll shop all the stores in town." He grinned and leaned back in his chair.

Brett remembered the payroll shipment that had been stolen from a Northern Pacific train several years back. The robbers had been captured, but the gold was never found. Rumor was they'd buried it somewhere in the Badlands. Brett had searched these hills with several other marshals but never found the lost gold. It figured there would still be stories circulating.

Most likely, the Sallingers had taken the money and used it to expand their ranch. Brett tossed coins on the table and stood. "Nice chatting with you, Ollie."

The old man nodded. "Reckon I'll sit here a while a drink more coffee." He smiled and lifted his cup.

Brett nodded and walked out of the café, worrying about Lottie. Was she safe at the orphanage? What would Lloyd Stout do if he returned and found her there?

He glanced at the sun's position in the sky. He'd been gone much longer than he should have. Settling the planks of wood for the steps across his lap, he nudged Jasper back toward the children's home, his thoughts and emotions swirling.

Chapter Ten

"You wouldn't believe the condition of that place, Quinn." Anna sliced off a circle of bratwurst and stuck it in her mouth, along with forkful of Leyna's sauerkraut. Guilt riddled her as the tangy, salty flavor teased her taste buds. Here she was eating a delicious meal when the orphans were eating who knows what. She had to win Quinn over to helping them. "Those poor children are filthy. They don't have decent clothes or shoes, and they look as if they haven't eaten a good meal in months. My heart nearly broke."

Quinn's mouth pinched into a straight line. "I can't abide people abusing children, but I don't know what we can do about it. Maybe talk to the sheriff."

Anna laid her fork down. "Leyna and I were talking. What if we started a foundation to help the children?"

"What's the point of that? Sounds to me like that Stout man would spend any money donated on himself." Quinn spooned three heaping spoons of applesauce onto his plate then proceeded to shovel it into his mouth.

"We find good people to run that place and kick out those bad ones." Leyna refilled Quinn's coffee pot, not the least bit sorry for interrupting their conversation.

"Good idea. But who is actually in charge of the orphanage? Who do we talk to about getting changes made?"

"I'll see if I can find out. Maybe one Saturday we could take a crew to town and have a workday." Quinn sat with his elbows on the table, sipping his coffee. "I don't know about this foundation thing, though. Much of our money is tied up in the ranch."

Ideas swirled through Anna's mind. "Maybe Grandma could get her church involved. The old ladies there like to sew for the unfortunates. Mother would be happy to help with it, I'm sure."

Her brother nodded. "That's not a half bad idea."

Anna smiled at his rare compliment. "I'll need to get a list of all the children and what size clothing they wear. But I don't know how agreeable the Stouts will be." She frowned at her brother. "Miss Stout didn't even want to let me in the house. Once I got in, I could see why. It's not much of a place. Though the rooms were fairly clean, the old furniture was threadbare, what there was of it."

"I imagine furniture wouldn't hold up too well in a house with—what'd you say?—a dozen or so kids."

"I don't really know how many children there are. The older ones haven't been around when we were." Anna spun kraut onto her fork. "And I don't think their furniture is ragged because of the little ones. It looks as if it was someone else's rejects."

"Might have been. Probably most all the furnishings in the home were donated, and folks generally don't get rid of furniture until it's past worn out." He stabbed a hunk of bratwurst.

Anna's gaze drifted to the parlor. They'd brought their furniture with them from Texas when they moved here. The horsehair couch was old but had many years of life left in it. She'd never considered redecorating the parlor before because it was still serviceable. But now…

Filled with an eagerness she couldn't contain, she turned her gaze back to her brother. "What if—"

"No."

"But—"

"No!"

Anna leaned back in her chair and crossed her arms. "You don't even know what I was going to say."

Quinn grinned. "I saw you eyeing our furniture with the look of a trout after a fat, ol' worm."

"Well…so what. It's old."

"It's fine."

"You're so stubborn." She tossed her head and looked out the window.

"That's the pot calling the kettle black." Quinn chuckled as he stood. "We'll find a way to help. Let me think on it—and don't go hauling off our furniture."

She watched him snatch his hat off the peg and leave. She speared another slice of meat and chewed it as if chomping up her frustrating brother. At least he agreed to find a way to help. That's something she could be thankful for.

"You could maybe get the townswomen to help out?" Leyna removed the bowl of kraut and Quinn's plate.

"Why do you suppose they aren't already helping out?"

"Could be they are."

"I've never organized anything before, but I can talk to the church women and see if they'd like to help." Anna shrugged. "But even if they did, I don't know if the Stouts would accept our help. Hattie seemed quite offended that I offered to wash those two toddlers."

"We will just have to pray about it. God will show us what we can do to help."

Anna nodded. She would pray, but her mind raced with all manner of ideas now that she had finally found a worthwhile project in which to invest her time.

The buckboard creaked and groaned over the rocky trail, knocking Anna's shoulder into Brett's. She glanced out the side of her eye at the handsome man. He'd been quiet ever since leaving the ranch. She supposed he was getting tired of escorting her to town.

If she allowed her imagination to take flight, she could pretend they were married. Anna Wickham had a nice ring to it. *Mrs. Brett Wickham.*

She heaved a sigh at her school-girl silliness. At twenty-two, she was closer to being a spinster.

Brett mumbled something, drawing her attention. The sun had browned his skin. His blue eyes and white teeth only enhanced his dark coloring. A scowl tugged at his features.

"Is something wrong?"

Brett rubbed the back of his neck and slid a glance her way. He went back to studying the trail ahead. "It doesn't matter."

"What doesn't?" Now he had her curiosity aroused.

He lifted his hat and ran his hands through his hair, the same color as the chocolate fudge she'd sampled in a Bismarck candy store.

"I probably shouldn't tell you, but you'll hound me all day if I don't. Several of the men are teasing me about being your nursemaid and not doing any real work."

Anna crossed her arms and leaned back against the hard seat. The men at the ranch all liked her so why would they tease about such a thing? She looked across the grasslands at the hills on the horizon.

"Look, this isn't about you." Brett turned toward her on the seat. "But I can't get anything done at the ranch when I'm escorting you all the time."

"Well, I never asked you to." No, but she'd asked Quinn if Brett could escort her. She forced a scowl, sure that it bettered the one he'd worn earlier. "I've been riding this country alone for nearly a third of my life. I'm not a baby and don't need anyone tending me."

She leaned in closer. "In fact, turn this wagon around and go back home."

Brett heaved a sigh, smelling of coffee. "I knew I shouldn't have mentioned it. And besides, look what happened last week with the bear."

"Well…well…that was an isolated incident."

This time he leaned in. "But you nearly got yourself killed. I'm here to see that doesn't happen again."

Up this close, his blue eyes had an almost navy ring around them. His breath wafted over her face. If she leaned a little closer she could kiss him. She wanted to taste his lips on hers. Would he mind?

She looked at his eyes again and saw that he was watching *her* lips. Anna's breath caught in her throat. The wagon dipped, knocking their foreheads together in a painful clunk.

How embarrassing! She faced forward and refused to look at Brett. Had he been about to kiss her? Disappointment battled with relief. What was she thinking?

Looking out across the landscape, she scoured the area, hoping nobody had seen them. Quinn would never let a ranch hand court her, not even one who'd saved her life. She needed to curb her infatuation with Brett, because there was no future for them together.

Having him as her escort didn't help matters. Maybe she should ask Quinn to let Claude drive her. But time sure would pass much slower than it did with Brett, even if he didn't talk all that much.

As they pulled up in front of the children's home an hour later, the two toddlers she'd washed the day before sat in the front porch rocker. Their sunken eyes widened at the sight of her and Brett. The dark-haired waif on the right lifted one hand and waved, but the blond looked frightened.

Brett stopped the buckboard in front of the door and climbed down. He lifted his hands to assist Anna, but she was tempted to climb down the other side alone. Realizing the pettiness of her thoughts, she placed her hands on Brett's shoulders. He lifted her at the waist and set her on the ground. Her hands ran down his arms in a daring gesture as he stared at her with that look of his that made her tremble. Was he thinking about their almost kiss?

Brett stepped away and hoisted a twenty-five-pound sack of flour onto his shoulder. His free hand rubbed across his chest, fingers splayed.

"You shouldn't be lifting such heavy things until your stitches have been removed. Did you hurt yourself?"

"I'm fine." He strode for the door, a scowl planted back on his handsome face.

The toddlers shinnied off the chair and darted through the open door. Anna knocked on the doorframe. Miss Stout soon answered, a damp dish cloth drying her hands.

"Oh, it's you again. What do you want now?" She eyed the bag on Brett's shoulder.

"May we come in and talk to you?" Anna said. "I have a few ideas for helping you and your brother with the children, and we've brought you supplies."

"Lloyd don't want you two coming around no more. I got in trouble for letting you in yesterday."

"Could Mr. Wickham at least put this sack of flour in your kitchen? He's had a recent injury and shouldn't even be lifting it."

Miss Stout's gaze flitted back and forth between them. "I didn't order no flour."

"It's a gift from the Rocking M Ranch. We've got sugar, bread, and a few other things in the wagon too."

The woman's eyes brightened at the mention of sugar, and she stepped back. "The kitchen's this way. I sure hope I don't get hollered at for this. At least I can make Lloyd a cake now. He does like his sweets."

Anna pursed her lips. "The donations are for the children, not particularly Mr. Stout."

"Well, I know that. I didn't mean nothin' by it."

Brett set the bag on the floor of the big kitchen. An old cast iron stove took up one corner with a worktable beside it. A basin of water and a stack of clean dishes and mismatched cups cluttered the counter. On the far wall was a large, worn table with two chairs at each end and benches on the sides. No paint, wallpaper, or pictures adorned the plain wood walls. The back door stood open like the front, and one lone window near the stove was open. A cool but comfortable breeze blew through the room.

"I'll fetch the other bags." Brett rolled his shoulders as he left the room.

Anna's gaze followed him. She turned her focus back on Miss Stout.

"I want to help you improve things here for the children. I thought I could measure each child to see what size they wear and then get my grandmother's sewing circle to make each child a set of clothes."

Miss Stout fiddled with the edge of her frayed apron. "Lloyd ain't gonna like that. He thinks we's the only ones what should take care of them young'uns."

Anna wanted to win this woman to her side for the sake of the children. "I understand, but you have what—a dozen children?"

"Eleven."

"Surely any woman with eleven children would need help. What's the age of the oldest?"

"I don't know for sure. Maybe twelve."

The two urchins from the porch peered around the doorjamb when Brett carried in the bag of sugar. He dumped it beside the flour and left again, the children scattering as he walked in their direction.

"How many little ones are here? I've seen two. Are there more?"

"Just one. He's asleep."

"How old are they?" Anna walked back into the parlor, looking for the little ones. She stepped back as Brett carried in a crate of various canned fruits and vegetables.

"Don't really know. "Two. Three maybe."

Anna spun around, making Miss Stout's eyes go wide. "How can you not know their ages? Where do the children come from?"

Miss Stout retreated back to the worktable. She picked up a mug and dried it, then set it aside and picked up another. "Lloyd generally finds the young'uns. Once in a while someone will bring us one. Nobody never tells me their age."

Hattie was getting defensive, so Anna dropped the age topic. "Do you mind if I measure the younger children for clothes?"

Miss Stout shrugged. "Guess it wouldn't hurt none. Junie, Suzanne, you two get in here."

The woman finished drying another cup and watched the doorway. When the children didn't come, she smacked the tin mug down hard on the counter. "Don't make me get my switch. You two get in here."

The patter of tiny bare feet announced the arrival of the two waifs as they ran into the room. Both looked frightened half to death.

Anna's heart melted. The poor dears. She knelt down and looked them in the eye. "Remember me from yesterday? We had fun when I gave you both a bath."

Junie nodded, but Suzanne only sucked her thumb and clung to Junie's shabby dress.

"Well…I know some nice ladies who want to make you new clothes, and I need to measure you so they know how big to make them. Is that all right?"

Junie nodded again. Anna made quick order of measuring the two and then the baby boy who slept in a dresser drawer on a dingy blanket. Anna wanted to be angry with the Stouts, but the fact of the matter was, they *had* given the children a home when nobody else wanted them. Granted it wasn't much, but they had a roof over them and food to eat. She tried not to judge the Stouts too severely for not doing a better job. Raising eleven children was a huge job, especially if you weren't related to them.

"Thank you, Miss Stout. I'll be able to send these measurements on ahead of the others so the women can get started on them." She hadn't exactly asked the sewing group yet, but she knew their hearts, having visited her grandmother and met her friends.

"Everything's unloaded. Are you done?" Brett stood in the doorway, filling up the whole opening.

"I suppose." Junie and Suzanne could already use another bath, but they'd probably go hide if they knew her thoughts.

Brett handed Anna up into the wagon and joined her. As the buckboard pulled away from the house, Anna looked over her shoulder. Junie and Suzanne were climbing back into their rocker.

Now that she thought about it, she hadn't seen a single toy. Maybe she could make dolls for the girls—if she'd ever learn to sew. "I need to go into town before we head home."

Brett peered at her with raised brows but guided the wagon toward Medora at the fork instead of the Rocking M.

As they passed the tiny schoolhouse a few minutes later, Anna got an idea. "Stop! Stop!"

Brett yanked back on the reins and spun toward her. "What's wrong?" His gaze quickly glanced at her then scanned the area around them as he reached for his rifle.

Anna giggled. "Sorry. I didn't mean to alarm you. I thought since we were at the schoolhouse that I could see if it would be possible to measure the other children. It would speed things up tremendously, because I want to mail a letter with their sizes to my grandma while we're in town."

Brett's sighs were getting familiar. He shook his head and helped her down. About a dozen children played in the yard, but she didn't see Jimmy and Emma. Brett followed her, dodging the lunch pails and containers lining the stairs. Inside, a young woman sat behind a desk. The room smelled of wood and chalk dust.

"May I help you?"

Anna introduced herself and Brett. "I'm helping gather clothing for the children at the orphanage. I was wondering if you'd mind my measuring the orphans while I'm here."

The pretty blond scrunched up her nose. "I don't see what that has to do with me."

Anna moved closer. "I just thought since you're the teacher I should ask your permission before approaching them."

The teacher stood. "I think there's been a mistake. None of the children from the orphanage attend school here. I was under the impression they were taught at the Home."

Chapter Eleven

Lottie sidled a worried glance at Brett. "Uh...we were led to believe the older children were at school."

The teacher wrung her hands. "Oh, dear. This is highly irregular. I'll have to talk to Mr. Richter, the school board chairman. Although I don't know how I'd handle any more children than I have now."

"Don't worry about it, ma'am. We'll find out what's going on. We must have misunderstood." Brett took hold of Lottie's arm and ushered her out the door. In spite of her bewildered look, she didn't fight him.

"Why did you say we misunderstood?"

As they descended the steps, Brett glanced over his shoulder to make sure the door had closed. "I'm not ready for that teacher to stir things up and alert Stout that we're suspicious of him."

She leaned against his side as they headed for the buggy, causing a stirring in his gut that he didn't want to acknowledge. "I knew something wasn't right over there. What do you think's going on?"

"I don't know, but I aim to find out." He helped her into the wagon and climbed in. He guided it on into town and stopped at the sheriff's office. They stepped inside, but the office was empty.

Lottie casually studied a wooden door with a small barred window that Brett assumed led to the jail cells. "Now what?"

"I don't know." He tried to rub the tension out of the back of his neck, halfway surprised that Lottie hadn't bucked at the idea of entering the sheriff's office. She'd marched right in as if she'd never once done anything illegal. Even now she seemed completely at ease. "Unless..."

"Unless what?"

He stared out the window for a moment, hoping to see the sheriff. He had questions for the man. "I could come back in the morning and trail the older kids. See where Stout takes them."

"I'll ride with you."

"No." He spun to face her. "It could be dangerous."

"I'm not afraid. I've been in dangerous situations before."

Brett clenched his jaw. He bet she had. He stared into her coffee-colored eyes, wishing things were different. What was he looking for? Guilt?

Her cheeks flushed a bright pink at his perusal, and she looked away. "Fine."

Lord, why does the only woman who I ever wanted have to be an outlaw?

If only…

He stormed out the door toward the post office with Lottie on his heels. "You're too soft…" His father's words haunted him again. Maybe he was right.

All Brett needed was evidence tying Jack and Lottie to the bank robbery, then he could go home and start a new chapter in his life. He had to get inside the McFarland house again.

His boots echoed on the wooden floor as he strode into the post office. "Got any letters for Brett Wickham?" he asked the postmaster.

The thin man shook his head. "No, haven't received nothing for you. Sorry."

Brett nodded his thanks. Lottie sashayed past him to the counter.

"I'd like to purchase two sheets of paper and an envelope with postage to Bismarck." She turned to Brett. "Do you mind waiting while I pen a note to my grandmother?"

He shook his head and went outside. Leaning against a post, he thought about Lloyd Stout. What could he be doing with the older children?

Lottie had told him that Hattie had said her brother was the one who usually brought the children to the orphanage. So…where was he finding them?

Brett marched back inside. Lottie peeked up from her letter writing and smiled. His insides turned to liquid fire, knowing that smile was for him alone. He was in big trouble.

Focusing back on the task at hand, he stopped at the counter. "Could you answer a question for me?"

"I'll try." The postmaster, a thin man with round spectacles, stacked a pile of envelopes he was sorting.

"Did you ever hear of any children going missing much in these parts?"

The man narrowed his gaze. "That's an odd question."

"Humor me."

"Well, not so much around here, but there *have* be stories over the past years of children around Dickinson and even as far off as Mandan and Bismarck going missing."

"Hmm…" With the train, a trip to Bismarck could be done in half a day or less. Stout could easily travel to another town, find a child, and bring it back to the orphanage with nobody the wiser and a set of grieving parents left behind wondering what happened to their beloved child. The lawman in him smelled a rat. Still, he had no proof.

Lottie sealed her envelope and handed it to the postmaster. Brett followed her outside into the bright afternoon, trying hard to ignore how the sun glistened on the golden hair that hung below her straw hat. Swallowing hard, he forced his thoughts to what he'd do with Lloyd Stout if his suspicions were right. If only he hadn't lost his badge. Although he was still a deputy marshal, he had no way to prove it, and he'd be risking Lottie finding out he was a lawman if he made a move on the Stouts.

A man dressed in a stiff white shirt and black pants jogged toward Lottie. "I thought I saw you in town, Miss McFarland. Got a telegram for you."

Lottie paid the man and opened the thin paper. She gasped and looked up at Brett. "My mother is coming home on Friday."

Brett knew she must be happy since her mother had been gone so long.

"Oh, dear. We have so much to do. We need to air out her room, and…" Her cheeks flushed. "You aren't interested in all that."

She snagged his arm and tugged him down the street. "I need to stop at the mercantile and get more fabric. I want to make dolls for those little girls. Did you notice they didn't have any toys at all?"

Brett shook his head. He hadn't thought of such a trivial detail, although now that he did, he wondered about it. Why wouldn't an orphanage have any toys? Maybe they were in a playroom instead of the parlor, not that the place looked big enough to have a separate play area.

Excitement glittered in Lottie's eyes. "I'm not a very good seamstress, but I hope it's not too late to learn. I never cared about sewing for myself, but I think making something for the orphans would be very satisfying."

Suddenly, she stopped and spun toward him. "Oh! I should telegraph ma and have her bring more supplies to replenish the ones we gave the children's home."

Just that fast, she was off in another direction, tugging him along as if he belonged to her and had nothing else to do but her bidding. He shook his head, frustrated that he didn't mind at all. Glancing heavenward, he cast another plea to God. So far, his prayers to distance his heart weren't working. If he didn't find evidence soon, he might have to leave and allow another lawman to do that task. He didn't like failing, but he could not—would not—allow himself to fall in love with an outlaw—and he feared that was close to happening.

He halted in his tracks, jerking Lottie to a stop. She looked at him. "What's wrong?"

"You go tend to your errands. I...uh...have several things I need to do."

Her warm smile added salt to his wounded heart. "All right. I'll meet you at the wagon in a half hour or so."

Spinning around, Brett strode away. Out of politeness, he nodded to a couple he passed as he crossed the street. Lottie had confessed her hatred for sewing before, so why was she willing to do something she disliked so that she could make dolls for the children? How could a cold-blooded outlaw care so much for a handful of dirty kids?

Oh, he cared, too, but then he wasn't a man on the run. Could it be Jack had forced Lottie to take part in the robberies? If she'd never killed anyone and was willing to testify against her brother, she might be able to get a light sentence.

But she'd benefited greatly from the money stolen in the robberies. She had one of the nicest homes he'd seen in the whole area, and a fine ranch that seemed to be successful.

At the buckboard, Brett unhitched the horses and led them to a trough. After they drank their fill, he found a patch of grass and hobbled the animals so they could graze for a short while.

Leaning against a tree, he watched a hawk gliding high in the sky. Lazy, feathery clouds drifted by as the warm sun burned the last of the morning's chill away. He thought of Taylor. His brother had been so excited to see him again and to share the news of his successful cattle drive. Taylor had a promising future. A pretty gal would have snagged his attention—if she hadn't already. The fact that he didn't even know if his brother had been sweet on a girl nagged at him. He should have known. Should have written more. Should have gone home more often.

But he hadn't, and his own stubbornness had cost him the last years he could have spent with Taylor. Lottie captured his gaze as she walked toward him carrying a large package, her green skirt swishing back and forth like a bell. She looked so young and deceptively innocent. She waved and smiled, making his outlaw heart do things he didn't want it to do.

Striding toward the horses, he struggled to keep the picture of his brother's limp body in his mind. Cold and dead.

No female thief was going to steal his heart. He refused to allow it.

Anna watched the North Dakota landscape slowly drift by as the wagon headed toward home. Brett's constant mood changes were more perplexing than trying to figure out the North Dakota weather. One moment he was smiling at her, the next, he was scowling. Anna wasn't sure if he actually liked her or merely tolerated her.

Oh, there were times she was sure he cared for her like when he'd stare deeply into her eyes, and then there was the time she thought for sure he would kiss her. But he'd never voiced an interest in her and seemed to only be doing his job. Anna sighed. Why did men have to be so perplexing?

What would it be like to have a man like her enough to not kowtow to Quinn? Maybe more men would come calling after her mother returned. Before she went to Bismarck, they'd even had Saturday visitors on occasion, but not for the past year. Anna wondered if her mother would stay on the ranch or just visit. Grandma was better but still had a hard time getting around. If only Grandma would move to the ranch, but she wasn't ready to give up her home and friends.

Anna's shoulder bumped into Brett's arm as the wagon dipped into another rut. Tingles shot through her body, and she rubbed her arm from shoulder to elbow. Why did his touch affect her so?

She shook her head, trying to dislodge the confusing thoughts of her escort and considered how to go about making a doll. She'd gotten plain linen for the faces and various yardages of different colored fabric to make clothes with. There was also extra heavy thread for the facial features, and even yellow and brown yarn for hair. Maybe they could make the dolls' hair and eye color match the children? That would work for the girls, but what about the boys?

A rabbit zigzagged across the road up ahead. She watched it until it disappeared under a juniper shrub. Off to her right, the Badlands' buttes rose up in a majestic display. She often thought that God must have been angry when he created this part of the country. While the Badlands held a craggy beauty of its own, most folks considered this area rugged and barren. And yet amidst all the rocks and boulders, God had created bountiful grasslands, perfect for raising cattle—if only they could survive the tough winters.

Bored with the silence, she turned to Brett. "Do you think you'll ever go back to your ranch?"

He stared ahead, his expression blank. "Probably."

"You never told me if you have any siblings."

A muscle in his cheek quivered. "I had a younger brother, but he's dead."

Anna laid her hand on his arm, drawing his gaze. "I'm so sorry, Brett. Quinn can be bossy and stubborn, but I'm thankful I have him. I can't imagine what it would be like to lose him. It's hard enough not having Adam at home, even though I know that one day he and Mariah will return."

Brett scowled and refocused on the road. Obviously, he wasn't in a talking mood. Again. She liked him more than any man she'd ever met, and yet she knew so little about him. And it looked as if she wasn't going to learn any more today. At least she no longer thought he was a rustler. Rustlers wouldn't attend church or show such an interest in parentless children.

She allowed her thoughts to drift to the orphans. What could Mr. Stout be doing with the older ones? She had no idea but was determined to find out.

Back home in her room, Anna stared in the mirror as she untied her bonnet. Did Brett find her pretty? She'd always wished she had blue eyes like Adam's. Even though he was her twin, she looked more like Quinn.

She brushed a leaf from her hair. She needed a bath to get the layer of dust off her after the long trip to town and back. Next time she took the wagon, she'd take a book. When Brett wasn't in the mood to talk, the trip was quite boring. One could only look at rocks and grass for so long.

She pulled open a drawer and tugged out her nightgown. Her gaze landed on the glimmering gold coins from the bank. They'd skipped her mind. She really needed to return them. After her bath, she'd see if Quinn had forty dollars in paper money to replace the coins. Then she'd pen a letter to the bank explaining how the double eagles accidentally fell into her reticule when that female outlaw knocked her down. Shivering at the memory, Anna laid the coins on her dresser and went to take a bath.

Chapter Twelve

The morning sun crested over the rocky buttes east of the Rocking M. Anna pushed Bella hard, anxious to arrive at the orphanage before Lloyd Stout could leave with the older children. Her mare eagerly responded to Anna's gentle nudge to gallop after being locked in a corral for days.

The cool morning breeze whipped dust in Anna's face and made her eyes water, but it felt exhilarating to be on horseback again. She'd never ride in a buggy or wagon if she didn't have to.

A herd of mule deer dashed away when Bella cantered through a pass and startled them. The animals scattered in three directions, darting back and forth, joining up again before they disappeared over the next hill.

Anna peeked over her shoulder and smiled, knowing she'd managed to sneak away without Quinn or Brett finding out. She'd left Leyna a note that she'd gone riding and wouldn't be there for breakfast. The slice of bread and cheese she'd eaten would sustain her for now.

As she neared the orphanage, she slowed Bella to a walk and allowed the mare to cool down. She located a nice little draw where Bella could graze and be fairly well hidden and dismounted. After securing her mare, Anna climbed up the top of the nearest butte and jogged forward until the roof of the orphanage came into view.

Ducking low, she hurried to a large red cedar tree guarding the valley below like a lone sentinel. A thin trail of smoke drifted up from the kitchen area of the orphanage. From her vantage point, Anna could see that the roof needed immediate attention, but if she were to tell Brett or Quinn that, they'd want to know how she knew. Better they find out for themselves.

Squatting behind the trunk of the cedar, she waited. Half an hour later, two older boys who looked almost in their teens came out the back door. One headed to the privy while the other began tugging tools out of a lean-to affixed to the back of the house and tossing them on the ground.

Soon, children of varying sizes came outside and searched through the pile of rusted shovels and picks until each found a specific one. Anna counted the children. Eight. With the three smaller ones left in Hattie's care that made eleven. So the woman hadn't lied about that.

Lloyd Stout exited the house and stretched. The largest boy came out of a dilapidated barn leading a healthy buckskin. Mr. Stout took the reins, looped them over the horse's neck, and climbed on—not without much effort on his part. He yelled something to the children, but Anna couldn't make out the words.

Anger bolted through her as the ragtag group of barefoot children plodded after their leader, each carrying a tool. Why, Mr. Stout's horse was better fed than those poor kids. She watched until the group went around a bend and she could no longer see them. She debated whether to follow on foot or horseback, and finally opted on riding Bella. At least the mare would be nearby if she needed a quick getaway.

Bella carefully made her way down a steep incline past the orphanage, and Anna easily picked up the trail. Obviously, the children had walked this path many times because there were multiple footprints both heading toward and away from the Home.

Close to a mile past the orphanage, the children diverted to a smaller path that led between two buttes. On either side of her were a multitude of holes someone had dug as if looking for something. She scowled, knowing that the children had most likely been forced to dig them.

As she crested the next hill, her heart nearly flew out of her chest. Lloyd Stout came into view, still mounted on his fine horse. He looked as if he were dressed to go to a business meeting rather than a day in the hills to work. Then again, Anna doubted he did much other than supervise. She could imagine him lounging on a blanket, eating and drinking, while shouting orders to the poor children, forced to do his bidding.

Her fist tightened around the reins. Mr. Stout motioned to his right and dismounted. Anna backed Bella up and secured her in a small ravine off the trail, then made her way toward the sounded of plinking and clunking. She managed to climb up a boulder behind where Mr. Stout had sat down on a big rock shaded by a trio of quaking aspens. The children were spread out in groups of two, one child with a pick and another with a shovel. The bigger child in each group wielded the pick and loosened the hard, rocky soil while the younger one shoveled the dirt.

What were they doing? They had to be searching for something, but what could be buried way out here?

Anna wanted to charge down there and rescue the children this very moment, but she had the sense to know that would be a dumb idea. Lloyd Stout could easily overpower her.

She backed away, knowing if she didn't return to the ranch, Quinn would go looking for her. If she told him what she'd seen, he'd be furious that she'd ridden this far from the Rocking M without a companion. Mounted on Bella, she headed for home. Maybe her best bet would be to tell Brett what she'd seen. He'd know what to do about the situation and wouldn't send her packing to Bismarck like her brother would.

She urged Bella into a gallop, knowing something had to be done for those needy children—and soon.

Brett carried the two bridles he'd repaired into the tack room and lit the lantern, illuminating the small area lined with saddles, harnesses, and head gear. Sniffing the scent of leather, an odor he never tired of breathing, he hung up the pair of bridles, proud of the job he'd done repairing them.

He looked around the small room. He'd searched the whole barn, twice, hoping to find a hidey hole for stolen loot, but he'd come up empty. Bouncing on the boards of the tack room, he looked for a loose one that could be easily pried up. But there were no scratches out of the ordinary, no place to hide anything. Every square inch was used for storing equipment. Latching the door, he turned and faced the house. He needed to get back inside somehow.

"Help me out here, Lord."

The other ranch hands were out rounding up cattle for branding. Though it was autumn, Quinn informed him they generally had a second round of branding. The first round was held in late spring, but this next round was to brand late calves and any new stock they'd accumulated over the summer.

Brett rubbed his chest, hoping he'd be of some help. He hated doing menial jobs but knew his body wasn't yet ready for the more vigorous ranch work. He grabbed a curry comb and brushed the burrs out of Jasper's tail, then his mane. His gelding sniffed his hand, hoping for a treat. "You'd like an apple or carrot, wouldn't you, ol' boy?"

Jasper nickered as if answering and bobbed his head.

"I'd like to ride out and head home, but I'll always be sorry if I don't finish this job."

But everyday that went by, he became less and less certain that the McFarlands were actually the Sallingers. They were just plain too nice to be outlaws. Oh, Quinn could be crotchety, but he was fair, and had been extremely patient and had encouraged Brett to not worry about taking it easy until he was totally healed. The two outer scrapes from the bear's claw had healed nicely, but the inner two were deeper and still pained him. How long before he could do a man's full day of work?

He snapped a lead onto Jasper's halter and led his horse outside, setting him loose in a small pasture with plenty of grass to feed on. His gelding bucked and leaped like a young colt, happy to be freed of the confines of his stall. Warm sunshine battled with the light chill, promising a glorious day.

Brett leaned his arms on the fence railing, watching as Jasper settled and ducked his head to graze. He twisted the lead rope in his hand. He had to get back to his own ranch before winter set in. There was so much that needed doing, unless the hands had been diligent to keep the place going. But with Taylor gone, Brett had no idea if the hands had absconded with his cattle or not. How long would a man continue working when nobody was paying him? How loyal were the men to Taylor?

He didn't have a lot of money but had saved most of what he'd earned—and he still had that bank draft for the cattle. Hopefully, that would keep the ranch running for a while. He needed to write to the foreman and let the man know he intended to pay everyone as soon as possible.

Hoofbeats drew his attention back to the present, and he turned around. Lottie rode in on Bella, pulling the mare to a stop outside the barn. The woman sat a horse well and rode like she'd been doing it all her life. A wide smile brightened her face, and the sun gleamed off the yellow braid hanging down her back. Why couldn't she be as ugly as three-day-old stew and mean as a cougar?

It would sure make things easier for him. Sighing, he walked toward her and held Bella's bridle as Lottie dismounted.

"Fine day for riding." Lottie smiled and patted her horse on the neck.

"Yep, it is." Brett led Bella into the barn, hoping Lottie wouldn't follow. He put the horse in her stall and swapped the bridle for a halter, then gave her a bucket of feed. Lottie followed and uncinched the saddle. She started to tug it off, but Brett reached for.

"I'll get it." His hand landed on top of Lottie's, and his gaze met hers. He should move away, but his feet were stuck, as if trapped in quicksand.

"Um...thanks." Cheeks flaming, Lottie tugged her hands free and picked up a brush.

Brett forced himself into motion, certain that his ears matched her face. What was he thinking, staring at Lottie like that? The problem was he enjoyed working side-by-side with her. What would it be like to do that everyday? To wake up beside her? To hold her close each morning?

Brett wished for a bucket of cold water to douse his head in. He yanked off the saddle. The only way he and Lottie would ever be together was if he joined her in a jail cell.

He kicked open the tack room door and slung the saddle onto the block where it belonged. This room reminded him of the one on his own ranch. Tending tack had always been something he found rewarding. Well-cared for leather would last years longer than if it were neglected. Was his ranch being neglected?

Lottie cleared her throat, and he turned. She leaned against the doorjamb, blocking his exit. "I have a confession. I didn't simply go riding, I went back to the orphanage."

Clenching his teeth, Brett glared at her. "You're not supposed to go there alone."

She shrugged. "I told you I could take care of myself." Her high-minded attitude seemed to shift as her expression softened. "Oh, Brett. You should have seen those poor children. That man has them digging all day, hunting for something."

Thoughts swirled in his mind. "I wonder what he thinks is out there."

"I don't know, but we've got to find out."

Brett shook his head. "It won't happen any time soon. We leave for roundup today. You know that."

Lottie crossed her arms and kicked at a tuft of hay. "I can't stand the thought of those children hurting and us not doing anything."

"I know." He stepped toward her, wishing he could offer more comfort than mere words.

"Maybe I shouldn't go on the roundup and ride into town instead and talk to the sheriff."

Brett took hold of her upper arms, drawing her gaze to his. "You'll do no such thing. Lloyd Stout could be dangerous. He obviously doesn't mind hurting innocents. Exactly what do you think he'd do to a beautiful woman, off all by herself? You'll go on the roundup, just like I will, and when we get back, we'll think up a way to help the children."

She glared at him, jerked away, and stomped out of the barn. Maybe he should say something to Quinn about his sister and her foolish notions. He shook his head. The boss was busy enough with getting things ready for a three-day roundup. Brett would just have to keep his eye on Lottie and make sure she didn't do anything else stupid.

As he brushed Bella down, his thoughts returned to the Bar W and all of the memories he'd made there—some good, some not so good. What would be the point of having such a place with no family to share it with?

Maybe he ought to just sell it. If he couldn't share it with the woman of his choosing, the Bar W would be a lonely place.

Brett shook his head, trying to dislodge the thought of Lottie living at the Bar W with him. Maybe that hit on his head during that bear attack had done more damage than he'd realized.

Chapter Thirteen

Brett lounged against a downed tree and studied the flickering campfire. His body cried out for rest after three days of herding cattle and branding. In the morning, they'd be leaving these hills and going back home. No, not home, but back to the bunkhouse—or cabin, in Jack and Lottie's case.

Lottie stood beside her brother laughing at something he'd said. She looked tired but exhilarated. At first, he'd been worried about her riding among the herd and doing a man's job, but she'd proved herself more than capable with her expert roping and even wielding a hot brand like a cowpoke. Sleeping outside didn't even appear to bother her. She would make the perfect rancher's wife, if only…

Why would Jack allow her to live among the ranch hands like this and to risk her life cutting cantankerous cattle from the herd? Brett didn't like the protectiveness surging through him. Was he simply trying to protect her so that he could see justice done? Or were his feelings more personal?

Getting emotionally involved would only make his job harder.

Brett nodded his thanks as Cookie handed him a plate of stew and biscuits. His mouth watered as he took a bite of the still warm bread.

Claude, the old-timer, eased down onto the trunk next to Brett. "Whew, long day, huh?"

Brett nodded, wondering how the man had lasted all day. Quinn had wanted to leave him at home, but Claude had insisted he still had it in him to do one more roundup.

"These old bones ain't what they used to be. Let me tell you, son, enjoy life while you're young. Don't end up an old codger with no place of his own." He shoved a spoonful of stew into his mouth. "Now, don't get me wrong, I love it here, but a young fellow like you should dream bigger than working for someone else all his life."

Brett contemplated Claude's words. The man couldn't know he'd been considering selling his ranch. Was this God's way of telling him he was wrong to go down that path?

"If you could do life over, would you change things?"

Claude wheezed a laugh. "I reckon most of us would. But it took a lot of hard livin' and getting rid of stubbornness to get me where I am today—and I don't mean here on the Rocking M, but right with God. I was a fool when I was younger. Thought I was smarter than everyone else, but now I know better."

Brett finished his stew then sopped up the remaining broth with his last biscuit. He needed to pray about the ranch. If he kept it, he'd always have a home. He'd lived on the range for the last five years, and while it was all right for a man his age, he couldn't see living that vagabond life the rest of his days. He wanted to settle. He wanted to go home.

Brett set his plate on the ground. "How long have you worked for the McFarlands?"

Claude looked up at the sky and scraped his wrinkled hand over his bristly jaw. "Don't rightly know. I reckon Quinn was around five or six when I started workin' for his pa. The twins were only babes back then."

"That must had to have been over twenty years."

Claude nodded as he yawned. "Yep. Good folks, them McFarlands. Not many would keep on an old man like me."

Brett watched Quinn as he unsaddled his horse. He didn't want to like him in case he turned out to be Jack Sallinger, but the man was more than fair with his employees. Sure, they worked hard but they ate well, had a decent place to stay with clean bedding washed weekly, and got Sundays off. "Does Quinn come and go much?"

Snorting a laugh, Claude shook his head. "That man don't hardly leave his land. The women have to twist his arm to get him to go to Bismarck to buy supplies."

Brett was more confused than ever. Things didn't add up. Standing, he stretched and looked at Claude. "Thanks for the advice."

The old timer's faded blue eyes twinkled, and he nodded. "Glad to be of help."

Brett dropped his tin plate in the pile of dirty ones and decided to stretch his legs before turning in. He checked on Jasper and gave the horse a brisk pat before heading out of camp. Stones clattered behind him, and his hand instinctively reached for his pistol as he spun around. The light from the campfire illuminated a person's shadow. A woman's shadow.

Lottie held up her hands. "Whoa, don't shoot me, cowboy." Humor laced her words.

Brett relaxed, glad that the darkness shielded his embarrassment at overreacting. "Sorry. Guess I'm jumpy because of that bear attack."

"Makes sense. Do you care if I walk with you?" She eased up beside him.

How could he explain that the last thing he wanted was to be alone with her in the dark?

"If you want."

They walked in silence for a short ways, the moonlight casting its faint glow on the rocky ground. Beside him, Lottie stumbled, and he grabbed for her.

"Thanks. Mind if I hold on to your arm? It's harder to see out here than I'd expected."

Yes, he minded, but he couldn't very well tell her that. "Sure. Go ahead."

She looped her arm through his, and Brett clenched his teeth at the sparks shooting through him. *Lord, help me not to be attracted to Lottie.*

"The roundup's gone well. I sure will be glad to sleep in my own bed though." Lottie giggled, a very pleasant sound to Brett's ears.

"You sure handled yourself well out here. I didn't know you were such a cowgirl."

"There are lots of things you don't know about me. And thanks for the compliment."

He knew she was an outlaw. What would she say if he told her that?

"Don't forget I lived over half my life in Texas. I grew up riding and chasing cattle."

"What did your mom think of that?"

"She tried to make me act more like a girl, but with two brothers, it wasn't easy. I wanted to be just like them, and my pa. Besides, Ma's not a half bad cowgirl herself."

Brett figured if they kept talking, he would forget about her clinging to his arm and what her closeness did to him. "How did your father die?"

Lottie tsked, much liked he'd heard Leyna do. Brett grinned in the dark.

"It was a terrible accident. He was returning home when a big storm hit. Rain turned to ice and made the trail slick. We think his heavily loaded wagon must have slipped off the edge of the trail where there's a steep drop-off. We found his body, the smashed wagon, and dead horses the next day."

"I'm sorry about that. Must have been quite a shock." Brett laid his free hand over hers.

"It was. I can still remember it. Adam and I were only fourteen. Adam took it really hard. In fact, we just found out last year that he blamed himself."

Brett stopped walking. "Why?"

"Pa had told him to replace one of the wagon wheels that was cracked. Adam was sketching that morning and got caught up in his drawing and didn't change it. All this time he's blamed himself, even to the extent that he quit drawing for many years."

"But it wasn't his fault, was it?"

Lottie's arm lifted and dropped as she shrugged. "I don't think so. How could we ever know for sure, but nobody blames him. It was an unfortunate accident."

"I understand now why Quinn is so protective of you."

Anna heaved a sigh. "I'll probably end up an old maid because he won't let any man get close enough to get to know me."

Brett couldn't help noticing how close *he* was to her. Was Jack aware that his ranch hand—a U.S. marshal, at that—was walking with his sister in the dark? He couldn't help smiling at the irony of it all. Yes siree, he'd captured Lottie Sallinger without as much as a fuss. The problem was…she had captured his heart. He swallowed the lump in his throat.

Of course, he had no proof he was a marshal, not without his badge. He'd been meaning to go search for it along the creek bed where the bear attack had occurred but hadn't been able to get away yet.

"So what are we going to do about the orphans?"

Brett halted and turned to face her. His shadow blocked the moon's light from her face, so he took a step sideways. "Tell me again what you saw."

"Oh, Brett. It was awful. That scoundrel has those poor children digging in the dirt, looking for something. I imagine they're probably shoveling dirt all day. It pains me to think about it. We have to help them"

"Did you tell your brother what you saw?"

She shook her head. "He's been too busy with the roundup. I can't sleep at night thinking about how awful things are for the orphans. I have to do something. I can't let them keep suffering."

She clutched his forearms. "They were digging with shovels—barefoot. Can you imagine how that must hurt?"

Her concern for the youngsters about did him in. He wanted to pull her into his arms and comfort her. "I knew something wasn't right there."

"Stout is using them like prisoners."

"Listen to me. I don't want you going there alone again. If you have to go, I'll go with you."

"What about Quinn and your job here?"

"I'll quit my job if I have to."

Anna smiled, looking up at him with those big brown eyes as if he were her hero. The light breeze whipped a strand of spun gold across her cheek. His mouth went dry, and he forced himself not to look at her lips. Oh, brother, was he in hot water.

Anna couldn't help smiling at Brett's protectiveness. Why, he sounded as if he really cared for her. If only he'd kiss her…

But something was holding him back.

"What do you think they could be searching for?"

Brett shrugged. "I have no idea."

"That area is rugged. As far as I know nobody has ever lived there."

Brett suddenly let go of her arm and snapped his fingers. "I know. I heard mention in town of a payroll shipment that some outlaws had buried in the Badlands around Medora. That must be what they're hunting."

Anna gasped. "I bet you're right. What else could it be?"

"I need to see for myself. I'll ride out at dawn the day after tomorrow if things work out and follow them like you did."

"I'll go with you."

"No, you stay home." Brett laid his hands on her shoulders and tightened his grasp as if he meant business.

"You can't force me to stay home. Besides, how will you explain your being gone to Quinn?"

Brett remained silent. Anna wished she could see his face, but his back was to the moon. At dinner, she'd watched him across the campfire. He looked even more handsome with stubble darkening his cheeks and his face tanned from the sun. Her stomach had done funny things, as if there were critters in it turning somersaults. Was she falling in love? Is that why she tingled all over whenever he touched her?

"I'll tell Quinn I want to ride out and watch the sunrise and want you to escort me—and we *will* watch it, so I'll be telling the truth. All right?"

Brett rolled his head, trying to work the tension out of his neck. "I guess that would work, but I want you to stay back if things go bad."

"What do you intend to do?"

"Nothing yet. I want to see what's going on, then I'll go to the sheriff."

"Thank you, Brett. It means so much to me that you're willing to risk your job to help those orphans."

Before she considered her actions, she stepped on her tiptoes and kissed him on the cheek. His stubble pricked her lips. A fire she never felt before ignited within herself, and she hurried back to camp, afraid to see Brett's response.

Chapter Fourteen

The morning after they'd all returned from roundup, Brett and Lottie lay side by side on their stomachs on the bluff overlooking the orphanage, after watching a glorious sunrise. There was no movement below, and only the occasional shout of a child could be heard. A dozen chickens roamed about in a small pen behind the house, and a goat was tethered to a cottonwood tree, with its twin kids butting heads and frolicking around her. One goat was hardly enough to provide milk for so many children. Brett's ire rose at Lloyd Stout—or maybe he was still angry with himself.

The cold boulder, not yet warmed from the sun's touch, chilled his bones. Maybe he was still upset with himself over his lack of response to Lottie's kiss. Why hadn't he stopped her? Told her it couldn't happen again?

It had been an impulse on her part, he was sure of that. He could tell she was embarrassed. She wouldn't look at him once they returned to camp and avoided him most of yesterday. Course, he'd been busy, helping to unload the chuck wagon and assisting Cookie in putting things away. And all the time he'd worked, he'd thought of Lottie.

He slid a glance her way. The sun glimmered on her hair like pure gold. He wanted to reach out and touch it, feel its softness. Gazing at her profile, he noticed for the first time that her pert nose turned up the tiniest bit on the end. Her thin brows matched her hair, and her appealing lips were pressed together.

He forced his attention back to the house. He was a goner. He'd stayed too long at the Rocking M, and now his mind would need a good scrubbing to rid its chambers of Lottie.

He'd heard of other lawmen falling for one of their captives, but he never would have believed it could happen to him. Gazing up at the sky, he made another appeal for help. *C'mon, Lord. I need to find evidence of that bank robbery, so I can finish this job and get on home. I've drawn a blank so far. You've gotta help. I can't act on my attraction to Lottie. It's wrong.*

Good thing he was quitting the U.S. Marshals after this. If a woman could get under his skin like Lottie had, he was better off staying on his ranch herding cattle than chasing outlaws. A man with his attention divided could get himself—or someone else—killed.

"Look!" Lottie hissed and scooted closer. "I told you so."

Brett watched a half-grown boy come out of the house and enter a lean-to. He tossed out a mixture of picks and shovels. Another boy, smaller than the first, went inside the rickety barn and soon returned with Stout's saddled horse.

One by one, children came dragging out of the house, rummaged through the tools, and took one. A trio of girls headed toward the privy, while the other children stood or sat on the ground. Lloyd Stout ventured out last, stretching and patting his oversized belly. It took him three tries before he managed to mount the horse.

Brett prayed he'd see enough today to have the man behind bars by tonight—as long as the sheriff wasn't in cahoots with Stout.

Lottie started to rise, but Brett threw his arm over her. "Stay down. They can see us too easily."

She looked at him with wide brown eyes. "They never saw me last time."

Stubborn woman. He needed to withdraw his arm but feared she'd get up again. Lottie turned her head to watch something to her right and nearly rested her head on his shoulder. Her warm breath teased his cheek. How could holding her feel so right when he knew it was wrong?

If truth be told, he'd wanted to pull her in his arms the other night and kiss her. Would she have welcomed his kiss? Somehow, he thought she might.

The children lined up and followed Lloyd Stout up a path and then disappeared from sight. Brett couldn't decide whether to follow on foot or horseback.

"Can I get up now? They're gone."

Brett peered over at Lottie. Her face was only a foot away. All he had to do was lean a bit...

"Get up, Brett. We don't want them to get away. They might not be going to the same place I saw them go the other day." Lottie squirmed until he rolled away.

Brett shook his head and jumped up. Being alone with Lottie was getting dangerous. They moved back from the edge of the butte and hurried back to the horses.

"I think we should ride instead of walking. They went over a mile the last time I watched them." Lottie mounted without waiting for a response. She nudged Bella forward.

Brett shook his head. "Let me go first."

Lottie sighed, but waited. "Why do men always have to go first?"

Brett grinned. "So we can protect you, Princess."

Anna's breath caught in her throat at the endearment. But did it mean anything to him?

The ranch hands had often called her names, especially when she was younger, but Brett never had. And why "princess?" Did he think she was spoiled? Hadn't she shown him she was willing to get dirty to help the orphans? Didn't she pull her weight on the roundup?

Anna pressed her lips together. At some point her feelings for Brett had sprouted from admiration to love. But loving a cowhand was a waste of time. Quinn would never allow them to court, much less marry, even if Brett desired that also. If her brother even suspected there was an attraction growing between them, he'd never let Brett escort her anywhere again.

She leaned back in the saddle, stirrups forward as Bella descended to the valley floor. Brett glanced back at her, probably wanting to be sure she'd made it down the steep hill. She wasn't a baby. Couldn't he see she was a woman well past marrying age?—and she was interested in him.

He slowed his horse as he rounded the bend, then urged him on around the corner. Anna followed. This time the children took a different trail, but their tracks were as easy to follow as before. Half an hour later, she followed Brett as he crawled out on another butte and looked down. A muscle in his jaw clenched.

"It's the same as before," Anna whispered. "The bigger kid works the pick, and the younger one shovels the dirt. They're looking for something. That's obvious."

Stout sat atop his horse, riding from one hole to another. "Dig it deeper. You ain't gonna find nothing in the topsoil."

"Just look at him..." Anna whispered, "...dressed in his nice clothes and riding that fine horse while those poor children do manual labor. If I weren't a God-fearing woman..."

"Shh."

"Are you going to do anything? Those children have suffered long enough."

Brett clenched his fist and scowled. "I'm thinking on it. I don't want the kids to get hurt."

One girl, who looked to be nine or ten, stood and pressed her hands into her back after wielding the heavy pick. Her gaze landed on Brett and Anna, and her eyes widened. She glanced at Mr. Stout and then went back to work.

Anna rushed backwards, sending pebbles clattering off the edge of the butte. Brett jumped back. She rubbed her hands together and wiped the dirt off her jacket and riding skirt.

"You think Stout saw us?" Anna asked, as she hurried toward Bella.

"Don't think so." Brett followed her.

"So…did you see enough?"

His angry glare made her want to never get on his bad side. "Yes. I need to get to town and tell the sheriff what we saw."

"All right, then. Let's go."

Excitement surged through Anna like a flashflood. For the first time in her life, she might actually make a difference in someone's life.

Brett watched Lottie dismount and march into the sheriff's office without even waiting on him. Again, it struck him odd how an outlaw could have the audacity to enter a lawman's domain without a speck of apprehension. Either she was very certain of her disguise as Anna McFarland, or she wasn't the woman he thought she was. And he was wondering that more and more, and hoping it was true. Why, if Anna truly wasn't Lottie Sallinger…

His heart soared at the possibilities. But he had that drawing in his pocket. And no evidence. How long should he keep looking?

He dismounted and looped his reins over the hitching post and followed Lottie into the office. She was already halfway through her spiel, like a country peddler. The sheriff's gaze darted to Brett and back to Lottie. She finally ran out of steam.

"So, you see, we've got to do something to save those children."

The sheriff scratched his jaw. "I don't know as any laws have been broken. Not sure what I can do."

"You can protect those orphans. He's mistreating them. Why, they don't even go to school." Lottie hiked her chin and shoved her hands to her slim waist.

"Tell me what you saw." The sheriff turned to Brett.

"Same as she did. Stout dressed in his fancy clothes, riding a well-fed buckskin, and those barefoot kids digging in the dirt with picks and shovels. We saw the Home too. The kids don't have decent clothes, and several of the smaller kids had runny noses. The law should protect such little ones."

"Guess I could go out there and talk to them after Lloyd brings the children back home."

Brett leaned against the wall of the small office. "I have a theory. I think Stout's looking for that lost gold shipment that's rumored to be hidden in the hills."

The sheriff twisted the end of his moustache. "You know, you might be right. I bet that *is* what they're doing."

"That money belongs to the railroad. I'm sure there's a reward for it."

"There's more." Brett pressed his hands on the sheriff's desk and leaned forward. "I've wondered where the children came from. The postmaster confirmed that youngsters have gone missing in nearby towns. I think Stout may be kidnapping them."

The sheriff sat up straighter. "I heard about that too. If you're right, that's an arrestable offense."

Lottie tossed her arms up. "Are you two just going to keep jawing while those children are suffering. If you're not going to do anything, I will."

She turned and strode toward the door. Brett blocked her way. "You're not going there alone."

"Y'all are just yakking while the orphans are killing themselves doing a grown man's job." Tears glistened in her eyes. She was really taking this whole thing quite seriously for someone who held up a bank. Must be that even outlaws had a tender spot—some bigger than others.

He held onto her shoulders. "We'll take care of this. Right, sheriff?"

The man held Brett's gaze and nodded. "Tonight. After dinner, when we're sure the children are at home. I don't want any of them getting hurt if things go bad."

Chapter Fifteen

"So, what should we do now?" Anna stood outside the sheriff's office; fingers of the morning sun touched her face. "We can't stay in town all day."

Brett stretched. "Don't know about you, but I'm hungry. How about we eat breakfast and then decide what to do?"

Anna nodded and walked beside Brett on the boardwalk. The sleepy town of Medora was barely awake, and only a handful of other people were out and about. Brett's stomached growled, and he wondered what the orphans had eaten for breakfast.

After downing a heaping plate of fried ham, eggs, biscuits, and gravy, Brett leaned back in his chair, sipping his coffee. He watched Lottie swipe the napkin across her mouth and held back a grin. She wasn't the daintiest of women, in fact, when she was in a hurry to get somewhere, she tended to swagger like a man. Could be because of that split skirt she insisted on wearing so often. And he'd seen her jump clear off the porch without even using the steps a time or two when she thought nobody was watching.

"So...what do you plan to do with the rest of your life?"

Her eyes widened at his pointed question. She shrugged. "I don't know. I guess I want what most women do—to marry the man of my dreams, raise a family, not have to cook."

Brett couldn't help smiling at that. "You don't like to cook?"

She glanced away, a pleasant pink blush on her cheeks. "I can fix a few things but haven't really had to cook since Leyna came to live with us. I'd much rather be helping with the horses—at least I used to be satisfied with that."

"And you dream about men?"

"What?" Her gaze zipped in his direction.

"You said you wanted to marry the man of your dreams, so I figured you must be dreaming about someone."

Her cheeks flamed, and her gaze flittered around the room like a hummingbird dashing from flower to flower. "I'd rather not talk about that."

What would cause such a reaction? Unless she was dreaming about... No. He couldn't allow himself to think that. It wasn't fair to her—or to him.

Lottie nibbled her lip, as if she were preparing to tell him a deep secret. She glanced at him and cocked her head. "Lately, I've been dissatisfied. Feeling the need to do more with my life."

"I understand. That's how I felt when I left home and became a..." Brett choked on his almost revelation that he was a lawman. He picked up his coffee and took a gulp.

Lottie leaned forward. "Became a what?"

He studied the other people in the room, hoping Lottie wouldn't press him further. A couple, two tables over, sat cramming food into theirs mouths as if they hadn't eaten in weeks. Two women dressed in calico chatted amiably over their coffee and cinnamon rolls. Silverware clinked, and the aroma of fresh cooked food filled the air, but didn't smell as good to him now as when he'd first come in.

Lottie touched his arm, drawing his attention back to her. "Became a what?"

"Uh...guess you could say I'm a drifter. Traveling from place to place."

Lottie smiled and ran her finger around the top of her coffee mug. "Sounds interesting to me. That's kind of what Adam and Mariah do. I've often dreamed of traveling like that. It must be wonderful to see so many different sights instead of being stuck on a ranch all the time."

Brett swallowed hard. "So you don't have any desire to marry a rancher?"

"No. Never."

He flinched at her adamant response. That certainly made things easier. Not that he ever would have asked her to marry him, but knowing she didn't want to marry a rancher eliminated him. So, why didn't he feel relieved?

"I guess I shouldn't say never." Lottie's lips tilted in a melancholy smile. "If I loved a man who was a rancher, I think I'd enjoy living on *his* ranch, seeing him daily, waiting for him to come home in the evenings. Life wouldn't be so lonely if you were with the one you loved."

Brett's throat tightened. She looked at him—almost as if she loved him. But it couldn't be. He couldn't allow it. Standing, he fished several coins out of his pocket. "We'd best get back to the ranch."

"You're right. I need to explain everything to Quinn. If the Stouts leave, I may have to stay with the children until we can find a new overseer."

"You gonna cook for them?" He couldn't help the ornery gleam in his eye.

"Ha ha." Anna stuck her tongue out at him, right there on Main Street. "Maybe I'll let you do the cooking."

He chuckled as he mounted Jasper. "I need to check if I have any mail since we're in town."

"That's fine. I want to go to the mercantile and see if they have enough clothes in stock so I can buy a set for each child. They need something now, and it will take too long to hear back from my grandma."

"Don't you need to check with Quinn before spending so much money?" He clicked out the side of his mouth, and Jasper moved forward.

Lottie tossed her head like a wild mustang. "The Rocking M is as much mine as it is his, I'll have you know. Pa's will left Mama one-fourth of the ranch and each of us three kids one-fourth."

Brett knew when to keep quiet. He shook his head and reined Jasper toward the post office, thinking what a woman that Lottie Sallinger was.

Disappointment resurfaced when he discovered he still hadn't heard from Marshal Cronan. He was about ready to cut his losses and leave town. The more he was around Lottie, the less he believed she was an outlaw. There had to have been a mistake.

He leaned against a post outside the mercantile and watched the people ambling up and down the dirt road and boardwalks. There were more people here today than usual, probably because the train had arrived while they were eating. A pretty blond woman who looked to be in her forties stopped across the street and looked in the window of the dress shop. There was something oddly familiar about her.

She slowly turned, and Brett's heart stumbled. Why, the woman looked just like Lottie, only older. The woman looked both directions then crossed the street after a buggy passed. He realized this was the same woman he'd seen with Lottie in the Bismarck store.

"There you are." Lottie exited the store and stopped beside him. "What's wrong? You look like you've seen a ghost."

He nudged his chin toward the woman and Lottie turned. "Mama? Oh, my goodness—" she glanced back at Brett. "Is it Friday already? How could I have not realized today is Friday?"

She tossed a small package into his arms and jumped off the steps, meeting her mother in the street. "I'm so sorry we didn't meet you at the train. We had roundup this week, and I completely lost track of what day this was."

Her mother hugged her again. "It's all right, darling. I was about to go to the livery and rent a buggy, but I thought I'd find something to drink first."

"There's a bucket and a dipper in the mercantile, or we could go to the café if you're hungry."

They walked arm-in-arm toward Brett. He looked back and forth, amazed at their similarities. Lottie was an inch taller than her ma, but they could almost be twins. Now that he thought about it, her mother must have been the woman he'd seen her with in Bismarck that first day. He'd been too focused on Lottie to pay any attention to her companion.

"There's someone I want you to meet." She pointed to Brett. "This is the man who saved me from the bear."

Mrs. McFarland started up the steps, and Brett reached out to assist her. She took his hand, then held it between both of her hands once she was on the boardwalk. "I owe you a great debt, Mr...uh."

"Wickham." Brett and Lottie said in unison, and Mrs. McFarland joined them in a chuckle.

"Thank you for rescuing my half wild daughter. You can't know how much that means to me."

Brett swallowed, wondering what she'd say if she knew that he had planned to arrest her son and daughter. "Uh...you're welcome, ma'am. I was happy to do it."

"You should see his scars, Mama, from where the bear clawed his chest."

Mrs. McFarland lifted one brow. "And you *shouldn't* be seeing them, young lady."

Lottie waved her hand in the air. "I see the men's chests all the time in warm weather. What's one more?"

Mrs. McFarland shook her head. "You see, Mr. Wickham, I've raised a hooligan."

His grin turn into a scowl as Lottie and her mother entered the mercantile. He liked the woman—but he didn't want to. It only made his job harder. Was she also involved? Hadn't she been living in Bismarck for over a year? Could be she was innocent and unaware of her son and daughter's misdeeds.

One thing for certain, his job sure got more complicated.

"Whoa!" Lottie stopped the wagon loaded with clothes and supplies for the children right before rounding the final bend to the orphanage. "What now?"

Brett glanced at Sheriff Jones and his deputy, Chester Brennan. "How are we gonna play this out?"

The sheriff leaned on his saddle horn and scratched his bristly chin. "I don't imagine Lloyd Stout will go easily. I can't say he's done anything illegal, but folks around here won't like him taking advantage of children. I think if we rattle him enough, he'll ride out of town of his own free will."

"And what if he doesn't?"

The sheriff sighed. "Don't know. I couldn't find any laws against child labor in this state. Maybe if we could prove he was guilty of using donations for himself instead of the children..." He shrugged one shoulder.

"Well, then, we will pray that he takes the hints and leaves." Ellen McFarland had insisted on coming with Lottie when she learned what was happening tonight. She had been adamant about not allowing her daughter to stay overnight alone at the orphanage.

Lottie hadn't taken too well to her wings of independence being clip so quickly and so efficiently. He'd heard them arguing clear outside. Jack had even considered riding along, but Lottie had efficiently told him everything was under control.

"Let's do this. Chester and I will go to the front door. You reckon you could cover the back incase Stout tries to sneak out?" The sheriff eyed Brett as if taking his measure.

"Yes, sir. I can do that."

"All right. We'll leave the horses here and go in quietly. Maybe take Stout by surprise. I don't want any of them youngsters getting hurt. You women stay here."

Lottie scowled at being left out, and Brett couldn't help grinning. He tipped his hat and winked at her then followed the two lawmen. It felt good to be back in action, even if it was unofficially. Sheriff Jones and Deputy Brennan walked along the side of the house and onto the porch. Brett heard their solid knock as he crept behind the house.

Three children were knocking small rocks around with sticks. Their eyes widened at his approach. Brett held up his finger and motioned to them to move away from the house. One child dropped her stick and raced into the rickety barn with the other two close on her heels. Brett heaved a sigh of relief to have them safe and out of the way, but he didn't like thinking that he might have frightened them. And where were the other children? Around the dinner table, he hoped.

"Who do you think you are to come here and tell me what I can or can't do." Brett recognized Lloyd Stout's voice from when he hollered at the children while he and Lottie had spied on the man. The murmur of the sheriff's voice echoed along the walls of the house, but he couldn't make out the softer words.

"That's ridiculous. I took these snotty-nosed kids in when nobody else wanted them, but I'm not going to jail for them."

Brett wondered what the sheriff had said to get such a reaction from Stout. There may be no laws to protect children, but Stout didn't necessarily know that. Maybe with enough pressure he'd leave, but that always meant he could sneak back. The children might never be safe from him.

He heard a ruckus and heavy steps running through the house and peered around the corner.

"No, Lloyd, don't leave me here with them."

"Turn loose of me, woman." Stout hollered, and the sound of banging furniture echoed out the back door. Brett imagined Stout had shoved his sister aside so he could get away. Brett's dislike for the man grew by the second.

The sheriff came around the front side of the house, his nose bloody, just as Stout burst out the back door waving a pistol. Brett couldn't fire without risk of hitting the sheriff and deputy. He hugged the house, and a second later, Stout rounded the corner.

Brett let his fist fly in the face of the surprised man. Stout grabbed his bleeding nose, but before Brett could react, Stout elbowed him hard in the chest, right where the bear had clawed him. He doubled over, clutching his chest and gasping for a breath free of pain. Stout lumbered around the boulders toward where the women were waiting. *Oh, no.*

The sheriff and his deputy glanced at Brett but rushed past him. Ignoring the inferno in his torso, he jogged after them, hoping Stout hadn't harmed one of the women. As he rounded the corner, he skidded to a halt at the sheriff's deep, rumbling chuckle.

Lottie stood in the wagon, holding a rifle on Stout. "Go ahead and move. After the way you've treated those children, jail is too good for you." Lloyd Stout held one hand on his bloody nose and the other in the air and glanced back as if he hoped the sheriff would rescue him.

Brett grinned. Good job, Lottie!

The sheriff hauled Stout, whimpering and complaining, back toward the house. "It may not be illegal to force children to work all day in unseemly conditions, but it is against the law to assault a sheriff. You're going to jail, Mister."

The children came out of the house, the bigger ones first, followed by the younger. They huddled in a group and watched, wide-eyed. Deputy Brennan saddled Stout's horse and Lloyd mounted, holding a handkerchief to his face.

"I don't know what's to become of me. Will I go to jail too, Lloyd?" Hattie wrung her hands around a small satchel and gazed up at her brother.

"Hush, Hattie, and get on." He held out his hand, and the woman managed to clamber up behind him.

The sheriff stopped in front of Brett as Lottie and her mother pulled up in the wagon. "Thanks for alerting me about this and helping in the capture."

Brett nodded. But he really hadn't done all that much. Stout had sucker-punched him and slipped past. Brett studied the ground. He was getting too old for chasing outlaws and the like.

Jimmy stepped out of the crowd, followed by Emma. Both children's faces were filthy, as was their ragged clothing. Never had he known the lack they had. "What's gonna happen to us? Are we going to jail, too?"

Emma's chin quivered, and Brett stooped down in front of her and her brother. "No, pardner. You did nothing wrong, but Mr. Stout *is* going to jail for being cruel to you."

Emma nodded. "Good. Him's a bad man."

Brett smiled and tousled her hair. "Yes, he is. And he won't be hurting you again. In fact, I brought two women who will take care of you tonight—and I do believe they have some gifts for you."

The children's gaze turned as one toward the wagon. For the first time since Brett had seen these youngsters, hope brightened their eyes. He rubbed his chest, aching both from the blow he'd taken and from the mistreatment the orphans had endured. Why was it that some people had so much and others so little?

Chapter Sixteen

Anna swiped her arm across her sweaty forehead. She and her mom had made several trips to the nearby creek taking first the girls to bathe, and then the infant boy. Brett oversaw the other boys, making sure they didn't shirk in their washing.

The orphanage sounded like the McFarland home used to when they'd open presents on Christmas morning, back in Texas when they were young.

"I got a red shirt and new pants!" a cute boy with freckled nose declared.

"Mine's blue and matches my britches." Jimmy ran his hand proudly down the front of his new top.

The girls, ages three to nine, twirled around and admired each other's dresses. Brett leaned against the doorframe, arms crossed and a gentle smile on his handsome face. He looked as pleased as she felt. Her heart danced with…love. Was that what she felt? Did she love him? Or did she simply admire him for the way he helped make sure that evil man could no longer harm these children.

Her mother braided Junie's hair, then tied a bow on each short braid. She looked over the child's head and smiled. "There you go, sweetheart."

Junie spun around to face Anna's mother. "Are you my new mommy?"

Anna's heart nearly melted. Her mother touched Junie's cheek. "No, darling, I'm here to help take care of you for a while."

Junie ducked her head. "I want you to stay. You's nicer than them other folks."

Ellen hugged the girl and wiped a tear from her cheek. Anna wrestled with her thoughts. How could a loving God allow children to be mistreated so?

Brett went outside and returned a few minutes later carrying two bundles that held the orphans' new nightshirts. She hoped the sizes were all right. Some of the clothes she'd picked out had been too big, but the children hadn't seemed to mind.

"Gather round, everyone. We have something else for you." Anna and her mother handed out the nightshirts and instructed the older children to get ready for bed. They helped the younger ones change into their nightclothes.

Suzanne started crying. "I don't wanna give back my new dress. I neber had a new one afore." She wrapped her arms around her chest and clung to the pink garment.

Anna smiled and knelt in front of her. "You don't have to give it back, sugar. It's yours to keep, and you get to keep the nightgown too." She held out the soft flannel gown.

"Truly?" Suzanne still didn't seem to believe her.

Anna pulled the girl's arms open and placed the nightgown in them. "See, you get both of them. One you wear at night and the other during the day. So…can we put the nightgown on now?"

Suzanne nodded, then Anna helped her swap clothes and carried her to bed. She wished she'd had the foresight to think about getting new bedding. It looked as if it hadn't been cleaned in months. Tomorrow they'd stay busy washing it all.

With the children tucked into bed, Anna joined her mother and Brett on the porch. They sat in rockers, resting after their hectic evening. "What do you think will happen to them now?"

Her mother looked at her. "I've been thinking about that very thing. I know a couple of middle-aged sisters who might be willing to watch the children until we can find another place for them to go or a new person to oversee the orphanage. Do you remember the Allen sisters?"

Anna leaned forward. The younger Allen sister had never married and had come to live with her widowed older sister after her husband died. Both were sweet, kind women who were always cooking and doing for others. They would be perfect, if they could handle eleven children.

Her thoughts swirled in her mind. Yes, things were getting better for the children, but why did they have to endure what they did? "I don't understand why God didn't help these children."

She sensed Brett's gaze on her and turned toward him. He cocked his head and smiled. "God did help them. He sent you to rescue them."

Anna ducked her head, confused by his piercing stare. "But why didn't he help them sooner? Why did they have to suffer such inhumane treatment?"

Her mother reached out and took her hand. "There will always be cruel people in this world who capitalize off the pain of others. You're not to blame for that."

"I know, but my heart still aches for them. If only I'd known about them sooner."

"We have to trust in God's timing. He sees things we don't." Brett's smile warmed her, like hot coffee on a chilly morning. He stood and stretched. "I need to take care of the horses. I'll sleep in the barn, but holler if you need me."

As he ambled past Anna, he patted her shoulder, sending fingers of fire radiating down her arm. His waffling signs of affection and periods of withdrawal confused her. Why...she couldn't even remember a time he had called her by her name, and yet, sometimes his sapphire eyes seemed to brim with affection. What was holding him back? Why did he pull away every time they made an emotional connection? Had another woman hurt him deeply in the past?

She glanced at the darkening sky, inky to the east with pink and orange clouds to the west, disappearing behind a tall butte. *Lord, you know my struggles. Is Brett the man for me? Please, Father, show me how to reach him. What to say to him.*

With only a little sign of interest on his part, her heart would be his...if it wasn't already.

Brett leaned against the depot wall and watched Lottie wave at her mother and the orphans as the train pulled out of the station, leaving only a smelly cloud of smoke littering the air. The engine wailed out a lonely farewell. Lottie stood with her arms clutched around her middle as if saying goodbye to the children and her mother threatened to squeeze the life out of her.

"It's too bad the Allen sisters felt they were too old to oversee the orphanage." Lottie swiped at a tear.

"At least they offered to help you mother take the youngsters to that children's home in Bismarck." Three of the older children had confessed they had been kidnapped, and their parents would be waiting at the orphanage in hopes of reclaiming their lost offspring.

Lottie dabbed her eyes and sniffed.

Brett handed her his handkerchief. "Are you sad because your ma is moving permanently to Bismarck or because the orphans are gone?"

"Both, I suppose. I've suspected for a long while that Mama would stay there with Grandma, but I wish she would have let me go and help with the children."

He struggled not to wrap a comforting arm around her shoulders. "She didn't want you to have to travel home alone again."

"I could have come back with the Allen sisters, or you could have come with me."

He shook his head. She was getting too dependent on him, beginning to care too much. He closed his eyes, thinking how she would be hurt when she learned the truth about him—and as much as he despised what she and Jack had done, Brett didn't want to hurt Lottie. Her soft hand squeezed his forearm.

"I know you miss the children too, but for me, it's different. I was so certain that God had brought them into my life so that I could help them and make a difference in theirs."

"You did. You probably saved their lives. Can't you see that? The whole town was oblivious to what was going on at that place—how those kids were being mistreated. If you hadn't figured it out, they'd still be there, and Stout would still be using them to search for that gold. I think your mother didn't want you to go along because she could see how attached you were getting to the kids and thought it would be easier for you to say goodbye here."

Her tears were his undoing. A lawman should keep his distance, but he couldn't stand to see her suffering and not offer comfort. "Come here."

She fell into his arms, her tears wetting his chest. She wrapped her arms around him and clung to the back of his shirt. He crushed her in a single hug, knowing this would be the only one he could ever offer her. She filled his being, made him long for things that could never be. In many ways, she was the woman his heart had been searching for, but no matter how much he loved her—and yes, he would admit it just this once—she'd never be his.

He loved Anna—not Lottie. It was sweet, caring Anna who had sneaked in and stolen his heart with her gentle spirit and spunky determination. He crushed her to his chest, his chin resting against her soft, sweet-smelling hair.

He'd searched the barn and all of the outbuildings several times while the other men were out with the cattle or horses, and he had even managed to look around the house when he brought firewood in to the various rooms. There had been no sign that the McFarlands had ever robbed a bank. Somewhere, somehow there'd been a mistake. The person who'd given Lottie's description must have seen Anna or someone who closely resembling her at some point on the day of the robbery and had her in mind when describing the bank thief to the sketch artist. It was time for him to leave. He slammed the door of his heart and set her away from him, already missing her closeness.

She blinked and stared at him as if she were confused. She heaved a heavy sigh. "Before we return home, I need to purchase a few blankets. We donated all of our spare ones to the orphans, and with winter coming soon, we'll need more."

The arriving crowd of train passengers had mostly dispersed, leaving only two other groups of people still at the depot. The stench of coal still hung in the air as Brett ushered her toward the mercantile. "I need to check at the post office to see if I've gotten any mail."

Lottie smiled. "Would you collect ours too, if we have any?"

"Sure." He nodded and tried to ignore her tender gaze. Swallowing hard, he strode to the post office. As soon as he walked in the clerk shook his head.

"Sorry. I still haven't received any mail for you." He shrugged one shoulder. "Anything else I can do?

"Yeah, got any mail for the Rocking M?"

The man clad in a white shirt and black pants turned and rummaged thru a small stack of letters, pulling out three. "Here you go."

Brett nodded his thanks and pocketed the missives. It was time to send a telegram to the marshal. Hopefully, the clerk was one who could keep his mouth shut. At the telegraph office, Brett penned his message and passed it to across the counter. The man scanned the note then glanced up at Brett.

"You a lawman?"

Brett glared at him. "Just read it back to me."

The clerk's gray eyes went wide, and he cleared his throat. "Dead end. Returning soon. Wickham."

"Sounds good. How much do I owe you?"

Brett paid him and left. The sun had crested and was already heading toward the western horizon. They needed to head back to the ranch soon. Brett scratched his chest where the last of the bear gouges was healing over. He'd always have some nasty scars, but they probably wouldn't look too bad once his chest hair finished growing back. He couldn't help smiling when he realized his panic at seeing his bald torso that first day. That had rattled him more than his injury had.

Shaking his head, he strode toward the mercantile, knowing it was time he returned to Bismarck. He still had the drawing of Lottie in his pocket, but he no longer believed she and Anna were the same person. Anna… A wave of melancholy washed over him. Her name was as pretty as she was.

Brett scowled and refocused. In Bismarck, he would find out the latest news on the Sallingers and then decide what to do. Letting Taylor's murderer run free still rankled him, but he might just have to let God deal with the Sallingers.

He blinked his eyes in the dimmer light of the store and found Lottie—no, Anna at the counter. Her smile when she saw him sent spirals of awareness swirling in his belly. Maybe there was hope for the two of them one day.

"They only had two blankets, so I ordered the others that we'll need, as well as a few more things. Might be a while before they arrive. I hope it won't get too cold before then."

Anna's cloak hung over her arm. Her rose-colored dress swished around her legs when she spun back toward the counter. She'd worn the dress for her mother, but he knew she'd rather be wearing her split skirt. She made a beautiful sight, with her hair caught up in that net thing that she'd worn the day he followed her to Medora on the train. He swallowed the lump in his throat. When had he fallen in love with her?

She gathered up the two wool blankets and handed them to him with a sweet smile. His gaze focused on the gold oval necklace with a fancy engraved M that she wore, and a fog blurred his mind. His heart stampeded, knowing the necklace was important. Where had he seen that before?

Anna plunked down two double eagle gold coins on the counter, and Brett felt the skin on his face tighten. He set the blankets on the counter and picked up one of the coins, not wanting to believe what his eyes were seeing. Running his thumb around, he found the notch that the Northern Pacific treasurer had etched into all the coins in a specific payroll shipment that he had personally delivered to the Bismarck Federal Bank the day before the robbery. The notch rested on the edge of the coin in the space between "twenty" and "dollars" at the bottom of the eagle side of the coin. All of the coins in that specific shipment were dated 1890, exactly like these. There was no doubt they were from the bank robbery.

Brett felt as if he'd been roped and dragged behind a horse through the Badlands for three days. How could Anna have these particular coins in her possession unless she'd taken part in the robbery?

The store clerk cleared his throat when Brett didn't release the double eagle.

"Is something wrong?" Anna stared up at him, and his gaze dropped to her necklace.

He closed his eyes as he remembered where he'd seen it. A cold numbness wafted over him as his hopes and dreams washed away like debris in a flashflood. When he opened his eyes, he was a lawman again.

He turned to the clerk. "I'm a U.S. marshal, and these coins were part of a robbery in Bismarck. I'm taking possession of them. They're evidence."

Both the clerk's and Lottie's mouths dropped open.

"What do you mean? Where's your badge?" Lottie stared at him dumbfounded.

"I lost it when that bear attacked me, but I *am* a marshal." He grabbed the other coin and took Lottie by the arm. She came with no resistance, and for that he was grateful. He didn't want to see her get hurt.

"Wait a minute. What about your order, Miss McFarland?"

Lottie glanced over her shoulder. "Put it on our tab, and I'll pay you next time I'm in town."

She still had no idea of the trouble she was in. Brett gritted his back

252 | OUTLAW HEART

teeth together. This was the hardest thing he'd ever had to do, except for taking his brother's body to the undertaker.

Lottie pulled at his grasp. "Tell me what's going on, Brett. Where are we going?"

"You'll find out soon enough." He marched her over to the sheriff's office, gaining a few curious glances from passersby. It irked him how Lottie trusted him enough not to question him further. Well…she wouldn't trust him much longer, and that thought was worse than the pain of the bear attack.

Sheriff Jones dropped his feet off his desk and smiled when Brett strode in. "Got those youngsters off on the train, did ya? Some of them looked pretty excited."

"I'm here on an altogether different matter." Brett plunked the coins on his desk while keeping a tight hold on Lottie.

"What's this?" The sheriff picked up a coin and looked it over.

"I didn't tell you before, because I was working undercover, but I'm a U.S. deputy marshal. Those coins were taken from the Bismarck Federal Bank several weeks back when the Sallingers robbed it. They're marked coins. Railroad officials anticipated a train robbery and marked the coins to make it easier to locate the criminals. The Sallinger Gang had been hitting the trains frequently, and the railroad decided to fight back. It worked."

He shoved Lottie in front of him. "This is Lottie Sallinger."

"What?" Lottie turned her startled gaze on him and tried to jerk her arm out of his hold. "Have you gone crazy?"

The sheriff looked as baffled as she did. "Look here, uh…Marshal Wickham, I've known the McFarlands ever since right after they moved here. That there's Anna. She's no criminal."

"I have more evidence." With his free hand, he fished the sketch of Lottie from his pants pocket and handed it to the sheriff.

The man unfolded it and laid the frayed page on his desk. He glanced up from the drawing to Lottie and back down several times. "Well, I'll be. It is her, and she's wearing that same necklace. I'd never have believed it if you hadn't had the picture."

Anna leaned over and stared at the sketch. For the first time, something like panic darkened her gaze. "There's been a mistake. I was at the bank that day, but outside, walking past. A female robber ran into me, and we both fell down and coins went sailing everywhere. It wasn't until I got home to the Rocking M that I discovered two coins had fallen into my reticule. Besides, Mother has in her possession a bank draft to replace these coins. Please, Brett, you have to believe me."

She was quick, he'd give her that. His ears were deaf to her pleading, though his heart was another matter. "I need you to lock her up, sheriff. I have to go after her brother."

Lottie spun around and slapped him on the jaw. Hard. Tears tracked down her cheeks, but she swiped them away. "How could you come into our home and accept our hospitality and then treat us like this? Why…I even saved your life."

"Don't forget, I saved yours too. I have the scars to prove it." He spun back to the sheriff, deadening himself to her pleas. "Will you lock her up? My own brother was killed in that robbery. He was an innocent victim. Help me capture Lottie's brother?"

"I don't see as I have a choice. Come along, little lady." The sheriff took Lottie's arm, and she went without a fight, but the glare she tossed over her shoulder froze Brett down to his toes. The sound of the cell door closing and locking was a death knell in his heart. The only woman he'd ever loved was an outlaw, and she'd never forgive him for what he'd done.

Chapter Seventeen

Anna sniffed and wiped her eyes again. She kicked and shook the locked door, barely rattling it. Crossing her arms over her chest, she paced the tiny cell, alternating between sobbing from a broken heart to explosive anger at Brett for what he'd done. How could he believe she was an outlaw after he'd gotten to know her and her family? Hadn't he seen their hearts...her heart? How she was willing to drop everything to help those poor orphans?

She leaned against the wooden wall, refusing to sit on the nasty bed that had held truly vile men. Why, Lloyd Stout had probably been locked up in this very cell and might still be here if the sheriff hadn't sent him on to Dickinson.

Anna kicked her heel against the wall. How could she have not known Brett was a lawman? Even when lying in bed injured there'd been something commanding about him...something that drew her like a moth to a lantern.

He was the thief, not her. He'd thoroughly stolen her heart and then tossed her in jail, as if she meant nothing to him. Was he that hardened?

No, she'd touched him, too. She could tell when he held her at the depot. His caress had been that of a man who cared. And hadn't he said his own brother had been killed in the robbery? No wonder he was so determined to find the robbers and convict them. But his craving for justice had blinded him to the truth.

She crossed to one wall, spun around, and back to the other. How long would she be locked up in here before Quinn learned about it and came to get her? Or would he be imprisoned too?

Anna blinked as another round of tears threatened. Her heart broke that Brett could think such evil of her. He was the only man she'd ever loved, and now he was dead to her. She leaned her head against the bars with an ache so deep in her heart that she thought it might shatter.

"Oh, Lord. Help me. You know I'm innocent. Please vindicate me.

Protect Quinn—and Brett. Don't let them kill each other." Her tears wouldn't stop, and she wiped her nose on her sleeve. The lovely pink dress would be ruined anyway after the filth of the cell. Something skittered along the wall. Anna spun around and jumped back. A mouse!

Desperation drove her on top of the dirty bed. Why did it have to be a mouse? A snake or spider didn't faze her, but ever since she was a child and a mouse had gotten caught under the covers of her bed, she'd been petrified of them. Weak from worry, anger, and now fear, she drew up her legs and leaned against the wall. Elbows on her knees, she rested her head in her hands, covering her face. The stench in the place was horrible. In the adjoining cell, someone had forgotten to empty the chamber pot.

What would happen to her? She'd seen the sketch and had been stunned at how much it resembled her. Even her pendant had been drawn in vivid detail. And with the gold coins as evidence, she stood a good chance of being convicted. Why hadn't she returned the money sooner? The forty-dollar bank draft hadn't even been delivered, since it was on its way back to Bismarck in her mother's possession with a note explaining what had happened. Anna had kept the coins because her mother hadn't wanted to travel with that much money on her.

"Oh, Lord," she sobbed. How would she endure prison? Being locked up, never to ride the plains and hills of the Badlands or to feel the sun on her face or the wind blowing her hair?

She gasped. Would she be hung?

She clutched her throat as her mind raced like a runaway horse. Would she ever see her mother again? Or Adam? Could her twin, wherever he was, sense her distress?

Heedless to her clothing and the mouse, she dropped to her knees. "Heavenly Father, I know I've often been wild and reckless, but I never robbed that bank. You know that. I've never done anything that warranted being locked up like this. Please help me. Help Quinn to evade Brett so he can rescue me."

She wanted to pray that God would punish Brett, but she couldn't. As much as she hurt, she knew he was only trying to do his job—to capture the outlaws who were responsible for his brother's death. The mouse scampered across the floor. Anna jumped up and climbed onto the cot again.

Blinking in the dim lighting, she realized something. The reason Brett had never used her name was probably because he thought of her as Lottie. Now she understood how his moods could change so fast. He had been attracted to her, but he'd been trying to keep his distance.

She wanted to hate him, but she couldn't. Still, it would take a very long time for her wounded heart to trust another man. To love another man.

Anna yawned. She closed her eyes, hoping this was all a bad nightmare, but the stench told her it was real. A fog of sleep descended, taking with it the horrors of the day.

Angry voices pulled Anna from her dreams of riding Bella through the grasslands, and she bolted upright. They echoed through the wall, and the shuffling of footsteps and loud bangs sounded as if men were fighting.

"We're innocent. I've told you that a hundred times."

Quinn! Anna stood and ran her hands down her wrinkled dress. She wiped her cheeks again. Her brother would have her out in no time.

A key jingled, and the door opened. Brett strong-armed Quinn inside, and the sheriff closed the door, locking it. She couldn't help glancing at Brett. His angered blue gaze softened, then widened. She knew her face was red and splotchy. She couldn't help hoping he'd hurt for what he'd done to her.

"Anna, are you all right?" Quinn took her by the arms and shook her. "Don't look at him. He's the reason we're here."

The outer door closed, taking most of the light with it. Her chin wobbled, but she held back the tears. She wouldn't admit defeat in front of her brother. He'd always thought her a child, but she'd prove him wrong. "I'm fine."

Quinn circled the cell, much smaller with his bulky frame in it. "I can't believe this happened. Why did Brett keep calling me Jack?"

"You mean you don't know?" In the shadows, she could see her brother shake his head.

"I was furious when he overpowered me and tied me up. He even got me off the ranch without any of the hands noticing. He's good, I'll give him that. Who would have thought he was a U.S. Marshal?"

The smidgeon of admiration in Quinn's voice surprised her, knowing her brother's temper. "He's convinced that we're the Jack and Lottie Sallinger. They robbed the Bismarck Federal Bank and killed his brother in the process."

Quinn paced back and forth. He ran his hand through his dark blond hair. "But what does that have to do with us?"

"I was there."

Quinn spun to face her, confusion wrinkled his brow. "What?"

"It's not what you're thinking. Mother and I were shopping and decided to get lunch. She needed to stop at the bank for money first. As I was reaching for the door, a female bank robber—Lottie Sallinger, I'm guessing—charged out the door and ran into me. We both fell down, and a bag of gold coins burst open and flew everywhere. I guess two accidentally fell into my bag somehow."

Her brother heaved a heavy sigh that tickled her forehead. "How come you never told me any of this?"

Anna held out her hands. "When would I tell you? You're always working. You never want to talk to me." Her loud shout echoed in the small area. She crossed her arms and turned her back, her gaze landing on the faint light shining in a tiny crack between two boards.

Quinn placed his hands on her shoulders and gently turned her. "I'm sorry, Anna. I know you've been lonely with Adam gone."

"I do miss Adam, but I miss you too. I love you as much as Adam." Quinn pulled her into his arms, and the unwanted tears flowed again.

"I'm sorry. All I know how to do is work. I'm not good with people."

"You are too good with people, or you wouldn't be such a great boss."

He chuckled. "I don't know about that. I promise I'll try to give you more of my time."

"Won't that be difficult if we're in different prisons?" She clutched him tight, remembering how not so long ago Brett had been the one comforting her. Was putting her behind bars hard on him? As much as she wanted to despise him, she couldn't. There was too much love in her heart for him, although she'd never look at him the same. In time, her love would die.

"We're not going to prison. We're innocent." Quinn patted her back.

"Do you truly think we'll get out of here?"

He nodded against her head. "Yes. I'll contact Mother tomorrow and have her get a good lawyer. They have no evidence against us."

Anna shuddered and cleared her throat. "Yes, they do."

Chapter Eighteen

"Sheriff, open this door. I have the right to contact an attorney." Quinn shook the bars of his cell, his anger evident.

Anna hated the bars keeping them apart now. Her brother hadn't like it when the sheriff had separated them last night, but at least Quinn, too, had a cot to sleep on, such as it was.

The key jingled on the other side of the wooden door. Balancing a tray of aromatic food, the sheriff stepped into the vault-like room that held the two cells. "Got you some lunch."

He slid a plate under the three-inch gap between the bottom of each cell door and the floor. Anna didn't know if she could eat. One night in the cell had been bad enough, but now the morning was gone and the long, dreary afternoon loomed ahead. There was nothing to do but watch Quinn pace and to stew over Brett's complete betrayal.

"I've contacted the U.S. Marshal in Bismarck and hope to hear from him soon. Maybe he can clear up this mess," Sheriff Jones said.

Quinn rattled the bars then leaned his forehead against them. "I'm telling you, sheriff, this is all a big mistake."

"That's what I told Marshal Wickham, but then he showed me that sketch."

"What sketch?" And how do you even know that man is really a marshal? Did he have a badge?"

The sheriff disappeared into the outer room for a minute then came back carrying a paper. Anna knew it was the drawing of her, and her mouth went dry.

Sheriff Jones passed it through the bars to Quinn. He unfolded it and stared, then he pivoted to look at her. "It looks just like you." He crossed to the bars separating them and stared at her pendant. "It's the exact same necklace as the one you're wearing. How could a mistake like this happen?"

Anna shrugged. "I believe it is the fault of a particular bank clerk. He saw me sitting on the boardwalk after I'd collided with that robber. Gold coins had spilled onto my skirt and all around me. He tried to have me arrested then, but another man told him I wasn't involved. He must have given my description to the authorities. Mother was there, but I don't know if a judge would believe her story since she's related to us."

Quinn forked his hand through his hair. "Going by this, I can see why Brett confused you for an outlaw, but that still doesn't justify what he did. After I went and gave him a job and all."

"Well, I can see where he might have gotten confused. Hopefully, we'll get this straightened out soon." The sheriff reached for the picture and pocketed it. "I'm sorry to have to keep you folks here."

Anna jumped as the heavy wooden door thudded shut. In the dim lighting, she decided to rescue her lunch before the mice could get it. Quinn did the same, and his cot groaned as he sat.

"What did he bring us?" He tugged away the cloth covering the plate. "Mmm...pot roast."

Anna watched her brother wolf down the meat and vegetables. She speared a chunk of potato with her fork and nibbled one end. Food didn't interest her.

"You won't have any of Leyna's cinnamon bread to snack on later, so eat up, sis."

"Do you think she knows? I wonder what the hands did when they couldn't find you."

Quinn lowered his plate to his lap and sighed. "I don't know. I hope they aren't out scouring the countryside thinking I've been hurt."

"Maybe the sheriff could let the people at the ranch know what's going on."

"Good idea. I'll ask him when he comes back."

Anna poked at a carrot. "What I don't understand is how Brett could believe us guilty of killing his brother and robbing a bank. Hasn't he gotten to know us? Can't he see that we're good people?" Frustrated, she flung the tear off her cheek.

"It's a lawman's job to be objective."

"I can't believe you're defending him, Big Brother."

"I don't know how he even associated us with the Sallingers in the first place."

Anna heard a rustling and noticed two mice in the neighboring cell. A shiver charged down her spine. She tossed a bread crust through the metal slats.

"Hey! Don't encourage them."

She quirked a sad grin. "I'm just hoping to keep them over there."

"That's fine. They don't bother me." Quinn stomped his foot and the mice dashed under his cot. "Eat. You don't know when we'll get another meal, and it might not be as good as this one."

Anna managed to swallow about a third of her meal, then she offered the rest to her brother. He stabbed her meat through the bars and made quick order of finishing it before sliding the plate back under the cell door. Anna lay back on her cot, and Quinn resumed his pacing.

The jangling of the cell door jarred Anna awake. She yawned and sat up, smoothing her mussed hair with her hand.

"I don't know how to tell you how sorry I am for the mix-up. Got a telegram from Marshal Cronan in Bismarck. Turns out the real Sallinger gang is in custody down in Deadwood. They tried to rob a stage that held a payroll shipment, but it was actually filled with deputies. They caught the gang red-handed, and you're free to go with my deepest apologies."

Thank you, Lord! "Hurry, please, I need to get out of this horrid place."

The sheriff looked as if he'd eaten a bushel of green apples as he stepped back and let her pass. Then he unlocked Quinn's cell. "Miss McFarland, your wagon and Quinn's horse are at the livery. Marshal Wickham saw to them for you."

"Right nice of him." Quinn's sarcastic tone almost made Anna smile. "Ready to go home?" His brown eyes mirrored the relief she felt.

"All I can think of at the moment is a hot bath." Anna stepped into the sheriff's office and stared at her filthy hands. Her dress was a mass of wrinkles and as dirty as her palms. She dreaded going outside looking like this.

"I can get the wagon if you want to wait here." Quinn must have sensed her discomfort.

As ready as she was to be free of this place, when she looked out the window and saw people walking by, she nodded. "That's very considerate. Thank you."

Locked up in the cell, she'd had nothing to do but think of Brett. Here in the light of day, his betrayal seemed even bigger, more painful. How did a woman get over such an event?

The thing that hurt the most was that he could think her capable of such a deed. She was certain she'd seen affection, maybe even love in his gaze. But now she must forget about him.

The problem was…she had no idea how to go about doing that.

Brett stabled Jasper in the barn at the boardinghouse he normally stayed at while in Bismarck and then headed to the marshal's office. Needing time to think and allow his heart to adjust after seeing Lottie in that cell, he'd ridden Jasper to Dickinson and caught the train there. He'd chosen to return and ask Marshal Cronan to send some other deputies to bring Jack and Lottie to Bismarck where they would stand trial. He simply didn't have it within him to do it.

The scrawny deputy who normally sat at the front desk was not there today. Brett heard the rustle of papers and the screech of Marshal Cronan's chair and knocked on the doorjamb. The marshal's gaze darted up, and his moustache twitched.

"Good to see you, Brett. Have a seat."

Brett obeyed, thinking how things had changed since the last time he'd sat in this chair. He'd been on the verge of an exciting change when he'd turned in his badge the day Taylor died. And he hadn't yet met the woman who now haunted his dreams.

"How you doin"?"

That was a loaded question. Brett shrugged. "All right, I guess. All things considered."

The marshal shook his head. "That was a mess in Medora, huh?"

Brett eyed the marshal. Did the man know he'd fallen in love with an outlaw? How could he, when Brett barely comprehended it himself?"

"Feels good to know the Sallingers are locked up, doesn't it?"

Brett nodded, still seeing Lottie's splotchy face with trails running across her cheeks where she'd wiped her face with hands dirtied from the jail cell. He hated thinking of her locked up where the sun couldn't glisten on her golden hair.

"What are you going to do now? Stay on the job or go back to your ranch?" The marshal locked his hands behind his head and leaned back, causing the chair to moan and groan under his bulk.

"I'm going home. It won't be the same without Taylor there, but I'm ready to settle down." His gaze traveled over the wanted posters stuck to the bulletin board out of habit, but he no longer had the heart to chase outlaws. In fact, the only way he knew he had a heart at all was that his was breaking. In spite of the fact that he'd fallen in love with the outlaw he'd been trailing, he done his job and had seen the Sallingers captured. But he couldn't stick around and watch Lottie be convicted. His heart ached at the thought.

"I don't suppose you'd consider waiting to retire long enough to go down with the team I'm sending to Deadwood to bring back the Sallingers? I figure you've earned the chance, even if you did chase a dead end."

"What?" Brett leaned forward in his chair, his mind swirling. "I left the Sallingers locked up in the Medora jail. How could they have gotten all the way to Deadwood in such a short time?"

Marshal Cronan leaned on his desk. "Where have you been, boy? I telegraphed the sheriff in Medora and told him to release that couple you'd arrested. We already had the Sallingers in Deadwood, caught red-handed trying to rob a decoy stage filled with marshals."

Brett's mouth hung open, his whole body numb. "But Anna McFarland was a dead ringer for that picture of Lottie. I tracked her right here from Bismarck, and she even wore the exact same necklace that Lottie wore in the sketch you gave me."

"Oh, that." The marshal sighed. "Seems the clerk who gave us that description was mistaken. He confused the woman Lottie ran into outside the bank with Lottie, and gave us her description. I don't have to tell you that he's been fired. In fact, I talked with the banker this morning." The marshal twisted one end of his thick moustache. "Two days ago, an Ellen McFarland met with the bank president and gave him a draft for forty cash dollars to replace two double eagles that had fallen accidentally into her daughter's handbag after she and that outlaw collided outside the bank."

Brett leaned back in his chair, taking it all in. Unbelievable joy battled with pure regret. His Anna wasn't a thief. Only she wasn't his Anna and never would be after what he'd done.

"You look like you've seen a ghost. What's wrong? I thought you'd be happy."

"I put two innocent people in jail. Why would I be happy about that?"

"If this gal is the spitting image of the drawing, how could you have known?"

Brett stood and reached into his pocket, pulling out the two double eagle coins. "And she had these in her possession." He dropped them on the desk. One spun around before hitting the other coin and falling down. The marshal ran his thumb over the notched edge. "These are the double eagles she mentioned in her letter. How did you get them?"

"I confiscated them when she tried to spend them in a Medora store." Brett huffed a laugh. "It's ironic, isn't it? I jailed Anna McFarland for stealing these coins, and then I took them from her when they legally belonged to her. I've sure made a mess of things."

The marshal stood and looked him in the eye. "I can see why you did what you did. You had two solid forms of evidence. Those folks are free now, so don't worry about it. I'll see that they get this money back."

Brett knew he would worry. He'd sacrificed his future for a mistake. "I'd turn in my badge but I lost it in that bear attack I wrote you about."

The marshal waved his hand in the air, stirring up the lingering smoke from his last cigar. He stepped around the side of his desk and held out his hand. "Don't worry about the badge. I've got plenty more. Looks like you've recovered all right from your injuries."

Rubbing a hand across his chest, Brett nodded. His chest had healed, but his heart was another subject.

"I wish you luck, Wickham."

Brett shook the marshal's hand and headed toward the boardinghouse. After a soak in a hot tub, he sat on the end of his bed, staring out the window. How had he made such a mess of things? If only he'd never gone in that Bismarck store and seen Lott—no, Anna, none of this would have ever happened.

But then he'd never have gotten to know her or fallen in love. Brett fell to his knees. "Oh, God, how could I have let my quest for vengeance go so far? I knew in my heart that Anna wasn't capable of the things I accused her of. Forgive me for charging ahead and taking things into my own hands. Please, God, let Anna forgive me."

For the next hour, he prayed and cried out to God. Never again did he want to walk in his own power without God's leading. But the thing God was now requiring of him was more than difficult, but he knew it had to be done.

He stood and walked to the window, knowing he'd be on the next train to Medora. He owed Quinn and Anna a huge apology. He had to make things right with them—and he hoped he didn't get shot in the process.

Chapter Nineteen

Lottie sat beside the creek with her rifle across her lap. She seriously doubted the bear would be back after Sam told her how he and Hank had found her and the cub and had chased them several miles away, but she wasn't taking any chances.

After spending twenty-four hours locked in a tiny jail cell, she couldn't get enough of God's creation. The night she and Quinn returned home after their release, she'd sat on the porch watching the sunset. Even later, she'd gone outside to stare at the stars.

Now, she watched the water gently lapping over the stones in the creek bed. Its soft sounds ministered to her aching soul. How could she miss Brett so much after what he'd done?

But hadn't he only been doing his job? Even if his train was on the wrong track?

She exhaled deeply. Hours of prayer, begging God to take away her love for him had been a futile effort so far. Maybe it took more time.

She longed to see him again but wasn't sure what she'd do if she did. Quinn was still mad, though seeing that sketch of her had soothed him some. A grin tugged at her mouth. It was her opinion that her tough brother was more angered over the fact that Brett had bested him and then sneaked him off the ranch with nobody the wiser. Few men were tougher than Quinn and big enough to outfight him.

Two gray rock doves drifted down to the edge of the creek and strutted around, their necks a shiny iridescent green and purple in the afternoon sunlight. They pecked at the ground for a few minutes as Anna watched. A magpie swooped down and landed off to her right. It squawked at her as if telling her this was his domain. He ducked his head at something shiny. Anna stood, wondering what would be reflecting the sun in such a way. The bird chattered but flew off a few yards as she approached it. Anna knew what she'd found the moment her fingers touched the slick metal. Brett's badge.

She wrapped her hand around it and didn't try to stop the tears. How could she still love him when he'd thought so little of her?

After a few minutes, she stuck the badge in her pocket. She would hide it away, knowing it would always be a memento of the man she'd loved. As she rode up to the ranch a short while later, she saw Quinn standing in front of the barn with Hank and Claude beside him. Quinn and Hank held their rifles toward the side of the barn, while Claude looked to be trying to calm her brother. What was going on? Had a coyote come looking for their chickens?

"Get off my land."

She reined Bella to a stop and slid off. As she hurried to her brother's side, a rider came into view. Anna gasped. Brett.

"I told you to leave. You've got a lot of nerve showing up here after what you did." Quinn lifted his rifle, showing he meant business.

Her rebellious heart leaped in recognition. Now all she had to do was decide if she wanted to shoot him or hug him.

Out of the corner of her eye, Anna saw Leyna come out onto the porch, holding her broom as if she wanted in on the action. Anna pulled her gaze back to Brett, and her heart somersaulted. He was so handsome. His blue eyes, so vivid against his tanned skin, couldn't seem to stray from her face. His expression begged for compassion. His longish hair hung down against his collar, while his Stetson was pushed back on his forehead, revealing the lighter skin along his dark hairline. Oh, how she loved this man, but could she ever trust him again?

Brett's outlaw heart lurched as Anna rode up. He needed to keep his wits about him, but his gaze kept straying to her. She looked so much better than the last time he'd seen her, and for that, he was thankful. It had nearly gutted him seeing her suffering so much. He held up his hand to Quinn. "Please hear me out. I've come to apologize."

"We don't want your apology. We opened our home to you and tended your wounds when you were half dead, then you toss my sister and me in jail."

Anna lifted her hand to her brother's arm. "Quinn put the rifle down.

You know you're not going to shoot a U.S. Marshal."

Quinn darted a glare her direction. "Stay out of this, Anna."

Brett reached for his shirt pocket. "Let me show you the sketch that started all this."

Quinn lowered his rifle but didn't relax his rigid stance. "I saw it. But after you got to know us, you should have known we couldn't do something like rob a bank, much less kill someone."

Brett pocketed the drawing with a sigh and leaned forward, arms resting across his saddle horn. "I'll admit I struggled with it all. I was ready to ride away, thinking there'd been some mistake—had even wired my superior that this was a dead end—when Anna plopped down those stolen coins at the mercantile. It was evidence I couldn't ignore."

Quinn sighed. "You could have talked to us about it."

Brett took a risk and dismounted. "A lawman doesn't discuss his case with the criminal he's investigating."

Quinn raised his rifle again. "We aren't criminals."

Brett lifted his palms in a sign of surrender. "I know that now, and for what it's worth, I'm deeply sorry about my error and the trouble it caused. You have no idea how sorry."

"You've said your piece, now get goin'." Quinn hiked his chin and glared at Brett.

Anna's brother would never forgive him. "I've repented to God, but I want you to know that if I sought vengeance for my brother's death instead of justice, I'm sorry for that too."

Quinn relaxed his stance. "I'm sorry about your brother. It must be tough to lose him."

Brett nodded. "Taylor was only twenty-one. He had his whole life ahead of him."

Quinn looked Brett in the eye. Caring for younger siblings was something Anna's brother could relate to.

"Well…thank you for letting me apologize. I want you to know I'm deeply sorry."

"We get the idea." Quinn looked at Hank, who stood inside the barn, and swiped his arm in the air. The cowhand lowered his rifle, and he and Claude disappeared into the barn.

Unable to read Anna's expression, Brett hoped and prayed she'd be willing to talk to him. He looked back at Quinn. "I'd like to have a private word with Anna, if you don't mind."

A muscle ticked in Quinn's jaw as he looked at his sister. Anna gazed at Brett with apprehension but nodded.

Quinn glared at Brett. "Don't break her heart again, or so help me, lawman or not, I'll come gunnin' for you."

Anna couldn't stop wringing her hands as she and Brett stopped by the pasture fence. She never dreamed she'd be walking with him ever again, much less so soon after what had happened.

"Anna…"

She loved her name on his lips. "You know, you never called me by my first name when you were here before."

Brett ducked his head. "I wanted to, but I had to keep thinking of you as Lottie, in order to keep my distance."

Hope flickered in her chest like a match to kindling. "Why did you need to keep your distance?"

Brett looked her in the eye, and a sad smile bent the edges of his mouth. "I think you know. It was all I could do not to fall head over heels in love with you."

Her heart clenched. So he didn't love her. She closed her eyes and willed her tears away. She could get through this without breaking down, and she'd forgive him so he could get on with his life. Without her.

"I'm so sorry for all the trouble I caused. If you only knew how I'd struggled, arguing with myself that you couldn't possibly be Lottie. It wasn't until I saw those coins that I actually believed you were her. In fact, I was ready to ride out that very day and go back to Bismarck, and then I saw the coins."

"Well…it's over now, so stop apologizing. Are you going to keep marshaling or go back to your ranch?"

He leaned his arm across the top of a fence post and stared at the horses grazing in the field. "I retired. I'm going home."

Anna tried to not show her disappointment. Had she read him totally wrong? Hadn't she seen love in his gaze, or had she imagined it?

"Well…I guess that's it then. I wish you good luck, and maybe if you ever get in this area you could stop by." She stiffened her spine and held out her hand.

Brett looked at it then at her face, his gaze questioning. He stood and took her hand, then wrapped his other hand over the top of hers. "Anna…I can't leave without telling you how I feel."

Her heart skipped a beat.

"I know I have no right to say this, but I'll always regret it if I don't. I love you." His warm blue eyes told her his words were true.

Anna gasped, and the tears she'd held at bay broke loose. "Oh, Brett, I thought I'd lost you." She fell into his arms, and he held her tight.

"I know, darlin'. I felt the same way." He rested his head on hers and watched a half-grown foal frolicking in the tall grass. This was what he wanted, her in his arms for the rest of his life.

She leaned back. "You have to know I love you too." Anna stroked his cheek, and he leaned into her touch.

"I don't deserve your love, especially after what I did."

She pressed her fingers against his lips, surprised at their softness. "Shh...don't say that. Love is a gift from God."

Brett recaptured her hand. "Isn't it amazing how God can take such a mess and work something good from it? If I hadn't had that drawing of you and then seen you in the store in Bismarck, we never would have met."

Anna nodded. "That's true, isn't it? God is truly amazing."

"You're amazing. I can't believe you'd forgive me so easily." He ran his hand down her soft cheek. "Anna, do you have it in your heart to marry a scoundrel like me?"

She couldn't stop her chin from quivering. Brett's loving gaze turned worried. She had to put the man out of his misery. "Yes, I'll marry you, Deputy Marshal Wickham."

He grinned, leaning in closer. "It's Mr. Wickham, ma'am. I turned in my resignation."

His lips touched her, and their kiss was all she had dreamed it could be. He held her tight against his solid chest, and she felt cherished and protected. To think she'd almost lost him. He deepened his kiss with a promise of many more to come.

Suddenly, a shot rang out, hitting the fencepost three feet away, sending splinters of wood flying. Anna and Brett leaped apart.

"Hey, that's my sister you're sparking with, mister." Quinn raised his rifle as if preparing to fire again.

Brett leaned his head against hers. "Your family sure keeps things interesting."

She returned his grin. "Yes, Mr. Wickham, they do at that."

Epilogue

Anna fidgeted with her autumn flower bouquet. Quinn paced the back of the church, waiting to escort her down the aisle. He'd asked her half a dozen times if she was sure that she wanted to marry the man who'd tossed her in jail. But she was certain. Not a doubt lingered in her mind.

Brett had offered to stay until spring to help on the Rocking M to make sure he'd smoothed things over with Quinn. In April, providing there wasn't deep snow, she and her husband would travel to his Bar W Ranch in southwestern North Dakota. While she was happy to spend time with her family, she was eager to have Brett all to herself. Being a newlywed and living in the same home as her watchful brother would present some challenges. She could only hope that Quinn would honor her and Brett's vows and not pester him once they were married.

She peeked around the corner and saw Adam and Mariah sitting on the front row, along with her mother and grandmother. Mariah looked over her shoulder, caught Anna's eye, and waved. Anna smiled back. Last night at dinner, Adam had broken the news that Mariah was with child. They, too, would be wintering at the ranch, and everyone would enjoy the new baby, come March. Anna couldn't help wondering how long it would be before she and Brett had a child of their own.

Only a handful of their friends had made the trip to Bismarck for the wedding, but Anna didn't mind. She rather liked the coziness of the small group in the chapel of her grandmother's church.

The organist started playing, and she heard a door open and close. Quinn looked around the corner of the chapel's entryway and then nodded at her. "It's not too late to change your mind, sis."

She smacked him on the sleeve. "I want to marry Brett. When will you get it through that fat head of yours?"

He grinned, looking so much like her father that a lump formed in her throat.

"Quinn, I know it hasn't been easy on you since Pa died, but I want you to know that I'm deeply grateful for all your hard work to make the ranch a success and your help with Mama to keep Adam and me on the straight and narrow. I hope one day that God will bring a beautiful woman into your life and that you'll find the happiness I have."

"Goodness, sis, you're gonna make me cry." He looped her arm around his. "Let's go make that scoundrel down there happy. He looks as nervous as a mustang fresh off the range."

She smiled, and as she rounded the corner, her gaze captured her beloved's. Brett looked so handsome in the black suit that matched his hair. She hoped all her children had his hair and beautiful blue eyes—all but one ornery tomboy who loved split skirts and riding full-gallop.

Brett's wide smile warmed her heart. She breathed a thankful prayer to God for forgiveness. Without it, today would never have happened.

Quinn acted as if he didn't want to hand her over, but she knew her brother was only pretending. "Make sure you get the ceremony right, preacher, or this fellow might toss you in jail."

The minister cast a bewildered glance from Quinn to Brett. The audience chuckled as Quinn sat down next to their mother. Brett took Anna's hand and turned her to face the preacher. Joy overflowed as she said her vows to love and cherish forever the man God had given her.

April, 1895

"All aboard!" The conductor waved at the final passengers who still lingered on the platform.

"You ready, Mrs. Wickham?"

Anna nodded, afraid if she voiced the words that she'd break into tears, and she didn't want her husband thinking that she loved her family more than him. But leaving her family, the Rocking M, Medora, and everything familiar to journey to the unknown was scary. At least Leyna was coming with her. Brett had said he'd starve to death if he had to rely on Anna's cooking, but she knew that he didn't want her to be too lonely. Leyna's cousin would be coming to cook for Quinn after Adam and Mariah left again next month.

Her family gathered around, and she hugged each one. Her mother had come to see the baby and to see her off. She clutched her twin, hating to turn lose now that she'd had him back for a time, but he no longer belonged to her. She released Adam and kissed baby Jonathon and hugged Mariah.

With tears in her eyes her mother handed her a large package wrapped in brown paper.

"What's this?" Anna reached for it and clasped her mother's hand.

"Mariah and I finished the quilt. You'd done so much work on it this winter, that we wanted it finished, so you could take it to your new home."

"Oh, thank you both." She fell into her mother's arms, wondering when she'd see her again. The train whistle wailed, and they stepped apart. "You will come and visit?"

Her mother nodded and wiped her tears. Brett helped Leyna onto the train and handed up her satchel. He came to Anna's side and relieved her of the heavy package. Anna gazed at Quinn. They'd become much closer since being locked in jail together, and now she hated to leave him. If only he had a wife and family. That item still topped her prayer list, but she knew God would be faithful.

"Goodbye, Quinn." Her chin quivered.

"Don't you dare cry, Sis, or you might see a grown man weep." He embraced her in a fierce bear hug then abruptly turned her loose. He looked at Brett and held out his hand. "You'd better take good care of her. I still have a loaded shotgun handy."

Brett smiled. "I'd give my life for hers and have the scars to prove it."

Quinn grinned and hugged Brett, both men slapping each other on the shoulder.

"Final call! All aboard."

"Goodbye, everyone. You'd better write." Anna allowed Brett to help her up the steps to the railcar, then hurried to her seat and plastered her face against the window. How was it possible to be so excited to be going to a new home when it was so hard to leave the old one? Brett settled in beside her and draped his arm over her shoulders.

"We'll be back, and they'll come to visit." He kissed her temple, sending tingles down her neck and arm. How could he still affect her so much after six months of marriage?

"I know. Don't fret. I want to be with you, remember?"

His gaze said he wished they were alone instead of on a crowded train. He dipped down and kissed her lightly on the lips.

Leyna tsked at them. She sat in the seat facing theirs, wielding her wooden spoon and an ornery grin.

A laugh slipped from Anna's lips. Brett chuckled and shook his head. Anna looked out and waved a final goodbye to her family as the train left the station.

The train shuddered as it picked up speed. They were on their way to a new future, and Anna couldn't wait to explore it.

STRAIGHT FROM THE HEART

Chapter One

Western North Dakota, 1895

Sarah Oakley glanced over her shoulder, listening for the sound of hoofbeats. How long before their uncle noticed them gone and came after them? A shudder snaked down her spine. If taking a beating would satisfy him, she could endure that for the sake of her siblings. But when he discovered what they'd done, she feared seeing them dead was the only thing that would soothe his vile temper.

Her arms ached from carrying the heavy load, a constant reminder of her foolish, impulsive decision, but it was the only way she could think to save her siblings.

They had to get away.

Far away.

"Hurry, kids. Walk faster."

"How come you keep looking behind you, Sissy?" Beth turned and walked backward for a moment then faced forward again.

"Because she thinks Uncle Harlan will come gunning for us." Ryan pointed his index finger at Beth and pretended to shoot.

"Don't scare your sister." The girl worried far too much for a six-year-old.

Beth leaned against Sarah's leg, forcing her to slow her pace. "Sissy, I'm tired. My feet hurt."

Sarah shifted her heavy bundle to her other arm and rested a hand on her sister's head. She couldn't carry both Beth and the bag of gold coins. "It's only a mile or two farther. On that last hill we topped, I got a peek of that giant smokestack in Medora. We'll be there soon."

"But that's what you said last time."

"You're lazier than a one-legged chicken." Eight-year-old Ryan tucked his hands in his armpits and flapped his elbows up and down. "Brock, brock!"

Beth gasped and began to cry. "Ryan called me a chicken. They're ugly."

Tears dripped down her sister's lightly freckled cheeks and onto her jaw. Sarah's shoulders and neck tightened. They were running for their lives, and her siblings couldn't quit bickering. She sighed and patted Beth's head. "Ryan, leave your sister alone."

Sarah glanced up at the sky, but darkening clouds blocked the sun. Lunchtime had surely passed by now, judging by the growl of her stomach. They should have left their uncle's shack first thing this morning, right after Uncle Harlan and his gang of three unkempt men rode west, but she had waited several hours, in case the men returned unexpectedly.

A cool breeze dried the sweat caused by her nervousness and the exertion of their quick-paced journey. The rugged path snaked through the thick grasslands of the Badlands. Sarah studied both sides of the trail, looking for hiding places in case she heard hoofbeats. After a moment, her gaze always settled back on the top of the tall smokestack, which looked so out of place surrounded by nature—almost as if God knew she would need it one day.

"I can't see that big chimney." Beth wrinkled her brow and nibbled her lip.

"It's still there. You'll see it when we top the next hill."

They could easily get lost in this rugged land where few people lived. On all sides of them, rocky buttes had jutted up through the dense grass. Some buttes were round-topped and grass covered, while others were rocky and rugged. An artist's palette of color stretched out before her, but she couldn't enjoy the beauty of nature today.

Too bad their dream of finding a home with their uncle had turned into a race to get away from him.

"Will Uncle Harlan be mad when he finds out we stole his gold?" Beth asked, glancing up at Sarah with wide blue eyes.

"He's an outlaw. He'll probably shoot us all," Ryan said. "Didn't you see the notches on his gun?"

Beth whimpered and clung to Sarah's pants, nearly pulling her uncle's big trousers off her hips. She braced the gold against her chest to free one hand and hiked up the pants she'd worn to disguise her feminine form.

Sarah glared at her brother. "You told Beth about Uncle Harlan?"

Ryan shrugged and pulled his gaze away from hers, a wry smile tilting one side of his mouth. She should have known he couldn't keep something like that a secret, especially since he'd been the one to overhear their uncle talking to his outlaw gang about the next bank they planned to rob. Sarah's stomach swirled. Her brother had thought it was a game to follow their uncle and see where he had buried his loot. Ryan didn't realize the action could have gotten him killed. Uncle Harlan didn't want them there in the first place. He'd jump at the first chance to rid himself of them.

Sarah looked up at the clouds. *What's going to happen to us, Lord? Why couldn't Uncle Harlan have been as I remembered him?* She had prayed their uncle would love and protect his brother's orphaned children, but instead, they were merely a nuisance to him.

She pursed her lips. Now they were running away with his bag of stolen gold.

"Since we've got so much money, I want a horse." Ryan eyed the sack in Sarah's hands.

"I'm turning the gold over to the Medora sheriff." She hoped to collect a reward that would be enough to take the three of them far away on the train so Uncle Harlan couldn't locate them.

"But I found it so I should get to keep it." Ryan scowled and tightened his hands around the canteen strap that looped over one shoulder, then his expression softened. "I could buy you a new dress."

Sarah pressed her lips together to keep from smiling. Blackmail wouldn't work on her. "The gold doesn't belong to us, you know that."

"Yeah. It's stealing if we keep it, and that's a sin." Beth made a face at Ryan.

He jumped in front of Sarah before she could grab him and gave Beth a shove. "Who asked you?"

Beth gasped and spun around, falling to the ground. "Ow, ow. My ankle." She grabbed her right leg and rocked back and forth.

Sarah dropped the bag of gold and the quilt she carried and knelt beside her sister, giving her brother a stern glare. What would they do if Beth was seriously injured? *Please, God. No.*

"How bad does it hurt, sweetie?"

Tears ran down Beth's face. "It hurts bad, Sissy."

Sarah closed her eyes. They'd gone too far to go back, and even if they did and reburied the gold, surely their uncle could tell it had been tampered with. They had no choice but to continue on to Medora. Sarah straightened. "Ryan, you carry the rifle and the gold."

"But that's too heavy. I can't—"

"You will." Fear that they'd be caught had already worn her nerves as thin as a paper dollar, but she had to remain strong. She reached out to Beth. "I'll carry you, and you can hold the quilt with our belongings."

In less than a half hour, Sarah's back and arms ached. Nearly out of breath from carrying the six-year-old, she stopped to rest as they crested the next rise. Beth was almost asleep with her head bobbing down and back up.

A jackrabbit darted across the trail and down the hill. It dashed a few yards away then stopped beside a juniper bush. Its ears twitched. Past the rabbit, a dilapidated shack sat partially hidden in a copse of aspen and pines. If not for the rabbit, she would have walked right past the place and never seen it.

She lifted her knee and shifted Beth in her arms. She gazed toward Medora. The smokestack rose up in the distance, appearing closer than it had been earlier, but it was still a long way off. An idea formed in her mind, but just as quickly she dismissed it. Nibbling on her lip, she studied the sky. If only the clouds weren't so thick, she'd be better able to determine the time of day. Maybe there was enough time—if she hurried.

No, she couldn't do it. She couldn't leave the children here and go on alone.

"Let's take a break and eat lunch in that old shack."

Beth yawned and turned her head from side to side. "Where?"

"Down there." Sarah pointed toward the structure. "We'll be out of sight should anyone ride past the trail."

They slid down the hill, sending pebbles cascading. Sarah brushed a spiderweb out of the doorway and peeked inside the shack, glad to see the layer of dirt on the floor was free of footprints. At least no people or critters had been there in a long while.

"It's dirty." Beth stared at the floor.

"And it stinks, too." Ryan wrinkled up his face.

"But it's shady and will protect us if we get rain."

Sarah set Beth down, and the girl held onto the doorframe, keeping her sore foot from touching the ground. Sarah rolled her head and shoulders, trying to work out the kinks.

Ryan plunked down the gold sack with the name of a Deadwood, South Dakota bank stamped on it. Sarah spread out the thin quilt that held their meager possessions, and her sister hopped over and plopped down. Sarah's gaze shifted back to the canvas bag and lingered a moment. Using the gold to buy the food and clothing they needed was tempting. They had done without so many basic things that others took for granted for so long.

"No." She shook her head. Guilt would drive her crazy were she to do such a thing. The reward for returning the gold should be sufficient to give them a new start. It had to be.

"No, what?" Beth jerked her hand away from the bandana that held bread she'd been reaching for.

"Nothing, sweetie. Just talking to myself."

Ryan flopped down and tilted back the canteen. He took several long swigs.

"Go easy on the water. We don't know how long that will have to last us." Sarah untied the knot in the bandana that held their only food. She tore off chunks and gave them to her siblings. It wasn't much but would have to do until they could find something better. Too bad she didn't have time to trap and cook that rabbit.

"Is this all we get to eat?" Ryan turned up his nose at the dry bread.

"We'll get more once we get to town." If things worked out right.

Beth nibbled at her bread, her eyelids sagging. Sarah sighed and looked around. The lopsided one-room shanty was about as ramshackle as her uncle's, but it provided protection. She glanced at Beth's ankle, but the girl's shoe covered it. If she were to remove the shoe and the ankle swelled, she wouldn't be able to get it back on. Better to leave it alone.

Dare she leave her siblings here while she walked to town? They could rest, and she could hurry to Medora and turn in the gold. The three of them could hide out here until the day the train arrived. But could she leave her siblings? Even for a short time?

Ryan munched his bread and yawned. The long walk had tired him out, too. Sound asleep, Beth slumped over onto the quilt, a bit of bread still clutched in her fist. Ryan leaned back against the splintery, gray wall and closed his eyes.

Sarah gazed at her exhausted siblings and then at the crooked door. Her train of thought made her body quiver. She couldn't leave them. But she had to. There was no other choice. She could get to town and back quicker without them. The decision made, she stood.

Ryan yawned and opened his eyes. Sarah picked up the rifle and handed it to him.

"I'm going into town alone. You watch over Beth. I won't be gone too long."

"You're leaving us?" Ryan jumped up, his eyes wide.

"Beth is too tired to go on. If I go by myself, I can get to town, collect the reward, buy some food, and be back before dark."

Ryan's lower lip trembled. Sarah rested her palms on his thin shoulders. "I don't want to leave you at all, but Beth needs to sleep for a while and to rest her ankle. We can't leave her alone and there isn't enough time to wait until she wakes." Ryan needed to rest, too, but if she suggested that, he'd only balk at the idea. "You're a brave boy. I can trust you to take care of your sister."

"I'll guard her." He dropped back down and laid the rifle across his lap.

Sarah tucked her uncle's shirt into the big trousers. She patted her hair, making sure it was neatly pushed under an old felt hat. "Do I look like a man?"

Ryan shrugged and yawned. "Not to me."

Sarah untied the rope holding up her pants and redid it. "I figured we'd be safer if folks thought I was a man with two young'uns instead of a woman."

Ryan took a sip from the canteen then lay down beside Beth with his arm around the rifle. They were so young to be left alone in a strange place. Was she doing the right thing? What would Beth do when she awakened and found Sarah gone?

She couldn't waste any more time arguing with herself. "Stay hidden and do not leave here, no matter what. It'll be close to dark before I get back, and I don't want to have to go hunting for you two."

He nodded but wariness haunted his blue eyes behind his false bravado. Forcing a smile, Sarah bent and ruffled his brown hair. "Those shooting lessons I've been giving you were timely. Be careful. Watch Beth closely, and don't fight with her."

Ryan saluted like a little soldier. Leaving them was one of the hardest things she ever had to do, but this was the best solution.

Half a mile later, Sarah stared at the gray clouds and lengthened her stride. If she didn't get to town before the storm hit she would get drenched. She shifted the gold to her other arm. Hurry. Hurry.

The toe of her shoe sent a rock skittering across the narrow trail. She welcomed the noise. Without the chatter of the children, the wilds of the Badlands seemed more frightening. Her gaze darted to the left and then the right. This was the first time she'd been truly alone since her parents' deaths. Only the wind and her shoes scuffling against the rocky ground made any noise. She'd kept so busy trying to keep her family together and finding food for her noisy siblings that she'd never noticed the quietness before.

On the farm there was always a dog barking, cows lowing, or chickens clucking. And there was her mother's soft humming as she worked in the kitchen. The quiet pressed in on her.

"'Yea, though I walk through the valley of the shadow of death, I will fear no evil: for thou art with me; thy rod and thy staff they comfort me.' Walk with me, Lord. Please take these fears away."

With each step, her fear lessened. She wasn't alone. No matter what happened, God was with her.

She looked skyward again. How long since she'd left Ryan and Beth? An hour? Two?

The walk was taking far more time than she expected it would. After she turned in the robbery money, would she be able to collect a reward today? They were nearly out of food. How would they survive if they had to wait for payment of the reward?

A whinny pulled her from her thoughts. About twenty feet off the path, a horse turned to look at her. Sarah tightened her grip on the gold. She hadn't considered until now that someone else might steal it away from her. She couldn't let that happen.

"Hello? Anybody there?" The only sound was the swish of the wind in the tall grass. Sarah scanned the small valley for the horse's owner. Why would someone leave their mount untied out here in the middle of nowhere? "Easy now, that's a good girl."

The sleek gray horse jerked its head but stood still. Its black nostrils flared and ears flicked as it watched her. The mare stuck its muzzle toward her open hand and stepped forward, and Sarah wrapped her hands around the reins. There were no human footprints in the dirt near the animal. Could the owner be injured? She climbed a large rock and cupped her hand over her eyes and searched the valley again, this time with a better view. There were no signs of another human being and no buzzards circling, indicating a person badly injured.

Maybe the horse ran off, and if that was true, she should take it back to town so that wild animals didn't harm it. With its reins dragging, the horse could easily trip or get tangled in a bush and then it would be stuck. Also, if the rider was missing, surely someone in town would recognize the mare and send a search party.

She might even get a reward for returning the pretty horse with the expensive tooled saddle. Her heart danced at the thought of what she could do with the extra money. If she rode the horse to town, she could get back to the kids even sooner.

She shoved the gold into one of the empty saddlebags, but the flap refused to close. Sarah tied it shut the best she could. The bag of coins was wedged in good and tight and wasn't going anywhere. A north wind tugged at her hat and sent gusts of cool air into the gaps on her uncle's shirt. Being so far north, even summer could be chilly at times. She tucked the shirt in, put her foot in the stirrup, and mounted the mare. "Thank you, Papa, for insisting I learn to ride astride, and thank you, Lord, for the horse."

Twenty minutes later, she passed a few shacks and then crossed the bridge over the Little Missouri River. She rode past the giant brick smokestack of an abandoned factory. The town of Medora was little more than a handful of buildings—a few brick, but most made of wood or stone—spread out in a valley sheltered by tall buttes on all sides.

Sarah rode down the wide street, looking for the sheriff's office. A man to her right shouted, and people stopped on the boardwalk. All turned to stare at her. She tugged her hat down, hoping her hair was still covered.

In the minute it took to walk the horse into town, a crowd gathered off to one side. A dozen men stood on the boardwalk outside the mercantile and barbershop. Shouts and angry voices filled the streets as the growing crowd surged toward her. Heart skittering, she glanced over her shoulder, hoping they were yelling at someone else, but nobody was on the trail behind her. She didn't understand their hostility. A thin man hurtled toward her and grabbed the reins. The mare jumped sideways and squealed at the sudden action.

"That's Mary Severson's horse." A scowling, red-faced man shook his fist at Sarah.

"Ja, dat vas the horse dat ran off after Mary vas shot," A tall, fair-skinned man bobbed his blond head.

Sarah's heart lurched. Had her uncle's gang robbed the Medora bank instead of the one in Wyoming like they'd planned? The shouts grew louder, and the horse pranced sideways. The crowd encircled her and closed ranks. The mare reared up, and Sarah clutched the saddle horn to keep from falling.

Big hands suddenly yanked Sarah backward off the horse. The crowd swarmed her.

A tall man grabbed the bag of gold and yanked it out of the leather saddlebags. He opened it and stared. "Look! He has the stolen gold and paper money from the bank robbery in his saddlebags."

The roar of the crowd grew louder. Sarah jerked and struggled against her captors, but she couldn't break free. They propelled her against her will toward the middle of town.

"It's not my gold. I'm returning it!" Sarah shouted, but her cries were drowned out by the crowd's
frenzy.

"String 'im up!"

"Get a rope."

"Shoot him. Hanging's too good for the likes of him."

Three blasts of gunfire echoed off the surrounding hills, and the crowd instantly grew quiet. Sarah jerked toward the sound, her arms hurting where the two men on either side of her held her tight. This couldn't be happening. Lord, help me.

"What's going on?" A tall, middle-aged man with a thick moustache that curled on the edges stood on the elevated boardwalk holding a rifle. A badge was pinned to his vest.

"That man. He's one of the robbers who shot Mary Severson and stole her horse and robbed the bank," a deep voice behind Sarah boomed out.

"Yeah," another man called, "he was riding Mary's horse and had the gold in his saddlebags."

"That right?" The deputy scanned the crowd as they yelled their affirmation in unison. "All right then, bring him up here."

The crowd parted, and the two men holding Sarah hauled her forward.

"Let me go. I'm innocent." She fought her captors, but they were too strong. Her heart pounded and her legs trembled. Why wouldn't anybody listen to her pleas?

Surely the sheriff would be more reasonable. When he learned the truth, he would set her free. He had to let her go. She had to get back to her siblings before dark.

Please, Lord. Help me.

The men plunked her down on the boardwalk as the noise of the crowd rose again. One man shoved her toward the deputy sheriff so hard that she collided against his chest. Her hat plopped off her head, and her hair cascaded down around her face.

The crowd, a horde of smelly, bearded men, gaped in stunned silence.

Quinn McFarland was so angry at his grandmother he could yank nails from a horseshoe with his bare teeth. The horse pulling the buckboard jerked its head and snorted, slowing its pace. Quinn relaxed his tight hold on the reins and clucked out the side of his mouth, urging the horse forward. He couldn't leave that poor woman alone at the depot, even if he only learned he was to marry her this morning.

But how could his grandma do such a thing without talking to him? Didn't he have any say in the matter? How does someone go about arranging a mail-order bride in the first place?

Quinn thought of how happy his twin siblings were now that they were both married. He hoped to get married one day, too, but to a woman of his own choosing, not one picked out of a catalog or a newspaper ad. And certainly not to one that his grandmother had chosen for him.

Zerelda von. . .Something, no less. He shook his head and pulled back on the reins of his temper, forcing himself to relax.

Since he moved Grandma Miles to the ranch, it seemed as if her main duty was to needle him into finding a good wife. She wanted grandchildren before she died—as if fathering a child was all he had to worry about.

"When am I supposed to find time to court a woman?" He smacked his gloved hand against his thigh. Every waking hour he'd worked hard to keep the ranch going well enough to support his family. Not that it mattered now that they'd all moved away—except Grandma.

Quinn stared at a red-tailed hawk soaring carefree in the sky. What he wouldn't give to have that bird's lack of cares. If only his mother hadn't died suddenly and he hadn't moved his grandma to the ranch, he wouldn't be in this predicament. But family cared for family. He loved his grandma but was tired of her meddling.

He steered the buggy down the hillside to Medora. The town was tucked in a cozy valley in the heart of the North Dakota Badlands. Medora made a charming picture for newcomers, but life in this part of the country was tough. It took a certain kind of man—and a much stronger woman— to be able to survive the harsh winters and sometimes scorching summers, not to mention the loneliness of ranch life. Somehow, he didn't think Miss Zerelda von. . .What's-her-name had it in her. She'd probably take one look at the tiny town and its lack of amenities and catch the first train back East.

Red hair, hazel eyes. That's what the letter had said. There couldn't be too many women with that coloring arriving by train in Medora. Quinn checked his pocket watch then guided the buggy toward the post office. There was time to run a few errands before he had to be at the depot to meet the afternoon train. Maybe by then he'd know if he wanted to keep the woman or send her back on the next train.

With women being few and far between out West, maybe he should accept the bird-in-the-hand. He'd make his grandma happy and get her off his back, but he'd be saddled with a woman he hadn't asked for, didn't know, and didn't want. Could he come to love a mail-order bride under such circumstances?

Maybe she was so plain she couldn't find anyone to marry her in her hometown. Or could be she was as crotchety as a hen caught in a downpour. But if she was a nice, godly woman, they could probably manage. Only he didn't know if he wanted to give up his one chance to choose his own bride.

He climbed out of the rig, his brain tired from arguing with himself. He hadn't done this much thinking since. . . well, he couldn't remember.

The June breeze whipped around him, hinting at cooler weather. A north wind like this could be a blessing in summer, but not so in the winter. He paused to take a swig from his canteen, but the lukewarm water did little to soothe his thirst. He returned his canteen to the wagon and entered the post office. "Afternoon, Mr. Simms. Got any mail for the Rocking M?"

"Good day to you, and yes, I believe I do." The postmaster, a thin man clad in a wrinkled white shirt and black pants, nodded his head. He turned, reached into a slot, and retrieved several letters.

Quinn took the stack and nodded his thanks. Outside on the boarded walkway, he stared at the depot. Should he keep the bride or send her back on the next train?

He watched two cowpokes chatting beside their mounts. A businessman in a suit strode down the boardwalk across the street then turned into the barber shop. Not a woman was in sight. Quinn heaved a sigh. Might as well keep the bride. It wasn't like he had many opportunities to meet women, and in two years he'd turn thirty. If he wanted to marry and start a family, the time was now. He'd just have to keep the woman. After all, it was what she wanted. Otherwise she wouldn't be traveling so far to marry him.

Relieved to have finally made one of the biggest decisions of his life, he thumbed through the mail. His hands stopped on one particular missive from Zerelda von Hammerstein. Ah. . .that was her name. The letter was addressed to him, so he flipped it over and opened it. He sure hoped she hadn't changed her arrival date and that he hadn't wasted nearly half a day coming to town. He shook open the single sheet of paper.

Dear Mr. McFarland,

After much prayer and talking with my minister, I have come to the conclusion that to marry a stranger would be a drastic mistake for me. I hope you don't take this offensively, for it is no reflection on your character. I simply can't marry a man I don't know. Please forgive me for getting your hopes up. As a result of my decision, I will not be arriving on the June 4th train. Please accept my humblest apology for any inconvenience my change of mind has caused you.

Best wishes,
Zerelda Ingrid von Hammerstein

Quinn sighed. He'd been left at the altar—no, he hadn't even gotten that far. He shook his head, his self-esteem plummeting.

I've been dumped by a mail-order bride I've never even met--a bride he hadn't wanted or even known about until his grandmother had informed him about her this morning at breakfast. And what about the funds his grandmother had mailed to the bride to pay for her trip here? The woman hadn't even been courteous enough to return the money. Quinn crumpled up the missive and tossed it at the buggy. Half a day wasted on fetching a bride who hadn't wanted him. How could her rejection sting when he'd decided to marry her only five minutes ago?

And what would he tell his grandmother? He retrieved the wadded letter and smoothed it out. He may be a tough North Dakota rancher, able to fight wolves, thieves, and rustlers without flinching, but he needed this evidence to prove to his five-foot short granny that his bride had dumped him and not the other way around.

Some man he was.

He crossed the dirt street and headed toward the mercantile to place an order. A local rancher, Theodore Roosevelt, strode out of the store and grinned at Quinn.

"Haven't seen you in a while, McFarland. How are things going?"

Quinn shook the man's hand. "Good as can be expected. What brings you to town, Mr. Roosevelt?"

"Call me Theodore." He smiled and shifted the crate of supplies he was holding to his other arm. "I'm staying at my ranch—the Maltese Cross—for a while. Came into town to get supplies." The man fingered his bushy moustache. "Sorry to hear about your mother's passing."

"Thank you. It was unexpected." Quinn clenched his jaw. The fever that took his mother two months ago came fast and swift, surprising them all. He didn't want to think about missing her—wondering if he'd done all he could to ease her burden after his pa had died. He gazed down the dirt street that would turn into a muddy mess if the storm clouds dumped the rain they were threatening. He turned his focus back to the rancher. "I haven't been to town in a while. How have things been going around here?"

Theodore slid his hat back on his head. "Heard there was a bank robbery yesterday morning. Most exciting thing that's happened in a long while around here—at least that's what the clerk in the store said. It was unfortunate that the banker's daughter got shot. Seems she had just ridden up to the bank to see her pa when the outlaws came running out. She was shot and fell into the street. Her horse ran off, following the outlaws' horses."

Quinn pursed his lips. "Sorry to hear about that. Do you know how Mary is doing?"

The big man shrugged one shoulder. "Not too good, so the clerk said."

A rider on horseback rode into view, followed by a crowd of people. The rider, a thin boy, looked from side to side as if wondering why so many people were watching him. Quinn wondered the same thing. Normally folks in Medora went about their own business.

He studied the rider and horse. Something was familiar, but he couldn't pinpoint what. Suddenly, he realized what was nagging him. Quinn glanced at Theodore. "That horse looks exactly like the mare I sold to Mary's pa."

"You don't say. From the way the townsfolk are acting, I would guess it is the same animal."

The murmuring crowd suddenly encircled the horse. The frightened mare tossed her head and whinnied. One man grabbed the reins while another man yanked the rider off the horse. Someone shouted the word "gold." Quinn nodded good-bye to Mr. Roosevelt, stepped off the boardwalk, and moved toward the crowd. What was going on?

Amidst the loud ruckus, the rider was hoisted by each arm and carried toward the sheriff's office. "Hang him," someone shouted, and the crowd roared in agreement.

"Get a rope."

"He needs to pay for what he did to Mary."

The crowd moved toward the Sheriff's Office. Two men deposited the small man on the boardwalk a few feet from the deputy sheriff.

One of them shoved the captive. Stumbling forward, the man flapped his arms like a chicken with clipped wings and fought for balance as he collided with the deputy. His hat flew off, and the crowd instantly hushed as a mass of black hair cascaded down past the man's—no, woman's—shoulders.

Quinn clenched his jaw at the rough way the woman was being manhandled. A skinny man squeezed past her and handed the deputy sheriff a canvas sack. "Look, she's got a bag of gold coins just like them ones that was stolen from our bank."

The deputy eyed his prisoner and his jaw twitched. "You come with me. For your own well-being, I'm locking you up. Sheriff Jones will be back in the morning, and he can straighten out this mess."

The woman dug in her feet. "But I'm innocent. I didn't do anything."

The deputy sheriff shook the heavy bag. "The evidence says otherwise."

Chapter Two

Quinn shoved his way through the unruly crowd, trying to get closer. The frightened young woman had looked straight at him, their gazes connecting for a split second before hers moved away, as if she was searching for someone to believe her. She was in the deputy's custody, so she was safe from the rowdy crowd for the time being.

He'd heard the words "stolen gold," but if the woman was guilty of a crime, why would she ride into a town she recently robbed in broad daylight? It had to be some kind of misunderstanding. Sheriff Jones would get to the bottom of it.

A gust of wind threatened to steal Quinn's hat away, and he glanced at the sky. A dust devil swirled at the end of the street, and the air smelled of rain. The clouds had thickened and blocked out the sun that had shone so brightly earlier in the day. He ought to head back to the ranch but didn't want to get caught in a downpour. If he'd been on horseback, he would have toughed it out, but he had the buckboard and wasn't about to drive it in a storm. Not after what happened to his father.

A raindrop tapped against his hat. He hurried his steps and headed toward the general store to place an order for some spices and other supplies his cook and his grandmother needed. He'd stay the night in town, and tomorrow morning he'd tend to some business and then ride home.

After checking into his room at the Metropolitan Hotel, he stared out his window watching the heavy raindrops pelt the street. That mail-order bride fiasco had cost him a day's work, the cost of the money they sent her, and a hotel stay. His gaze traveled to the jail. He couldn't get that young female outlaw off his mind. Would the sheriff let her go? Was she locked up in the same jail cell Quinn had been confined to after he and his sister had been mistakenly arrested for being outlaws the previous year? He wouldn't wish that on any female.

He leaned his head against the cool glass as the darkness of that day crowded in on him. He'd hated that hot, clammy cell that stank like an outhouse. He had hated not being able to see the sky or feel the warmth of the sun on his skin. Was that what the young woman was now experiencing? If she was guilty of her crimes, she deserved confinement, but if she wasn't. . .

He shook his head and sighed. He had his own problems, mainly being how to keep his grandma from ordering another mail-order bride for him. As soon as he returned home without his bride, the meddling woman would probably start searching the ads. Then again, he could just forget to bring her a newspaper.

Quinn grinned for the first time that day.

"Hey in there! Why won't you listen to me?" Sarah shook the flat bars of the cell that reminded her of wooden lattice, but they held firm. "I'm innocent, I tell you. I didn't rob anyone. I was returning that gold."

She swallowed, her throat raw from yelling so much. She pulled her bodice free from her sweat-dampened chest and fanned it as she paced the tiny, dark cell, her mind racing. Had Ryan and Beth stayed at the shack when she hadn't returned before dark? Had last night's storm frightened them?

A moan escaped her mouth. What if they'd gone back to Uncle Harlan's or attempted to get to town? He could use them as hostages and threaten their lives if she didn't return his gold. Or, what if they were lost in the Badlands?

Tears burned Sarah's eyes, but she refused to let them fall. Had Beth been scared of the storm? Had she awakened this morning and been frightened when she realized her big sister hadn't returned? The little girl had been so fearful that Sarah would be taken away, just like their parents had been, that she'd hardly let her out of sight for the past few months. She shook the black bars of the cell again, but they didn't give.

"God, please, help me. I have to get out of here."

Something skittered across the floor. Sarah jumped back, her heart hammering. A mouse sniffed at something on the dirt floor then dashed under the cot she'd spent the night on.

Her thoughts turned back to bigger problems. Why wouldn't that deputy listen to her? At least the sheriff was due back in town this morning. Maybe he'd be more compassionate and willing to hear her out.

The lock on the entrance to the sheriff's office clicked and the door opened. A tall man with dark hair walked in and stared at Sarah. He leaned against the wall opposite her cell, and his silver badge, which matched his dull gray shirt, reflected in the lantern light.

"I'm Will Jones, Medora's sheriff."

She pressed her face against the slats, glad that he had returned. "I'm innocent. Please, you have to believe me, Sheriff Jones."

The man held up his hand. "I've heard the story."

She had to make him believe her. "I was heading into town and found the horse. I rode it to Medora, thinking maybe it had run away from here or one of the area ranches. I didn't steal it. Only rode it so I could get to town and back to my brother and sister sooner. Please, they're little and alone in the hills. Last night's storm probably scared them half to death."

"If they're so helpless, why'd you leave them alone? Why weren't they with you when you came into town?"

Sarah rubbed her palm against her forehead, hoping to chase away her growing headache. "They were exhausted. Beth had twisted her ankle, and she was too heavy for me to carry all the way. I left them in a deserted shack and hurried to town, thinking I'd get back to them before night fell. Could you at least send someone for them and bring them here?"

The sheriff leaned against the wall and swatted his hand in the air as if batting a fly. "So, the gold was in the saddlebags when you found the horse?"

"What? No. We found it back at my uncle's cabin where we've been staying since our parents died."

"Your uncle? What's his name?"

"Harlan Oakley."

"Never heard of him. Where'd he get the gold?" He lifted one foot and pressed it against the wall behind him.

"My brother, Ryan, overheard our uncle and some men talking about the banks and trains they'd robbed. After Uncle Harlan and the other men rode out yesterday morning, we dug up the gold. I was hoping if I returned it, I might get a reward. I need to get my family away from my uncle and his cronies."

The sheriff pursed his lips, and in two steps, he was at the bars. He grabbed hold of them. Sarah swallowed hard and stepped back.

"So I'm supposed to believe that you already had the gold and then just happened to find a horse that ran away during a robbery the day before. Did you know the woman who owned that horse was shot? The doc doesn't know if she'll pull through. I'm working on getting descriptions of the thieves, but one of them sounds similar in size to you."

"Well, it wasn't me." Sarah grasped the slats of her cell and leaned her forehead against the cold metal. "If you'd let me go, I could show you where I found the horse and take you to my brother and sister. They'll verify my story."

He straightened. "How old are these mysterious young'uns?"

"Beth is six, and Ryan is eight."

"I'd really like to believe your story, ma'am. You seem like a nice young woman, but you were caught red-handed, and you'll have to stay here for now. I'll see that you get some grub in a little while." The sheriff shook his head and turned away.

"Nooo! Please listen. I've got to get back to my brother and sister. They've got to be scared and confused, and they don't have much food. If I don't get out of here they could die." Sarah trembled at the thought of all the things that could happen to two unprotected children in the wilds of the Badlands.

Without a backward glance, he shut the door, sealing her in again.

"Don't leave. Wait!" Never had she felt so helpless, not even after the fire that had destroyed her home and killed her parents. "God, why aren't You helping me? We've been through so much already, why this? You know I'm innocent."

The lone lantern cast eerie shadows that danced on the wall across from the two cells. The room smelled of smoke—and the unemptied chamber pot she'd been humiliated to use. If only there was a window to let in fresh air.

A dark panic she'd never before experienced closed in around her. The tears she'd held at bay for so long now flooded down her cheeks. She sat on the cot, elbows on her knees, and a wail escaped, sounding like a panicked animal caught in a trap.

"God, help me. Watch over my brother and sister. Keep them safe, and get me out of here."

Quinn stood outside the hotel, absorbing the warm sunshine. A bird chirped in a nearby tree greeting the new day that smelled fresh and clean after yesterday's storms, but Quinn could hardly enjoy its tune. What would his grandmother say when he returned without his bride? Would she nag him half to death until he found another woman to marry?

He exhaled a frustrated sigh. How could a grown man—a rancher who'd forged a life out of a wilderness—be afraid of his granny? His grandma had always been a strong woman, but mourning her daughter's death had made her frail, and she'd often taken to her bed. A mother shouldn't have to watch her child die, Grandma had said. Now that she was starting to get around again, he didn't want her to have a setback.

He shook his head and crossed the street, dodging a puddle, and headed toward the mercantile. He missed his mother, too, but he had a ranch to run and did his grieving in the saddle. He passed the sheriff's office and recalled the woman's frantic gaze from the day before—a gaze that had haunted his dreams last night. Was she still in jail?

It had been a long while since he'd chatted with Sheriff Will Jones. Will had locked up Quinn and his sister when a U.S. Marshal had turned them in as outlaws. After they'd been found innocent and released, he and the sheriff had become friends. Maybe a quick stop to say howdy was in order. Quinn had a burning desire to know what had become of the young woman, and there was only one way to find out. Had she been sent happily on her way, or was she even now incarcerated in that dark, stuffy cell?

He spun around and headed back to the sheriff's office. The door rattled as Quinn stepped inside. Will looked up from the papers on his desk and smiled, weary lines clinging around his eyes. Will gestured toward the chair opposite his desk.

Quinn sat and crossed his arms over his chest. He stretched his legs out in front of him. He still didn't like this place, but at least the office was brighter and less claustrophobic than those two gloomy cells. "Haven't seen you in a coon's age. How you doin'?"

"I've had better days." Will proffered a crooked smile. "I've had worse ones, too."

"I imagine you have." Quinn stared at the door separating the office from the cell room. "What became of that gal that your deputy dragged in here yesterday?"

"She's locked up in back." Will rubbed his nape. "I don't know what to believe. She came riding into town on Mary Severson's horse, carrying a bag of stolen gold, and claims she's as innocent as a newborn babe." Will picked up his coffee and took a sip. "The problem is. . .I'm half inclined to believe her. But all the evidence says otherwise."

"It wouldn't be the first time you had an innocent female in your jail."

The sheriff spewed coffee onto the floor and chuckled. "You're never gonna let me live that down. You still mad about that?"

Quinn shook his head. "Nope. It's water under the bridge now. Anna's happily married to that ex-marshal who arrested us. I still can hardly believe that, but Brett's a good man. So, what makes you think this gal is innocent?"

Will scratched his chest, wrinkling his shirt. "Just a hunch. There are no eyewitnesses that can place her at the crime." Will glanced at the closed door to the cell room. "She claims she has a younger brother and sister out there somewhere waiting for her to return."

Quinn bent his legs and leaned forward. "You think she's telling the truth?"

The sheriff shrugged. "I sent my deputy out to look for them, but he didn't find any trace of two kids."

Quinn stared out the window. The sun shone bright on the two small trees across the street, and a light wind tickled leaves still damp from last night's storm. He hated the thought of an innocent woman in that cell, unable to see the sun or feel a breeze on her face, experiencing the same fears his sister had endured until he, too, had been arrested and was able to comfort her. But maybe the woman was guilty. How else could she have had stolen gold in her possession?

Will leaned forward and laid his arms across his desk. "I have a bad feeling about this one. The townsfolk were ready to lynch her yesterday. The odd thing is that bank bag she had in her possession had the name of the Deadwood Federal Bank on it. I telegraphed the Deadwood sheriff, and they had a robbery over a month ago, but there wasn't a woman involved."

Loud footsteps pounded on the boardwalk, and a heavy-set man dressed in a three-piece brown suit strode past the window. He halted in front of the sheriff's door.

"Great. Here comes trouble." Will leaned back in his chair and crossed his arms.

The man flung open the door and stormed inside. He glanced at Quinn and then focused a glare on the sheriff. Quinn recognized Medora's bank president, Lars Severson. The wealthy white-haired man had often tried to push his own agenda at town meetings.

Sweat trickled down Severson's temple. He marched forward, put his hands on the desk, and leaned toward the sheriff. "I want to know what you plan to do with that outlaw who shot Mary and stole her horse."

Will stood, forcing Mr. Severson to look up. "I haven't decided yet. Witnesses have testified that Mary's horse ran off without a rider following after the outlaws' horses, but a few folks say one of the outlaws was on it."

"My Mary lies half dead in her bed, and you can't decide what to do with the outlaw who shot her?" The man's beefy face turned the color of a beat. He pounded his fist on the sheriff's desk, rattling an empty coffee cup. "I demand justice."

Will shoved his hands to his waist. "Now see here, there's no proof this woman was with the outlaws who shot Mary. She claims she found the horse and the gold. . .but not at the same place." Will glanced at Quinn as if the story sounded highly unlikely once voiced out loud.

"I want that woman to pay for her crimes."

"You want to send an innocent woman to prison or see her hanged?" Will asked.

The banker's white brows crinkled. "Of course not, but there's plenty of evidence that the woman in your jail is a thief."

"Nobody has stepped forward who can identify her as one of the outlaws, and there was no mention of a woman being among the gang of robbers. I'm not convinced she was." The sheriff stared at the banker until the man looked away.

A distant memory clawed its way to the front of Quinn's mind. "I can think of a way to get rid of this headache." Both men swung their gaze on him, and he struggled to keep a straight face. Maybe he could defuse the tension with a bit of jesting.

"How?" Will asked. "I'm open to any ideas at this point."

"I remember reading in the newspaper about a woman outlaw who was captured in Montana. Since there were so few women around those parts, the sheriff auctioned her off to the highest bidder."

Will stared at him. "You're joking, right?"

"Nope." He may have been joking about auctioning off the woman in Will's jail, but the tale he told was true. "That sheriff didn't want the hassle of keeping a woman in his jail until a judge rode through."

"That's preposterous, Sheriff." Banker Severson looked from Quinn to the sheriff. "Surely you aren't taking him seriously, are you?"

Quinn shrugged. "I'm merely telling you what another sheriff did in a similar situation. But you've got to admit there are few women around these parts. Do you really think a jury made up of men from around here would convict a pretty gal?"

Will seemed to consider that. "Probably not."

"Why not give her the choice of marrying now and getting out of jail or trying her luck at a jury trial? That way if she is innocent, she won't pay for a crime she didn't do, and the jail will be free for more serious criminals."

"Why. . .that's unseemly—unchristian," the banker sputtered. "What could be more serious than shooting an innocent girl and robbing a bank?"

Will gave Quinn a furtive wink and rubbed his jaw and glanced toward the closed door that led to the cell area. "That's not a half bad idea. Women are hard to come by in these parts."

The banker pounded his fist on Will's desk again. "I demand justice. That woman must account for her misdeeds." Mr. Severson glared at them then turned and stomped out the door.

Quinn chuckled. "He just might have your job for that."

"It was worth it. Did you see the look on his face?" Will hooted and pounded on his desk. "That man has been a thorn in my side ever since he came to town. I'm real sorry Mary got shot, but I'd rather lose my job than send an innocent woman to prison or see her hanged."

Will walked to the window and stared out. "Uh oh, looks like Severson is making a stink already. Half a dozen men are headed this way."

Quinn stood and joined him at the window. Sure enough, they were about to be swarmed. Will spun around, grabbed his rifle, and pulled a box of cartridges out of his top desk drawer, preparing for a fight. Quinn checked his revolver out of habit, knowing already that it was loaded. "We can't let them lynch that woman."

Will nodded. "It's days like this I wish the jail had a back door."

Chapter Three

Quinn cocked his gun and watched the growing crowd. Half a dozen men shouted and shoved at one another as if each wanted to be the one to pull the trap door and lynch that poor girl. Will opened the door and stood there, blocking the entrance.

"Stop right where you are, or someone's gonna get hurt."

The men at the front of the crowd halted, surprise lifting their brows. Men in the back plowed into them. More pushing and caterwauling ensued.

Tom Gallagher, a local rancher, shoved past another man and stepped forward. "I'll marry that gal. It don't matter to me what she's done. She's right fair to look at, and I need a woman at home."

A smelly, hairy man who resembled a bear fresh out of hibernation stepped in front of Mr. Gallagher. "Nuh-uh, I's here first. Heard Lars Severson myself say the sheriff was marryin' her off. She's my woman."

Pete Samson wiped his sleeve across his whiskery face. "Nope." He spat a wad of tobacco juice at Will's feet. "I reckon I was first. She's mine."

Will's confused gaze darted to Quinn's, and he shrugged one shoulder.

"What are you talking about?" Will asked. "I thought you were a lynch mob."

The bear tugged off his dingy cap. "Nope. That was yesterday. Today, I reckon we all got our hearts set on marryin' that little gal—and I'm first in line."

"No you're not," Tom Gallagher hollered. "I need a wife to watch after my two young'uns. You only want her for, well. . .never mind."

"It don't matter why I want her. I just do." The two men shoved at each other like schoolboys wanting to do a favor for a pretty teacher.

Pete stared at the two, then grinned and stepped past them. "Reckon I'm first now, Sheriff."

Several men still standing in the dirt street yelled that they wanted to marry up with the outlaw, too. One man punched another, and a jaw-breaking brawl started. Sheriff Jones pointed his rifle over their heads and pulled the trigger. The blast of the gunfire froze the crowd as the familiar odor of gunpowder scented the air in a cloud of smoke. Men with fists raised slowly lowered their arms and glared at their neighbor.

"Nothing has been decided yet. Go home." Will held his rifle across one arm.

"But Banker Severson was griping to anyone who'd listen. Said you was gonna auction that gal off. I'll give ya two dollars for her." A man Quinn had never seen before jingled some coins in his hand.

Will growled. "We don't sell people around here. Go home before I lock up the whole kit and caboodle of you."

"If'n you're gonna lock me up with that gal, then go ahead." The bear held out his hands as if waiting for Will to slap irons on him. Several men chuckled.

Will aimed his rifle at the man's belly. "Head back to the hills, mister."

Irritation sparked in the man's eyes, but his gaze lowered to the rifle. He backed away, mumbling something Quinn couldn't make out, and sauntered across the street.

Quinn bit back a chuckle. Yesterday they were ready to lynch the poor gal, and now they wanted to marry her. The crowd of fickle men had been disappointed. That was obvious. Twenty men to one woman. No wonder they all went half crazy for a chance to have one of their own. His mail-order bride's refusal stung again. Yep, it sure would be hard to find a woman to live on a ranch, two hours' ride from town.

Will shook his head and remained outside the doorway. "Look what you started."

Quinn shrugged. "Men out here are lonely. I was only trying to help." He leaned one shoulder against the doorframe. "But you can't turn that poor girl over to the likes of any of those men. Gallagher's not so bad. He needs a woman for those kids of his, but he's got that hair-trigger temper and those rambunctious boys."

Will rubbed the back of his neck. "I wouldn't let that poor gal marry a one of those hooligans."

"Well. . .why not find a man you would let her marry—if you're sure of her innocence."

Will's eyes sparked and one corner of his mouth tilted up. He stepped back into his office and laid his rifle on the desk. "I think I will. How'd you like to meet your new bride, McFarland?"

"What?" Quinn scowled at Will. "That's not funny."

Will placed his hands on his desk and leaned toward Quinn. "Do I look like I'm joking? That little gal is as pretty as a mustang. I feel in my gut that she's telling the truth. You need a wife, so why not marry her? Would solve a lot of problems—for both of us."

Quinn turned to leave. "That's just plain crazy, Will. You don't even know if she'd be willing to marry simply to get out of jail." He walked to the open door and noted that the crowd of men outside had grown to more than a dozen. Most weren't family men who worked hard and made a good living, but rather the bums, trappers, and cowpokes that hung out at the saloon. It didn't take much thought to realize why they wanted a woman.

"She seems willing to do about anything to get out of jail. Think about it, will you?"

Coming home with a bride would solve one of his problems. It would get Grandma off his back, so he could focus on his work. He turned to face the sheriff.

"Did you see her yesterday?" Will's eyes brightened. "She's a comely little thing. You want to have a look up close before you decide?"

Quinn clenched his teeth and scowled. Will made it sound as if he were buying a horse. But his curiosity had been aroused. He wasn't one to make impulsive decisions, especially when an outlaw was part of the deal, but what did it hurt to have a look at the woman?

Muffled cries came from the back room where the woman was jailed. Quinn stared at the door that led to the cells. Was the woman as frightened as Anna had been in there? "I'd like to see her." The words came out before he could lasso them back.

Will stared at him for a moment then grinned. "She'll give you an earful. She's a feisty little thing."

Quinn wished he'd kept his mouth shut. He needed to get his supplies and head home. But he wasn't in any hurry to disappoint his grandmother.

"I need to talk to her anyway. C'mon." Will stood and shuffled across the room, digging a key from his pocket. The latch clicked, and he opened the door.

That sound was enough to make Quinn sweat. The feeling of being totally helpless—of knowing he was innocent, but no one believed him—hit him full force in the chest. For a moment, he wasn't sure he could walk through that door again.

"You comin'?" Will called as he peered around the doorway. He grinned. "Got cold feet, McFarland?"

Quinn narrowed his eyes at the man and sucked in a breath. He strode to the door and halted. The dank odor of mold and a chamber pot assailed him. He'd never been afraid of anything except losing his good reputation when he had been locked up for a crime he hadn't committed. Quinn stepped halfway across the threshold. He could see plenty well from there.

Will chuckled and faced the prisoner. The memory of Anna alone in the cell before Quinn had been arrested hit him suddenly as his gaze landed on the red-faced waif. Why, the girl couldn't be out of her teens yet. Quinn's irritation with Will grew. Wasn't imprisoning one woman enough for him?

She wiped her eyes and hiked up her chin as her confused gaze darted between Quinn and Will. She grabbed the bars, and her gaze turned frantic. "Please, I'm innocent. You've got to believe me."

Bile rose to Quinn's throat. She wasn't a hard-edged criminal, but a frightened young woman. Her haunted eyes held desperate fear, not the cold, hardened guilt of an outlaw. She was as innocent as Anna had been. He knew it in his gut.

Will shook his head. "I want to believe you, miss, but there's the gold and horse you had in your possession. Horse stealing is a hangin' offense in these parts."

"But I didn't steal it. I found it, and I was returning the gold. It didn't come from Medora. You can clearly see that if you look at the bag it was in." Her gaze darted to Quinn as if he could help her.

"You need anything, miss? More water?" Will asked.

She glared at him. "I only need to get out. Ryan and Beth are depending on me. They must be terribly frightened and half-starved by now."

Will heaved a heavy sigh and nodded for Quinn to head back into the office. Quinn was glad to be away from that dark hole. The door clanked as Will pulled it shut, sending a shiver down Quinn's spine.

"Now you see why I can't marry her off to just anyone—if I decide to go that route. She's too young and naive."

"You don't even know if she'd want to marry. She's a still a kid." Quinn leaned against the wall across from Will's desk. He glanced at the locked door, glad he was on this side of it.

"She said something about her parents dying." Will leaned back in his chair and propped his feet onto his desk.

Quinn stared out the window, knowing the pain of losing one's parents. He needed to get going. Grandma would be fit to be tied that he hadn't come home yesterday. Too bad he didn't have a good enough excuse to stay gone a whole week.

"What are you grinning about? I don't see anything funny." Will laced his hands behind his head and leaned back in his chair.

Quinn stared at the wanted poster above Will's head. He was glad the girl's pretty face wasn't up there. Her eyes had looked like yesterday's storm clouds one moment and then turned soft and sincere. . .pleading, the next. Her long, dark hair reminded him of a wild mustang when she'd flipped it over her shoulder.

"I said, what's so funny?"

Quinn took a deep breath and told his friend what his grandma had done. Will's eyes went wide.

"That's not the worst part. The bride didn't come. Wrote me a letter saying she'd changed her mind."

Will slapped his leg and hooted with laughter. "Dumped by a bride you didn't even want. Oh, that's a good one."

Quinn straightened. "Don't tell anyone. A man's got his pride, you know."

"Are you threatening a lawman?" Will grinned wickedly, then suddenly sobered. Quinn glanced out the window to see if something had drawn his attention.

"So"—Will's feet dropped to the floor and he leaned forward—"let me get this straight. Your grandma ordered you a bride who didn't show. Now you've got to go home and tell her. No wonder you've been dawdling in my office so long."

"I'm not dawdling. I'm paying a friendly visit." Quinn picked up his hat from Will's desk. "I can see I've worn out my welcome."

"Hold on. I can help."

"How?"

Will grinned again. "I've got a gal in my jail who needs a husband."

Quinn narrowed his eyes. Suddenly he realized what Will meant. "Oh, no. You're not going to pawn her off onto me. I never said I'd marry her. I just wanted a look at her."

"Hold on." Will held up his calloused hand. "Let's think this through. You need a bride—"

"No. I don't." Quinn rolled his eyes. He didn't need a bride, especially an outlaw one, although Anna would love that story.

"I saw how that gal affected you. She's frightened and alone, like your sister was when she was locked up. I've got a feeling she's innocent. Even if she isn't, a good man like you could keep a woman on the straight and narrow."

Quinn's gaze darted to the closed door. Anna had been so scared and heartbroken to be locked up in jail. The woman's pleading eyes called to him. He felt sure she was innocent, but what if she wasn't?

"You said yourself that women are hard to come by out here. You'd better take the bird-in-the-hand."

"Don't you mean bird-in-the-cell?" Quinn cocked a brow.

Will shrugged. "You want to marry her or not? I've got plenty of others ready to jump at the chance."

Quinn gritted his teeth. He didn't like being coerced into doing something, but he couldn't get that tear-streaked face out of his mind. That gal had looked scared to death—and innocent. If she was guilty, she wouldn't be putting up such a ruckus, and the thought of one of those mangy men getting their hands on someone so naive stuck in his craw. "How do you even know she'd want to marry me? I have to be ten years her senior."

Will waved his hand in the air. "That doesn't matter. Herbert Simms is fifteen years older than his wife. You'd be doing me a huge favor, Quinn. How can I arrest real criminals if I have a woman in my jail? I couldn't subject her to that."

The girl was comely, and if he married her, one of his problems would be solved. Quinn grinned. "It would almost be worth it to see Grandma's face. She's expecting a hazel-eyed redhead."

"Wish I could be there to see her reaction. But this ain't no laughing matter. Marriage is for life. So . . . you willing?"

Quinn swallowed, unable to believe he could actually go through with such a crazy plan. He wasn't one to be impulsive. He preferred to think through things and look at them from all angles. He couldn't explain why, but he felt marrying this woman was the right thing to do. Swallowing hard, he nodded. "I'm willing. . .if she is."

The outer door opened again, and Sarah jumped off the cot, hit by a wave of dizziness. The lack of sleep and appetite, along with the stagnant air and worry for her siblings had left her woozy. She held on to the bars as the sheriff and that handsome man entered again. The other man was taller than the sheriff with shoulders so wide he looked uncomfortable in the narrow walkway. His brown hair matched his dark eyes, which held a mixture of curiosity and apprehension. He twisted his western hat in his hands.

He leaned against the doorjamb, with one foot barely over the threshold, as if he were afraid to come in further. He glanced over his shoulder. Perhaps he didn't like small, confining spaces. Well. . .neither did she.

The sheriff stopped in front of her and stared as if taking her measure. She'd just finished braiding her hair and tying it off with a piece of fabric she'd torn from the tail of her shirt.

Sheriff Jones cleared his throat. "You say you're innocent, Miss Oakley, and I'm inclined to believe you. The law out here is—shall we say—a bit more flexible than back East, and there are times a sheriff has to go with his gut, and mine says you're not guilty."

Sarah's heart jumped. Was he going to release her?

He rubbed his hand over his cheek. "I have a proposal for you, miss. Well. . .I don't but he does." The sheriff used his thumb to point at the stranger, and his lips tugged up in a cocky grin.

Sarah narrowed her gaze and glanced at the tall man. How could he help her? Was he a lawyer?

Sheriff Jones cleared his voice. "Here's the thing, ma'am, I got nobody who can identify you as the thief who shot Mary and stole her horse."

Sarah hiked up her chin. "That's because I didn't do it."

"Be that as it may, here's the deal. You can sit in this cell until the circuit judge from Dickinson comes around in a month or so, or. . ." The sheriff glanced at the other man, who looked at Sarah then pursed his lips and nodded.

Her heart thundered and her knees shook. No matter what the alternative was, she had to take it.

"Or you can marry up with this man and get out of jail today."

Sarah's mouth opened, but no words came out. Surely the sheriff couldn't be serious. Marry a stranger?

She glanced at the other man—the one who was willing to marry her. Why would he want to wed a woman he didn't know? A woman in jail, no less. He was handsome enough to marry any woman he wanted. She looked him in the eye and swallowed back her fear. He was the key to getting out of here. "Why?"

He glanced at the sheriff and twisted the hat in his hand. The lantern cast flickering light across his face. "Why what?"

"Why would you want to marry me?"

He studied his hat for a moment. With his head ducked down, Sarah saw that his hair had a curl to it. "I've got my reasons."

"There's no point in you wasting away in jail when you can marry Quinn. He's a good man and owns one of the best ranches in this area. He's got, what"—the sheriff glanced sideways—"a couple of thousand acres?"

"Four thousand."

"And he's got one of the finest cabins I've seen. He's an honorable man and raises some of the best cattle and horses in these parts."

Sarah's mind raced but nothing made sense. She looked at the sheriff. "You're saying if I agree to marry him"—she pointed at the stranger—"then I can go free? Today? I wouldn't have to come back to stand trial?"

Sheriff Jones nodded. "Yep. I don't much like having a woman locked up in my jail. Causes all kinds of problems. I figure if you marry up with Quinn, he'll keep you out of trouble and my jail will be free for real outlaws."

"Does he have a last name?"

"McFarland," the sheriff and her potential husband said at the same time. The sheriff chuckled, but Mr. McFarland scowled.

At least he understood this wasn't a laughing matter. "I do have one question," her would-be spouse said, as he stared her in the eye.

Sarah swallowed the lump in her throat and resisted the urge to flee to the back of the cell. He looked fierce enough to make a person do what he wanted. Would he be mean to her if she married him? To Ryan and Beth?

"I have an ailing grandmother. She's got her mind set on finding me a bride before she dies. If I marry up with you, will you treat her kindly? Take care of her while I'm out working the ranch?"

Ahhh. . .so that was it. Sarah nodded and clung to the slats of the cell, relieved that what he asked was something she could easily agree to. "Yes, I'd be happy to care for your grandmother—if I decide to marry you. Mine died before I was born, and I've always wanted one."

Mr. McFarland visibly relaxed and nodded his gratitude. Sarah licked her lips. Maybe she was pushing her luck, but she had to know. "Are you a God-fearing man, Mr. McFarland?"

He blinked then glanced sideways. The sheriff grinned. A muscle ticked in Mr. McFarland's clean-shaven jaw. "I believe in the good Lord, ma'am. It's just that He and I aren't as close as we should be."

Was any person ever as close to God as they could be? His answer wasn't what she'd hoped for, but it would suffice. "You wouldn't ever hit a woman or child, would you?"

His expression, which had barely softened, turned hard. His dark eyes glinted. "I resent that question."

The sheriff turned to him. "Now, Quinn, it's a fair question. She don't know you, and she's considering becoming your wife."

"Of course I wouldn't. What decent man would?" Mr. McFarland crossed his arms, pulling his shirt tight across his wide shoulders.

Sarah's mouth went dry. If he treated her as nice as he looked, she'd be all right, but she knew that handsome men could be as hurtful as ugly ones. Hadn't her uncle proven that?

"Do you like children?"

The sheriff snorted and seemed to be holding in his laughter. He looked at Mr. McFarland with his brows raised. "You want kids, Quinn?"

Mr. McFarland's eyes widened. "Well. . .I hardly think this is the place to discuss such a matter."

Oh, dear. They had misconstrued her inquiry. Sarah was grateful for the dimness of the room. She hadn't considered how he'd take that question. She opened her mouth to explain but slammed it shut. He was her only way out of this cell. If he knew she had two siblings, he might rescind his offer. If he misunderstood, so be it.

She wasn't sure but thought he might be blushing. "So. . .do you like children?"

He straightened. "I reckon I like them as much as any man. I've got the cutest nephew in the world." A soft grin tilted his lips.

"I guess we ought to give the gal some time to think on your proposal, Quinn." The sheriff nudged his chin toward his office, indicating Quinn should head out of the cell room.

He nodded at her. With her whole being trembling, Sarah watched him turn, slow and easy. So in control of his big body. She had no real choice. She had to get out of jail and get back to Ryan and Beth. This Quinn McFarland was her only option. She'd hoped to marry for love like her parents had, but that wasn't to be. According to the sheriff, this man had a nice home and a good ranch. Ryan and Beth would have plenty of food to eat and a decent place to stay.

But was it far enough away that Uncle Harlan couldn't find them?

Would they be safe on an isolated ranch?

The sheriff reached out to close the door.

"Wait. I–I'll marry him."

Chapter Four

"Will you take this man to be your lawfully wedded husband, ma'am?"

Sarah stared at the skinny parson who waited with lifted brows, a worn Bible tucked against his chest. Was this truly what she wanted?

Dodging his stare, she let her gaze skip past the sheriff, and she peered around his sparse office, so unlike a church, where she'd always wanted to be married. Instead of stained-glass windows, there were dingy panes looking out on a muddy street. Instead of her family to celebrate what should be the most joyous of days, stern-faced outlaws glared at her from the wanted posters on the walls.

Mr. McFarland peered down at her, looking as if he'd swallowed a wormy apple. Could she actually marry this stranger? Was he having second thoughts, too? He may have another option, but she didn't. She nodded, before he could change his mind.

"You'll have to say the words out loud, miss." The parson rubbed a finger along his thin moustache. He looked more like a gambler than a minister.

She hated marrying a man she didn't know, but he was her only chance to get out of jail. Sarah cleared her throat. "Yes, sir, I will take him as my husband."

The parson nodded. "All right then, I reckon you two are hitched." He glanced at Mr. McFarland and grinned. "You can kiss your bride now, Quinn."

Heat engulfed her cheeks. Sarah could feel the warmth emanating off her husband's—oh, that word was hard to swallow—arm as he stood beside her, not moving an inch. The back of his hand had bumped hers during the brief ceremony, and he'd jerked away. He didn't want to touch, much less kiss her.

"I reckon we can skip that part, Parson. We've a long ride ahead and need to get on the road." Mr. McFarland shoved his hat on his head and handed the man some coins from his pocket.

Skipping the kissing part was the right thing to do since this wasn't a love union. So why was she disappointed that he felt the same way? They were united together for life. Was it foolish to hope he might grow to like her one day?

In the light of the office window, Sarah realized her husband's hair was a dark blond and not plain brown as she'd thought earlier, and his eyes were such a deep brown that she could barely make out his pupils. He had nice eyes, when they weren't glaring.

"You ready?" He caught her watching him.

She turned to the sheriff. "Am I free to go?"

He nodded. "Yes, Mrs. McFarland. You sure are. I'll escort you two until you're clear of town, just so you don't have problems with anyone."

"I'm obliged, Will." Her husband spun toward the door. He strode outside, then turned back quickly and held the door open for her.

Sarah forced a smile and walked outside, blinking against the sun she hadn't seen in nearly a day. Her stomach gurgled. She was hungry but anxious to be on their way. Please, God, let Beth and Ryan be where I left them.

"I've got to pick up my buckboard from the livery and get supplies at the mercantile; then we can head out." He glanced down at Sarah's pants and grimaced. "You got any clothes besides those?"

She knew how bad she looked in her uncle's baggy clothing, especially after being locked up in that grimy cell. She could do with a bath, but she didn't want to take the time, not that he'd given her that option. "I have a dress back where I left my belongings."

"Only one?" He pursed his lips.

Sarah nodded. She'd had another one, but she could hardly tell him that she'd cut it down to make Beth a dress. Her husband turned and walked away. Sarah stood where she was, watching the townsfolk watching her. A few people gathered outside a building across the street, glaring at her. A man riding a horse stopped in the middle of the road and stared. Sarah wiped her sweaty hands on her pants, and peered over her shoulder at the sheriff, who stood a few feet away. Were these people still bent on lynching her?

Mr. McFarland glanced back, spun around, and stalked toward her.

She flinched as he stopped in front of her. Had she upset him already? He studied her and then scanned the crowd of townsfolk. He offered her his arm. "May I assist you, ma'am?"

Grateful for the protection he offered, Sarah looped her hand around his arm. It was rock hard, and her hand shook at his overpowering nearness. The sheriff walked on her right side, and she felt cocooned between them. Other than her pa, she'd never had a man stand up for her. This was something she could easily get used to. She alone had borne the burden these past months of finding shelter and food and caring for her siblings after their farmhouse had burned with their parents inside. It was nice to have someone watching out for her again.

They walked into the mercantile and all talk stopped. Her husband strode to the counter, all but dragging her along. "Are my supplies ready to go?"

The plump, white-haired woman behind the counter nodded her head and looked Sarah up and down. Mr. McFarland's jaw tightened. He turned to Sarah. "I want you to pick out a new dress, and some fabric to make several more." His eyes narrowed. "You can sew, can't you?"

Sarah nodded, grateful for his generosity but anxious to be on her way. She needed to know her brother and sister were all right. He leaned toward her. "Be sure to get any, uh"—he leaned closer, his warm breath tickling her ear—"unmentionables that you might need. We don't get to town all that often."

He stepped away, his ears and neck as red as she was sure her cheeks were, and looked back at the clerk. "Make sure she gets a sturdy pair of shoes, too. I'm going to fetch my wagon. I want her ready to go when I get back." He strode out of the store without a backward glance.

"I'll rest here while you shop." The sheriff smiled and leaned his hip against the countertop.

The clerk nodded, but Quinn was already gone. Sarah was sure he didn't often shop for ladies' clothing and couldn't help grinning at his embarrassment.

The sheriff chuckled. "Quinn lit out of here like his britches was on fire. What a day he's had. First, he gets married, then he has to buy a lady's unmentionables."

The clerk twisted her mouth. "Maybe such unmentionables should remain unmentioned, Sheriff."

Will Jones chuckled. "Maybe so, ma'am. I'll just stay here by the counter while you two do the shopping."

Sarah looked around the store. It was smaller than the ones she'd been in before, but most everything anyone would need was crammed on a shelf or cabinet or stuffed in a corner. Her heart pounded with excitement at having a new dress. It had been so long.

"I don't know where to start." She'd never been able to buy whatever she wanted before. Her parents' farm had provided most of the things her family had needed, and they had traded for other necessities. A man and woman to her left eyed Sarah with speculation, the man whispered something, and then they hurried out the door.

"Our ready-made dresses are in the back. We don't have too many since most folks in these parts make their own." The clerk didn't seem fazed in the least that her customer had so recently gotten out of jail. She was probably counting up the big sale she was about to make.

Sarah held her breath as she looked at the four dresses hanging on a narrow rod—one blue, one dark green, and two brown calicos. She'd never had a store-bought dress before. She loved green and reached out to touch the garment but then looked down at her dirty palm. Her hand dropped to her side. Tears blurred her view of the dresses. After all she'd been through, why should something so small make her cry?

"You know, I've got a room in back where you could freshen up if you've a mind to."

Sarah smiled at the woman's gracious offer. "That would be wonderful. Thank you."

She followed the clerk to the back of the store. As they walked toward a curtain separating the store from another room, the sheriff pushed off the counter and strode toward her.

The clerk sashayed around Sarah and stopped in front of her, crossing her arms over her ample chest. "Now, Sheriff, the lady would like to freshen up. Surely you can't deny her that after all she's been through."

Sheriff Jones studied both women as if he thought they were up to something.

"I'm not going anywhere. I just want to get this layer of grime off me. Please." Sarah begged with her eyes for him to grant her this one little favor.

He flung the curtain aside and glanced at the store's closed back door that she'd have access to once the curtain was shut again. Finally, he nodded. "Don't forget there's a town full of men out there who were ready to lynch you yesterday." He strode back toward the counter. "Or marry you."

Had she heard correctly? She shook her head. Surely there hadn't been more than one man willing to marry her.

The clerk slid the floral curtain shut, blocking Sarah's view of the sheriff. A colorful ceramic pitcher with painted flowers sat in a matching basin on a worktable next to the wall. The older woman poured water into the basin and laid a washcloth and a bar of scented soap on the table.

"This is a special soap. I only carry a few bars, but I want you to have it."

Sarah batted back tears. After being jailed, this small kindness nearly destroyed her composure. "Thank you so much."

"I'm sure you deserve it. I don't know what this world is coming to when they put girls in jail. No sir." She shook her head. "Now go ahead and strip down. I'll get some fresh under things and that green dress you were eyeing. It might be a tad long, but you can hem it once you get a chance. My man is gone on a delivery and won't be back until this afternoon, so no one will bother you back here. I'm Mrs. Johnson, by the way."

She dashed away before Sarah could utter another thank-you. The scent of leather mixed with the odor of spices, pickles, and coffee made her stomach rumble. An abundance of canned items were stocked on shelves that went all the way up to the ceiling of the storage room. It looked as if Mrs. Johnson had already stocked up for winter, even though it was still months away.

Sarah wiped away the grime that had collected over the past two days. She slipped out of her uncle's smelly clothes, grateful to be rid of them. They'd make good fuel for someone's fire.

Standing in her frayed undergarments, Sarah flinched when the curtain moved, and she stepped back beside a cabinet, lest the sheriff see her. Mrs. Johnson slipped through the curtain, taking care to keep it closed around her. "Here you go."

On her arm were stockings, a chemise and drawers with eyelet trim, and a pretty petticoat. Sarah reached out and rubbed the soft cotton fabric between her fingers. The unmentionables she and her mother had made were from rough flour sacks. "I've never had anything so beautiful."

314 | STRAIGHT FOR THE HEART

Mrs. Johnson smiled congenially. "Most men won't say so, but they love seeing their woman in pretty things."

Sarah's eyes widened at the thought of Mr. McFarland seeing her half-dressed. "I suppose I'd better hurry. My. . .uh. . .husband will be back any minute."

Mrs. Johnson chuckled as she laid the green dress on a chair. "I'll gather up another three sets of undergarments for you, if that's all right. Two for warm weather and two for when it gets colder."

"Don't you think that's too much? One or two would be sufficient."

"We have some long winters here, and it's hard for the ranchers to get to town. It's better that you have too much than too little."

Sarah shrugged. "I suppose you're right."

Mrs. Johnson slipped around the floral curtain again. Sarah dressed quickly, enjoying the feel of the fresh cotton dress and soft, clean undergarments. She could only hope her husband wouldn't be angry at her for buying so many things. But he did say to get whatever she needed.

She smoothed down her dress, wishing it didn't drag on the floor. She picked up the front of her skirt and peeked around the curtain for Mrs. Johnson. Sheriff Jones craned his neck as if checking to see if she was still there. She couldn't resist waving. He shook his head, and a grin tugged at one corner of his mouth.

"Try these on. I think they're your size."

Sarah stared at the lovely boots Mrs. Johnson passed to her. The soft black leather was cool to the touch. "I can't buy these. They're too much." Reluctantly, she handed them back.

"Nonsense. Your husband said to get you a sturdy pair, and these are the best we've got. Go ahead and try them on."

Sarah sighed and slipped on the new boots. They fit as if they were made for her.

"You look lovely, my dear. Let me do something with your hair. I'm sure you'd like to wash it, but this cornmeal will have to do for now." She sprinkled on some cornmeal and brushed it through Sarah's tresses. In a manner of minutes, Mrs. Johnson had coiled Sarah's hair and pinned it up. The woman handed her a mirror. "Have a look."

Sarah held it up, staring at herself. Melancholy battled with delight. Not since before her parents died had she looked so nice. If only her mother could see her. Would she be angered at how Sarah had left her brother and sister alone? Or would she be proud of Sarah's efforts to keep the children together?

"That husband of yours won't know what hit him when he sees how lovely you are."

Sarah smiled and checked the mirror again. Would Quinn think she was pretty?

"Now, let's hurry and pick out some fabric before your Mr. McFarland returns. He seemed anxious to be on his way."

The sheriff's brows lifted, and a low whistle escaped his lips. "Wow. If I'd have known you'd clean up so well, I'd have married you myself."

Heat rushed to Sarah's cheeks. "Why, Sheriff, I do believe that was a compliment."

The rogue grinned and pushed his hat back on his forehead as if to get a better look.

Ten minutes later, Sarah had enough fabric to make two more dresses, as well as clothes and undergarments for both Ryan and Beth. She added a brush and comb and some hair ribbons to the pile. She wished she could get new shoes for her siblings, but how could she explain that? She hoped Mr. McFarland wouldn't question why she'd purchased so much fabric, because she wasn't ready to let the cat out of the bag quite yet.

Boots clomped on the boardwalk, and Sarah spun around to face her husband. He stopped a few feet into the doorway. His gaze moved past her then rushed back. His mouth dropped open. Quickly enough, he slammed it shut, but his gaze traveled her length from head to toe. A slow smile tugged at his lips. "Well. . .that's an improvement."

Sarah pressed her hands against her chest, embarrassed at his perusal. She'd never had a man look as if he was so pleased with her appearance. "I was hoping that you meant for me to wear the store-bought dress so that I'd look nicer when I meet your grandmother."

"Honestly, I just didn't want you to have to wear those filthy duds any longer."

"More likely, he didn't want to have to smell them all the way to the Rocking M." The sheriff chuckled.

Mrs. Johnson gasped, grabbed a nearby broom, and swatted the sheriff's boots. "What an awful thing to say. You ought to be ashamed of yourself, Will Jones."

Smiling, the sheriff danced out of her way. He grabbed the two large packages that Mrs. Johnson had wrapped in brown paper and hurried out of the store with the clerk at his heels. Mr. McFarland pulled some paper dollars from his pocket and paid the woman when she returned. He glanced at Sarah with one brow lifted when the woman quoted the exorbitant total.

Sarah tried to soothe herself with the thought that her husband had purchased several crates of supplies himself, too, but it wasn't working. She cringed at the thought of spending so much of his money and for deceiving him about the children. But would he have married her if he'd known about Ryan and Beth ahead of time?

"Ready to go?"

Sarah avoided his gaze and nodded. The sheriff might have been joking about how she smelled, but what he'd said was true. She'd cleaned up some and the rose-scented soap helped, but she still needed a bath. She'd been afraid to bathe at her uncle's. Afraid his partners would see her, so she only had when they were all gone.

Mr. McFarland took her elbow and steered her toward the door. "Don't let what Will said bother you. You can have all the baths you want when we get home. I've been wrongly accused and in that jail before, so I know what it's like."

She peeked up at him. Why in the world had he been in jail? Was that why he'd been so willing to marry her?

He lifted her up onto a solid buckboard with a padded seat and back rest. "Are you all set? Did you get everything you needed?"

"Yes. That was very generous of you to allow me to purchase so many things. Thank you." Sarah was grateful that Sheriff Jones's comment had distracted her husband from the large packages that the sheriff had set among the crates of supplies he helped load.

Mr. McFarland grunted a response as if uncomfortable with her gratitude. The wagon swayed as he climbed in. His big body took up much of the bench. Sarah scooted to the right, bumping the edge of the seat.

He clucked to the horses, and they started forward. The townsfolk gathered on the boardwalk, a few waving, but most grumbling and glaring. Mr. McFarland and the sheriff had spoiled their lynching. Sarah reached up, her hand touching her throat. Would she ever be welcome in this town.

Her husband turned the wagon in the opposite direction of the Little Missouri River and the big smokestack that had guided her to town. Away from Ryan and Beth.

Chapter Five

Quinn slapped the reins on the horses' rumps, and they walked faster. He rubbed the back of his neck, as he considered how he'd explain Sarah to his grandmother.

"No, wait." Sarah clutched Quinn's arm, and he looked down.

"What's wrong?"

"I need to go the other way—to collect my belongings."

"I just bought you two parcels of things. I thought you realized that I purchased those items so you wouldn't have to return for your other dress." Was that so hard to understand? He needed to get home. Work was waiting. He couldn't be traveling all over the Badlands to pick up an old dress.

Sarah sputtered then glared at him. "There are other things I need besides my dress."

"Can't you get them at the store?"

"Um. . .no, I can't. They're things especially dear to me. All I have left of my parents. Please."

Quinn stared out the corner of his eye at her then sighed. Pulling tight on the left rein, he turned the buckboard in a wide arc then snapped the reins again. "Where are these belongings of yours?"

"A little ways across the river. It's not too far." She nibbled her lip and clenched her hands so tightly together in her lap that her knuckles turned white.

They rode back through town, receiving stares again, as they headed toward the river. Quinn shook his head. He hadn't been the center of so much attention since he and Anna had been jailed.

"Thank you for what you did—marrying me, I mean. I want you to know that I truly am innocent. This has all been a horrible mistake."

Quinn stared again at his wife, unable to believe how pretty she looked once she'd cleaned up. She seemed as if she was struggling not to squirm. His heart jolted. She had blue eyes. In the dimness of the jail, he'd thought they were gray or even brown. He'd always hoped if he married that he'd wed a woman with eyes the color of the summer sky. A tiny flame deep within him sparked to life.

Her long black hair was pinned up in a womanly fashion, but he'd seen it down, hanging clear to her waist, and that's the picture that remained in his mind. Her skin wasn't porcelain white like one of the dolls Anna had as a girl but had been kissed by the sun into a light brown. He wouldn't admit it out loud, but he'd done all right for himself.

Still, she couldn't be anywhere near his age. "Just how old are you, ma'am?"

"Nineteen."

He scowled. There was nearly a decade difference in their ages. "You're mighty young."

"What about you?"

"Twenty-eight."

She raised a hand to her chest. "My, but you're positively ancient."

Her teasing made him grin; then he sobered. "That a problem for you?"

"No. Is it a problem for you?"

He pursed his lips. She was young enough to take care of him in his old age. He nearly chuckled out loud. "I reckon not."

In her efforts to stay away from him, she'd scooted clear over to the right of the seat. She'd seemed apprehensive of the men in town who'd watched her outside the general store. Did he frighten her? "You can relax. I won't hurt you."

Her gaze darted to his, and he could read the questions in her eyes. Eyes that he could get used to staring into. He focused on the trail ahead. They passed the old meat processing plant that the Marquis de Mores had closed nearly a decade earlier. The giant building with its sky-high smokestack was a sad reminder of a failed dream.

"What is that place? It looks empty."

"It is. A French marquis came here back in '83 when the big cattle bonanza was still in full swing. He had a vision to butcher cattle here and ship refrigerated beef back East. He was one of the first to do that." He looked over his left shoulder. "Don't know if you can still see it, but that big two-story building up there in the hills was his home."

Sarah glanced in the direction he pointed. "So, what happened?"

Quinn shrugged. "Two bad winters all but destroyed the herds of cattle around here. And with the competition from other beef producers around the country, the marquis went bust and took his family back to New York, or wherever it was they came from."

"That's sad." Sarah looked back at the abandoned plant.

That was life, as far as he was concerned. Some benefited from living in the Badlands, but most were victims of the harsh winters and hot summers in one way or another. Still, he was grateful for the town the marquis started. Without Medora, it would be a long trip to the next closest town.

They crossed the river and rode on in companionable silence for the next few miles. He had to admit he kind of liked having a pretty woman at his side, and he couldn't wait to see his grandma's expression when he returned with a blue-eyed brunette instead of a redhead. But what was he going to tell her? How could he explain that he married a stranger just to get her out of jail? It sounded ridiculous when he thought of it that way.

He simply couldn't leave that sad, red-faced waif in that dark cell. Maybe he'd been quick to marry, but he didn't have time to socialize and court a woman like they wanted to be. He didn't even know a woman he would have fancied courting. But now he had a wife.

It sounded weird even in his mind. His wife. Sarah McFarland.

"Over there's where I found the horse I rode into town. It was standing off the road, eating grass. I was tired and nobody answered my call when I hollered. I figured it must have gotten loose in town and wandered out here."

He looked where she pointed, and sure enough, the grass was broken down as if a large animal had walked through it. He started to turn his head back to the road when he spotted a pile of manure. So a horse had been there. Sarah's story was far-fetched, but maybe she was telling the truth. But even if she'd found the horse, it still didn't account for the gold she had in her possession.

She worried her lower lip and fidgeted in the seat for the next fifteen minutes, always scanning the area on his side of the wagon. Was she looking for something?

A short while later, she motioned to his left. "Pull over there, and I'll get my, uh. . .belongings."

Quinn glanced around, wondering where she could have stored them. There was nothing but rocky buttes, ridges, and grass for as far as he could see. He stopped the wagon and set the brake, but his wife scurried down without waiting for his help. Picking up his rifle, he stood, watching her shuffle down the incline beside the road. He jumped to the ground, not liking how she trotted off unarmed into the wilds without any hesitation. Didn't she know any number of critters might be down there, awaiting prey for dinner? Was she trying to ditch him and get away?

He was halfway to her when she disappeared into a rickety old shack he just noticed. He heard high-pitched squeals and quickened his steps. Voices? Someone else was in the shanty. Quinn slowed down and raised his rifle. Could she be leading him into a trap? Had she led him straight to her outlaw den? If so, they sure weren't very successful outlaws.

His wife's soft voice carried out the door. He couldn't hear her words, but the happy tone didn't indicate she was plotting his demise. He thought about moving closer, but there was no place to take cover if shooting started. He ducked behind a pine tree less than half his width and kept his Winchester ready.

Sarah stepped outside carrying a rusty rifle pointed toward the ground and a faded old quilt in one arm. Her belongings, he surmised. That's what she'd made all that fuss over?

Behind her, a young boy and even younger girl stepped out of the shanty. Their gazes darted from side to side. Quinn's concern about outlaws shifted to cold shock. His mouth sagged open, and he couldn't do a thing about it. There was no chance on earth that those were her children. Although both kids had the same blue eyes as Sarah's, the boy's hair was brown while the little girl's was blond. Quinn's mouth went dry. These were her belongings? His wife had deceived him. He scowled. "What's going on?"

"Children, this is my husband, Quinn McFarland."

Both of the kids gawked at him. He steeled himself not to squirm under their scrutiny.

"This is Ryan, and this is Elizabeth." Sarah touched each child's head in a loving caress. "Ryan is eight, and Beth is six. They're my brother and sister."

His anger burned like a grassfire in a heavy wind. Hadn't Will mentioned something about some children? So she hadn't been lying about them either. No wonder she was so desperate to get out of jail that she'd agreed to marry him. He was a fool to hope maybe she'd seen something in him that she'd liked. That he was a cavalier knight who'd swooped in and rescued the innocent maiden. Instead, she'd played him like a pawn on a chess board.

"Are we going to live with him?" The little girl's worried gaze darted between Quinn and Sarah.

Sarah nodded her head and smiled softly at the child. "Yes—"

"No!" Quinn hollered.

The color drained from Sarah's face as she stared at him with disbelief.

The little girl started crying and grabbed Sarah's skirt. "Don't leave us again. You promised you'd never leave me, but you did."

The boy crossed his skinny arms and glared at him. Quinn felt like an egg-sucking dog. Like a low-down, yellow-bellied snake. What kind of a man refuses to care for needy children? Especially a man who'd helped raise his own siblings. They'd caught him off guard, was all. He'd barely gotten his twin sister and brother raised and married off. He hadn't wanted a wife, and now he was strapped with two children too. He didn't like losing control of his life. His throat closed as if he was the one with a hangman's noose tightening around it.

"No?" Sarah's eyes sparked like blue fire. Beth whimpered and sniffled into her sister's skirt. "How can you refuse to care for two orphans?"

Hadn't he asked himself the same question? He ducked his head, shamed by his outburst, his shoulders weighted with guilt. "Sorry. Of course, they can come. I was merely taken off guard. That's all." He motioned toward the pile of fabric in her hands. "Is that all of your stuff—or do you have any more surprises for me?"

Sarah furrowed her brow. "That's everything."

He stepped forward and took her bundle and rusty rifle before she decided to turn the weapon on him.

"You two get in the back of the wagon." Sarah motioned the children up the hill.

"I want to sit with you." The girl's whine sent a chill down Quinn's spine. What had he gotten himself into?

Sarah leaned over and whispered something to her.

What else could he do but take them along? It was a miracle the two youngsters were still alive after a stormy night alone in that old shack. Why, the door didn't even look as if it closed. And there were holes in the roof.

The boy—Brian? Rowan? What was his name?—scowled at Quinn as he stomped past him.

Quinn pursed his lips. He deserved the boy's ire. He'd probably spent the last day and night protecting and comforting his little sister while worrying himself half sick about his older one. The scrawny lad looked exhausted and dark rings shadowed his eyes. When was the last time they'd all had a good meal? Or a bath?

He looked heavenward as he thought of his wife in that cell, frantically worrying about her siblings. No wonder she'd be so desperate to get out.

He swung the wagon back toward Medora with Sarah and her two siblings aboard. How could a man lose control of his life so fast? Quinn hunched over, resting his elbows on his knees. He peeked in the back of the buckboard. The girl had curled up on the worn quilt, but the boy sat with his back against the side of the wagon, his arms on his knees, glaring at Quinn.

Well, he certainly deserved the boy's contempt after his foolish outburst. But any man would be angry to marry a woman and find out she had two kids she hadn't told him about. It didn't matter that they were siblings and not her own children. They were a responsibility he hadn't bargained on. He needed more children on the ranch about as much as he needed a three-legged horse.

But wouldn't his grandmother be delighted to have children in the house again? He wasn't sure how she'd respond to him marrying a woman in jail, though. She'd probably say he deserved the kids after marrying in such haste. This was all the fault of Miss Zerelda von Something-or-other. If she hadn't agreed to come in the first place, or if she'd at least honored her agreement and married him, none of this would have happened. Maybe it was all a bad dream and he'd wake up in the morning with everything back to normal.

He sniffed a laugh. Yeah, sure. And tomorrow the sky would be green.

Sarah was as angry as a hen drenched in dishwater. How dare Quinn say her siblings couldn't come with them? Yes, he'd changed his mind rather quickly and looked plenty chagrined for his angry eruption, but it was obvious to her that he didn't want the children. Well, like it or not, he was stuck with them. She could only hope he wouldn't make them all miserable.

An hour later, out of the corner of her eye, Sarah saw Beth moving. Her sister had been asleep since shortly after leaving the shack. Beth jerked up, and her frantic gaze darted around until it settled on Sarah. She smiled, hoping to soothe her little sister's concern.

"I gots to go, Sissy."

Quinn glanced sideways and sighed. "Whoa, hold up." The wagon stopped, and he set the brake. He lifted his hat and swiped the sweat off his brow with his sleeve. "Do your business quickly. We need to be getting home."

He climbed down, strode to the back of the wagon, and reached out for Beth. She spun around, shinnied over Ryan and the crates of supplies, and flew into Sarah's lap. If Sarah hadn't still been so angry, she might have laughed at her husband's surprised expression. She set her sister aside, climbed out of the wagon without waiting for his help, and then lifted Beth down. Ryan stood and stretched then jumped over the side of the wagon and walked out into the tall grass.

"Watch out for prairie rattlers."

Sarah's heart pounded, and she glanced around. She might tolerate mice but snakes were another thing. Ryan jogged a ways past them, and Sarah and Beth finished quickly.

"He don't like us, does he?" Beth looked up at Sarah as they walked back to the wagon, and she realized her sister wasn't limping.

She turned and knelt down. "It's not that, sweetie. I didn't tell him about you, and he was merely surprised. Men sometimes get angry if you surprise them."

"Like Uncle Harlan did?"

Sarah nodded. A shiver ran down her back as she remembered her uncle's short temper. She rubbed her right wrist—the one he liked to grab hold of when he wanted to scold her for some minor thing she or the children had done.

"Papa never got angry."

Sarah smiled, glad her sister only had good memories of their father. He had never hurt them, but he'd shouted a time or two when she and Ryan had done something stupid. "Give Mr. McFarland time, and he'll see how sweet you are. Then he won't be able to keep from loving you like I do."

Sarah hugged Beth, hoping desperately that what she'd said was true. Would Quinn's grandmother be happy with her and the children? Or would she be angry at the big surprise her grandson would soon be popping on her?

"How's your ankle?"

Beth stared at the ground. "It don't hurt no more."

Sarah twisted her lips. Beth probably faked her twisted ankle so she didn't have to walk so far. Her sister might be small, but she was clever.

"Why don't you pick some wildflowers while we wait for Ryan?" Beth nodded and skipped toward a nearby patch of flowers. Sarah glanced over her shoulder. Where was that boy? "Ryan?"

"Coming." He plowed through the grass like a crazed bull and stopped in front of her. "Why were you gone all night? Beth was scared during that storm."

"It's a long story." Sarah sighed. "I had no choice about returning before now. I'll tell you later, but we'd better not keep Mr. McFarland waiting. He's anxious to get home."

"I watched over Beth. Even held her last night when she was scared of the dark and crying for you."

Sarah smiled and tugged her brother into her arms. "I appreciate that. I knew I could depend on you. I'm sorry I scared you and didn't get back before dark. Just wait until you hear what happened."

"Tell me now."

She turned Ryan back toward the wagon, determined not to rile her husband any more this day. Every man had his limit, and she sure didn't want to find out what her new husband's was. Beth scurried around gathering yellow, scarlet, and purple flowers. When she'd gathered a handful, she hurried over to Quinn. He checked one of the horses' hooves and stood, patting the large animal's rump.

Beth nibbled her lip and watched him. When he turned her way, she lifted the flowers up to him. "These are for you."

His questioning gaze sought out Sarah's, and she held her breath. Quinn stooped down and rested his forearms on his knees. "Why, thank you, ma'am. Nobody ever gave me flowers before."

Beth turned and flashed Sarah a wide smile. Quinn lifted her sister into the buckboard without complaint. Ryan climbed in back and glared at Quinn again.

He sniffed the flowers. "Well," he said, as Sarah approached, "looks like I've won over one of them at least."

Chapter Six

The buckboard jostled and dipped to the left into the dried rut of a previous wagon, then bounced free of it a few feet down the trail. Sarah's shoulder bumped Quinn's, and he peered sideways at her. He ought to be furious with her deception, but now that he'd gotten over his surprise, the honest truth was he admired her for caring so much for her siblings that she'd marry a stranger. Still, his pride took another shot that she hadn't wanted to marry him because she liked what she saw.

He glanced in the back of the wagon. Ryan and Beth were both asleep. "I've got a young brother and sister, too."

His wife's blue gaze darted in his direction. Her dark brows lifted.

"Twins, actually. Adam and Anna will be twenty-five in another month. Both are married."

"Didn't you mention that one has a baby?"

"Adam, and his wife is Mariah." A smile tugged at Quinn's lip as he thought of Jonathon. "They live at the ranch when they aren't traveling."

"Traveling?" Sarah picked up the canteen lying on the floorboard and took a swig.

"Adam is a gifted artist. They tour the West, and he draws pictures for a man in Chicago who owns a gallery, who sells them. Mariah writes dime novels."

His wife choked and nearly spewed the water she'd been drinking. She coughed several times. "You're teasing. She does not."

"Honest. She does." He lifted a hand in the air and couldn't help grinning at Sarah's expression.

"I've never heard of such a thing. It sounds so exciting."

Quinn shrugged. "I've read a few of her novels. They're not bad, even though she generally has a woman saving the day."

Sarah dabbed at her mouth and scowled. "What's wrong with that?"

"Not too realistic if you ask me."

She didn't say anything but looked out over the Badlands. He'd like to know what she was thinking—if she was one of those women who thought they could outdo a man. Hadn't he just saved her? And in doing so rescued her siblings from certain death?

"What about your sister? Does she live on the ranch, too?"

"No, she and her husband live on his ranch down south, 'bout a day's ride from here." Quinn guided the horses off the main trail and onto the one leading to the ranch. Yesterday's storms were long gone, except for the muddy trail, and the sun now shone down in full force. He lifted his hat, swiped the sweat from his brow, and scowled when he realized Sarah wasn't wearing a hat. He'd have to see if one of Anna's old ones was still around or buy her a new hat next time he came to town.

What was he going to tell his grandma about her?

"Does your sister have any children?"

He shook his head. "Brett and Anna married last fall, and several months after that, Adam and Mariah's cute little son was born on the ranch."

"How old is he?"

"A couple of months. He was born in March."

"I imagine you must enjoy him."

Quinn nodded. "Yeah, but I haven't seen them since early last month." He peeked at his wife and thought again how pretty she had cleaned up. He'd looked right past her in the store, not once thinking the pretty lady at the counter could be her. Yes sir, he'd done all right for himself as far as looks. He sure hoped she had a good temperament.

But what she think about marrying him? Women had funny notions when it came to weddings. Had she been disappointed in her only choice of husband? If Will had given her a choice of men, would she have picked him or someone else?

"Would you tell me about your grandmother?"

"Sure," he said, surprised that she'd asked. He leaned forward, elbows on his knees, and held the reins loosely in his hands. "My grandma and grandpa moved from Texas to Bismarck about a year after my dad moved us up here. Grandpa died four years ago, but Grandma stayed in Bismarck because of her friends and church. About a year and a half ago, she fell and broke her leg real bad. My mom left the ranch and went to live with Grandma so she could care for her. Mom never came home much after that."

"Must be hard with her that far away. I sure miss my mother."

Pursing his lips, Quinn watched a hawk circling in the sky. After his father's death, he and his ma had gotten closer because they had to work together to keep the ranch running. He had missed her when she left them to tend Grandma, and now she was gone forever. "Ma died several months ago."

Sarah gasped and turned toward him in the seat. "I'm so sorry. What happened? I mean. . .you don't have to talk about it unless you want to."

Quinn stared straight ahead, ignoring the compassion in her eyes. He'd cried at the funeral and didn't want to go down that road again—especially not in front of his new wife. "She took sick with a fever. It was so fast it stunned us all. I brought Grandma to the ranch to live with me after that. She didn't really want to come, but I didn't want her all alone and didn't have time to be traveling back and forth to Bismarck." He didn't mention that he hadn't wanted to be alone either.

"I'm sorry for your loss." Sarah peeked over her shoulder at the children in back. "We lost our parents when our farmhouse burned down in late April. The children were at school, and I'd gone into town on an errand. We don't know what happened." She turned away and dabbed at her eyes.

Quinn thought about the irony of the situation. He was struggling with his own mother's recent death when about the same time the woman who would become his wife was enduring a similar loss, only worse.

Sarah's shoulders quivered. He leaned forward and looked at her. She turned farther away, dabbed her face, then hiked up her chin. He considered putting his arm around her, but she'd already gotten control of her emotions. Good. That strength of backbone would do her well out here.

"Sorry about your folks." Quinn steered the buckboard onto the trail leading to the Rocking M and pulled the wagon to a halt. He waved a hand in the air. "As far as you can see in three directions is Rocking M land."

"You're blessed, Mr. McFarland. The bank took our farm after the fire."

He wondered how they'd gotten by but figured that was a topic for another day. "Call me Quinn. Mr. McFarland was my pa."

Her cheeks turned a rosy red. "And you must call me Sarah."

He liked her name. It was a strong name. Sarah, as in the wife of Abraham, mother of the Hebrew nation. He clicked the horses forward.

Abraham and Sarah had been united until death, but could a marriage such as his last? Maybe he'd be better off not getting his hopes up. Sarah obviously married him for one reason only—to get out of jail so she could get back to her siblings. He'd been a loner pretty much ever since his pa had died. It was best he cut his losses and protect his heart.

"Grandma hasn't been well since Ma's death. It took something out of her to watch her only child die. Having you and the children there will be an encouragement to her. I want you to know that I don't expect anything from you—except to care for Grandma. We'll think of this as a business arrangement." He glanced at Sarah, but she stared straight ahead, her lips pressed together. "I don't want you to think you're stuck with me forever. Once Grandma passes, if you want to leave, I'll give you enough money so that you and the children can start over somewhere else."

Shock rolled through Sarah, forcing her to look away from her husband for fear she might cry. Had he found her so lacking already, without even giving her a fair try, that he was ready to be rid of her the first chance he got? Or was it because she hadn't been honest about the children?

She crushed a fold in her skirt as disappointment surged through her. Why, God? You freed me from jail and provided a home for us. So why does he wish to be rid of me so fast?

She blinked, pushing the tears away. This was merely another obstacle she'd have to climb over. In the meantime, the children would have a home and food to eat. And hopefully, Uncle Harlan wouldn't find them. At least her husband—she nearly choked at the word—would provide for them to start over, if he was true to his word. But where would they go?

If only they could find a permanent home. She was tired of not knowing what was ahead. She longed for security and thought she'd found it with Quinn. But it wasn't to be.

"What did your father do/" Quinn glanced at her then focused on the trail ahead.

Her heart ached so badly that she didn't want to talk to him. Some protector he turned out to be. Still, if she remained silent, he'd suspect something was wrong and most likely question her about that. She'd rather talk about her parents.

She peeked over her shoulder at the children still asleep in the back then faced forward again. "My father had a farm outside of Grand Forks. He grew mainly sugar beets."

"Got downwind of a sugar beet farm once. Phew. That's stinky stuff." He waved his hand in front of his nose.

"I can't say that I miss that much." But she did miss her parents. How could life change so quickly? One day she was an innocent young woman looking to capture the eye of tall, blond Peder Ericksen. The next day she was homeless with two grieving children to provide for. The neighbors who took them in had been kind and sympathetic, but when those same neighbors sought to separate them, Sarah asked Peder to marry her. She'd never forget the shock in his pale eyes. When he said no, they'd caught the first train heading west in hopes the kind uncle she remembered from her youth would give them sanctuary.

She pressed her lips together. How could a man change so much in a few years?

Should she tell Quinn they might be in danger? That her outlaw uncle could very well come hunting for them?

Show me what to do, Lord.

"I don't guess you're used to all these hills after living in the flatlands."

"No, but I like it here. The landscape is so interesting, and the view over every hill is a little different." She looked out across the rugged terrain. Flat-topped buttes stood guard over valleys of rocky grasslands. Covering her brows to block the sun, she stared at some black dots moving in the distance, a cloud of dust following. Buffalo. She'd never seen one before but heard they weren't nearly as abundant as they used to be.

Quinn nudged her arm. "Look over there on that far hill."

She turned and scanned where he pointed. "What are they? Deer?"

"Elk."

"At first glance, this place looks barren, but there are many surprises." Wildflowers danced in the light breeze, a pleasant contrast to the browns of the rocky hills. She heard a rustling behind her, and Beth crawled up to the back of the seat and leaned her arms on it.

"Are we about there? I'm hungry."

"It's not much farther. We have a cook name Elke. She can fix a snack to hold you until suppertime."

"Elke's a funny name."

Sarah spun around on the seat. "Beth, we don't poke fun at people's names. That was rude."

Beth hung her head for a moment then grinned. "Well, it is funny."

Quinn chuckled, and Sarah glared at him. He didn't need to be encouraging Beth.

"Elke is German. She's the cousin of our previous cook, who went to live with my sister when she moved to her new husband's ranch."

"What is Elke's last name?" Beth asked.

Quinn scratched his hairline and honestly looked perplexed. "You know, I'm not sure. I've called her by her Christian name ever since she arrived."

"We will find out, and you will call her by her last name. Is that clear, Beth?"

Her sister nibbled her lower lip and nodded. Quinn looked as if he'd like to argue with Sarah but wisely kept his mouth shut.

"What's that up there?" Beth stuck her arm between Sarah and Quinn and pointed.

"That's the sign to the Rocking M Ranch. We've been on my land for a while, but that's the official entrance."

"It looks funny standing there all by itself. Where's the fence?"

Sarah's eyes widened. If Beth kept this up they would never make it to the ranch house.

"I suppose it does look odd," Quinn said. "But most of the land out here isn't fenced. My ma wanted a sign, so my brother and I put one up."

They drove under the sign that was supported by two tall beams. Sarah enjoyed the quiet of nature after being in the noisy town. Even better were the wide-open spaces and the feel of the sun on her face. A cool breeze kept her from getting too hot, but she wished she'd thought to buy a bonnet at the general store. Maybe she could make one for her and Beth if there was enough fabric left after making her sister a dress.

They crested another hill, and she sucked in a breath at the sight of the huge cabin that came into view.

"Is that your house?" Beth stood and leaned forward over the back of the bench. "It's really big."

Quinn nodded and a satisfied look encompassed his handsome face.

"Yep, that's home."

"I've never seen a cabin so big," Beth whispered as if in awe.

Sarah experienced the same amazement at her first view of the cozy home situated in a valley that was surrounded on all sides by tall buttes. This was a place that cried home—shelter. The safe haven she longed for...but it was only temporary. Why would God send them to this place only to have it taken away once they'd become settled?

"Pa wanted Ma to have a home she could be proud of. We had a big house back in Texas, and he wanted her to have a large one here. It wasn't easy, though; we had to have much of the wood shipped in since there are so few trees around here. It took a lot of hauling."

Her father had provided a nice home for their mother and them, but it was all gone in a puff of smoke. She never knew how fast things could change.

Now that they were actually here, nervousness twittered in Sarah's stomach. She crushed the fold of her skirt in her hand. How long would they be here? A few weeks? Months? Would Quinn's grandmother send her packing when she learned that Sarah had been in jail?

Sarah lifted her chin and took a deep breath. One thing for certain, she was going to do everything possible to see that Quinn's grandmother recovered from whatever it was that ailed her and that she lived a long, healthy life. Then maybe they could stay long enough for Quinn to come to care for them. And if he cared, maybe then he'd keep them.

Chapter Seven

With home in sight, the team picked up their pace and headed for the barn. Quinn still didn't know how to explain to his grandma everything that had happened. He didn't want to upset her and cause her to be afraid when she learned Sarah had been in jail.

Then again, Sarah was hardly intimidating. No, her wide, expressive eyes took in everything and emanated an innocence that couldn't be faked. Still. . .how could he explain why he'd married a woman who'd been jailed for bank robbery? He hardly knew why himself.

Maybe it was the fear in her eyes. How they pleaded for someone to believe she was innocent. Or maybe it was that long dark hair swirling past her shoulders down to her waist. The only women he'd seen with hair down had been his ma and sister, and that was hardly the same thing.

Something in him had wanted to be her hero. To rescue her.

He'd been a fool. A man alone for too long. He'd given in to a moment of insanity. How could any good come from such a harebrained idea?

He guided the wagon toward the barn. "Whoa. . ." He set the brake and turned on the seat to face Sarah before one of the ranch hands showed up. Ryan sat up and rubbed his eyes and looked around; his anger was subdued for the moment, replaced by open curiosity.

Beth jumped up and down. "Sissy. . .I got. . ."

Sarah looked at him. "Where is your necessary?"

"She can use the one behind the house." He nudged his chin toward the cabin.

Sarah looked at Ryan, and the boy rolled his eyes. "Oh, all right. C'mon, Beth." He helped his sister off the wagon and the two walked toward the house. Beth glanced over her shoulder as if checking to make sure Sarah wasn't leaving.

"This is going to sound crazy, but I reckon you need to know this." Quinn lifted his hat and ran his fingers through his hair. "Yesterday morning, my grandma informed me that I was to ride into town and meet my mail-order bride at the train station. That was the first I'd heard about her."

Sarah's eyes widened, and she opened her mouth but didn't say anything. What was she thinking?

He plunged ahead before he lost his nerve. "She didn't show up. But there was a letter at the post office saying she'd changed her mind." Quinn looked away so she wouldn't see his embarrassment. Where were the ranch hands? He yanked off his hat and fiddled with the brim, working up his nerve to continue.

Sarah laid her hand on his arm, drawing his attention back to her. "I'm sorry. That must have made you feel terrible."

He didn't want her compassion. He was a crusty ol' rancher. Too hardened by life to need a woman. And yet something within him longed for Sarah to like him—to need him.

He looked down, hating that the sting of the bride's rejection still pained him. "I want you to pretend to be the mail-order bride."

Sarah's brows lifted in surprise but quickly dipped down into a scowl. Quinn held up his hand. "Hear me out before you say no. Grandma hasn't been well since Ma died. I'm afraid if I tell her you were in jail that it would cause her undue worry and make her worse."

His wife's pretty lips pressed together so tightly that they turned white. She breathed loud breaths through her nose like a riled-up mustang. Finally, she looked at him. "I'm afraid I can't pretend to be your mail-order bride. It would be lying."

Irritation surged through him. "Seems a little late to be getting self-righteous." Hadn't she deceived him this morning?

"I'm not self-righteous. I don't believe in telling falsehoods." She stuck that cute little nose in the air.

"Uh-huh. And I suppose you always refer to your brother and sister as your 'belongings'?"

A rosy pink stained her cheeks and she looked away. "I told that sheriff I had siblings, but he didn't believe me. He thought it was merely a ploy to get out of jail."

"But you didn't tell me. You should have said something before we married. It's a lot to expect a man to take on two children. He has a right to know about that before he marries." His gut twisted. Sheriff Jones had mentioned something about two siblings, but he'd thought they were just something Sarah had made up so she could get out of jail.

She spun toward him. "And would you have married me if you'd known?"

Quinn resisted the urge to back away from the fire in her gaze. "Maybe." He shrugged. "We'll never know now, will we?"

Sarah looked down, suddenly contrite. "I'm sorry. But I couldn't take a chance that you might change your mind. I had to get out of that jail and back to Ryan and Beth. Their lives were at stake. Can't you understand that?"

Yes, he could. Far more than she'd ever know. He'd been the only father figure for Adam and Anna since the accident that claimed their pa's life. He'd have done about anything to protect them from harm.

One of the horses whinnied as if questioning why he hadn't freed him of the harness. Quinn stood and shoved his hat back on. "I understand, Sarah. But surely you can see how I want to protect my grandmother from worrying about being safe in her own home, which she would if she knew I married an outlaw."

"I am not an outlaw." Sarah stood, coming only up to the bottom of his nose. "And I do understand, but I still won't lie to your grandmother. That's no way to start a relationship."

Quinn heaved a sigh, thinking their own relationship had started with falsehoods, but kept that thought to himself. "All right. Let's go up to the house so you can meet her."

He jumped down and came around to help his wife. She placed her arms on his shoulders as he lifted her down. She didn't weigh much more than a young calf.

He started to let go but she held on, drawing his gaze to hers. "I won't tell her how we met. I will leave that up to you, if possible."

"Fair enough." Quinn offered her his arm and guided her toward the house. His esteem for her grew. He'd asked a stupid, impulsive thing of her. He didn't believe in telling falsehoods either and had surprised himself by asking her to do so. The fact that she'd refused elevated his opinion of her. Maybe she had been telling the truth all along?

Disappointment weighted down Sarah's shoulders as anxiety swirled in her stomach. How could Quinn have asked her to lie to his grandmother? She'd thought him to be a man of fine character. He hadn't leered at her like many of the other men in town had—at least once they'd decided not to lynch her. And he married her when he didn't have to. Why should it bother her so much? Most people lied every day. But that wasn't how she'd been raised, and in her heart, she knew telling falsehoods was wrong.

She turned her thoughts to Quinn's grandmother. Would the woman be shocked to learn Sarah wasn't the mail-order bride she was expecting?

Beth ran around the side of the house, her gaze searching until it landed on Sarah. The girl hurried to her side. A door banged, and Ryan jogged toward them, apprehension in the boy's blue eyes. He looked longingly toward the barn. Ryan had always wanted a saddle horse, but his pa had said they could only afford the mule needed for pulling their plow. Maybe Quinn would teach him how to ride.

"Listen," she stooped and whispered, "don't mention Uncle Harlan or his gold for now."

The children both nodded, and their footsteps echoed on the wooden porch. Quinn opened the door and stepped aside to allow her to pass through first. Sarah smiled at him, knowing many men would have plowed inside without being gentlemanly.

The pungent scent of something cooking hung in the air, reminding her of how little she'd eaten in the past few days. Her eyes took a moment to adjust to the dimness of the room. Beth took her hand and leaned against Sarah's skirt. A large parlor held western-style furniture that Sarah assumed must have accompanied the family from Texas. The horsehair sofa looked old but still serviceable. A low, rectangular table sat in front of the sofa, with two chairs on the other side of the table. The parlor connected with the dining room, making one very large room. A table with seating for ten people boasted a vase holding colorful wildflowers. Too bad the flowers Beth gave Quinn had already wilted.

The door shut behind her, and Quinn strode past them. Ryan came around to Sarah's other side and stood close but didn't hang on her like Beth did.

"Grandma? I'm home."

Home. If only this comfortable cabin could become their home, too.

"Coming." A gray-haired woman glided into the room, a big smile on her face. Her gaze landed on Sarah, and her smile faltered.

She doesn't like me. Sarah wanted to flee out the door, but there was no place to run to. They were stuck here, no matter how bad things might be. Quinn's grandma looked at him and raised her white brows.

He shuffled his feet but held her gaze. "Grandma, this is Sarah, my wife."

Surprise widened the woman's eyes then the charming smile returned. "Welcome, dear. You don't know how happy I am to meet you." She hurried forward, not looking sick at all, and held out her hand.

Sarah took it, and the older woman laid her other hand atop Sarah's. "I've prayed long and hard for you, my dear."

Sarah glanced up at Quinn. He actually looked as if he was blushing, but she couldn't tell for certain. She turned back to his grandma. "I'm Sarah Oak—"

Quinn cleared his throat, and Sarah realized her mistake. She smiled. "I'm Sarah McFarland, ma'am. It's a pleasure to meet you." The new name sounded odd on her lips.

"I'm Martha Miles, but you may call me Martha—or Grandma—whichever you'd like. And who are these fine youngsters?"

Sarah patted Beth's head. "This is my sister, Beth, and my brother, Ryan."

Martha clapped her hands together. "I'm so delighted that there will be children in this house again. Where is your luggage?"

"I'll get their things if you can show them to their rooms." Quinn glanced at Sarah. "I need to tend to the horses then I'll bring in your *belongings*." A soft smile tugged at one corner of his lips.

Was he teasing her? Surely not.

"Come this way. We have enough bedrooms that you can each use one for now. Of course, once Adam and Mariah return, things will be more crowded." She opened a door to a room that held a double bed. Several framed drawings of cattle scenes decorated the wall. There was one chair as well as a small desk.

"Ryan, this is Adam's room. You may sleep in here for now."

Her brother's eyes widened. "By myself?"

Sarah wasn't sure if he was frightened or in awe.

Grandma Miles nodded. "When Adam and Mariah return, you will need to share a room with your sister, or maybe you'd prefer to sleep in the bunkhouse with the ranch hands."

Her somber brother actually smiled.

Across the hall, they entered a small whitewashed room. A colorful quilt decorated the single bed and matching curtains hung on the lone window. A small wardrobe sat in one corner of the room and a wingback chair in the other. Sharing the small bed with Beth, who wriggled in her sleep, would be awkward, but they'd slept on far worse in the past few months. Maybe she could talk Ryan into switching rooms so she and Beth could have the larger bed, but she doubted he'd want this room, which looked as if it was decorated for a girl.

Grandma patted the bed and gazed at Beth. "This will be your room, sweetheart. It was my granddaughter Anna's before she married."

Beth's brow crinkled. "But I want to stay with Sarah."

Grandma leaned over. "Sarah will be just down the hall. She's married now and needs to sleep with her husband."

Sarah was certain her eyes must have widened as much as Beth's. Her heart throbbed. Why hadn't she considered that before? How was she going to get out of this quagmire?

Beth leaned against Sarah, and she realized she needed to comfort the girl. "This is our home now. I'm not leaving you again. I promise."

Beth looked as if she wanted to remind Sarah that she'd made that promise before but hadn't kept it.

"Can you imagine this whole room is yours? I've never even had a room of my own before." Sarah patted her sister's head.

Beth considered that and looked around. "Can I leave the lantern lit when I sleep?"

"Of course you can, dear." Martha smiled.

"And the door open?"

Martha nodded. "If it makes you feel better, you certainly may. Would you like to try out the bed?"

Beth grinned and reached for the white metal frame. Sarah grabbed her sister's shoulder. "Perhaps it would be better to wait until she's had a bath."

Grandma Miles ran her gaze over the child and pressed her lips together. "You might be right. Let me show you to your room, then I'll have Elke—she's our cook and helps with other things we need—heat up some water for you to bathe in."

Sarah followed the older woman down a short hallway and through an open door. A large bed filled one wall of the room, and Sarah swallowed. She had to force herself not to gawk at it. Curtains fluttered at the open window, drawing her attention. She nearly gasped at the view. Coal black cattle grazed peacefully throughout the wide valley. One butte looked as if someone had sliced off the slide, revealing colorful layers of orange, tan, and even black. Shadows crept along the ground, eating up the light, where the sun had started to set behind the tall buttes.

She heard a rustling and turned back to survey the room. A sofa rested across from an unlit fireplace, and a large wardrobe all but covered one wall. A braided rug in blues, greens, and white warmed the wooden floor and gave the room a cozy touch.

Grandma Miles picked up a housecoat and some slippers. "The room belonged to Quinn's parents. He insisted I move in here when I first arrived, but I never liked this room. It's far too big, and I have trouble getting into that high bed."

Sarah wasn't sure where this conversation was leading so she remained silent.

"I'll move my things into Quinn's room. You two will be sharing this one now."

Quinn halted in the hall outside his grandmother's room. Sarah stood looking out the window. Why was she in there? He assumed she would stay in Anna's room or maybe Sarah and Beth could share the double bed in Adam and Mariah's room for now. He kicked open the door to his room. Sarah could stay there, and he'd move to the bunkhouse. He set the two large bundles his wife had purchased onto his bed. Now he understood why she'd bought so much fabric. She must have planned on making her siblings some clothes. What they wore wouldn't be good enough for piecings in one of his grandma's quilts.

He stopped in the hall, wondering what the two women were talking about. Beth clung to Sarah's skirt, but Ryan was nowhere to be seen. He hoped the boy wasn't getting into trouble. Quinn shook his head. He had some fences to mend where Ryan was concerned. The boy still hadn't forgiven him for his initial outburst.

"You and Quinn will be sharing this room now."

Quinn's heart jolted at his grandmother's words. Oh no! Why hadn't he considered that?

Of course, his grandma would assume the newlyweds would room together. He ran his hand over the back of his neck. Sarah wouldn't like this development. And neither did he.

"I don't want you to have to move on my accord, Martha. I can sleep with Beth for the time being."

"Nonsense," Quinn said, stepping into his parents' bedroom. "A man and wife should share a room." He hoped he sounded sincere when he felt anything but that.

Sarah turned and stared at him with wide eyes. He swallowed hard. If he insisted they not share a room, Grandma would suspect things weren't on the up-and-up.

"I'll move my things into your room." Grandma marched toward him, carrying her robe and slippers; a twinkle he hadn't seen since his mother's death danced in her brown eyes. "A redhead, huh?" she whispered as she passed. She deposited her things on his bed and turned. "While your wife and the children have their baths, I'll move your clothing into the big room."

Quinn nodded and started removing his clothes from the wardrobe. Grandma hurried out of the room and down the hall.

Sarah stopped outside his door. "Do something. We can't share—" She looked down at Beth. "Sweetie, why don't you go see what Ryan is doing?" Beth glanced from Sarah to Quinn and back then walked toward her brother's room.

"We'll have to make the best of things, Sarah. I don't want Grandma thinking we're not a true married couple."

She leaned forward. "But we aren't. At least that's what you said. Have you changed your mind?"

Crossing her arms, his wife's eyes shot blue fire at him. Did she have any idea how pretty she was when she was angry? For a moment he almost changed his mind. He almost said he wanted a real marriage. But Sarah would leave one day—just like the siblings he'd raised. Just like the parents he'd loved so much. And he was the one who'd opened the door for her to go—once Grandma had passed. "We'll share this room, Sarah. We are married, after all."

Chapter Eight

Sarah lifted her arms and allowed the new nightgown to fall over her body. She'd never had one so soft or so pretty. Oh, how good it felt to be clean again. But even better would be sleeping in a real bed after spending so many nights on a hard pallet. If not for the fact that Quinn expected to share that bed, things would be wonderful. But if not for her husband, they wouldn't even be at the Rocking M Ranch, and she'd still be locked up and her siblings alone.

She spun around the big room. Never had she seen a bedroom this size. Why, it was even larger than the parlor had been at their farmhouse. Thoughts of her former home sobered her, and she dropped onto the sofa. A bear skin rug, complete with the head, lay between the fireplace and sofa. No fire burned, because the nights weren't cold enough. She stuck her feet underneath her gown, not wanting to touch the rug, and stared at the logs sitting ready for a match. Lord, thank You for this wonderful home. Please heal Quinn's grandmother of what ails her so that we can stay here a long time. And help me. I don't know how to be a wife.

A soft knock sounded at the door. Sarah jumped to her feet, raced across the room, leapt onto the bed, and crawled under the covers, her heart pounding.

"It's only me, dear. May I come in for a moment?" Grandma Miles pushed open the door and stuck her head in. "Oh, I didn't expect you'd be in bed already. We can talk tomorrow."

"No, please come in. I just—" It wouldn't do to explain that she was hiding from Quinn. "I was thinking about today and all the changes it brought." She climbed off the bed and held out her hand. "Come and sit with me."

"I peeked at the children. Both are out cold." Martha smiled and ambled over to the sofa and sat down. She turned to face Sarah. "I wanted to let you know how happy I am that you're here."

"Thank you." Sarah held her quivering hands in her lap, hoping the older woman wouldn't ask how she'd met her grandson.

"Quinn is a good man. He's carried the burden for this family since his father died. He helped raise his siblings, and now he's caring for me." She looked down at her hands a moment; then a soft smile graced her wrinkled face. "I'm glad he has someone to take care of him now."

Not knowing what to say, Sarah remained quiet. Her gaze darted to the partially open door, and she picked a pillow off the sofa and held it against her chest. "I'll do my best to make Quinn happy and to help you."

Grandma patted her hand. "I'm sure you will. I'll admit that I'm curious how you and my grandson came to be married. It's obvious you aren't the mail-order bride I sent for, but that can wait for another day."

Sarah's heart skipped a beat. So, she knew without being told that Sarah wasn't the bride she'd been expecting. What else did she know?

Grandma leaned in closer. "I do have to admit that I'm delighted to have the children here. They are such sweet things." She patted Sarah's hand. "Well, I'll let you get your rest. Tomorrow, I'll get my other things out of here. Then the room will be all yours and Quinn's. And I believe we might have some old clothes in a trunk somewhere that may fit your brother and sister."

She pushed up and walked to the door. "I'm so glad you're here, Sarah. I look forward to getting to know you better."

The door closed, and Sarah's heart warmed. She felt as if she'd made a new friend. And even better, Quinn's grandma didn't seem ill at all. Could there be something wrong that wasn't obvious? At least she could uphold the woman in her prayers and relieve her of some of the burden of the household chores.

Sarah moved to the door and peeked out. She'd seen no sign of her husband since supper. He'd shoved away from the table after the meal, muttering something about being behind on his chores. She'd wanted Ryan to help him, but the boy wouldn't leave her side.

A soft light shone out from under the door of Quinn's old room. Sarah tiptoed to Beth's room and peeked inside. The lantern had been turned down to a gentle glow, casting dancing shadows around the room. Beth lay on her side with her hands under her cheek. Sarah leaned over and kissed her then pulled up the colorful quilt.

She hurried to Ryan's room at the beginning of the hall. Stopping at his door, she peered into the dark parlor. Elke had fixed a delicious dinner of bratwurst, sauerkraut, applesauce, and braided bread with flavorful seeds in it. The scent still clung to the air. Sarah hoped she hadn't made a pig of herself by taking a second helping.

She opened Ryan's door and peeked in. The faint light of a half-moon illuminated his face as his soft snores filled the room. Sarah smiled and closed the door. When was the last time the children had rested so soundly—so worry free?

The front door opened, startling Sarah. She rushed down the hall, into her room, and dove under the covers. If she pretended to be asleep, maybe her husband wouldn't bother her tonight.

The thud of Quinn's boots moved closer, each step sending her pulse racing faster. She might be married, but she sure didn't feel married. His steps stopped at the door as if he was afraid to enter. Or maybe he was disappointed to find her sleeping. She carefully opened one eye a slit and peered at him.

He looked to be studying the floor. She hadn't gotten the impression he was a man of indecision, but he seemed hesitant to enter. Finally, he glanced over his shoulder toward his old bedroom and sighed. He stepped across the threshold and shut the door.

His footsteps softened as he crossed the braided rug at the end of the bed then clicked against the wooden floor next to where she lay under the covers. Her heart stampeded like a runaway horse. Could he hear it? Could he tell she was faking sleep?

With both eyes shut, she felt him watching her. Thank goodness she'd pulled the sheet up to her neck. The longer he stood there, the more she trembled. Finally, he walked toward the sofa, leaving behind the scent of leather and dust.

The sofa creaked as he lowered his heavy body onto it, and a boot flopped onto the floor, followed by another. She turned over and peeked out again. Quinn ran his hands through his thick hair, leaving swirls where the edges curled up. She wondered why he didn't keep his hair cut shorter like most curly-haired men would, but she liked it longer. Would it be as soft to the touch as her own was?

He stretched and then stood. She closed her eyes, lest he see her watching him, and heard him pad toward the chest of drawers. A soft whoosh sounded, the light faded, and darkness enveloped the room. Sarah's heart nearly jumped out of her chest. Would her husband come to bed now? She was as far on her side as she could be without falling off the edge, but her husband was a big man.

She heard a rustling near the fireplace and waited. Her ragged breathing would give her away if he was paying attention. He exhaled another sigh, and the room grew quiet.

Sarah waited, but he didn't come. He couldn't be sleeping on the sofa or it would be creaking under his weight. Then he must be lying on that smelly bear rug. Something in Sarah's stomach twisted at the unfairness of their situation. She was small. Her husband worked hard and needed his rest. Tomorrow, she'd sleep on the sofa—and hope and pray that his grandma didn't choose to pay her another before-bed visit.

Quinn rested his elbows on the table and sipped his coffee as he studied his makeshift family. Beth cast him shy smiles whenever he caught her eye. She was a darling. Her dark blond hair had been plaited and hung in two braids down the front of her faded dress. Had Sarah's dark hair been blond when she was a child?

Ryan still glared at him, but the hardness had left his blue eyes. The boy had no idea how much the two of them had in common. Having lost his own father, Quinn knew how Ryan was suffering. He wanted to make things easier for him. But how?

Silverware clinked against plates as the women and children finished eating their pancakes and sausage. Grandma dabbed at her lips and cleared her throat. "I think today we'll search that trunk in your bedroom, Sarah. I'm sure there are some clothes that we could alter to fit Ryan and Beth. That would give them something else to wear until we can make some new things out of the fabric that you got at the mercantile."

Beth's eyes lit up, but Ryan scowled and looked down at his shirt, as if he didn't see anything wrong with the patched flannel.

"Thank you. That would be nice. The children are in desperate need of new clothes." His wife's gaze darted in his direction then away, like a butterfly flitting from flower to flower.

She hadn't said anything about him sleeping on the floor, but then he'd been out of the room before sunup, so there'd been little chance for them to talk. He rolled his neck, working out the kinks. He was too young for his back to hurt, but after a night on the floor, he felt like an old-timer.

Halfway through the night, he'd seriously considered climbing out the window and finding a bed in the bunkhouse, but then the hands would wonder why he wasn't with his new bride. He didn't want to face the humiliation in those questions. Just their harmless teasing about being a newlywed was enough.

"What do you plan to do today, Quinn?"

He glanced at his grandma. Somehow the question didn't feel as innocent as it seemed. "Work. Same thing I always do."

"Perhaps there is something Ryan could do. He needs to learn the ways of a ranch if he's going to be living here."

Quinn caught the spark of hopefulness right before Ryan's eyes dulled again. The boy would be more trouble than he was worth, but Quinn's pa had taught him, and it was only fair that he teach Ryan. Quinn couldn't very well tell his grandma that the boy wouldn't be around all that long. "Sure. I can put him to work. That is, if it's all right with Sarah."

Ryan's head jerked toward his sister. There wasn't a doubt that he'd rather be helping Quinn than sorting and trying on old clothes. Maybe he'd do, after all.

"Of course, that would be fine. Ryan would love to learn to ride, and he knows some things. He did chores back at our farm." Sarah's eyes sparkled, nearly taking his breath away. He hadn't seen her so happy since she'd been reunited with the children.

"You'll have to do what I say. There are many things that can hurt someone who's not paying attention and doing what he's told. If you can't mind me, you'll have to stay in the house with the women."

Ryan's eyes narrowed. Quinn could tell the boy didn't like being ordered around, but he also didn't want to stay with the women all day. Finally, he nodded.

Quinn stood, hoping he wasn't making a mistake. His wife would blame him if something happened to her brother. Ryan rose and followed him to the door. Quinn removed his hat from the peg on the wall and reached for the knob. Adam's old hat still hung on his peg. Quinn grabbed it and stuck it on Ryan's head. "My brother bought a new hat last time he was here. You can have his old one."

Ryan's eyes widened and a smile tugged at one corner of his mouth. He pushed the too-big hat up on his head.

Quinn looked at the boy's shoes. "We'll have to see if we can find you a pair of boots. All ranchers need boots."

The boy straightened and nodded. He glanced back over his shoulder at his sister with a half-smile.

Sarah waved. "You work hard and be obedient."

Ryan nodded and looked up at Quinn. "What are we going to do?"

"Do you know how to ride?"

Ryan shook his head, but a sparkle danced in his eyes. "Not by myself. I rode our old mule back home, but Pa always led it or rode in front of me."

"Then let's start there."

Two days later, Ryan ran into the kitchen. He skidded to a halt in front of Sarah. She looked up from where she was helping Beth make sugar cookies. "Sarah, I rode by myself today!"

Quinn followed Ryan, unable to keep the proud smile off his face at the boy's enthusiasm. Who would have thought teaching the boy to ride would be the thing to break down the walls between them?

Quinn crossed the room and snatched a cookie from the cooling rack. Instead of scolding him like Grandma or Elke would have, Sarah smiled, doing funny things to his insides.

"Thank you," she mouthed.

He nodded. He felt a tug on his pants and looked down. Beth stared up at him with big blue eyes. "I wanna ride a horse. It's not fair that Ryan gets to, but I don't."

Quinn reached down, and Beth jumped up into his arms. The girl's unconditional love warmed his heart and made him wish her big sister felt the same. He took the end of her braid and tickled her cheek with it. Beth giggled and rubbed her face against his shirt.

"You won't like it. Horses are big and scary." Ryan scowled.

"Horses are big, but most of them aren't scary." Quinn lifted his brow at Ryan, hoping he'd understand that frightening his sister wasn't all right. He patted Beth's back. "If Sarah doesn't mind, I'll teach you to ride, too. My sister, Anna, is an excellent horsewoman."

"Truly?" Beth said, with awe in her voice. "Can I, Sissy?"

Sarah nodded. "It's probably a good idea for you to learn, but we'll have to do it at a time so as not to take the men away from their work."

"When's that?" Beth looked at Quinn.

"After dinner some evening."

Grandma entered the kitchen and picked up a platter of biscuits off the counter, her eyes twinkling. "Wash up, you two. Lunch is ready."

Quinn could tell she already loved her new family. She seemed to have twice the peppiness this week over last. Having Sarah and the kids here had been a huge boost to his grandma and seemed to have revived her spirits and her health. And she hadn't yet asked him how he came about marrying Sarah. But she would one day. He just hoped by then she'd be so in love with Sarah and the kids that it wouldn't matter.

Elke squeezed past him, carrying a soup tureen filled with beef stew, and his mouth watered at the fragrant scent. He set Beth down and snagged Ryan on the shoulder as the boy reached out to snitch a square of corn bread. "You heard your sister. Let's wash up."

"You snuck a cookie," he said, scowling.

"You're right. Sorry that I was a bad example."

Ryan looked chastised and followed him out to the mud room where a bucket of fresh water and clean towels awaited them. The boy washed quickly and snatched a towel. Quinn dipped his hands then flicked the water on Ryan. He jerked his head and giggled. Ryan tossed the towel at Quinn and dashed into the kitchen before Quinn could get him again. Splashing had become a game between the two of them.

Quinn rinsed his hands and dried them then used the towel to clean the dust off his face. When he lowered the towel, he was surprised to see Sarah leaning against the doorjamb, watching him with a raised brow.

"Splashing again?"

He grinned and shrugged. "Ryan enjoys it. I'm for anything that keeps him from frowning."

"Thank you. I appreciate how you and the ranch hands have taken him under your wing. I know he has to be in the way at times."

Quinn tossed the towel toward a peg on the wall, not a little proud that it caught and stayed there. "Everyone has to start somewhere. But who would have thought riding lessons would thaw the boy so quickly? After my initial outburst when I first saw them, I wondered if I'd ever get on his good side."

Sarah's pretty lips pressed together. "Losing our pa was really hard on Ryan. And then our uncle was just plain cruel. I'd never have gone to him if I'd known how much he'd changed. When I was a child, he was a fun man to be around."

"People change. Adversity can make a person cold and hard while others learn from their problems and get stronger." Somehow, he knew Sarah was a survivor. Even though she'd been forced into a marriage she hadn't wanted, she'd never once treated him with scorn. She'd simply accepted things for what they were and had gone about making things easier for Grandma and Elke.

A rosy stain covered her cheeks as he continued to stare. His stomach twittered as if a moth had found its way in there. Finally, Sarah dropped her gaze.

"I want you to know how much I appreciate you taking us in." She fiddled with the edge of her apron then looked up. "I'm sorry I didn't tell you about Ryan and Beth before we were married. That wasn't fair to you. I was afraid—"

Quinn grabbed her hand, surprised at its softness. "I know why you didn't tell me. I'll admit I was angry at first. I don't like surprises, but you did what was necessary to protect your siblings. That's something I know a lot about."

Sarah cocked her head and smiled. "Yes, I'm sure it is. Your grandma has told me how you helped raise your brother and sister."

That was a fact that most everyone knew, but when his wife said it with pride in her voice, embarrassment warmed his neck. His stomach gurgled.

Sarah grinned. "Hungry, huh?" She tugged him through the kitchen, dropping his hand right before they entered the dining room.

Quinn watched her glide toward her chair. Comfortable chatter filled the room as his wife took her seat. He no longer regretted marrying her—but he was fast coming to regret making his marriage a business arrangement.

Chapter Nine

"Come closer and watch me, Ryan." Holding two new horseshoes, the boy approached cautiously on Quinn's right. He lifted the mare's rear hoof between his legs and held up a tool. "This is a hoof pick. It's used to scrape out packed dirt, manure, and small stones from a horse's hoof."

Quinn cleaned the hoof and removed the old shoe. Ryan watched with something that looked like admiration on his face. "Hand me those nippers. You use them to trim the hoof wall." He quickly trimmed the hoof and used a rasp from his back pocket to smooth it out.

"I've already sized the shoes for this mare, so all that's left is to put on the new one." Ryan handed him a shoe, and Quinn tapped it on with a nailing hammer.

"What about the nail points sticking through the shoe?" Ryan asked as he bent closer, blocking the light.

"Clinch the nails—bend the ends—to keep the shoe from coming off. After that, smooth things with the rasp, and then you get to do that three more times." He dropped the mare's hoof, patted her rump, and rubbed his lower back. Ryan picked up the old shoe and examined it.

Quinn smiled and lightly squeezed the boy's shoulder. At least Ryan was no longer flinching whenever he touched him. Since acquiring a new family, Quinn had chosen chores that kept him closer to home. For someone who'd been a loner for so long, it was a big change. He bent and lodged the horse's front hoof between his legs, dug out a stone, and grated down the hoof. "Hand me the rasp again."

Ryan did as asked and stood beside Quinn watching each thing he did. Adam had never been so interested in ranching. He'd done what had to be done but would slip off and draw pictures if their pa didn't keep a close eye on him. Ryan wanted to learn everything. He'd probably asked Quinn a hundred questions. With the new shoe nailed on, he lowered the hoof and patted the mare again. Why couldn't women be so easy to handle? "See, it's simple."

"Maybe to you." Ryan shrugged.

"It will be to you one day, too, after you've shod a few dozen horses."

He finished the last two hooves and then let the boy lead the horse into the corral and release her. Ryan was a quick learner. His coloring and features hardly resembled his big sister, except for those brilliant blue eyes they all had.

The odor of cattle hung on the cool breeze, reminding him of all the chores that needed doing. This spring's crop of calves still needed to be branded. The new yearlings needed to be halter broke. His wife needed a real husband.

He shook his head, leaned on the corral, and lifted his foot to the first rail. Had it been a mistake to marry Sarah? Weren't she and the kids much better off?

Ryan closed the gate and mirrored his stance but remained silent. Quinn's thoughts veered to Sarah and how she had insisted he sleep on the bed. Ever since their second night together, she'd dressed in her nightgown before he'd come in and had slept on the sofa, wrapped up in a quilt. Sure, he was resting better than when he'd been on the floor, but the guilt was driving him crazy. She should take the bed, but she was too stubborn. What would she do if he picked her up in her sleep and put her in it? He grinned, but then realized that would mean he'd be sleeping on the floor again. He shook his head. There was no easy answer.

A squeal sounded from near the house, and the mare nickered and turned her head toward the noise. Quinn looked over his shoulder and saw Beth run around the side of the house. He pushed away from the railing and moved toward her. Was she hurt? Scared?

Sarah followed, laughing, and Quinn's bunched up muscles relaxed. She growled and lifted up her skirt and ran after her sister. "I'm gonna get you."

"Nuh-uh." Beth spotted him and ran in his direction. "Save me, Quinn! Don't let the mean old bear eat me."

Quinn reached out and caught Beth as she lunged for him. He spun her around then held her against his chest. "I'll protect you from that mean ol' critter."

Beth giggled and looked at her sister.

Sarah halted a few feet from him, her chest heaving. Her cheeks were a rosy red. "Looks like you've got my dinner, cowboy."

"Yep."

"What's a poor bear gonna do?"

Ryan slipped up beside Quinn, staring at his sisters as if they'd gone loco.

"Eat Ryan." Beth pointed at her brother, who peered back with interest.

Sarah's eyes gleamed, and she tiptoed toward Ryan with her hands making bear claws. A smile tugged at the somber boy's lips. "She can't catch me." He dashed toward the barn with Sarah close on his heels.

"C'mon, Quinn," Beth squealed and bounced in his arms. "We gotta save Ryan."

Grinning, Quinn jogged toward the barn. Inside, Sarah tackled her brother, and both landed in a pile of fresh hay that was ready to be forked into the clean stalls. Ryan laughed as Sarah tickled him.

"Let me down." Beth kicked, and he set her on the ground. The little girl dove on top of her sister.

Quinn leaned one arm on a stall gate, wishing he had the freedom to jump in and play with them. They reminded him of the days when his family still lived in Texas. When he was a boy and had horsed around with Adam and Anna—before they moved here and their father died and everything changed. He missed those carefree days. Maybe one day he'd feel comfortable enough to wrestle with Sarah and the kids like that.

But then Sarah and the kids weren't staying.

Ryan jumped up and dashed past Quinn with Beth on his heels. Quinn grinned at the two, who more resembled scarecrows with all that hay in their hair than children. Chuckling, Sarah sat up and plucked stems from the cuff and pocket of one of Anna's old dresses. She rested her arms on her knees, a wide grin on her face. "It's so good to see them laughing again. I have you to thank for that."

Quinn pushed away from the stall and strode toward her. He reached out his hand, and she glanced up. After a moment she placed her hand in his, and he drew her to her feet. Sprigs of hay stuck out from his wife's dark hair, and her thick braid rested over her shoulder, hanging down the front of her dress. He couldn't help grinning.

"What's so funny?"

He may be just a rancher, but he knew better than to answer that question. He lifted a hand and pulled out a stem near her ear. Then another off of the top of her head. His wife swallowed. Did he affect her like she did him? He'd never been drawn to a woman before. Never allowed himself to get close enough to get to know one. And now he was married—sort of.

His wife had filled out a little in the week that she'd been at the Rocking M. Her cheeks were rosy, and she'd lost that wary look. She was filling a place in his heart that he hadn't known was empty. He'd been lonely but hadn't noticed until Sarah and the kids arrived. He'd worked hard all day and spent his evenings doing bookkeeping or reading up on cattle breeding or diseases. He hadn't had time to be lonely. And now that Sarah was here, he was lonelier than ever. As much as he didn't want to admit it, he wanted her to care for him—not because he'd provided her family with a home and food, but because she saw something in him worth desiring.

His wife nibbled on her bottom lip. Quinn plucked a stem of hay from the top of her head and ran his hand down her soft hair. It was black as a raven's wing. Her lightly tanned skin seemed fairer than it actually was in the shadows of the barn. Her questioning sky blue eyes peered up at him.

His breath caught in his throat as he thought about kissing her. Would she welcome his affection? It was unwise to be thinking such thoughts. She would leave him one day. But he couldn't help leaning toward her. She lifted her face up to his.

A piercing scream echoed behind him, and Quinn spun around. Beth ran toward him with Ryan right behind her. "Save me again, Quinn!"

Beth dashed behind him and wrapped her arms around his waist. Disappointment soared through him at the missed kiss.

But maybe the little girl had saved *him*. Saved him from making a big mistake.

Martha lifted a linen baby gown from the top of the trunk and handed it to Sarah. "This was Adam's. He and Anna were so tiny when they were born, it's a miracle they survived. Anna took her matching gown and some other baby things with her when she moved to Brett's ranch, hoping it wouldn't be long before she was with child."

Beth leaned against Sarah's arm and fingered the thin fabric. "It's small enough to fit a dolly."

"Go get your doll and let's see if it does." Grandma smiled and ran her hand over the little girl's head.

Beth glanced up at Sarah, her eyes shimmering with unshed tears. Sarah pressed her sister against her side as the scent of smoke and the vision of a burned home still smoldering assaulted her. Just when she thought she was over her grief, it washed over her again like a spring flash flood.

"Beth doesn't have a doll anymore."

"It burned up in the fire like Mama and Papa." The girl's lower lip wobbled and a tear streaked down her cheek.

"I'm sorry, dear." Martha pressed her lips together, as if she, too, struggled not to give way to tears. "We'll simply have to make a new doll. I have a box of scraps in my room. Would you like to come and look at them after we finish here and see if you can find something that would make a nice doll?"

"Can Sarah come, too?" Beth looked back and forth between the two women.

"Of course, she can." Quinn's grandmother dug further down in the trunk and pulled out two folded garments. She shook out a blue calico and held it up to Beth. "It's a bit big, but we can alter it to fit you."

Beth's eyes lit up. "Look, Sissy, Grandma's giving me another new dress."

Sarah's gaze caught Martha's, and a soft smile flitted on the older woman's lips. "It's been a long while since a child has called me Grandma. It's a sweet sound to these old ears."

"Why don't you try on the dress, Beth? Then we can pin it up."

Beth quickly shed her old garment and slipped the new one over her head. Martha got her pin cushion, and Sarah pinned up the sides of the garment while Martha measured.

"Now the second one." Martha shook out a brown calico with a pinafore that would make a sturdy play garment.

Beth shed the blue dress and pulled on the second. She stood on one foot and then the other.

"You remind me of Anna at your age. The poor child hated trying clothes. She'd much rather be out riding a horse or chasing cattle."

Beth scratched her neck where the dress pressed against her throat. "Quinn's gonna teach me to ride like he did Ryan."

Martha laid the blue garment on Sarah's bed. "That's a good thing to know, even for women and girls. I used to help my husband with roundup back when we lived in Texas, and Anna helped here."

Sarah smiled as she measured the second dress. "I think this one will be fine in the side. I'll take the hem up a little and have it ready for you to wear tomorrow."

Beth clapped her hands. "Goodie. Can I go play with the blocks now?"

Sarah buttoned up the back of Beth's faded calico and hugged her sister. "Yes, you may, but stay on the porch. If you want to go see the animals or something else, you come and get me first. All right?"

Beth nodded and skipped out of the room. A warm sensation filled Sarah's chest. Quinn had made her sister's happiness possible. He may have had second thoughts about making their marriage real, but the result for her siblings had been the same. Both were happier than they'd been since the fire.

Martha held a knitted baby blanket against her chest. "I hope to be able to use this again one day soon."

Her sly smile sent a shaft of guilt spearing through Sarah. How could she tell this sweet woman that there wouldn't be any children from her marriage? That her husband wanted a business arrangement and would send her packing once Martha was gone?

She couldn't. Sarah forced a smile. "Maybe one day."

"Adam's little Jonathon is a cherub. He's got his father's coloring, much like your blue eyes and dark hair. Adam always hated that he didn't look much like Quinn and Anna, even though he was Anna's twin." Martha seemed to stare off in the distance, as if she were looking right at Adam. She blinked and turned back to Sarah, an ornery smile tilting her lips. "I certainly hope to see Anna's and Quinn's children before I leave this world."

Sarah patted Martha's arm. She didn't want to give the woman false hope, but surely it wouldn't be long before Anna had a baby. "I'm sure you will."

Sarah picked up the scissors from Martha's sewing basket and carried ss to the sofa. She flipped the garment inside out and snipped the on the side seams.

Only she could tell Martha the truth. That her marriage was a lie. eked over her shoulder at the woman she was quickly growing to Martha was kind and generous, opening her home and her heart to 1 and the children. She'd never asked how Sarah had come to marry grandson, but rather just seemed happy that she had.

Sarah heaved a sigh. Everything here was perfect. The home was ged but had most everything they needed. Elke was a good cook, and ey were getting used to eating all the German specialties the woman njoyed making. Ryan had even started eating sauerkraut.

Quinn ran the ranch with expertise. He worked hard and was gone nearly all day. Most times they didn't see him for the noon meal because he was out on the range tending the cattle. Now that Ryan was riding well, he often accompanied Quinn at least half of the day. The exhausted boy was little trouble and fell asleep most nights on top of his bed with his clothes still on.

The top of the trunk thunked as Martha closed it, and Sarah jumped, stabbing her finger with a pin. She sucked the blood off so that it wouldn't stain the fabric, stared at the cold fireplace that took up nearly the whole wall. The room held the scent of wood smoke and furniture wax, giving it a cozy, homey feel.

Martha ambled over and sat beside Sarah, holding the brown dress. She picked up the scissors lying between them and snipped the threads that secured the hem. "Is everything all right between you and Quinn? I mean, I'm sure you and he didn't marry for love, since you'd never met before you were married, but are you happy here?"

"Oh yes. I love it here." Sarah couldn't tell the whole story, but that much was true. Life at her uncle's shack had been a daily struggle to survive. She had to hunt for food because he said she owed him. Then she had to clean and cook the meat, if she was fortunate enough to even kill something.

"I'm glad. I'll admit I was quite surprised when my grandson came home with you and the children, but you've been a delight and pulled me out of my grieving."

Sarah laid her hand over Martha's. "I'm sorry about your daughter. I wish I could have met her."

"Parents shouldn't outlive their children." Martha rested her hands in her lap. "Things were very difficult when Quinn's father died, and my grandson had to grow up overnight. He had a ranch to run, a grieving mother to help, and twin siblings who needed guidance. He's a good man."

Sarah nodded, thinking again how Quinn had been willing to marry her even though he didn't know for sure if she was an outlaw. Not many honorable men would have taken that risk. She'd always be grateful that he most likely saved her brother's and sister's lives.

"We used to hold church here each Sunday, but after his pa died, it was as if something in him closed off. He didn't want to feel anymore."

"Why are you telling me this?"

"Because I want you to understand him. To know that he's a good man who has endured a lot of pain and is afraid to open up. You, my dear, are the only person I think who can get him to do so."

Sarah watched Martha return to her sewing. The older woman had no idea of the burden that she'd just dumped on Sarah. If her marriage to Quinn was a love-match, then maybe she could help him, but she was only a fake wife. One to keep his grandma from ordering another mail-order bride.

She thought of all she'd lost, and the pain of losing this home hit full force. How long would they be here? A few months? A few years?

Long enough for the children to get settled. Long enough that leaving here would cause them great disappointment.

I can't think about that day, Lord. It takes more energy than I have. Help me to make things easier for Martha. Keep her healthy and happy and show me how to make my husband fall in love with me.

Just how did a woman go about making that happen?

Chapter Ten

"You missed a spot." Sarah pared the peeling off the potato in one long swirl.

"Where?" Beth turned a potato over in her hand, her palm effectively covering the last of the peeling.

Sarah lifted her sister's thumb. "Right there. It's hiding from you."

Her sister giggled and cut off the last spot.

Sarah leaned her head back against the rocker. Sitting on the porch watching the birds flittering on the railings or the men working a new horse in the corral helped pass the time while she did monotonous chores. A comfortable breeze tugged at her skirt and cooled her legs. Off to her left, two magpies bickered and flapped their wings.

Russet buttes surrounded the cozy valley, forming a natural shelter from the heavy winds that sometimes threatened to blow away anything not tied down. Clean sheets snapped on the line, absorbing the fresh scent created only by the sun and wind. The few trees in the area followed the creek line nearly a quarter of a mile away, offering shade to those willing to take the time to walk down there. Maybe she should take the children to play in the water one afternoon while the temperatures were warm.

Sarah sighed and picked up another potato. If only she could relax and enjoy the peaceful setting, but Quinn's words still haunted her. She couldn't let herself get attached to this place, no matter how comfortable it was. Homes were temporary. How many times had her parents moved before settling on the farm? Fire destroyed homes. People destroyed homes. As long as she and the children were together, that was where home was.

Sarah lifted her face to the breeze and sniffed. A hint of something filled the air, so unlike the stench of sugar beets. Sage, maybe.

A rider appeared at the top of the hill, following the trail she and Quinn had taken from town. She shaded her eyes as he drew closer. The roan horse moved into a trot, and Sarah's heart lurched. Uncle Harlan owned a roan gelding. Had he found them already?

Ryan was safe out on the range somewhere with Quinn. She set three finished spuds in Beth's bowl, her hand shaking so badly that she dropped one.

"I'll get it." Beth jumped up and set her smaller bowl in the rocker next to Sarah's.

"Why don't you go inside and wash the pealed potatoes and give them to Elke so she can put them to soak. We don't want them turning brown before we're ready to use them."

She glanced at the rider again and let out a relieved sigh. Now that the man was closer, she could tell he was too thin to be her uncle. Thank you, Lord.

He rode toward the house at a comfortable lope, looking too relaxed to be someone bringing trouble. He stopped his horse in front of her and tipped his hat, gazing at her with a curious, but friendly stare. Had he heard that Quinn had married a jailbird?

"Guten tag. I am Howard Heinrich. I am owner of the ranch south of here."

Sarah nodded and smiled at his thick German accent, which sounded similar to Elke's. "I'm Quinn's wife, Sarah McFarland."

The man grinned, revealing yellowed teeth. "I heard about you when I was in the town. Quite a story that is."

Sarah narrowed her eyes, not sure what he wanted.

"I do not mean harm. I bring mail. Neighbors here do that for one another." He reached behind him, pulled a small packet from his saddlebags, and thumbed through the letters. He handed three to Sarah.

"Would you like something to drink?" It was the least she could offer after his kindness.

"Danke, Frau McFarland, but I wish to be home before the dark." He tipped his hat and clucked out the side of his mouth to his horse. He reached the top of the hill and disappeared down the other side before the dust settled on the trail.

Sarah glanced at the mail. Two letters were for Quinn and one for his grandmother. She found Martha in the kitchen, rolling buns for supper.

"You've got a letter." Sarah held it while Martha wiped her hands on her apron.

"Mr. Heinrich must have stopped by." She smiled and squinted then pushed her spectacles up her nose as she took the letter from Sarah. She slit the envelope with a knife and unfolded a single sheet of paper. "It's from my husband's brother."

Sarah hoped the note brought good news but couldn't help wondering how many more relatives the family had that she didn't know about.

"John is coming for a visit and is bringing Tom and Florinda Phillips with him." Martha laid the letter on the table next to a bowl of dough. "They come most every year to get away from the heat of the city. Of course, half the time it's as hot here as in Chicago."

"When will they be arriving?" Sarah had barely gotten used to living on the Rocking M and now visitors were coming. Would they ask how she and Quinn met?

Martha glanced at the note again. "Oh, dear. They'll be here next week. There's so much to do."

"The children and I will help get things ready." Sarah patted Martha's shoulder, happy to do whatever she could to help. She didn't want her to stress over this sudden news and take to her bed, even though she hadn't been in bed a single day since they'd arrived. Sarah suspected the illness Quinn had mentioned was actually Martha grieving over the loss of her daughter, and her Bismarck home and friends. Sarah remembered the three babes her mother had lost before Beth and Ryan had been born. After each loss, her mother had been downhearted and had barely eaten for a long while. Grieving was a process that men didn't have the time or patience for and often didn't understand. "Where should I put these letters for Quinn?"

"On his desk in the parlor. I need to make a list of everything we'll have to do before John comes." Martha stared off as if deep in thought. Sarah tapped the other two letters against her hand.

Beth walked through the mud room, lugging a bucket with two inches of water with Elke following close behind her. "Elke helped me get water, and I'm gonna wash the 'tatoes, Sissy."

"That's being a good helper." Sarah smiled. Her sister probably had more water running down the front of her frock than in the bucket. She needed to make Beth an apron to protect her new dresses.

As Elke passed by, Sarah lightly touched her arm and leaned toward her. "Thank you for letting Beth help. I realize it makes more work for you."

The shy, fair-haired woman with pale blue eyes kept her head down, but a soft smile graced her lips. "I like kinder, Frau McFarland. I was oldest of nine."

"Nine?" Sarah regretted her impulsive response, but it didn't seem to bother the quiet cook.

"Ja, we have big family." Elke helped Beth onto a chair and then poured a small amount of water into a basin. Beth washed the potatoes and then dropped them into the bucket of water.

Sarah walked through the dining area and into the parlor, trying to imagine what it would be like to have been raised in such a large family. Maybe that was why Elke wasn't married. The woman had to be in her early thirties. Maybe she liked children—as long as they weren't hers.

She placed the letters on Quinn's desk, noting the neatness of the few items arranged on it. The only thing even partly messy was an open book. She glanced down to see what her husband had been reading and wrinkled her nose at the chapter heading. "New Methods in Castrating Cattle."

Martha followed her into the parlor and stared up at a family portrait on the wall. Sarah recognized the gangly adolescent as Quinn. A handsome man stood behind a blond woman sitting in a chair. Adam and Anna stood in front of their older brother. Anna's light-colored hair matched Quinn's and their mother's, while Adam's was dark like his father's.

"Quinn's father dreamed of owning a ranch where city folk could visit and find rest from the hectic life of the big towns. Ian received an inheritance from a wealthy uncle who lived in Ireland. He was the only heir and used the money to buy this ranch and to move his family here." She looked down and fiddled with the hem of her apron. "I didn't want them to leave Texas, but there been had a long drought. Times were tough, and there were still some problems with Indians sneaking across the Red River from Indian Territory and raiding ranches."

Sarah lifted her brows. Had Martha ever battled Indians? Ever shot one to protect her family? She stared at the portrait, trying to see a resemblance between Martha and her daughter. "Ellen was very pretty."

"Yes. She was a sweet woman who endured a hard life. Things up here weren't much easier than they'd been in Texas." She motioned toward the horsehair sofa and both women sat.

"You're a McFarland now. I doubt Quinn will tell you about his family history, but you ought to know. His father built this wonderful home, and things were going well. They were building up their herd by selling off longhorns and purchasing hardy cattle that fared better in the colder winters we have. Then Ian died in a tragic accident."

"What happened?" Sarah shivered as a vision of the fire seared her memory. She and her husband had suffered similar losses.

"He was returning from town with a wagon of supplies and a bad storm set in while he was gone. His wagon wheels slipped on the ice—we think—and the wagon went off a cliff. Thank the good Lord none of the children were with him."

Sarah laid her hand over Martha's. "I'm sorry."

"It was a long time ago, but Quinn's life changed that day. He went from being a fairly responsible adolescent who liked to hunt and fish to helping raise the twins and being in charge of the ranch. I think he's always felt that he failed his father by not opening the ranch up to city folk, other than family and a few cattlemen who come occasionally. You can see why I'm hoping you and he will be very happy together. He desperately needs some happiness in his life."

"I suppose that's why this home has so many bedrooms." Sarah wanted to encourage Martha, but she wouldn't give her false hopes about her marriage.

Martha nodded. "Yes. We can put John and Mr. Phillips in that empty room with the two beds. I'm afraid we'll need to move Beth into Ryan's room as long as the company is here. Do you think that will be all right? They're both still young enough to sleep together."

"It will be fine. We all shared a—" She caught herself before saying mat. She didn't want Martha to know they'd slept on buffalo skins on the hard floor of her uncle's shack. She didn't need the woman's pity. "We slept together for a time after my parents died."

"That will make things easier. We can put Florinda in Anna's old room."

"Florinda?"

Martha's lips pulled into a tight grimace. "Yes, she's Tom Phillips's daughter and usually accompanies him when he comes to visit. He's a well-known beef supplier and buys cattle from Quinn and then ships them to a Chicago slaughterhouse that he owns. Florinda has always been a bit. . .flighty. I think the only reason she comes is because of Qui—" Martha suddenly looked as if she'd swallowed a fly. "Well, never mind."

Because of Quinn. That's what she'd almost said. Sarah was certain of it. Did this Florinda have designs on Quinn? Sarah wondered why a city woman would want to visit such an isolated ranch. Surely she would be bored here, but then she must like it if she'd been here before. Or maybe she just liked Quinn. What would Florinda do when she learned he was now married?

The idea of another woman attracted to her handsome husband made Sarah's stomach swirl as if she'd downed a glass of sour milk. Had Quinn been attracted to their guest? If so, why did he marry her? Would she have to do battle to keep the husband who already wanted to be rid of her?

"They're coming! I see them." Beth ran through the open front door, her braids flying behind her.

Ryan tugged at the collar of his new white shirt. "I don't see why we have to wear our fancy clothes just 'cause company's comin'?" He fidgeted on the steps.

Sarah wished she'd been able to purchase new shoes for him and Beth, but at least Martha had insisted they draw an outline of the children's feet, so Quinn could drop it off at the mercantile. Next time someone went into town, the new shoes, ordered from a cobbler in Dickinson, should be waiting.

Martha hurried through the parlor in the tan and gold church dress that Sarah had ironed for her the day before. The older woman, eager to see her husband's younger brother, looked excited, even vibrant, and not a bit sick. Sarah mumbled a thank-you to God for that.

She smoothed down the front of her dress, glad that she was able to complete the dark blue calico before their guests arrived. Her hands trembled. She'd worked herself into a tizzy the past few days worrying about Florinda Phillips. So what if the woman had designs on Quinn? What could she do now that he was married?

Sarah took a deep breath. She knew she shouldn't worry so. God had provided this home and family to care for them, and He would work out their future.

Beth bounced up and down, and Sarah rested her hand on the girl's shoulder. "Settle down. Those folks aren't coming to see us." She couldn't understand why Beth was so excited. Maybe it had to do with the cookies they would be serving once their guests had settled in.

Quinn guided a handsome black surrey with a folding leather top into the yard, pulled by one of the prettiest horses Sarah had seen. She couldn't help thinking how she had arrived on an old buckboard filled with supplies. Two men sat in the backseat, but Sarah's gaze was drawn to the beautiful woman in the front, leaning against Quinn's shoulder. Her neatly styled blond hair was covered by a small hat that held no purpose other than decoration. Her frilly lavender dress looked out of place against the browns and greens of the valley.

"Whoa, Charlie. Hold up, boy." Quinn hopped down, hurried around to the other side of the buggy, and offered his hand to Florinda. The woman gave him a coy smile then set her hands on top of his shoulders, forcing him to take hold of her thin waist and lift her down. She giggled and took his arm, ignoring everyone on the porch as she gazed longingly at Sarah's husband.

Sarah clenched her teeth. How could she endure this preening woman for two full weeks? Quinn glanced at her, and she lifted one brow and stared back. He looked down, as if watching the steps to make sure he didn't trip—steps he dashed up and down a dozen times each day.

The two men climbed out of the buggy. A tall, thin man looked around the ranch, but the shorter, balding man, who looked twenty years older than the other man, made a beeline for Martha.

"Oh, John. I can't believe you're actually here." Martha held out her arms.

He hurried up the stairs as soon as Florinda's skirts had cleared them and wrapped his arms around the older woman. "I was so sorry to hear about Ellen. I would have come to her funeral if I hadn't been in New York."

Martha patted his chest. "It's all right. She was probably buried before you even received our telegram."

"How are you doing?" he asked.

"Fine. Much better now that I've moved to the ranch. I needed to be with family."

Florinda narrowed her eyes and curled her lip as she regarded Sarah. Her hazel gaze darted from Beth to Ryan before settling, adoringly, back on Quinn. Sarah couldn't help wondering if Miss Phillips thought they were the hired help.

Mr. Phillips joined them on the porch and stood beside his daughter. He had kind gray eyes, and a thick head of light brown hair. He stood about three inches shorter than Quinn.

Sarah's husband wriggled his arm away from Florinda's and stepped toward Martha. "You remember my grandmother, Martha Miles. You two met three or four years ago in Bismarck."

Florinda's smile would have won a grinning contest, if there were such a thing. "How nice to see you again." She gently shook Martha's hand.

"It's a pleasure to have you visit the Rocking M."

"Yes, well. . .thank you." Florinda's gaze flitted over the front of the house, and Sarah felt like the woman would rather be just about anywhere except an isolated ranch in the Badlands.

Quinn crossed over to stand beside Sarah. He cast a quick glance her way and cleared his throat. "Uncle John, Mr. Phillips, Florinda, I'd like to introduce my. . .wife, Sarah."

Sarah couldn't help taking a small pleasure in the way Florinda's brows shot up. At the same time she hadn't missed how Quinn had hemhawed when he introduced her. Was he ashamed of her?

"Well now, this is a surprise. Congratulations, my boy." Uncle John slapped Quinn on the shoulder and gave him a rough hug. "It's about time you married."

He turned to Sarah. "Welcome to the family." Before she could shake his hand, he engulfed her in a bear hug, making Sarah feel loved and accepted. She already liked the man. "And are these your children?"

Martha slapped her brother-in-law on the arm. "Oh for heaven's sake, John, she's far too young to have children that age. They are her siblings, Ryan and Beth."

With introductions completed, Uncle John followed Martha and Mr. Phillips inside. Florinda seemed to have gathered her composure and grasped hold of Quinn's left arm, giving Sarah a derisive glare. Quinn glanced from Sarah to Florinda as if unsure what to do. He shifted his feet, looking uncomfortable with Florinda's overt attention. Sarah wasn't about to let the woman get away with such an action, and she took hold of Quinn's right arm.

"Will you please escort us into the house, husband?" If Quinn seemed surprised at her overly emphasized spousal reference, he didn't show it.

Sarah clung to him, ready to do battle for the man who didn't want her. Maybe she simply needed to prove to the flirty woman that Quinn belonged to her, even if he didn't realize it yet.

Chapter Eleven

Sarah set the sugar bowl on the table and then stopped in front of the open window. She allowed the wind to cool her body, hot from helping Elke in the kitchen, while she struggled to calm her emotions, equally as steamy. Fortunately, this evening's breeze was from the north and not the south, where the cattle were currently grazing. She took several deep breaths and then took her seat between Quinn and Beth. Florinda sat across from them, alternating glares at Sarah with cocked-head smiles at Quinn. Did the woman not realize how obvious her flirtations were?

Learning that Quinn was married and no longer available seemed to have no effect on Miss Phillips. Sarah understood flirting. She had worked to catch the eye of a few boys back during her school days, but this was different. What could Florinda hope to gain?

A cold shiver snaked up Sarah's spine. What if Florinda discouraged her father from buying cattle from Quinn if he didn't shower her with attention? Surely Mr. Phillips wouldn't allow something so petty to keep him from making a wise business decision.

"I thought we'd ride out and look at the cattle tomorrow, if that's all right with you two. The weather's not too hot yet, so it shouldn't be a hardship for you city slickers." Quinn grinned at the men and then sipped his coffee.

"Perhaps they would like a day to rest from their travels," Martha said.

Elke set a platter heaping with fried chicken on the table. Sarah's mouth watered as she eyed the golden crust. She knew it was tasty, because she'd sampled the little crispies that had fallen off as Elke took the chicken from the skillet. At least their nauseating guest hadn't affected her appetite. She couldn't help grinning the next time Florinda glared at her.

"I feel fine and would like to see the cattle tomorrow. How about you, John?" Mr. Phillips looked at his friend.

"Sounds good to me as long as it doesn't rain."

At Martha's request, John said a quick prayer, and the food was passed. Florinda took one chicken leg and a tablespoon of potatoes, minus the gravy, and green peas. Sarah didn't let the other woman's puny appetite affect her and filled her plate. She was famished. She'd worked hard all day preparing the rooms, cleaning house, and cooking.

While the men talked weather and cattle prices, Martha attempted to engage Miss Phillips in conversation. "What have you been doing with yourself lately, Florinda?"

Ryan, sitting to Miss Phillips's left, finished off a thigh and licked his fingers with a smack. Sarah lifted her brows at him, and he ducked his head and retrieved his napkin from the floor where it had fallen.

Miss Phillips scowled at the boy as she dabbed her lips with her cloth napkin. Her expression softened when she turned her gaze on Martha. "Oh, the usual. Last year I completed finishing school at Miss Muriel Murdock's Academy for Fine Ladies. We learned culture and sophistication." She lifted her nose and looked at Sarah's plate. "Something you most likely know nothing about."

Martha cleared her throat, obviously displeased with the verbal attack. Sarah nearly bit clear through the chicken bone. She glanced at Quinn who was engrossed in his conversation and completely missed how she had been insulted.

"Some people have to work for a living and can't go to those fancy schools." Ryan squinted at Florinda; his lips looked as if he'd sucked on a lemon.

Sarah wanted to run over and hug her brother for defending her, but she stayed in her chair and took a bite of potatoes—with plenty of gravy.

"Well, things are different out West." Martha took a sip of buttermilk. "Most young ladies around here marry early. People don't have money for such luxuries as finishing school. You're a fortunate girl to have been able to attend such a fine academy." Martha caught Sarah's eye and smiled at her as if letting her know she understood how Florinda irritated her.

Sarah endured the rest of the meal, grateful to leave when it was time to help the children get ready for bed. Florinda smirked as Sarah stood, and Sarah didn't take time to analyze the crazy thought that sprinted across her mind, but she leaned over and kissed Quinn on the cheek, all the time looking at Florinda. The line in the sand had been drawn.

Quinn jerked around and looked at Sarah with confused eyes. She leaned her arm across his shoulders, her soft cheek rubbing against his bristly one. "If you'll excuse me for a moment, I'm going to put the children in bed. I'll be right back, so don't you go anywhere."

One of his brows lifted, but he quickly schooled his expression as if he was onto her. "I'll be right here waiting." He grinned and winked as she straightened, sending her stomach into spasms. Maybe she had eaten too much, after all.

Martha and the men chuckled. Florinda's perpetual scowl deepened. Feeling lighter than she had all day, Sarah took Beth's hand and helped the yawning girl out of her chair. "Come along, Ryan."

Her brother snagged another biscuit and stood. "'Scuse me," he mumbled. He shoved the bread into his mouth and walked around the table.

Sarah considered how being so close to Quinn had affected her. He smelled fresh, having bathed in the creek before going to town to fetch their guests. He had a scent all his own, a manly one that never failed to stir her whenever he came near. His dark blond hair, which was normally covered with his western hat, swirled in appealing curls. His forehead was a shade lighter than the rest of his tanned face. She'd tried not to like him too much, but he was a good, kind man. He worked hard, cared for his grandmother—even loved Martha enough to marry a woman he didn't know just to make her happy. At least that's what Sarah had decided was the reason.

She sighed as she walked into Beth's room. Having to stake her claim on her husband was exhausting. Still, there was something exciting about shamelessly cuddling him like she had. She couldn't help smiling. Maybe she'd simply have to kiss him again.

A plan formed in her mind. If she laid claim to Quinn and showed more affection, maybe he'd start liking her more. What could it hurt?

Quinn led three horses out of the barn and looped their reins over the hitching post in front of the house. John and Tom stood on the porch talking with Martha and Florinda. Quinn double-checked his rifle, making sure it was loaded. He didn't expect trouble, but he would be prepared just in case.

Florinda looked past her father, and her face lit up when she saw Quinn. He pursed his lips. He'd never liked her blatant attention and always wondered what game she was playing. Every time she visited the Rocking M, she would sidle up close and try to get him to notice her. Oh, sure she was pretty, if you liked fancified women. Her blond hair reminded him of his mother's, and her clothing resembled something Mariah, his sister-in-law who was from Chicago, might wear. But that was the only way Florinda was similar to the other women.

Instead of joining them on the porch, he checked the saddles on each of the horses, even though he knew they were fine. A shadow darkened the ground behind the horses, and Quinn sighed. Looks like there was no avoiding Miss Phillips this morning. At least they'd be gone all day.

Quinn glanced up and saw Sarah standing four feet behind the horses with a bundle in her arms. A shy smile graced her lips, and he remembered again how she'd kissed him the evening before. He'd be as stupid as a prairie dog to not realize what she was doing, but the thing that surprised him was how much he liked her attention. He'd never had a woman cuddle up to him, other than one of his relatives and Florinda, and that was not the same thing. Not even close.

Sarah's cheeks turned red, and he realized he'd been staring. He patted the horses' rumps as he walked between two of them toward his wife.

"Elke packed a lunch for you men. I thought I'd bring it to you so she wouldn't have to. She's busy in the kitchen." Sarah studied the ground then looked toward the porch. Her thin brows dipped down, and she refocused on him.

"Thanks. We'll appreciate the food later on." He took the bundle and tied it over his saddle horn then walked back to Sarah. Florinda glided down the steps and aimed for them.

Something like panic crossed Sarah's face, and she visibly swallowed and stepped closer to him. His heart thumped at her nearness. He wasn't sure what had gotten into her last night at dinner, but he liked it. Whatever it was hadn't carried over to their bedroom, though. By the time he finished talking with the men and had retired, she was sound asleep on the settee with a quilt wrapped tight around her. He'd watched her for a few minutes before taking off his boots. In her sleep, she looked younger, innocent. A desire to protect her surged up through him with the speed of a barn fire.

She reached out and fiddled with a button on his chest. He took a deep breath and stood still. "Have a good day, and come back safely." A soft smile pulled at her lips, and she peeked up at him as if she had more on her mind. Sarah stood on her tiptoes, leaning closer to him. He bent down, and she placed a gentle kiss on his lips then awkwardly wrapped her arms around him in a hug. He squeezed back, shocked at the sensations racing through him.

He'd been a loner for so long that he hadn't realized how lonely he was. "You don't have to worry about Florinda," he murmured in her ear. "I tolerate her because I need her father's business."

Sarah's eyes widened, and a shy smile graced her lips. She nodded and darted away like a spooked bird. Florinda approached with her arms crossed and narrowed her eyes. Was she suspicious about his relationship with Sarah? What did it matter if she was?

"I was hoping to talk to you. Hoping that we could spend some time together." Florinda's expression softened, and she batted her lashes at him. "It's been so long since I last saw you."

"I'm a married man, Miss Phillips. I don't think it would be proper for me to escort you around the ranch like I have in the past."

"But—"

"You're free to walk around the ranch yard alone, but don't venture farther than you can see the house." Quinn tipped his hat to her and mounted his horse. He knew Florinda would try to persuade him to change his mind if he gave her the chance. Even though his sister had volunteered in the past, his mother had always made him escort Florinda on walks whenever she visited, probably hoping he'd fall for the pretty gal. But she was too shallow for him, too obvious in her attentions, and someone like her would never be happy stuck on a ranch for months at a time. He'd thought the same thing about Sarah at first, but she seemed to love it here.

Quinn cleared his throat. The men laughed at something his grandmother said and then they stomped down the steps and mounted their horses. Quinn glanced at Florinda, still standing where she'd been observing him and Sarah. Was she jealous?

He smiled at that thought. She'd never had competition for his attention before. He could imagine Florinda's shock if she knew the truth about his marriage. Her astonishment would only last a moment before it molded into smug superiority. Miss Phillips already looked down on Sarah, although he had no idea why.

Sarah was as sweet as the day was long. She treated his grandmother with kindness and respect, and Martha seemed much improved having Sarah around to help her and the children to pamper. Marrying her had been a wiser decision than he first realized. Too bad he'd wanted to keep things businesslike.

He rode up the hill and looked back over his shoulder to see if his wife was still outside. Sadly, she wasn't. Her sudden attempts at affection had been a pleasant surprise. Did she think if she treated him more like a husband that he'd let her stay after his grandmother was gone?

The idea sounded better and better.

"Which way, Quinn?" Uncle John stared at him with raised brows, and Quinn felt his neck warm as if the men could read his thoughts.

"Let's head south. Just follow that trail." John and Tom rode ahead of him, and Quinn thought he heard one of them mumble, "Newlywed." He nudged his horse into a canter and passed the men. He thought again how Sarah had pressed her hands against his chest as she leaned up to kiss him. His heart had pounded like he'd run a mile-long race. He'd be lying if he said he hadn't liked her advances. Her cheek was so soft, and her lips warm.

But was Sarah's behavior simply an act for the sake of their visitors? To prove to Florinda that they were truly married?

He pressed his lips together. If that was the case, he would be sorely disappointed when his guests left.

Chapter Twelve

Sarah stepped onto the porch and covered her eyes, looking for Ryan. The boy had wanted to ride with Quinn and the men, but Quinn had said no since they'd be discussing business. Her brother had stomped off to the barn, pouting. The tenseness in her shoulders relaxed when she saw him sitting on a bale of hay, just outside of the barn, mending tack with Claude. The old man had taken a shine to Ryan and had been a good influence on him.

Beth was in the kitchen helping Martha make dinner rolls for supper. Florinda had retreated to her room after Quinn left. Sarah would love to know what conversation had passed between the two of them, but it mustn't have been pleasant since Miss Phillips had been puckered up like a prune when Quinn rode out. Sarah shook her head. How could any woman be so flirtatious with a married man? It was shameless and obviously a topic that had been overlooked at that fancy school.

She was thankful to have a few minutes to herself and headed to her bedroom to do the dusting. With company coming, she hadn't cleaned it, knowing no one would venture in there. At least she'd be away from Miss Phillips's scowls. She crossed through the empty parlor and into the hall.

Florinda sashayed out of her room, nearly colliding with Sarah. "Oh, it's you."

The woman had a way of getting under Sarah's skin worse than a chigger. She swallowed back her irritation, knowing the woman was Martha's guest. Sarah forced a congenial smile. "Was there something you needed?"

"Don't think you can fool me. I can tell there are no true feelings between you and Quinn." Florinda narrowed her eyes. "What were you? One of those forlorn mail-order brides? Quinn would never have married you if he'd seen you first."

Her words cut like a freshly sharpened knife. Sarah knew they stung now, but the pain would be stronger later, after she had time to consider them. She lifted her chin, wishing she were taller. "No. He saw me before we were married—more than once, in fact."

"Well, he must have been desperate. Not many women would want to be stuck in such a rustic place as this all winter."

"Then why are you so interested in my husband?"

Florinda laughed and waved her hand in the air. "Oh, you wouldn't understand. Quinn's a handsome man, and I've always been able to wrap him around my little finger."

Sarah smothered a gasp that tried to slip out. Surely that wasn't true. The stuffy heat of the dim, narrow hallway didn't help the situation. A rivulet of sweat trickled down her temple. Could it be possible that Quinn hid his true feelings for Florinda?

Florinda uttered a harsh laugh. "Quinn will never be satisfied with you. You're nothing but a tumbleweed bride—scrub brush plain. I've planned to marry Quinn ever since the time we met years ago at his grandparents' ranch in Texas, and I won't give him up without a fight."

Sarah straightened, looking Miss Phillips in the eye. "You're too late. Quinn is already married, and we're pledged to each other before God and the church." Quinn may not want her, but she'd never tell Florinda that. She'd do everything in her power to keep him. She had to—for the children's sake.

Miss Phillips waved her hand in the air like a fan. "I plan to make myself available to Quinn for when he tires of you." She eyed Sarah up and down. "Which won't be long, I'm sure."

Sarah clenched her fists under her apron skirt. It was true. There was nothing special about her appearance. She'd even overheard one of her uncle's gang say she looked two days of hard riding from pretty—at least she thought they were talking about her. Why would Quinn want her when he could have a beauty like Florinda—even if the woman was as prickly as a cactus?

Miss Phillips lifted her chin, spun back into her room, and slammed the door. Sarah stood there stunned. Never in her life had anyone directed such a vicious verbal attack toward her and made her feel so insignificant. Not even her uncle seemed as awful as Florina. Sarah had always been a peacemaker, and most folks liked her because of her kind ways. Worry swirled in her mind like a dirt devil, spinning and gyrating up negative thoughts. Did Quinn regret being forced to marry her?

Would he send her and the children packing even before his grandmother died? Which didn't look to be anytime soon. Or was she doomed to live her days in a marriage with a husband who didn't love her?

She rushed to the settee and flopped down, tears streaming down her cheeks. She hugged a pillow to her chest and cried. After a few minutes, she lifted her head and dried her eyes.

Nothing would be accomplished by giving in to her worries. There was only one thing that would help. She lifted her face toward the ceiling. Please, Father, show me how to make my husband love me, not Florinda. And teach me how to be gracious even to her.

"Good afternoon, Quinn."

The sound of Florinda's voice so near made Quinn cringe. He continued uncinching his horse and tossed the saddle over one shoulder. Maybe the odor of sweaty horse would drive the woman back to the house. She was more persistent than a swarm of gnats.

He nodded to her as he passed by, walked into the barn, and slung his saddle and pad over a block in the tack room. He grabbed a grooming brush and turned to exit the stuffy area, but Florinda blocked the doorway. Why was she sticking closer to him than a sand burr?

Maybe if he quit avoiding her he would find out. "Did you need something?"

Florinda's pink lips wrinkled in a pout he was sure some men found charming. But he wasn't one of them. "You've been so busy since I arrived that we haven't had time to talk."

"A ranch is a busy place."

She spun the handle of a lacy pink parasol that rested against one shoulder. "I've missed chatting with you. It's been two years since I last saw you."

So? he wanted to say. And when did they ever chat with each other? She gabbed, while he tried to talk with the men or get away from her. He'd never seen her do an ounce of work—never once offered to help his mother the previous times she'd visited. As far as he was concerned, she was as useful as one of those odd French poodle dogs that one of his grandmother's wealthy friends in Bismarck owned.

He resisted heaving a sigh. Some host he was. "What did you want to talk about?"

Her lips twisted in a wry grin. "Tell me how you met Sarah."

"Why?" He narrowed his eyes. What did that matter? Florinda already looked down on his wife. She didn't need more ammunition.

"Oh, just curious. She doesn't seem the kind of woman you'd choose to marry."

Sweat trickled down his temple from the closed-in room. He didn't normally stay in the small, windowless area any longer than was necessary. Besides not having ventilation, it reminded him of when he'd been locked up in Will's jail for a crime he hadn't committed. He moved closer to the door, but Florinda didn't back up. She gazed up at him as if he were her long lost love. He swallowed the lump that rose to his throat.

He wanted to shove his way past her, to completely ignore her, but her father had bought a lot of cattle from him over the years. He couldn't afford to lose Tom's business because of a row with his daughter. At least near the door he could breathe in fresher air. "Tell me what you want, Florinda. I have work to do."

She cocked her head and batted her lashes. "I want to go riding with you. To see your ranch."

He didn't have time for casual riding, but if it meant keeping Tom's business, he'd have to make time for it, unless he could discourage her. "You know we don't have any sidesaddles."

For a moment the young woman's composure seemed rattled. "Couldn't you borrow one from someone?"

He shook his head. The nearest neighbor was nearly an hour's ride from him, and none of them owned sidesaddles. "If you want to ride, you'll have to do it astride."

Florinda's lips pursed. "All right, I'll manage. If it means spending time alone with you."

Florinda alternated between pouting and struggling to stay on her horse as the caravan traversed the rocky countryside. John and Tom drove the supply wagon, and Tom cast concerned glances at his daughter every few minutes. Sarah held back a smile, not wanting to take too much pleasure in the other woman's discomfort, but she had brought it upon herself by trying to get Quinn to ride alone with her. Sarah swatted at a mosquito on her hand and then adjusted her felt hat.

She rocked along, comfortable on the bay mare Quinn had saddled for her. If they stayed, would he give her a horse of her own? She'd never had one before but had learned to ride on her father's big mule. The little mare was much less intimidating.

Beth waved with one hand while keeping a hold on the saddle horn with the other. Sarah felt sure her sister was safe riding in front of Quinn. He wouldn't let her fall.

Ryan rode alone on her right on a black gelding with a white diamond on his face. Her brother looked happier than she'd seen him in months. He saw her watching and smiled. "This was a good idea Quinn had, wasn't it?"

She nodded, remembering how Quinn had approached her about riding with him and Florinda.

"I'm in a bind," he'd said. "I'm hoping you'll help me out. Florinda asked me to take her riding, but I don't want to go alone, and I've got the ranch hands all working on projects." He stared at the ground a moment and then looked up with those coffee brown eyes. "Would you go riding with us?"

That he didn't want to be alone with Miss Phillips set Sarah's delight soaring. Other than to care for his grandmother, it was the first thing he'd ever asked of her. "What if we took the children, too?"

Quinn nodded and smiled, stirring her heart. He smiled so rarely that when he did it was a magnificent sight. "Good idea."

When they'd told the children at dinner about the ride the next day, the men had begged to come along. Ryan mentioned an overnight ride, and the next thing she knew, a camping trip to sleep under the stars had been planned. Florinda was the only one scowling at the table. Sarah sighed. She'd hoped the prissy city gal would decide not to go, but that wasn't the case. At least Florinda wasn't out riding the range alone with Quinn, leaving Sarah to wonder what was happening.

Camp was set up alongside a tributary of the Little Missouri River. Cottonwood trees sheltered them from the warm summer sun, and an abundance of knee-high grass kept the stock well-fed. Quinn had gone hunting for some meat for dinner while Tom and Uncle John attempted to start a fire. Sarah grinned at their feeble effort. If they didn't improve, everyone would be eating cold biscuits and cheese for dinner.

Two rough tents had been erected for the women from quilts strung over rope that had been tied to tree branches. Sarah laid out additional quilts and wool blankets for her and Beth to sleep on and then put several in Florinda's tent also. With that chore done, she turned to check on the children. Both of them had headed down to the creek as soon as the supplies had been unloaded from the pack horse. She could barely see the top of Ryan's head.

Florinda sat on a log, looking completely out of place in her frilly blouse and the brown split riding skirt Quinn had insisted she wear. Her fancy hat was tied down with wide lavender netting and secured in a showy bow under her chin. She flicked a leaf off her lap.

Ryan approached Miss Phillips, holding something behind his back. Beth followed her brother, giggling with her hand over her mouth. Sarah's stomach tightened. What were those two up to?

Her brother stuck out his hand and dropped something into Florinda's lap. She looked down, and her bored features transformed into horror. She soared to her feet, dancing and screeching so loud that the horses tethered to a nearby line backed up and snorted. Laughing, Ryan and Beth disappeared in the nearby bushes. Uncle John jumped up and jogged toward the horses.

Tom Phillips spun around and raced toward his daughter. "What's wrong?"

"Oh! Th–those horrible monsters."

Tom's gaze surveyed his daughter from head to toe. "Are you hurt?"

Florinda dusted her skirt with jerky hands and scanned the ground. Sarah knew the moment she spotted the frog.

"There! They put that horrid creature on my lap. Oh, Father, I'll probably get warts now." She fell into Tom's arms and he loosely patted her. His questioning gaze collided with Sarah's, and she pointed to the frog. Tom's mouth swerved to one side. He stepped back, looking embarrassed and annoyed. "It's only a toad. It can't hurt you."

Sarah grabbed the innocent frog and couldn't resist holding it up. "I'll take him back to the creek. I'm sorry it frightened you."

Florinda shrank back. "Those rotten children should be punished for scaring me half to death."

Tom patted her shoulder. "Now, now, they were only having some fun."

Puffing up, Florinda glared at Sarah. "Their behinds should be paddled good and hard."

Sarah narrowed her eyes and walked past Uncle John, doubting Florinda had ever had a spanking. He pounded two rocks together in an attempt to spark some kindling to life. "Elke put some matches in the crate with the cooking pots."

John straightened and gave her a perplexed but humorous stare. "We have matches? You knew that and let us make a fool of ourselves for the last half hour?"

Sarah grinned. "I didn't want to spoil your fun."

He chuckled and shook his head then walked toward the crates of supplies. Sarah set the frog on the creek bank and took in the tranquil setting. Water bubbled along the rocky bed, gurgling its way to the mouth of the Little Missouri. She probably should punish the children. But they were merely playing and having fun. She rubbed her neck. What would her mother have done?

Tears blurred her eyes as she remembered her parents. She'd never wanted to be fully responsible for the children and didn't know how to handle a situation like this one. If only her mother could give her advice— could hug her one more time. She'd never even had a chance to say good-bye.

Beth giggled off to her right, and Sarah turned to see her siblings squatting in the dirt near the creek bank. What were they up to now?

"Look at this huge one." Beth dangled a squirming worm in the air.

"Yep, that fellow's big and fat." Ryan took the worm and placed it in an empty can.

Sarah tiptoed nearer. "What are you two doing?"

Beth jumped and studied the ground, as if afraid to look Sarah in the eye. Ryan shrugged one shoulder. "Digging up worms. Quinn said he'd take us fishing."

Sarah eyed the two, not sure if she believed them. Beth looked too suspicious. "You are not going to put those in Miss Phillips's lap."

Ryan glanced up, shaking his head. "Of course not. Her screaming nearly broke my hearing."

"Mine, too." Beth rubbed her ears.

Sarah shoved her hands to her waist. "She wouldn't have been screaming if you hadn't dropped a frog in her lap."

Beth's eyes glistened with tears. "I told him not to do that."

Ryan's head jerked toward his sister. "You did not. You were just afraid to touch the frog and made me do it."

Sarah sighed and stooped down. "It doesn't matter whose idea it was. You will both go apologize right now or you won't have dinner."

Ryan scowled but Beth nodded.

Sarah glanced up at the sky. Oh, Lord, give me patience and wisdom.

The fragrant scent of cooked prairie chickens filled the air, making Quinn's stomach growl. The traps he and Ryan had set earlier had captured five birds. Sarah and Beth scurried around getting the food items Elke had sent with them ready. Nobody would go hungry tonight.

Ryan held up a plump burlap sack stuffed with grouse feathers that he'd picked up off the ground. "That's all of them."

"Good job. Grandma will be happy to have more feathers for stuffing pillows. Put the sack in the wagon and wash up. Dinner's about ready."

The boy nodded and cast him a shy grin. "That plucking contest was fun."

Quinn ruffled Ryan's hair. "It was indeed. You almost beat your sisters."

Ryan's face puckered. "I would have if you hadn't let Beth help Sarah."

"I don't think she was as much help as you believe she was." Quinn chuckled, as he remembered watching Tom and Uncle John yanking feathers as fast as they could. When they returned home, he could imagine the stories they'd be telling their friends and associates. Florinda had turned up her nose and strode off to read a book when asked if she wanted to participate. She didn't have one-fourth the gumption that Sarah did.

Ryan walked toward the wagon, the sack of feathers over one shoulder. The boy was certainly thawing. Quinn was grateful for that. He still regretted his initial outburst when he first saw the children that day he and Sarah were married. He wasn't one to lose control. The campfire flickered and popped as he stared into it.

"Dinner's ready." Sarah held out a plate to him.

Quinn grasped it, and for a moment, Sarah didn't release the other side. It was as if they were connected. His gaze captured hers, and he felt as if sizzling lightning connected them. Why did she move him like no other woman had? She wasn't gorgeous in the face like Florinda, but she had an inner beauty and kindness that Miss Phillips would never have. Did Sarah feel anything for him?

He blinked, surprised at the train of thought that rippled through him. He pulled the plate from Sarah's hand and stepped back as if he'd been burned. When had he started caring for her?

Questions filled Sarah's gaze, but she turned away.

"I fixed a biscuit for you." Beth handed a plate to Florinda, who eyed it with unhidden speculation.

"I—uh—thank you." Miss Phillips lifted the roasted thigh and leg of the prairie chicken and peered under it, then set it down. She stirred her spoon cautiously through the cabbage slaw that Elke had sent, examining it, and then picked up the biscuit and studied it for a moment.

Beth hurried back to Ryan, snickering. The boy's eyes flickered with delight, and both kids spun toward Florinda. Quinn's gut tightened.

She lifted the top half of the biscuit off and stared. Quinn was ten feet away, but he was certain he saw something move. The young woman's eyes went wide and her mouth opened, but no sound came out. She leapt to her feet, dropping the tin plate to the ground, and shrieked. Everyone in camp jumped, except Quinn and the kids. Beth covered her ears and grinned. Ryan rolled in the dirt near the campfire, laughing, as Sarah spun around. Three fat worms wriggled off the biscuit and onto the ground.

Tom hurried toward his daughter, but she pivoted and marched red-faced toward Quinn. "You will take me back to the ranch this instant. I will not stay here and allow those hooligans to frighten another ten years off me. This is no place for a lady."

Chapter Thirteen

With a lantern spilling light over the creek bank, Sarah washed the last of the dinner dishes. She rinsed them in the creek and dumped out the sudsy water. She gave each plate and fork a final rinse then put them in the bucket to dry.

Tom had offered to return home with his daughter, but Quinn insisted that he take her since Tom wasn't familiar with the ranch and might get lost in the dark. Sarah was pretty sure Tom was relieved. Both he and John were enjoying themselves immensely. Camping was so far removed from their normal routine of office work and dealing with beef buyers. She understood their reluctance to leave a place with no responsibilities or pressures.

Somehow, Sarah felt Florinda had gotten exactly what she wanted—a ride alone with Quinn. And in the dark, no less. She shouldn't be jealous, but when Florinda had claimed her fear was too great to ride alone, Quinn had allowed her to sit in front of him. Sarah couldn't stand the thought of her husband's arms around that woman. Florinda was probably leaning back against Quinn's chest, enjoying every minute and gloating in the dark.

She should have gone with him. But the children had been so excited about sleeping under the stars. They'd whined and complained about it when they'd lived with Uncle Harlan, but on the Rocking M, it was a great adventure. Still, she'd sent her siblings to bed without dessert, much to their complaint. They deserved a harsher punishment for disobeying her and for scaring Miss Phillips again, but she couldn't bring herself to spank them.

Sarah shook her head remembering how Ryan adamantly argued that she hadn't told them not to scare Miss Phillips but rather not to put any more critters on her.

She picked up the bucket and lantern and made her way back to camp.

Uncle John and Tom had already bedded down. Ryan wiggled around on his pallet as if he couldn't get comfortable. Sarah peeked at Beth and found her little sister was sound asleep.

She set the lantern on the wagon's tailgate and put the bucket behind it. Out in the darkness a horse nickered. Sarah jumped. As always, her first thoughts raced to Uncle Harlan. Had he figured out that she took the gold to Medora? Was the story still circulating of the rancher who married a jailbird? What if he had heard about it and was on his way to the Rocking M right now?

All security fled, and she yanked a rifle from the buckboard. She stepped into the shadows and aimed toward where she'd heard the horse.

"H'lo the camp."

Ryan and John sat up in unison and looked around. Tom and Beth slept on.

"Who's there?" Sarah called, clutching the rifle with trembling hands.

"It's Slim. Quinn sent me up here to help y'all with breakfast tomorrow and to get packed up and back to the house." Bushes rattled as he passed between them and into the light, leading his horse. One of the tethered horses nickered to Slim's mount. The cowboy tipped his hat. "Evening, ma'am."

Sarah exhaled a relieved breath. "C'mon in. There's coffee left."

She poured him a cup while he unsaddled his horse and spread out his bedroll a few yards from the campfire. She handed him the tin cup, then crawled into the tent. Sarah rebraided her hair as she stared at the flickering flames of the campfire. Why had Quinn sent Slim instead of coming back himself?

Probably because Miss Phillips wouldn't release her hold on him. No doubt the persnickety woman had wrangled some other chore for Quinn to do. Now that she had him to herself, Sarah was certain Florinda would make the most of it.

She lay down but doubted she would sleep much. Too many worries swirled in her mind. Quinn had wanted their marriage to be one only on paper. Could Florinda steal Quinn's love?

Sarah flipped onto her other side as she realized how ridiculous that thought was. If Quinn had affections for Miss Phillips, he never would have married another woman. Still. . .Florinda was beautiful to look at, and Sarah was just as she'd said—a tumbleweed.

She flopped onto her back and stared up at the stars through the open end of the tent. There were millions of them sprinkling the raven sky like little diamonds she'd once seen in a store. Quinn might not love her, but he was an honorable man. He wouldn't share his affections with a woman when he was married to another.

God had put her and Quinn together. Sarah was certain of it. The Lord had answered her prayers in a manner she never could have imagined and provided a home for her and the children. He wouldn't let them be cast out because of a spoiled, selfish woman.

"Thank You, Father, for calming my fears. Forgive me for worrying overly much and not trusting You to take care of us. I ask You to forgive me for being jealous of Florinda, and help me to be nicer to her. Thank You for keeping Uncle Harlan away, and please don't let him find us." She shivered at the thought of what he might do if he did.

An unwanted tear ran down the corner of her eye. "Please show me how to love Quinn, and make him learn to care for me, so we can stay here forever."

The closer they rode to home, the more anxious Sarah became. It was stupid. She knew that, but her fears threatened to overpower the peacefulness she'd felt that morning as she prayed by the creek.

"Are you cold, Sissy?"

"No, I'm fine. Why?" Though it was late June and normally a one-blanket night, sleeping outside had felt much cooler than in her cozy bedroom. She wished she'd thought to bring a shawl along.

"You're shivering." Beth squeezed her arms around Sarah's waist. "I'll keep you warm."

She patted her sister's hand. The ranch yard was quiet as they rode into it. Ryan trotted his horse over to the corral and climbed down, but Sarah guided her horse and stopped next to his. Across the yard, the front door opened, and Quinn strode out with Florinda on his arm. Her heart dropped, and her whole body felt weak, as if she'd lived through a train wreck. Had she lost him already?

Quinn smiled at her, and unwound Florinda's arm so quickly that the prissy woman dressed in pale green nearly stumbled. She grabbed hold of the porch post and scowled. Quinn didn't notice as he bounded down the steps and jogged toward Sarah. His warm smile set Sarah's hope back on track.

"Let me help you down, Beth." The little girl nearly leapt from her seat behind Sarah and hugged Quinn's neck.

"I didn't like it when you left."

"Neither did I, sweet thing. Elke has some cinnamon rolls on the warmer. Why don't you wash up and go get one?"

Beth grinned at him and kicked her feet. Quinn set her down, and she took off like a top. His gaze turned upward, and a shy smile tugged at one corner of his mouth.

"I missed you." He lifted his hands, stunning Sarah.

He missed her? Ignoring Florinda's glare, she fell into his arms and wrapped herself around her husband. Was he serious? Or was it all a show to get Miss Phillips to leave him alone?

Quinn gently pushed her away from his warm chest and stared down. He brushed a strand of hair from her face and tucked it behind her ear, making her knees go weak. She loved his dark, expressive eyes and longed to run her hand through his hair. He leaned down, pushed her hat back on her head, and claimed her lips. Sarah was so surprised that she stood there stiff as a step for a moment until her senses returned. Then she kissed him back, showing him that she longed to be his true wife. Quinn inhaled sharply through his nose, as if her response surprised him.

He set her back far too soon and stared into her eyes. Sarah's heart ricocheted in her chest. She was afraid she was falling in love with a man who didn't want her. But his kiss had felt anything but phony.

He smiled, and it actually reached his eyes. "I'm sorry Florinda ruined our campout, and I hope you realize that there's nothing between her and me. If I've given you that impression, I'm sorry. You're my wife, Sarah, and that's what's important."

Quinn smiled openly as he tucked her under one arm and held her close. "Ryan, come and tend your sister's horse."

The boy jogged toward them, casting curious glances their way as he grabbed the horse's reins.

"Be sure to brush her down and feed her."

"Yes, sir." He nodded and led the mare toward the barn.

Sarah grinned, pleased to see her brother responding so well to Quinn's orders. When he first arrived, he hardly wanted anything to do with the man, but now he shadowed her husband whenever he could—almost like a father and son.

With her arm around her husband's narrow waist, Sarah allowed Quinn to guide her up the steps. She nodded at Florinda, whose lips looked as if they'd tasted lemonade without the sugar. She crossed her arms, stomped one foot, and sashayed back inside. Sarah wished that she and Florinda could be friends in spite of their mutual attraction to Quinn, but it was obvious that Miss Phillips didn't share that desire.

The cabin smelled of cinnamon and fresh baked bread. Even though they'd eaten breakfast at the camp, now that her worries had been calmed, Sarah's stomach begged for food.

Florinda must have gone to her bedroom, for she was nowhere in sight. In spite of the woman's immature display, Sarah couldn't help grinning up at Quinn. Gloating was wrong, she knew that, but her heart overflowed with so much happiness at her husband's surprising greeting that she couldn't hold it all in.

Martha hurried toward them, dressed in a brown and gold calico. "Welcome back, dear. I missed your company and those ornery children. Beth's in the kitchen, having a snack. Perhaps you'd like to join her when you're finished with my grandson?"

She looked up at Quinn, enjoying his nearness and the feel of his solid body. He smiled. "I'm glad you're back, but work is waiting. I'll see you at lunch." He cast a quick glance at his grandmother, bent down and kissed Sarah's cheek, and then all but bolted for the barn.

Martha tugged Sarah's arm around her own and patted her hand. Her eyes twinkled. "Well, things are certainly looking up between you and my grandson. It's amazing what a little competition can do."

After breakfast the next morning, Sarah sat on the sofa in the parlor, helping Beth with her alphabet. She wrote an M on the slate. "What's that letter?"

Beth grinned up at her. "That one's easy. It's a M, like the Rocking M on Quinn's sign."

"That's right. How about this one?" She wiped off the letter and replaced it with a Q.

A rustling sounded from the hall, and Sarah looked over her shoulder. Florinda strode into the room with her fancy hat affixed to her head and tied under her chin with a big bow. She set a satchel on a chair, laid her parasol beside it, and narrowed her eyes at Sarah. "I'm leaving. Have someone get a buggy and drive me into town."

Sarah set Beth on the floor. "Go to the barn and find Quinn, please." The girl bounded out the door, casting an odd look back at Miss Phillips.

Sarah set the slate and chalk on the sofa and stood. What could she say to make Florinda reconsider? Would her leaving affect her father's decision to buy cattle from Quinn? The men had been talking numbers and prices yesterday evening, but nothing had been settled, as far as she knew.

"Please, won't you sit down and talk about this? There's no need for you to leave." Sarah locked her fingers together to keep her hands from shaking. "I was hoping we might become friends."

Florinda lifted her nose and tossed her head. "That's not possible."

"But why? What have I done to make you dislike me so?"

"Surely you realize that I have had my eye on Quinn for many years."

"How could I know?" Sarah shook her head. "Honestly. I knew nothing about you when Quinn and I married. I'll admit that I don't understand your interest in him, when it's obvious that you don't like it here."

Miss Phillips turned up her nose. "I can barely stand to visit this rustic place, but I had plans for Quinn in my father's beef production company."

"He would never be happy in a city. He's a rancher at heart and needs the wide-open spaces, and this ranch needs him."

"Well. . .it's neither here nor there now. I probably should have set my sights for Adam. At least he had the sense to leave this godforsaken place."

Loud footsteps sounded a moment before Quinn, John, and Tom entered the parlor. Mr. Phillips strode to his daughter's side. "What's this I hear about you leaving?"

"It's true. I can't stay here another day."

Tom scratched his head. "Well. . .you can't travel alone." He turned to face the other men. "I'm sorry, but it looks like I'll be leaving today. My daughter can't travel unescorted. Go ahead with the numbers we talked about. I'll send my man out here in mid-September, unless I hear different from you. All right?"

Quinn nodded and held out his hand. "Thank you. I'll make sure you get quality beef."

Florinda squirmed and fiddled with her net bow. John stared at his friend, looking disappointed and perplexed.

Tom pursed his lips and stared at the floor; then he looked at John. "I'm sorry our trip was cut short, but—"

John laid his hand on his friend's shoulder. "Think nothing more of it. Family comes first. I'll see you when I get back to Chicago."

Tom nodded and walked to Martha, who'd just entered the room. "I'm sorry to be leaving so soon, but I thank you for your wonderful hospitality." Tom hurried down the hall to his room.

"I'll get a buggy ready and take you to town." Quinn tipped his hat at Florinda.

"I'd prefer someone else drive us."

Sarah's heart ached for Quinn at Florinda's rude tone. Now that Miss Phillips had conceded her loss, she no longer wanted to be around him.

"No problem." Quinn pressed his lips tight and glanced at Sarah. She tried to soften things with a smile. "I'll have one of the hands drive you to town."

Quinn spun around and stalked out of the room in wide, long-legged strides.

Now that Florinda was leaving, would he continue showing affection to Sarah? She was asleep when he finally went to bed last night and had only seen him at breakfast. He'd smiled at her but hadn't touched her since greeting her in the yard.

Sarah collected the slate and chalk and put it in a desk drawer. Florinda paced in front of the window, waiting for her father. Sarah couldn't help feeling sorry for the man who had to cut his plans short because of his daughter's whims. Maybe if Florinda's mother were still alive things would be different.

"Can I offer you some refreshment before you leave?"

The young woman spun around. "No, you may not. And I would appreciate if you would leave my sight immediately."

Sarah cringed at Florinda's command but didn't want to upset their guest further. "As you wish. I will pray that you have a safe journey home."

She hurried into the kitchen and ran straight into Martha's arms.

"Now don't fret, dear. That girl never liked coming here." The older woman patted her back and leaned close to Sarah's ear. "I'm tired of her childish games."

"I'm sorry. I never meant to cause problems for you and Quinn."

Martha pushed away. "You didn't, and I won't have you thinking that. Quinn's been the happiest I've seen since Anna's wedding. You're good for my grandson, and you need to know that."

Sarah forced a smile, grateful for Martha's encouragement. "Thank you."

Martha patted her cheek. "Give Quinn a bit more time. I can already tell that he has feelings for you. He simply needs to realize it himself."

Chapter Fourteen

Quinn sat at his desk, calculating how much he'd make from the sale of one hundred twenty head of cattle to Tom Phillips. The amount would more than see them through the next winter and leave plenty of stock so that he'd have a good crop of calves next spring, as long as the winter wasn't too harsh.

Balancing everything wasn't always easy, but it was doable. He laid down his pen and leaned back in the chair. Thank goodness Tom had more sense than his spoiled daughter.

Lamplight flickered across his ledger pages. In spite of having more people at the ranch to provide for, things were going well. He thought of the two pair of Percherons in training. In another few weeks he would be receiving final payment for the four large stock horses.

Yep, things were going well, but he still had a dissatisfaction that he couldn't shake. Was it because of Sarah?

His mouth curved up as he thought of how surprised she'd been when he'd kissed her the morning after the campout. And she had pleasantly amazed him by kissing him back quite soundly. Her mouth was as soft as a horse's muzzle, and she felt good in his arms. He'd been a fool to want a marriage in name only, but then, he hadn't really wanted a marriage at all. Yeah, he'd willingly married Sarah, because it had seemed the right thing to do at the time. He got a wife and got Grandma off his back and got Sarah out of jail. What would have happened to Ryan and Beth if he hadn't married Sarah?

Quinn ran his hand through his hair, not wanting to think of how bad things could have been for the children. Maybe Sarah would be willing to consider a true marriage. She certainly hadn't liked how Florinda threw herself at him.

"What are you grinning at?" Sarah's soft voice floated out of the surrounding darkness a moment before he saw her.

He straightened, knowing he couldn't tell her his thoughts. Or could he?

Sarah shrugged. "Never mind. I only wanted to ask you something."

"Shoot."

"Well. . .I've been having evening devotions with Ryan and Beth ever since our parents died. Pa used to lead them, and I've tried to keep that one thing going when everything else was going haywire."

Quinn stood and crossed the room to her. "That's good that you have. I'm sure it's helped the kids."

"It helped me, too. It would have been so easy to get angry at God for all that happened." She glanced up at him, her blue eyes swimming with tears. "I would have been completely alone if not for God."

He placed his hands on Sarah's upper arms. "You have us now. You're not alone anymore." Sarah's smile warmed a place in his heart that had been cold for a long time.

"I don't want you to be alone either." She placed her hand on his chest. "Don't think I haven't noticed how you try to keep yourself apart from everyone else. You don't have to bear your burdens alone, Quinn. I'm here to help, and God will help."

He knew she was right. At one time, he was close to his heavenly Father, but the pressures of life and the busyness of the ranch had pressed in, and before he knew it, he'd quit praying and seeking God.

"Martha mentioned she'd like to hold family devotions before the children went to bed." Sarah nibbled the corner of her lower lip and glanced up at him through her lashes. "We were wondering if you'd be willing to lead them."

Quinn stiffened and walked back to his desk, putting space between him and Sarah. Who was he to be leading folks in devotions? Yeah, maybe he stood up in front of the ranch hands on Sundays when they couldn't go into town and read from the Bible, but teaching children. . .what if he said the wrong thing? And how could a man who'd been waffling between believing in God and chucking all he'd learned out the window lead others in their walk with the good Lord?

"I don't think that would be a good idea."

"What's not?" Sarah's brow puckered. "Having devotions or you leading them?"

He remained silent, not wanting to admit that he was a failure in the spiritual realm. He'd turned his back on God when things had gotten tough, and it didn't seem right to go crawling back now that times were better.

Sarah strolled toward him. "You don't have to make up your mind now. Just think about it. Please. Ryan could use a man's example in this area, too. You've been such an encouragement to him." Sarah laid her hand on Quinn's arm. "Ryan has opened up and isn't so angry since you've been showing him how to do ranch work. Thank you for that."

She stood on her tiptoes and leaned toward him. Quinn's heart raced double-time having her so near. He leaned down, and she placed a warm kiss on his cheek. "Good night, Quinn."

Her gentle smile stayed with him long after she'd gone to bed. He paced the length of the parlor and back several times, finally stopping in front of the window. The glow of the lantern reflected back at him, as he stared into the inky darkness outside.

Closing his eyes, he thought of Sarah's words. "You don't have to bear your burdens alone, Quinn. I'm here to help, and God will help."

Sarah had made things easier for his grandmother and had taken over many of the household chores. She'd freed him from worrying about Grandma so he could concentrate more on the ranch, and she'd reminded him that God was there to help, too. Perhaps it was time he reacquainted himself with his heavenly Father. Time he quit running from God.

He knelt in front of a chair and bent his head. "Lord, I don't deserve to ask for Your mercy. I've been stubbornly operating on my own since my pa died, but I need Your help. I miss Your closeness. Forgive me, Father God."

Sarah ran the needle through the two pieces of fabric. She loved sitting on the porch and sewing. All too soon winter would wrap them in its cold fist, and they wouldn't be able to enjoy the outdoors like they could now. She checked on her sister and smiled. Beth sat at the far end of the porch, playing with a litter of kittens.

"I don't like to say it, but I'm glad to have Florinda gone. My stomach was all a-swirl when she was flitting around." Martha selected a triangle of fabric and compared it to the one she'd just stitched. She shook her head, picked another one, and started sewing. "I don't know why she comes here. She's always bored, even when she visited my home in Bismarck."

"I feel badly for the shameless way I acted when she was here. I should have been kinder to her." Sarah's hands dropped to her lap. Some Christian she was. Her first chance to act as hostess and all she could do was to fight like crazy to keep her husband from noticing a prettier, more sophisticated woman.

Martha smiled. "I rather enjoyed watching you fight for my grandson's attention—and if I'm not mistaken, I believe he enjoyed it, too."

Heat rushed to Sarah's cheeks. She closed her eyes and laid her head against the rocker. "Was I that obvious? I'm mortified."

"Don't be." Martha squeezed Sarah's hand. "It warms my heart to see Quinn so happy."

"You think he's happy?" Sarah looked at Martha. Her gray hair was neatly packed into a bun pinned at her nape. Wisps of white danced around her face, and soft brown eyes held hers.

"Oh, yes. I guess you could say he's thawed since you and the children came here. For so long, he focused only on the ranch. It hurt his relationship with Anna and Adam and even with his mother. I think that's why Ellen stayed in Bismarck after I broke my leg. She and Quinn were quite close at one time, but then he seemed to pull away. Maybe he didn't feel as needed with the twins finding mates and getting married. I'm so thankful he has you now."

Sarah considered whether to tell Martha the truth about her relationship with Quinn. But how could she steal Martha's joy? No, she and Quinn would have to work it out on their own.

Resuming her stitching, she thought about the previous evening when she'd talked with Quinn. She'd gone in there fully planning to tell him about her uncle and the danger she might have brought to the Rocking M, but instead she'd asked him about devotions. How could her plans go so haywire?

Tonight. She'd find a way to warn him tonight. They'd been at the Rocking M close to a month now, and surely Uncle Harlan had returned home and discovered the gold gone. He wouldn't know which way they'd gone, but most likely he'd assume it was Medora since it was the closest town. Maybe by the time he got there, talk would have died down.

She could only hope. *Please, Father, don't let him find us. And keep everyone at the Rocking M safe.*

Ryan rode up to the front porch and pushed his hat back on his face. The sun had lightened his hair and darkened his skin, adding to the patch of freckles on his nose and cheeks. He looked so happy and at ease in the saddle. "So, are we going riding like you promised?"

Beth set down a plain white kitten with a tabby tail and ran over to join them. "Yeah, you said you'd take us riding after lunch if Quinn couldn't."

"I was hoping to complete the main squares today." Sarah ran her hand over the colorful quilt pieces in her lap, but it could wait until this evening. Keeping her promise to the kids was more important.

"You go ahead. I can finish this." Martha gently removed the sewing from Sarah's hands.

"Looks like we're going riding." She grinned at her siblings.

"Yippee!" Beth clapped her hands together. "Do I getta ride my own horse?"

"No, you'd better ride with me until Quinn has time to help you more." Sarah stood and stretched, ignoring Beth's pout. She ducked inside and took Anna's old hat from the peg it rested on. Life at the Rocking M was busy, but not like it had been at Uncle Harlan's place. She'd worked from dawn to dusk, hunting, skinning, or plucking their food and trying to keep the kids away from the outlaw gang.

Ryan helped Beth climb onto his horse, and they rode toward the barn. Sarah followed, but a shiver sent goose bumps across her arms as a memory swept across her mind. Eddie, the youngest member of the outlaw gang, had constantly leered at her and tried to catch her alone. She always kept the children close, fearing to be alone with him, but his pale blue gaze unnerved her—and not in a good way. Not like Quinn's steady gaze did.

But Eddie was gone, and she was a married woman for now. She twisted the gold band that Martha had given Quinn to give to her. Somehow wearing it made her feel more married.

Sarah helped Ryan saddle the bay mare, and with Beth in front of her,

Sarah followed her brother up a hill. They rode for a good half. Tendrils from Beth's blond hair tickled her face. The sun threatened to toast them, but the ever-present breeze cooled her body. She'd miss these days when the weather turned frigid and snow covered everything, like flour whenever Beth helped with the baking.

They rode for nearly an hour when Beth looked over her shoulder, her blue eyes pleading. "I'm hot. Can we go splash in the creek?"

It was often hard to say no to the little imp, but today she didn't have to. "I think that's a grand idea. You want to join us, Ryan?"

The boy scowled. Ever since Quinn had taught him to ride, he hadn't wanted to get off a horse. Why, he'd probably sleep in the barn if she'd let him. At least he was happy. After a moment his expression softened. "Sure. Why not."

At the creek, they watered the horses, and then Ryan led them to a patch of grass to graze. Beth quickly shed her shoes and socks and tiptoed into the gurgling stream. At its deepest point, the narrow creek didn't even reach Beth's knees.

Ryan ran back to join them, a wide smile on his face. His boots flew in different directions and his socks quickly followed. He rolled up his pants, revealing legs as pale as the ivory fabric in her quilt. He hopped in, heedless of the rocks on the bank and in the water.

Sarah smiled, so delighted that he was a carefree boy again. Quinn had helped make that happen, and she owed him. Beth giggled and cupped a handful of water and tossed it at her brother. Not to be outdone, he splashed wave after wave at Beth. She squealed and jogged in the opposite direction.

Cottonwoods created a pleasant canopy overhead, allowing dappled sunlight to filter between the branches. The wind whispered through the leaves. Sarah reclined on a sun-roasted boulder near the water and watched the dancing limbs overhead. When her parents had died and they lost their farm, she thought nothing worse could ever happen, but it had. Being so helplessly locked up in jail and fearing for Ryan and Beth had been worse. But she never could have imagined how landing in jail could have turned out so wonderful. Her mother had often told her that the Bible says "all things work together for good to them that love God, to them who are the called according to his purpose." She'd remained close to God in trying times and had prayed for Him to help her get out of jail and to protect the children, and He'd sent a handsome cowboy to rescue them.

She loved watching Quinn move, long-legged but so smooth. And his eyes—almost so brown you couldn't see the pupils. Then there was that curly dark blond hair that she longed to twist around her finger, and his deep voice, which sent vibrations all through her when he talked. She heaved a sigh.

A strange feeling, not unlike the warmth of a mustard plaster, heated her chest. Her eyes bolted open. She loved her husband! The awe of her discovery stunned her. He'd provided a home and protected her and the kids, and somewhere along the way, her admiration had turned to love. Martha's constant boasting about her grandson's virtues hadn't hurt any. She rubbed her hand over her chest, almost expecting to feel heat. Things couldn't be any better—unless Quinn loved her, too. Was that too much to hope for?

Beth squealed, and she splashed through the water with Ryan roaring after her. Sarah smiled, happy to see the kids playing together instead of bickering.

Her thoughts flicked back to her husband. If only Quinn loved her. . .then maybe they'd never have to leave the Rocking M. Please, Lord, show me how to make my husband fall in love with me.

A twig snapped behind her at the same moment something stepped between her and the sunlight. Beth screamed, but this wasn't a fun squeal. Sarah opened her eyes and bolted up.

No!

Eddie stood beside her, a sickening grin pasted on his whiskery face. Uncle Harlan held Beth, who squirmed and kicked, while Jim wrestled with Ryan. He smacked her brother across the face, and Sarah jumped to her feet. "Don't you hurt him."

Eddie grabbed her arm. "We ain't gonna hurt nobody unless you don't cooperate. Then"—his gaze traveled down her chest—"well, we'll just see."

Sarah's whole body trembled, and her mind raced. How could they get free without one of them getting hurt? Lord, help us.

Chapter Fifteen

Quinn walked out of the barn and headed for the house, ready for supper. Tantalizing fragrances had been emanating from the house for the past hour. Even the enticing odors of beef stew and corn bread that Claude was cooking for the ranch hands had pestered him. Tomorrow he'd tell Sarah to pack him a bigger lunch. He worked hard and had a man-size appetite.

A cloud of dust coming from the direction of the creek snagged his attention. He squinted in the sunlight and saw a black horse at full gallop. As it neared, Quinn pursed his lips. He'd told Ryan not to run a horse into the ranch yard—and he had Beth with him. Quinn couldn't let this slide. The boy should know better than to endanger his little sister just for fun.

Quinn lifted his arms to keep the gelding from racing into the barn. Ryan had sense to pull back and slow the animal. Beth nearly fell off as the horse all but slid to a halt. Quinn reached for her and realized she was crying. She clutched his neck and buried her face in his shoulder. He clenched his jaw and glared at Ryan.

His heart skipped. Ryan was crying, too? "What happened?"

The boy tossed his leg over the horse and dropped to the ground. He swiped his sleeve over his eyes and sniffed. "Uncle Harlan and his men have Sarah. They want to swap her for the gold."

Gold, he knew about, but who was this Uncle Harlan? "Beth, go inside and tell Grandma what's happened. Can you do that?"

Beth leaned back and wiped her eyes. "Yes. Will you get Sissy back?" Her chin and lower lip quivered.

"You bet I will." He hugged the girl and set her down. Her feet were pedaling her toward the door almost the second they hit the ground, keeping pace with his runaway heart. She dashed up the steps and through the door.

Sam and Hank walked out of the barn, covered with sprigs of hay, which they'd been piling in the loft. Quinn nodded with his head for them to join him. "Sarah's been kidnapped."

Both men's eyes widened. With his hands on his hips, Quinn turned back to Ryan. "Tell me everything you know about this Uncle Harlan."

Ryan's face paled, and he studied the ground. "Sarah took us to live with him after our parents died. There were people back in Grand Forks who would have kept us, but we would have been split up. Sarah wouldn't stand for that, so we snuck away one night."

The boy swiped his eyes again and looked up at Quinn. "We didn't know that he was an outlaw."

Quinn straightened, knowing how devastating it must have been for Sarah to learn that when she had hoped that her uncle would care for them. He patted Ryan on the shoulder. "So, what did you do?"

"Things weren't too terrible until three men showed up. Sarah had to hunt every day to find meat for them to eat. She worked awfully hard, but Uncle Harlan always griped at her." Ryan's eyes turned hard. "One man kept pestering her and trying to get her alone."

"You're doing good. Keep going, please."

Ryan shrugged one shoulder. "Sarah wanted to leave, but we didn't have anywhere to go. One day I followed my uncle and discovered where he hid his loot. The next time he and his gang left on a robbing spree, we dug up his money and headed to Medora."

Quinn held up his hand, indicating for Ryan to stop. "Sam, saddle up my horse and three others. Hank, go find Claude, and both of you get your rifles and any ammunition you've got. I want you two to guard the house."

The men left as ordered, and Quinn nodded for the boy to continue.

"The walk took a lot longer than Sarah thought it would. Then Beth twisted her ankle—" Ryan scowled. "But she was faking so Sarah would carry her."

"Never mind that. Finish your story."

He shrugged again. "Sarah left us at the shack where you found us and went to town alone. She said she was going to turn the gold in to the sheriff and get a reward, so we could take the train and get away from Uncle Harlan. We were going to start over."

Quinn crossed his arms and stared off in the distance. Why hadn't Sarah told him she might be in danger? She should have told him. His feelings for her had grown more than he could have believed they ever would. But she hadn't trusted him enough to tell him the truth.

And she hadn't played fair when Florinda had been there. Sarah teased him with her soft caresses, tender looks, and sweet kisses. She shot straight for his heart and scored a bull's-eye. He loved her.

He wanted to slam his fist into a wall, but that would only make him ache more. She should have told him. But he couldn't dwell on that now.

"How many men did your uncle have with him? Do you know how much gold he had?"

Ryan straightened and reached over to pet his horse. "Two men besides my uncle, and four hundred and fifty dollars in gold and paper money. I know, I counted it before I told Sarah about it."

Quinn considered the money in a locked box hidden in his bedroom. There wasn't half that much in it. But maybe it was enough to barter for Sarah's life—to distract the outlaws so that he could save her. He closed his eyes. He had to save her. She'd become important to him. Her soft caresses and stolen kisses had broken down walls that he'd erected years ago. He looked skyward. Lord, I need Your help here. Show me how to save my wife. I love her, Lord. I can't lose her.

He faced Ryan again. "Do you know where the outlaws are now?"

The boy nodded. "Uncle Harlan said they would meet you at that grove of quaking aspens, about a mile west of here. Do you know where it is?" His blue eyes turned hopeful.

"Yep, I do. Take care of your horse and then get inside and stay there."

"But I want to go with you." He grabbed the horse's reins but took a step toward Quinn. "I know how to shoot. I should have protected Sarah."

Quinn pulled him into a hug. "You couldn't fight off three men by yourself. You did what needed to be done. Beth is safe because of you, and I have the information I need to help Sarah. I'm leaving Hank and Claude here to help guard the house. Can you help them?"

Ryan nodded and led his horse to the barn, his back straighter than it had been a few moments ago.

Sam brought his saddled pinto and Quinn's horse out of the barn. Slim and Johnny followed with their own mounts, while Hank and Claude headed for the house. "Make sure your rifles are loaded and be ready to ride in two minutes."

He raced past the two cowpokes, leaving the front door open for them, and ran into his bedroom. First, he located the hidden box and counted out the money he had stored there. Seventy-three dollars was a far cry from what Sarah had stolen from her uncle, but would it be enough to satisfy the man?

He fished around in one of the dresser drawers and found two leather pouches. Maybe he could trick them into thinking he had more money. He filled one with all the paper dollars and gold eagles he had.

Quick footsteps echoed down the hall and stopped at his door. His grandmother stared at him with concerned eyes. "What's this about Sarah gone missing?"

"She's been kidnapped. Do you have some fabric remnants I could have?"

Grandmother blinked and glanced at the pouches. She nodded, disappeared for a moment, and then hurried back into the room with several long strips of calico. "Will this do?"

Quinn nodded. He snatched the cloth and stuffed it in one of the pouches and tucked a few paper dollars and gold coins into the top of the pouch. He shook the pouch and the coins clinked. That would have to do.

He strapped on the pistols that he rarely wore when working the ranch. His gaze lingered on the settee where Sarah slept each night, and his jaw tightened. He'd bring her back, and they would talk about this fake marriage of theirs.

"Are you going to tell me what's happening?"

Quinn shook his head. "No time. Ask Ryan." He pecked her on the cheek and strode down the hall.

Lord, I promised You I'd do better, and I've been trying. But I need Your help. Please, Lord, help me rescue Sarah without her getting hurt.

Sarah pressed her hands into her lap. She couldn't quit shaking. Uncle Harlan paced around one tree and then another, stopping to look east every few minutes.

She knew Quinn would come for her, and that scared her to death. What if he got shot because of her? What if the children hadn't made it back home?

She shook her head. No, she couldn't think that. The creek was less than a quarter mile from the house, and you could see the cabin almost the whole way. They made it, and Quinn would be here soon.

She pulled her legs up, making sure her skirts covered her ankles, and laid her head on her knees. *Please, Lord. Help me.*

Uncle Harlan stopped walking and stared eastward again. Then he climbed up on top of a big boulder and looked around. Jim, one of the outlaws, lay next to a smoldering campfire, sound asleep. She could hear his snores from clear across the grove of trees.

She pulled her bound hands to her mouth and tried to bite through the prickly rope. Her wrists ached, and her hands were turning red and going numb. Footsteps snapped a stick and came her way. She looked up, and a chill charged down her spine. Eddie leaned against the nearest aspen; a smirk twisted his lips.

"I told you I'd catch you alone one day." He flicked ashes off the end of his cigarette and watched her uncle as he strode down the path and disappeared around a tall boulder.

Sarah's gaze darted to where she'd last seen her uncle, but he was gone. Her stomach roiled, and her hands trembled.

Eddie tossed down the stub of his cigarette and stomped it out; then he moved toward her like a mountain lion stalking its prey. Sarah backed up until her spine collided with a thirty-foot high butte. The stone felt as cold as Eddie's eyes looked.

Lord, no. Help me.

He grabbed her elbow and pulled her to her feet. She opened her mouth to scream, but his dirty hand slapped across it. "Keep quiet, and you won't get hurt. I just want to have some fun. You teased me enough with those looks back at our hideout; now it's time to reward me for my patience."

Sarah kicked and struggled to fight him off, but even with one hand plastered across her mouth, he was too strong. Tears blurred her eyes. Her strength was quickly dwindling.

He shoved her to the ground behind a row of juniper bushes and looked back over his shoulder. With a huge grin on his face, he knelt beside her. Sarah turned into a dust devil, twisting, kicking, and striking out wherever she could.

"Whoa, hold on now."

He shoved back her flailing bound hands and sat down on her belly. A breath gushed out of her, but she kept swinging her arms. "Get off."

Eddie chuckled. "You're a feisty little thing. If I'd known that sooner, I wouldn't have waited so long to press my affections."

He grabbed her hands and forced them over her head. Sarah continued to try to buck him off, but her strength was nearly gone. Eddie leaned down and captured her lips with his.

Sarah squealed and tried to jerk her head away. Suddenly, Eddie froze, his eyes rolled up, and he fell across her torso. Her breaths came in staccato gulps. Above her, Uncle Harlan's furious gaze caught hers. He held his pistol in his hand, butt facing out.

"I'm sorry, Sarah. I never meant for this to happen, but I want my gold back." He hoisted Eddie off of her and tossed him aside as if he were a sack of potatoes.

"Let's get back to camp."

He pulled her with him, and she barely managed to get her rubbery legs to work. As she passed Eddie, she saw a stain of blood along one side of his head, but she couldn't find it within her to feel sorry for the outlaw. He'd scared her half to death, and if he'd had his way with her, Quinn would never have wanted her.

Sarah shuddered. Her uncle led her back toward the campfire, then suddenly stopped.

"Where's Jim?" He looked around and then stepped backward, scanning the grove of trees and the buttes above.

As far as she could tell, there were no signs that anyone had disturbed their campsite. But where was the other outlaw? Was he laying a trap to snare her uncle so he could get at her?

She had to get a hold of her runaway thoughts. *Help me, Lord.* Send Quinn to save me, but don't let him get shot.

Her uncle finally shrugged and took her back to where she'd sat before. He pushed down on one of her shoulders. "Sit there, and this will all be over as soon as I get my money. I'll disappear and forget that my own kin robbed me blind."

He looked more disappointed than angry, but Sarah couldn't work up any sympathy for him. How many people had he killed to get that gold?

Fear and the relief to be free from Eddie made Sarah's limbs weak. She wanted to curl up and sleep and hope that when she woke up, this would all have been a bad dream.

Maybe if she could get her uncle talking, she could get him to set her free. They were kin, after all.

"What happened to you, Uncle Harlan? You're so different than I remember."

He spun around and stared at her. After a moment, he sighed loud and hard and scratched the back of his neck. "After Tilde died, something in me broke. I was never the same. She was my rudder and kept me on the straight and narrow. But when she died, my heart went with her."

"It's never too late to get back on the straight and narrow." Sarah's heart softened toward him. She knew the pain of losing someone you dearly loved. "Pa always hoped you'd come back and help him work the farm. We prayed for you every evening."

"You prayed for me?" He halted his jerky movements and stared at her with wide eyes.

Sarah nodded. The shadows were growing as the sun dipped behind the western hills. It would be dark soon. She had to get away before Eddie came to.

"Well, your prayers didn't do no good."

Something crashed on the other side of the trees as if a person or animal was coming their way. Harlan spun around and yanked out his pistol. "Who's there?"

Nobody answered, but Sarah couldn't be sure because her heart pounded in her ears.

Uncle Harlan crept in the direction of the noise. "Jim, was that you?"

He kept walking and passed behind a boulder. The second he was out of sight, Sarah pushed to her feet and bolted down the trail toward home. She ran past a line of trees, glanced over her shoulder to see if her uncle was following, and someone grabbed her and threw her to the ground.

She squealed, but another hand slapped across her mouth. She bucked and twisted.

"Stop it, Sarah. It's me."

She froze and looked at Quinn's concerned gaze. He eased up his hand and she gasped for air. He leaned down and kissed her then hauled her up and shoved her behind a boulder.

"Stay there and be quiet. Don't move until I come back."

Quinn crept forward until she could no longer see him. Sarah peered around the big rock.

"We've got your two partners," Quinn said. "You're surrounded, Oakley. Drop your weapon."

Harlan fired in their direction, and the bullet ricocheted off a rock to Sarah's right. She ducked down but couldn't bring herself to quit watching. The campfire behind her uncle made his silhouette a clear target. Quinn fired, hitting the dirt at her uncle's feet. He jumped back, tossed the gun to the ground, and raised his hands. "All right, I give up."

Quinn strode toward him and made quick work of tying him up. "Sam, bring the others out," he yelled and then spun toward her.

Sarah's heart pounded harder with each step he took. She was safe. He'd rescued her again.

She stepped out of the shadows and into her husband's arms. He crushed her against his chest, placing kisses on her head. After a moment, he set her back and stood so that the light of the campfire illuminated him.

"Are you all right?"

She nodded, but tears blurred her vision. She held out her hands.

"Here, let me get that off of you." He pulled a knife from his boot and cut the ropes.

She rubbed her chafed wrists and rolled her aching shoulder. Quinn lifted her in his arms, and she looped one arm around his broad shoulders.

"You scared me half to death—once I got over being angry with you."

Sarah blinked. "Why were you angry?"

He pursed his lips. "Because you never told me about your uncle."

"Oh. I tried to, but you didn't seem to believe my story about how I ended up in jail. I was afraid you wouldn't believe the gold tale either."

Quinn looked up for a moment then back at her. His face was inches from hers. "I'm sorry, Sarah."

She brushed her hand along his jaw, feeling the stubble of his day-old beard. He closed his eyes as she fiddled with his hair that ran along his collar.

"Sarah," he ground out the words on a growl. "You sure know how to drive a man crazy."

His eyes opened, and a fire blazed in them that took her breath away. He cupped the back of her head and brought her mouth to his. His kiss was one of promise and it left her breathless. His mouth roamed over her cheeks and eyes, then returned to claim her mouth again.

Too soon, he pulled away, his breathing ragged. "When we get back home, we're going to have a talk about this marriage in name only stuff."

Sarah smiled and stroked his bristly jaw. "It was your idea."

"I know. I can be an idiot at times."

Sarah placed a finger on his warm lips. "Never say that. You're my hero. You've rescued me twice, and I'd love nothing more than to be your wife in every way."

His lips found hers again, and he let her know that he felt the same way.

Epilogue

"I cannot believe you two met at the jail." Anna clapped her hands and grinned at her husband. "Can you imagine that, Brett?"

Anna's handsome husband shook his head. "Female jailbirds must run in the family."

His wife smacked him on the arm as the other adults in the parlor laughed. "I was only in jail because of you."

"That was the only way to keep you still." Brett's eyes twinkled, and he picked up his coffee cup, dodging his wife's playful smack again.

Sarah liked Quinn's sister and brother-in-law the moment she met them, and Anna pulled her into a hug, saying she was so happy to have another sister. Sarah sat on the sofa beside her husband, her hand in his. She was still uncomfortable with showing affection when others were around, but she was learning to accept it.

Martha yawned and stretched her arms out in front of her. "Tomorrow's a big day. We should all go to bed soon."

Brett stood from the side chair he'd been sitting in and crossed the three feet to his wife in one long step. He held out his hand, and she allowed him to assist her up, her eyes twinkling. Sarah knew just how she felt. Now that she was completely in love with Quinn, it was hard not to smile at him all the time.

Anna wrapped her arm around her husband. "Before we go to bed, there's something we'd like to tell you." She glanced up at Brett and he nodded, a proud smile on his face. "We're going to have a baby."

Martha squealed so loud that Sarah jumped. She hoped the children didn't awaken, because they'd been so excited about Sarah and Quinn's second wedding—a real wedding—that they could hardly go to sleep. Both children knew the significance, and that it meant they would never have to leave the Rocking M.

Quinn dropped Sarah's hand and jumped to his feet. He wrapped Martha and his sister both in a big hug and shook his brother-in-law's hand. "Congratulations! Do you think you might have twins?"

Anna patted her stomach. "Could be. It's early yet, but I'm already starting to show, not that you can tell with all these petticoats I'm wearing."

Sarah's cheeks warmed at Anna's casual reference to her body in mixed company. How long would it be before she and Quinn could make a similar announcement? Ever since her uncle and his gang had been captured last week, Quinn had slept in the bunkhouse. He wanted a new wedding and a fresh start for them—the same thing that Sarah had hoped for, and tomorrow was that day. She quivered at the thought of being Quinn's wife in all ways, couldn't wait to show him how much she loved him.

Anna yawned. "Grandma's right, this baby needs its rest." She turned to Sarah. "Welcome to the family, again. I'm looking forward to getting to know the woman who managed to lasso my big brother."

Brett wrapped his arm around his wife and guided her out of the room.

Martha gave Sarah a hug. "See you two in the morning, though I doubt I'll sleep a wink. You'll make such a lovely bride, dear. And I'm so happy that you and this hooligan grandson of mine are taking your vows again now that you've fallen in love." She squeezed Quinn's hand and pulled him down so she could kiss his cheek. "Good night, you two. Don't stay up too late."

As soon as she disappeared down the hallway, Quinn pulled Sarah into his arms. His kiss was warm and almost desperate. All too soon, he pulled away. "Do you have any idea how much I love you, Mrs. McFarland?"

Sarah couldn't help smiling and patted his chest. "If it's anything like what I feel for you, then I do."

Quinn heaved a satisfied sigh. "Do you feel like taking a quick trip out to the barn?"

Sarah lifted one brow. "What's in the barn that can't wait until tomorrow?"

Her husband's dark eyes danced with mischievousness. "Come with me, and you'll see."

She nodded, and they walked hand-in-hand out the door. A thousand stars shone bright against the inky sky like tiny lights, but even they dimmed in comparison to the light warming her chest. How was it possible to be so happy? *Thank You, heavenly Father, for making this possible. For sticking me in jail so Quinn could rescue me. And thank You for my husband and his family.*

The barn door creaked open, and Quinn dropped her hand to light the lantern. Sleepy horses ignored them as they walked down the dirt aisle. Quinn stopped at the last stall, and a familiar gray head peered over the gate. Sarah caught her breath and looked up at her husband. His wide grin made him even more handsome, and he shrugged.

"Mary Severson is doing much better, but she doesn't want to ride anymore and has decided to stick to a buggy. Her father decided to sell her horse so it wouldn't be a reminder of the day she got shot." Quinn shuffled his feet and stared at the ground, then peeked at her as if embarrassed. "I just thought that since this horse brought you to Medora—to me—that you might like to have her for a wedding present."

Sarah gasped and threw her arms around his waist. "Oh, yes, I love the mare. Thank you so much." He pulled her tight against him and kissed the top of her head. After a moment she pulled away. "But I didn't get you a wedding present."

Quinn's smiled turned roguish. "You can give me my present tomorrow night."

Sarah's eyes widened and a warmth rushed to her cheeks. "Thank you for the horse. She's a perfect gift."

He leaned down and kissed her again. Sarah knew she'd found her home. It wasn't a farmhouse or a cabin, but a place next to her husband. Next to Quinn. Wherever he was, that was home.

The sun shone brightly through the stained-glass windows of the little church, painting everything it touched in a rainbow of color. A small group of ranch hands, townsfolk, and family had gathered to see Sarah and Quinn married—again.

She peered over her shoulder, and Quinn's sister waved at her. She was so glad that Anna and Brett had been able to attend the wedding. A telegram arrived from Adam and Mariah, sending their regrets from California, best wishes, and the promise to spend the winter at the Rocking M.

Even Sheriff Jones had given them a surprise wedding gift in the form of an official pardon. The gang that had robbed the Medora bank had been captured in Wyoming when they tried to rob a train filled with soldiers. One man had confessed to the Medora robbery and several others in exchange for a lighter sentence. At least Quinn could marry her knowing she was completely innocent of the crimes she'd once been accused of.

Sarah held a small bouquet of flowers tied with long ribbons that draped over the same Bible that Quinn's mother had used when she was married. It would always be special to her. She peeked at her husband and warm tumbleweeds swirled inside her, making her arms and legs go weak. She clung to his arm as he promised to love, cherish, and honor her—"till death do us part."

Beth giggled and squirmed on Sarah's left, looking pretty in her new dress and shoes. Ryan stood next to Quinn, dressed reluctantly in new trousers and shirt. Sarah's only regret was that her parents weren't there—that her father never got to walk her down the aisle. And that her wayward uncle would probably spend the rest of his life in prison.

"Sarah Jane Oakley, do you take this man to be your lawfully wedded husband?"

She grinned up at Quinn. "Oh, yes, I sure do."

His eyes twinkled with delight, and a soft smile danced on his lips. He squeezed her hand tight, so different than the last time they were married.

The plump minister grinned. "By the powers vested in me by God and the state of North Dakota, I now pronounce you man and wife."

Quinn's grin lit up his whole face. "I intend to kiss you this time—to make up for last time." He bent toward her, without waiting on the minister to say the words.

He thoroughly kissed her until the minister coughed.

"Yuck," Ryan called out, raising chuckles among the attendees.

Quinn grinned against her lips. "Is that good enough, wife?"

Sarah shook her head. "It will do for now, but I think you can do better. I know you can."

His eyes twinkled and he nodded.

"Let me present to you Mr. and Mrs. Quinton James McFarland."

The ranch hands whooped and tossed their hats in the air. Grandma fanned herself and reached out for Anna's hand. The small crowd of townsfolk clapped and cheered.

Sarah walked down the short aisle on her husband's arm. He was more than she could ever have hoped for. Quinn hadn't been looking for a wife, and she hadn't wanted a husband, but God had other ideas. He'd given her a man to love and had provided a wonderful home for her family. She looked at the image of Jesus in the colorful window on the side of the church. *Thank You, Lord, for Your bountiful blessings!*